Deviant Way

a Novel

O

by Richard Montanari

SIMON & SCHUSTER

New York   London   Toronto   Sydney   Tokyo   Singapore

SIMON & SCHUSTER
Rockefeller Center
1230 Avenue of the Americas
New York, NY 10020

SIMON & SCHUSTER and colophon are registered
trademarks of Simon & Schuster Inc.

Designed by Hyun Joo Kim

Manufactured in the United States of America

10 9 8 7 6 5 4 3 2 1

Library of Congress Cataloging-in-Publication Data

Montanari, Richard.
        Deviant way : a novel / by Richard Montanari
                p. cm.
        I. Title
        PS3563.05384D48 1995   95-6786
        813' .54--dc20   CIP

ISBN 0-684-80357-7

"I Feel So Good" by Richard Thompson, copyright © 1991 Beeswing Music.

Acknowledgments

MANY THANKS TO ALL FOR THEIR HELP, SUPPORT AND SUGGESTIONS— my editors, Michael V. Korda and Chuck Adams; my agent, the indefatigable Elizabeth Ziemska at Nicholas Ellison, Inc.; my friends and family; the Wednesday Night Group for liking the early stuff; and, for piping in the sunlight, the ladies at the Noble Road Community Library. For my excesses—geographic, social, legal and otherwise—a wink to the city of Cleveland.

For Dominic and Darla, who said I *could*

I feel so good I'm gonna break somebody's heart tonight,
I feel so good I'm gonna take someone apart tonight,
They put me in jail for my deviant ways,
Two years, seven months and sixteen days,
Now I'm back on the street in a purple haze,
I feel so good, I feel so good,
I feel so good I'm gonna break somebody's heart tonight.

—Richard Thompson, "I Feel So Good"

Part One

○

Delirium

1

SHE WAS A REDHEAD, TALL AND SLENDER, A LIBERTINE IN training if I ever saw one: Norma Kamali suit, twenty-three, Camry owner, loved her job, hated her boyfriend, never been properly fucked. Regard the redhead she said from across the room. Regard the regal redhead who doesn't just give it away.

Eyes like a cat.

We had watched her for the better part of an hour as she fielded the advances of the happy hour boys, dancing the occasional dance with the ones who looked well-heeled, her expression alternating between the bored-and-too-beautiful-for-you look that women like her worked hard at in such a setting, and the working-girl ennui that inevitably made its way to the top.

There were thousands like her across the city that night, this night, every night. Budget microwave meals for dinner, a quick shower and meet the girls for a drink. To wear the good lingerie or not, that was the question. She was strangling her twenties and she wasn't married and she had no children and she read a lot and she masturbated a lot and wondered what was wrong with the world that she didn't have the American dream yet.

She was bored and beleaguered.

She was ready for the beast.

                    o   o   o

SAILA LEANED FORWARD. "SHE WEARS A ROSE," SHE SAID, A HINT OF LACE PEEKing around the bodice of her dress. "What do you think?"

"I think I can smell her," I said. "It's bohemian sex she's wanting. Mr. Goodbar. *Very* exciting."

"She looks so young. Like a child."

The redhead glanced at me. Or did she? She gazed in my direction, then quickly looked away. She was talking to one of her suited throng, laughing at all the funny parts, trying to fill in the multitude of lulls. Sip, sip, sip. A Mai Tai now. She looked at her watch until the suit got the message. The music changed into a slow song.

"Do you think her legs are strong?" Saila asked.

I really didn't know the answer, but I knew my cue when I heard it. I turned my drink in its napkin and straightened my tie.

Saila put her finger into the middle of my back, stiffly, like a gun. "Bang-bang, kitty cat," she said. "I want to know every detail when you get back."

"Bang-bang, dirty mother," I answered.

And took my leave.

o   o   o

I MADE MY WAY ACROSS THE CROWDED BAR, DRAWING ADMIRING LOOKS FROM the women, along with a medley of sneers and envious glances from the men. I was used to it, though. This *jealousy.*

As I neared the redhead I noticed that her teeth were perfect, her breasts were small and firm, her legs shapely and strong-looking. She regarded me with a half-smile in the moment before I spoke to her.

"Hello," I said.

"You've been watching me," she answered.

"I have."

She regarded me further. Cautious, observant.

"And why *is* that?" she asked before sipping her drink.

Chit-chat-chit-chat. "It's purely physical, I assure you," I said.

She smiled. "I mean, let's face it . . . you could have any woman in here. Why me?"

She was going to press me on this. I would break her with her own mindless cocktail chatter. I leaned very close and said: "Does the daffodil question the advance of the honeybee?" It was very bad Broadway and the redhead lapped it, like the cat she was.

"Who *are* you?" she asked, looking me up and down.

"I'll show you." I extended my hands as another slow song began. "Dance with me."

She looked into my eyes, then at my lips, then back into my eyes. She smiled fully and I knew then that I had her. Without a word she took my hand and led me to the dance floor. I glanced at Saila. She was stirring her drink, looking at the floor, smiling.

We began to slow-dance, the redhead and I. Something by Lionel Richie.

"Are you with her?" she asked, nodding in Saila's direction.

I pulled back and looked into her eyes. She was beautiful. Her face was delicately featured, absolutely symmetrical. Her eyes were an emerald green. "Now . . . do you think I'd be up here dancing with you if I was on a date?"

Another smile. *Perfect* teeth.

"You never know," she said. "There's all kinds of people . . ."

She really had no idea. "Well, if she *was* my girlfriend and she saw me up here dancing with a beautiful woman such as yourself, I think she'd be rather upset, don't you?"

The redhead blushed. I loved it when they blushed, it meant there was still some girl left. She pulled me closer and I started to get hard, the warmth of her body and the tease of her perfume running roughshod over my senses.

"I think you're full of shit," she said. "But don't stop, okay?"

"Don't stop what?" I asked as I flexed the muscles in my loins, nuzzling my erection up against the curve of her stomach. The redhead noticed the pressure against her abdomen and flexed back.

And then this woman who had not laid eyes on me one hour earlier put her head on my shoulder and kissed me on the side of my neck.

Softly, like a lover.

And thus she was ours.

I fucked her in the back seat of her car, in a dark corner of the parking lot, while Saila drove to the motel and waited. I pushed her skirt up around her waist and brought her to just this side of orgasm, promising her the rest and more if she'd only come to the motel with me for an hour. Just an hour. An hour in a king-size bed where I could probe her deeply, properly, finding those places that made her scream.

And she came with me. They always did when they let me inside their minds, even for a few moments.

But by the time I got the redhead to the motel, Saila was ready for her: wet and flushed and violent, her hair tossed to one side like a mad Egyptian, her eyes blazing with the thrill of the game.

Out came the cameras, the makeup, the steel.

Out came the animal.

And the redhead—she of the delicious legs and wild auburn mane, she of the promising career and Lord & Taylor charge card— died screaming.

And coming.

Just like the others.

2

"AND SO YOU CHASED HIM?" THE WOMAN ASKED.

"Yep," Paris replied.

"And you were . . . um . . . completely . . . um . . ."

She waved her hand in front of his face as if saying the word out loud might cause him to lose control and sexually assault her right there in the bar.

"Naked," he said.

The woman covered her mouth with her heavily jeweled hand. "You're *kidding*."

"Nope," Paris said. "Buck-shriveled-naked, running down the middle of Carnegie Avenue at two in the morning."

The woman threw her head back and laughed, and, for the moment, erased a few of the hard years she'd spent holding down barstools. Jack Paris had seen her up and down the avenues for at least a decade—on the job, off the job, sometimes doing the job. She had this style that was right out of the fifties: tube tops and flowered party dresses all summer; beehives and plenty of eye shadow all year round. Paris was sure that over the past ten or fifteen years she'd slept with a lot of cops, been abused by a lot of cops. She was sweet, but she was used up in a way that only the corner-tavern life could impose upon a woman. It was a fucking shame.

But she still hung out where the cops hung out. Because sometimes they drank free and, at least in her younger years, and sometimes these days if the lighting was right, so did she.

Her name was Nedra.

"So, did you get him?" she asked, posing with an unlit cigarette: Bette Davis, waiting for a light.

Paris grabbed a pack of matches off the bar, struck one and lit her cigarette. He took one for himself, a Salem Light, hesitated, put it in his mouth, then returned it to the pack. "No," he said, blowing out the match. "But I got three offers of marriage."

Nedra laughed again, loud and throaty.

The Caprice Lounge was starting to fill up with second-shift cops from the Third and Fourth Districts. They all looked tired to Paris, a little browned around the cuffs. Cleveland had been averaging a homicide every thirty hours for three years, and although it was only mid-March, it looked like they were going to beat the quarterly stats by a half-dozen killings. At least, that's the way it looked from Paris's perch at the Homicide Unit. Drive-bys were up, robbery homicides, too. Tavern shootings, usually the province of the hot summer months, had averaged one a week all winter. The Brick City Lords—a drug gang that Paris had battled for almost five years in a zone car—had recently declared war on a Jamaican posse, part of Cleveland's Caribbean crime wave. And then there was the other shit: the carjackings in broad daylight, the stabbings over who spilled what drink on whose fucking pantleg, people getting shot because they looked at somebody wrong or because somebody bitch-slapped somebody else five years ago. Lucasville and Mansfield were busting at the seams and there seemed to be a never-ending train that kept dropping the new criminals on Public Square.

But even though the Caprice was located at Fifty-fifth and Chester, ground zero in the combat zone, it remained a virtually crimeless area. No cars were ever stolen from its unprotected, poorly lit parking lot. There were no drug sales for at least three blocks in every direction. At times, it was even considered to be a rap-free zone, with boom boxes and car stereos being dutifully dimmed out of respect for the aesthetic sensibilities of the dozen or two law enforcement types who seemed to be permanently rooted inside.

In the thirty or so years the Caprice Lounge had been a cop bar, it had only been robbed once. For every other establishment in the neighborhood, the number was in the dozens.

∘   ∘   ∘

DANNY LAWRENCE, A PATROLMAN FROM THE FOURTH DISTRICT, STOPPED BY and shook Jack's hand. Paris motioned to Victor to set them up again.

"What's doin', Danny?" Paris asked.

Lawrence was dressed in his civilian clothes. His uptown, officer-you-gotta-be-doing-*something*-off-the-meter clothes. He was also knee-walking drunk. "Fuckin' McGuinn, man," Danny said. He tried to light a cigarette, but it fell out of his mouth, onto the floor. He kept talking anyway. "Upstairs is up my ass about these smash-and-grab punks at the Galleria. Three *months* they're in my face. If I see 'em I'm gonna fucking *cap* 'em. Swear to God." Danny turned to Nedra, tried to focus his eyes, unsuccessfully, and slurred, "If you'll 'scuse my French, ma'am." Danny Lawrence was twenty-six and fair, Errol Flynn–handsome. Nedra blushed like a schoolgirl.

"Certainly," she said.

Paris steadied Lawrence, guiding him to a barstool. "Don't worry about it, Danny. How long can McGuinn have? Another fifteen, twenty years, tops." Carl McGuinn was a captain at the Fourth District. Hardass, Irish lifer. Nobody liked him because he was an old-school liberal as well as the cheapest prick in the department. "Doesn't matter anyway. Eighteen months, you're gonna make detective third."

Danny sat down hard and zeroed in on the whiskey glass that Vic Ianelli had placed on the bar in front of him. After a few moments, he knocked it back in one furious gulp. "So tell me, Jack," Danny began unsteadily. "How'd you know when it was time?"

"Time? Time for what?"

"You know," Danny said. "Time to . . . give it up. Time to get married."

"Me? You're asking *me* that question?"

"Well, you were married, right?"

"*Oh* yeah. Twelve years."

"You had to be happy for a while, no?" Danny tried a second cigarette, but that one fell out of his mouth too. "No?"

"Yeah, we were," Paris said. "But things change. People change. And it takes a certain kind of woman to be a cop's wife."

"Yeah?" Danny asked. "What kind of woman?"

"I'm not really sure. But I sure as hell didn't find her." Paris, having found himself unwillingly in the middle of a conversation about his ex-wife, decided to have that cigarette after all. "Why? Are you in *love*, Danny? Is that what this is all about?"

"Head over high heels, Jack." He clutched his heart with what looked like real pain.

"Live with her first," Paris said, drawing deeply on his cigarette. "That's my advice to you, Danny. Live with her. Spend a couple of years in the same bathroom, the same kitchen, the same car, the same bed with the woman. See how enchanting she is when she snores and farts and makes noises when she eats and uses your razor to shave her legs. She ends up with legs like Sharon Stone and you end up with a face like Manuel Noriega. If you still think that's cute after a couple of years, go for it."

"But I know *now,* Jack."

"No, you *think* you know now," Paris amended.

"I *do* know," Danny slurred, trailing off, sounding unconvinced. He looked balefully at Nedra, who reached out and smoothed the hair across his forehead. "I *do . . .*"

"Sure you do," Paris said, catching Victor's eye. "Sure you do . . ."

The barman nodded. He would start watering Danny's drinks.

o o o

PARIS LEFT THE LOVESICK DANNY LAWRENCE IN NEDRA'S MORE THAN CAPABLE care and made his way to the men's room. As he washed his hands he caught his reflection in the barely silvered mirror, or what passed for a mirror at the Caprice. At least a dozen times, Paris had told Vic and Marie Ianelli, the owners, that cops were probably the vainest people on the planet, they needed a better mirror. There was even loose talk about a fund to improve the lighting in the Caprice's johns, in hopes that Vic would get the message. But regardless, a bare bulb on a bare wire remained, and looking into the mirror at the Caprice was like looking into a flattened-out saucepan.

Paris noticed with a spike of dismay that some of the silver that was missing from the mirror was starting to show up in his hair. He brought himself close to his reflection; a droopy, fun-house face stared back. Bleary eyes, heavy lids, a midnight shadow. He poked at his hair.

He knew that all men, regardless of race, color, religion or country of origin, have one thing that they rely upon to get them laid throughout their lives. For some guys it's an athletic ability or a talent of some sort. Rock stars and jocks who are ugly enough to clog a fucking drain get laid all the time. For some guys it's their intellect. Others, their looks. And yet, for others, it could be their shoulders, their cars, their dicks, their apartments, their eyes, their attitudes—who the fuck knows with women?

The point was, if you're a man, and you get laid more than once in your lifetime, there's a reason. And for Jack Paris, it was his hair. He had great hair. Al Pacino hair. And a quick sense of humor. He could always make a woman laugh.

Except, of course, a woman named Beth Shefler-Paris.

19

The day he lost the ability to make her laugh was the day she walked out.

○   ○   ○

ON HIS WAY BACK TO HIS DRINK PARIS SAW ANGELO TUCCI, AN OLD-TIME PLAYER from Murray Hill. They shook hands and embraced briefly. He also spotted a pair of new recruits, female rookies, hovering around the video games. One of them, a pixieish but solid-looking little blonde in her early twenties, smiled at Paris when he walked by.

Before he could spin around—a long-rusted pickup line spewing drunkenly from his lips—his beeper went off.

○   ○   ○

HE LOOKED AT THE PHONE NUMBER IN THE LIGHT THROWN BY ONE OF THE CIGA-rette machines. At first he didn't recognize it, but two and two added up in short order. It was one of Tommy's harlots. He dialed the number. Tommy answered before the phone had rung twice.

"Yeah . . ."

"Tommy, it's Jack."

"Hey, Jack, how ya doin'?"

Paris could hear Tommy's signature hump music in the background. Isaac Hayes. "From two hours ago? I'm fine, Tommy. What's up?" He knew very well what was up.

"Good . . . good . . . So what's goin' on?"

"I'm not doing it."

"What . . . Come on . . . I didn't say a fuckin' thing . . ."

"Like I don't know what's coming?" Paris said. "Jack, I'd like to introduce you to Tommy. Tommy, this is Jack. What . . . we just met over here?"

Pause. "Okay, so you're Joe Friday," Tommy said, his voice starting to take on that pleading tone that Paris had heard before. "Just this once."

"No."

"Jack, please. Be the primary detective on this one and it's Danish for a month."

"No."

"Two months," he said, his voice dropping to a whisper. "Jack, she's wearing a garter belt. I got a dick of death on me . . . forget about it . . ."

"Okay, let's talk about your dick, Tommy. One of my favorite subjects, right?" Paris was quiet for a while, working him. "Two months?"

"My mother's eyes, Jack."

"Danish from where?"

"Uh . . . shit . . . I don't know . . . Lonesome Dove, okay?"

"Ungers," Paris said. He loved doing this. Ungers was at least another ten minutes out of Tommy's way.

Silence.

"Well . . . gotta run," Paris said.

"All right, suck my blood, Jack."

"Uh . . . I think you're the one getting something sucked here, pal. Tough duty, is it? Putting in for hazard pay, are you? Because if you can't handle it, I'd be glad to relieve you. Code three and I'm there in six minutes."

Tommy laughed.

"I want bear claws, starting tomorrow," Paris said. "I want them fresh, I want them wrapped in one sheet of that wax paper with the serrated edge and I want them delivered with a smile."

"You're a prince, Jack."

"Yeah, that's me. Prince of the city. Where and who?"

"See the man. Red Valley Inn on Superior. Black-and-white's already rolled."

"Bear claws, Tommy," Paris said as he scribbled down the information and the time of the call.

"I love you, Jack," Tommy said, starting his shit. "And I'm not just talking a summer thing. I love you for the man you are, the man you've helped me become. I *will* call you in the city."

"Go fuck yourself, Tommy."

"Don't have to," Tommy Raposo replied, and hung up the phone.

o   o   o

PARIS FELT HIS BACON CHEESEBURGER ABOUT TO TRAVEL NORTH.

"*Could* be skin," Ocasio said. He held the translucent, pinkish strip high into the air, suspended from his large forceps. He turned it around and around. The flap of skin—which measured two inches across and four or five inches long—slapped together wetly as Ocasio taunted Paris, whipping the pelt from side to side. "On the other hand, it could be beef jerky." He thrust it at Paris. "Wanna bite, Jack?"

Morrison and Dolch, the two hyenas from the Special Investigation Unit, let out a snort and a barrage of adolescent cackling. They always thought whatever Ocasio said was hysterical as hell, especially if it caused Jack Paris to grab his ever-roiling stomach.

"What the hell's the matter with you, Reuben," Paris said. He felt the bile start to rise in his throat. "I mean . . . how many times are we going to do this?"

"I don't know, Jacquito," Ocasio said with a generic Latino accent, even though the closest he had ever been to a Spanish-speaking country was two weeks in Los Angeles. "Maybe as long as you keep throwing up at crime scenes. You're too *easy, padrone.*"

"Number one, that's evidence you're messing around with, and number two, it's probably part of a huh-human buh-being." Paris dry-heaved twice.

"Yeah? So what's your point?" Ocasio said. "What are you saying? You like your redheads without the skin? Is this a calorie thing?"

More guffaws from the Tweezer Twins.

"Jesus, man," Paris said resignedly, breathing deeply. "It's amazing we have any kind of solve rate at all."

Reuben Ocasio smiled and, for Paris, it ruined what little there was to like about his face in the first place. Yellow teeth, backed up by a shitload of silver; bits of cigar tobacco on grayish-brown gums. Paris shook his head and walked out of the oppressive motel room, the late-winter chill helping to calm the mixture of pickles, ketchup and Maalox stirring around at the base of his throat.

Ocasio had joined the coroner's office four years earlier, the year Paris had gotten his gold shield, and from day one he had played with Paris's better nature, especially during the days, weeks and months following Paris's full-contact divorce. The two men had nearly come to blows one night at the Black Mountain Tavern, a cop bar on Payne, over something stupid like a crack Reuben had made about Paris's ex-wife and a small-time doper named Grady Pike. Then, two weeks after that, Reuben Ocasio put in twenty hours of overtime to close one of Jack's cases. Paris found it difficult to hate the man completely.

But the sick shit—the leaving of spleens in lockers, the intestine-

on-a-roll sandwiches wrapped up in Sub Shoppe sandwich paper—
made Paris want to shoot the asshole.

∘   ∘   ∘

HADN'T HE KNOWN THE MOMENT HE WALKED INTO THE ROOM? HADN'T HE
known as soon as he rounded the corner and saw her face? That ag-
onized mime face: perfect, beautiful, silent. Paris had seen Emily
Reinhardt up close. It was his case and, in almost six months, he
hadn't turned up a single lead. He knew that whoever did that was
an artist, a journeyman in the techniques of sexual torture, and
wouldn't strike just once. Paris knew that one day he was going to
walk onto another crime scene and see that death mask staring up
at him again from an ever-widening pool of red.

And then there was Maryann Milius. Greg Ebersole's case.

Three women now. Bodies torn to shit, their faces made up like
runway models. Foundation, eye shadow, rouge, mascara, powder,
lipstick.

Conclusion, Inspector Paris?

Cleveland had a serial on its hands, its first in a dozen years.

And who was going to put it together? Raposo? Too fucking
busy with his tailor and his stockbroker and his harem. Ebersole?
Maybe. Except Greg had been shutting down the Caprice quite a bit
himself these days and he was getting sloppy.

Paris lit his last cigarette.

Reuben already knew. Or he would soon. Then, of course, the
Plain Dealer would have it. Then Channel 5 and their Crime Watch
or Cop Watch or whatever the fuck it was.

But in the end, and probably within the next forty-eight hours,
the task of setting a trap for this psycho was going to fall to one
man: Jack Paris.

∘   ∘   ∘

THE WOMAN'S FACE, LIKE THE OTHERS, WAS FREE OF BLOOD: WHITE AND
wooden against the navy-blue carpeting. Her lipstick was fresh,
deep red, glistening in response to the flashbulbs exploding around
the room. Her body was nude, except for the remains of a black
lace camisole which had been cut clean away at the shoulder
blades, and a pair of high heels, now flecked with red. The patch of
skin had come from the woman's right thigh. It bore a tattoo. A pair
of roses.

The comforter lay on the floor to the right of the bed, unstained and folded, as if set carefully aside. It looked incongruously pristine, as if it were on sale at JCPenney's amidst a display of blood and torn flesh. The sheets were gathered at the foot of the bed as witness to a session of violent sex. Bloody sex. The killer was either monstrously large or had used an object on the woman. The blood from the wound that had most likely caused her death—the deep razor cut to the top of her spine—had spread to a diameter of four or five feet and looked black against the dark blue of the carpet. Paris noted that the death blow could have easily been dealt from behind in the throes of passion.

He slipped on a plastic glove and began to look through the woman's purse as the forensic activity in the room died down and the lab boys and the team from the coroner's office wrapped up, taking the body with them. Paris pulled out a small, red leather wallet, bulging with plastic, the snap all but torn off. He looked at the driver's license and was once again taken aback by the woman's face. She was striking; deep red hair, full lips. Natalie Wood–beautiful, Paris thought, even in the shitty little picture laminated in scuffed plastic.

The dead woman was Karen Schallert, twenty-three, five six, one-twenty. Lived in Lakewood on Bunts Road. He pulled out a stack of business cards, but none of them were hers, all belonged to men. Andy Sipari, attorney-at-law. Robert Case Meldrum, insurance agent. Joe Najfach, Prestidigitator Deluxe! Marty Jevnikar, service manager, Parma Porsche-Audi.

Paris searched her purse further. A half-finished bag of M&M's. Peanut. A pair of matching combs of different widths. There were a few cosmetic basics like lipstick and a small perfume atomizer. *Joop!* it said on the side. But Paris found no mascara, no rouge, no powder.

Because, he thought, the killer carried his own. And he was putting it on these women after he hacked them up. Paris's stomach flipped at the thought of this guy playing Barbie with the corpses. He absently made a note about funeral parlors.

And drove back to the Caprice.

o   o   o

DRUNK. STARING AT THE SIDE OF THE RED VALLEY INN. HAD TO BE FOUR, four-thirty. Long after the lab boys had left, long after the yellow tape had secured the crime scene until morning. This one, it appeared, even rated a cop at the door, stationed there to protect all the juicy evidence that wasn't going to add up to shit. Paris parked his Olds Calais alongside the motel, cut the engine, dimmed the lights and unscrewed the cap on his fresh pint of Windsor. He flashed his badge to the uniform, who nodded in deference to Paris's gold shield, his seniority.

Paris stared at the door to 127 and tried to imagine the scene from earlier in the night. A tall, dark-haired man had rented the room. Thirtyish, mustache, tinted glasses. He wore an Irish tweed walking hat that covered most of the upper part of his face. There was, of course, no register to sign at a place like the Red Valley Inn. The Valley was strictly pay and play, no questions, no paper. The night clerk had gone to the room after receiving a number of complaints about the TV being on full blast. He knocked on the door around one, and found the body a few minutes later.

Paris sipped from the bottle, the liquor washing over his stomach in hot, bilious waves. He closed his eyes until the fire passed.

He imagined the tall man opening the door, all charm and credit cards and cologne, letting Miss Karen Schallert, twenty-three, late of Lakewood, Ohio, into his room. His abattoir. He imagined them making love, Karen Schallert a bit nervous at first, surprised by the man's size, but then becoming so aroused that he entered her with ease. And had she enjoyed it? Did she think she had made the right decision, making it with this guy who was, most likely, a total stranger? A total stranger in this age of AIDS and crack wackos and fucking psychopaths?

What did she think when she saw the razor?

Paris hit the bottle lightly, replaced the cap and stepped out of the car. The night was clear and still, the traffic on Superior had diminished to a peppering of only the most desperately addicted—food, cigarettes, dope, sex, booze. He walked to the back of the motel parking lot and ran his flashlight around the base of the two giant Dumpsters parked there. Beer bottles, a few candy wrappers, some detritus from the nearly two dozen fast-food restaurants that populate Superior Avenue near the freeways.

To his left, one of the motel doors opened suddenly and a burst of drunken laughter skittered across the parking lot. Paris clicked off the flashlight and stepped into the shadow of one of the Dumpsters.

A black woman, overweight, clearly inebriated, stumbled out of room 140, paused on the sidewalk for a moment, straightened up slightly when she saw the uniformed officer, then turned quickly and yelled into the room: "Wutchoo *doon,* bay-be?" She struggled to maintain her balance, as if standing on a log, or stuck in a wind tunnel, propped up by a violent oncoming breeze. "Less go, bay-be. Jin-juh *hongry.*" She turned, smiled once in Paris's general vicinity and fell back into the room. After a few seconds, someone inside closed the door.

Paris recognized the woman. Her street name was Ginger Snapp. And before all the gravity, the crack, the booze and the fast food she had been beautiful, tall and busty, a fan dancer down at the New Era Burlesk on Prospect. Paris had picked her up occasionally when he had worked vice in the early eighties. They had even partied a few times, smoking joints in the alley behind the Caprice, playing soul music on a transistor radio. Ginger had also been a material witness when her onetime pimp—a particularly fragrant piece of shit named Luis Estancia—had washed up on the Seventy-second Street pier with a 9mm slug in his stomach.

Ginger Snapp, Paris mused, a phantom ache returning to his loins.

He was getting really fucking old.

o   o   o

THE NIGHT FELL SILENT ONCE AGAIN AS PARIS DIRECTED HIS LIGHT ALONG THE line of trees that bound the rear of the motel's property. Nothing. Nothing *moving.* A few fifty-gallon drums, a couple of chained-down picnic tables, the remains of an old cast-iron barbecue. If he had a brain, Paris thought, he'd pack this in until morning. How the hell was he supposed to—

The sound came from directly behind him. Inches away. The sound of heavy boots on broken glass. Paris turned quickly, but the tall man in the Irish walking hat was already upon him, running his straight razor across Paris's neck.

"You wanted to fuck her too, didn't you?" the man said, his voice gravelly and wet. "Admit it, Jack."

At first, Paris thought the man had pinched him—the contact seemed so light, so *minor*—but a scant moment later, the blurt of bright red blood that slapped against the side of the rusted Dumpster told him all he needed to know.

The man had severed his jugular vein.

Paris fell to his knees and screamed.

The man came at him again, swinging the razor in broad, muscular arcs, striking Paris's face and chest, chopping away the flesh in burger-sized chunks. For Paris, the pain soon coalesced into an excruciating red knife in the center of his brain.

He screamed again.

Soon, in his mind, his scream became a brain-rattling bell and the bell became the telephone and it was the phone, not the sunlight or his pounding skull or his fear, that brought him raging back to consciousness.

It rang again. Screamed again. Loud and insistent. Belligerent.

Paris looked around, terrified and disoriented, clutching at his neck. He was in his apartment and it was at least noon. He sat up, grabbed the receiver—his heart still racing furiously, his head a huge, violent echo chamber—and brought it to his ear. "Mull-oh?" he managed.

"Daddy," the young voice shouted. "I *knew* you'd still be there."

"Huh-whuh," Paris said, his mouth thick with wool.

"Dad-eeeeeeeee!"

It was Melissa, his daughter. And *man,* did she sound pissed. "Whuh, darlin'," he said. "Whuhsuh matter, sweetie?" He sat up, attacked by the noonday sun streaming through the high jalousie windows. He had to get some fucking *drapes.*

"You were supposed to be here already," she said, clearly on the verge of tears.

"Wait, sweetie," Paris said. "Wait for Daddy one second . . . I'll be right back . . . Don't hang up, okay?"

Silence.

"Missy?"

"All right." Her voice sounded so small, so betrayed that Paris's heart clogged with shame. He bounded over to the bathroom, barking his shin on the coffee table en route, and doused his entire head with ice-cold, rusty water. He caught a glimpse of himself in the mirror on the way out and was nearly frightened by the look of the jowly, red-eyed man staring back.

And then he remembered. Today was his birthday. His forty-third. Except the ashen-faced guy in the mirror looked a lot closer to sixty at that moment.

He glanced into the kitchen and tried to determine if he could at least get the water on the heat before his daughter disowned him right there on the phone. But he decided that the instant coffee would have to wait as he stumbled back to the couch, the quarter-bottle of Windsor staring up at him in mockery. Paris's stomach did a brief pirouette when he saw it.

"Sweetie?"

"Yes, Daddy." This was a very, very solemn Melissa Adelaide Paris.

"Um . . . where was Daddy supposed to be, honey?"

"The Olive Garden," they said in unison.

And then everything came flooding back at once. Melissa had saved her money for six months to take her father out to lunch on his birthday at the Olive Garden restaurant on Chagrin Boulevard. Beth was to drop her off at noon and he was to take her back to Hathaway Brown School at one-thirty. He had known about it for weeks. Beth had even called to remind him about it three days earlier. He was going to try and explain it to Melissa, but the woes of an overworked, boozy Cleveland homicide detective didn't carry much weight these days, especially with slightly cynical eleven-year-old girls. "What time is it now, sweetie?"

"It's, like, twelve-oh-five already."

"Uh . . . Daddy's on his way, okay?" Paris said, scrambling for his pants, hoping they weren't too creased. "You just wait right there, okay punkin?"

More silence. Big, cold, Beth-silence.

"Okay, sweetie?"

"Where am I going to *go?*" Melissa said softly. "It's not like I have a car or anything."

Eleven going on thirty, Paris thought. She knew how to work

him. Just like her mother, the realtor of the century. "Love you. On my way."

Manfred, who truly was every bit the cur Jack Paris felt—and probably the man's one true friend and overburdened confidant of late—rolled over with a subdued woof and went back to sleep.

3   "ANDIE'S ON LINE ONE," CAME JENNIFER'S VOICE OVER the intercom.

Matt Heller took a deep breath, loosened his tie and held his finger over the blinking clear plastic button. He closed his eyes for a moment, imagining an outcome, visualizing, hoping. Will she? *Would* she? He picked up the receiver and hit the button with all the authority he could muster. "Hi babe, what's up?"

"Are you sitting down?" she asked. When Andrea Heller started off with that rhetorical question, it was usually good news. When she started with "You're gonna kill me," it usually meant a fender bender, a broken computer printer or that she had set the entire deck ablaze with the Charmglow. But he knew his wife's moods as he knew his own, and that underlying fizz of Andie-ebullience in her voice was a good sign for Matt Heller and his naughty little plan for the evening.

It was serendipity.

"You got L'Etoile," he said, heading her off at the giant, career-move pass. L'Etoile was a chain of upscale fragrance mini-boutiques that Andie had been stalking for six months. The account probably meant another three or four thousand dollars gross into the annual Heller household coffers.

"I got L'Etoile," she echoed.

"Unbelievable!" Matt's shout was loud enough to draw a glance and a smile from Jennifer in the outer office.

"Excuse me?"

"I mean, I *knew* you could do it, babe." They laughed at the incredible antiquity of that routine. All through Andie's meteoric rise to regional sales representative for cosmetic giant Cinq, Limited, they'd run that by each other. Often for the mini-plateaus in Matt's career, as well.

Couldn't have been luck, they'd accede to each other. Had to be you.

And while Andie's job kept her on the road four or five days per month, the two had often thought, although never sharing it with each other, that it was just that time apart—and not some magic formula that their divorced friends kept bugging them for—that kept their marriage alive and spitting. Seven years in May.

"So . . . what? Primo Vino at seven-thirty . . . braciole and a bottle of some ridiculously expensive Merlot?" Matt asked.

"What about . . . I don't know . . . What about somewhere a little more . . . private?" Her voice dropped a sexy half-octave and sent a ripple of excitement down Matt's spine.

"Oh, we're feeling private, are we?"

"Ummmmmaybe . . ." Andrea singsonged the word, a girlish ploy she knew her husband found absolutely maddening. Like when she purposefully wore her plaid skirts and knee socks. Or a hair ribbon. Or barrettes. Or the nurse shoes, his favorite.

"I see," Matt replied. "Then how about the Terrace Room? Nobody goes there much anymore. It's dark and private."

"That'd be great," Andie said. "Haven't been there in years."

"Not too déclassé for a woman of your international reputation?"

"Screw you," she whispered.

"You know, if you whisper it, it's not a curse anymore," Matt said, smiling. "If you whisper, it's more like an invitation."

"I know."

"Let's make it six-thirty then."

"You are *so* bad," she said. "I'll see you at seven-thirty. I've got a few things to wrap up here and I want to stop at Severance Town Center."

"What if we . . ." Matt began. He was pushing it. He was going to blow it.

"What?"

"Nothing."

"Come on, tell me."

She knows, Matt thought. But it sounded as if she might be up for anything. "I was wondering if . . . uh . . ." he started, hoping he wouldn't have to finish the sentence.

"We'll see," Andie replied, all shyness and sass.

"Oooooh," Matt said. "Can't wait."

"And . . . honey?"

"What?"

"We're going to have fun."

She *was* teasing him. "See you tonight."

"Love you."

"Love you."

31

"Bye."

"Bye."

      o   o   o

THE KNOCK BROKE HIS CONCENTRATION. HE WAS AN ENGINEER, A MATHEMATI-cian. He couldn't afford to lose concentration.

"Yeah?"

"I'm going to lunch." It was Jennifer. "Do you want something?"

"Uh . . . no thanks," Matt answered. He was trying to make his voice sound . . . what? Normal, he guessed. Not easy to do when you've been interrupted while masturbating in the office bathroom in the middle of the day. He felt like a bigger pervert than usual.

"Are you okay?" Jenny asked.

Matt rolled his eyes, his erection already beginning to wilt. "Yes Jenny, I'm fine."

He watched the shadow of her shoes beneath the door hesitate for a moment, then disappear. He waited until he heard the office door close before he went back to the business at hand.

This time, Andie and he were on vacation somewhere. It was summer, the middle of the night, and they were staying at a two-story TraveLodge that wasn't more than one-quarter full. There were less than a dozen cars scattered around the parking lot.

Andie had told him to go out to the parking lot and sit beneath their sliding glass door. She said she wanted him to see something. Matt had grabbed a pair of beers off the dresser and hurried down to the car like a hormonal teenager.

After fifteen minutes or so, after sitting in their sensible Chevette and sipping his sensible Bud Light and watching Andie walk around the room, teasing him in her working-girl tweed suit and high-heeled pumps, Matt noticed a man sitting in a car to the left and in front of him.

The man, it seemed, had been watching Andie too.

Matt thought about getting out of the car and going back to the room, hoping he could get there before his wife started actually stripping, but the idea of this stranger watching Andie excited him. He wasn't sure why. Maybe it was because he just wasn't sure how far Andie would go.

Was this fair to Andie? he thought.

He didn't know, but he didn't move.

For the next twenty minutes the two men watched Matt Heller's wife take off her clothes, slowly, piece by piece, drawing out the part where she bounded about the room in her black lace camisole—a present from her husband. Andie then slipped out of the last piece of lingerie in front of the mirror and brushed her hair, her breasts rising and falling, rising and falling. She stood briefly in front of the sliding glass door, her hourglass figure silhouetted against the white walls of the motel bedroom, and closed the curtain.

And although none of this had ever happened—nor had any other of Matt Heller's bulging Rolodex of voyeur's fantasies about his wife—the prospect that it might someday never failed to arouse him.

Even at the office.

Maybe tonight, he thought as he laid his head back and closed his eyes.

Maybe tonight.

4 SHE WAS BIG AND SHE WAS SMALL IN THE DOORWAY TO the restaurant. Big because she was getting so tall, so angular. She would be a woman before Jack Paris knew it. Small because here she was on her own—no Beth, no Jack, no mom or dad. Just a dressed-up little girl with a purse full of hard-earned money, waiting for her father. Her juicehead father who can't even keep a date with an eleven-year-old.

As Paris walked across the lot, smoothing his stained tie and wrinkled shirt, he wondered how anyone this precious and beautiful ever sprang from his drunken passions. He would never let her down again.

Melissa Paris screwed up her mouth, tapped her foot and stared at her watch as her father opened the door. A pint-sized Beth. Her hair, a deep mahogany in color, seemed to have grown considerably since he had seen her last, even though it had been just a few weeks. It fell to her shoulders now, silken and luminous in the midday sun. She wore a gray spring coat and black patent leather shoes.

Girl shoes, Paris noted with relief. No heels yet. Thank God.

"Hi sweetie," he said, planting a wet kiss on the top of her head. "Sorry I'm late."

"Twenty-one minutes late," she said, trying to hold on to the mad-look for all it was worth, but rapidly losing ground to the corners of her mouth which were starting to turn up into a smile. Paris hadn't been able to get that smile out of Beth in years, but his daughter still loved him, still trusted him. "Did you forget?" she asked.

Paris cleared his throat. "Forget? Are you kidding? What kind of guy forgets his own birthday?"

"A cop," she said, matter-of-factly.

Paris bent down to her level, noticing that it wasn't quite the trip it had been just a short time ago. "You know . . . you can still be arrested for being a wise guy," he said. "Just because you're a detective's daughter doesn't mean you get any special privileges."

Melissa gave him a big hug. "Sure it does, Daddy," she said. "Besides, they don't arrest *angels*."

The hostess approached them. "I see your gentleman caller has finally arrived," she said, drawing two menus from behind the desk, saving Paris from any further scrutiny. The woman exchanged a wink with Melissa. "Will that be smoking or nonsmoking?"

Melissa turned and glared at her father, supplying him with the answer. "Uh . . . nonsmoking please," Paris said, his voice thick and phlegmy with the previous day's tobacco consumption.

"Yea!" Missy exclaimed, and took off after the hostess.

Paris followed them, already craving a Marlboro Light.

o o o

HE SCANNED THE *PLAIN DEALER* BUT FOUND NOTHING ON KAREN Schallert's murder. Generally, these days, murders were relegated to page 2 of the Metro section and, unless they were spectacular or involved someone of celebrity, warranted no more than a few column inches. Paris had gotten to the scene at around one-thirty, far too late to make even the late-morning edition. He took out his notebook and scribbled a note about calling Mike Cicero, the best of the *PD*'s crime reporters.

"Daddy!"

Paris looked up. "Yeah, honey?"

"You're *working*, Daddy!"

Paris had gone easy on his daughter's budget, ordering just a small sausage sandwich and coffee, even though she had encouraged him to order whatever he wanted. Missy, never the picky eater, had ordered, and already devoured, her favorite: spaghetti with meatballs and a large chocolate milk.

And as much as Paris didn't want to exhaust Melissa's cache of babysitting cash, he really couldn't face too much food just yet. He folded the paper and picked up his sandwich. A whiff of garlic and onions nearly sent a wave of nausea over him, but he took a small bite anyway. "So how's school?" He wiped his lips with his napkin.

Melissa rolled her eyes. "You already asked me that."

"I did?"

"Yes."

"Oh," Paris began, "and what did you say?"

Another glance at the ceiling. "I said it was fine and that I was going to be in a play and that we went on a field trip to Hillside Dairy and we had to watch them make cottage cheese." She wrinkled her nose.

"That sounds great, punkin," Paris said absently, stirring his coffee.

"And I told you that I took my third karate class."

"*Karate* class?" Paris dropped the spoon.

"*Heee-yah!*" Melissa shouted, then smiled, drawing her hands into a defensive position.

"Since when are you taking karate lessons?"

"Since three weeks ago."

"Man . . . nobody tells me *anything* around here." Paris shook his head.

"I almost flipped Ricky Singer already," Melissa said, pantomiming the motion.

"Great . . ." Paris said, trailing off, aghast at the news that his daughter was mixing it up with the neighborhood bullies.

"So tell me," Melissa asked in her strange, formal tone, now that she seemed to have her father's undivided attention, "how is Manfred?"

"Manny's fine, honey."

"Do you take him out for runs?"

"Of course."

"*Daddy . . .*"

"What?"

"I don't mean walks," she said. "I mean *runs.*"

"Well . . . occasionally we break into a . . . you know . . . *trot*like sort of rhythm." He could see that she wasn't buying it. "Okay, I'll take him out for a *run* tomorrow. I promise."

"Dogs have to run."

"I promise." Paris held up his hand and rested the other one on the place mat, in lieu of a Bible. "Cross my heart."

"Pinkie swear?" Melissa asked.

"Pinkie swear," Paris said. Observing the solemnity of such an oath, as was their custom, they dutifully locked fingers across the table. Melissa then reached into her purse and pulled out a long, white envelope.

"Here, Daddy."

Paris's heart stammered briefly as he took the birthday card from his daughter. She really was remarkable, he thought. Most kids would not have been able to sit all through lunch without giving away the fact that they had a birthday card on them. For Daddy. Most kids would have boiled over. But Missy was cool and methodical. Her cop half.

On the front of the card was a cartoon of a man, at least ninety years old, leaning on a pair of crutches. Beneath him it said: "Two, four, six, eight . . ." Paris opened the card. The sentiment continued: ". . . *boy,* did you depreciate!" Melissa had started giggling the moment Paris lifted the flap on the envelope. By the time he read the card, she was all but collapsed with laughter.

"Oh you think it's *so* funny, don't you?" Paris asked, his own smile rushing to the surface.

"Yes," Melissa said, full of false composure. "I do." More laughter. She then reached into her school bag and produced the big surprise of the afternoon. A brightly wrapped package that was the size and shape of—although almost certainly not—a carton of cigarettes.

"Melissa *Paris,*" Jack said.

"It's from both of us," Missy said. "Maybe you won't be late for appointments now. Maybe you can make notes for yourself."

Paris opened the package and was not all that surprised to find the Panasonic microcassette recorder inside. He had casually mentioned it to Melissa six months earlier, and his daughter never forgot a good gift idea.

"Thanks, honey," Paris said, leaning over and placing a kiss on his daughter's forehead. "Tell Mommy thanks too."

"The batteries are already inside. It's ready to go. There's a tape in there too."

"I'm not the least bit surprised," Paris answered. He opened the card once again, this time finding a little more humor in the sentiment. "And who taught you what 'depreciate' means?"

Melissa's slight hesitation answered the question. And because she never lied to him, she just raised her shoulders and stared at the table.

"Did you buy the card with Mommy?" Paris asked, somehow thinking he was changing the subject.

"You really just want to know about Robert, don't you?"

"Huh?"

"Oh, *please,* Daddy . . ."

He had never been able to fool her. Not with "Peekaboo." Not with "Which hand has the gum?" Not even with "Find Daddy in the leaf pile." Paris avoided her eyes. "Is it that obvious?"

"Um-hmm."

"And he never calls himself Bob?"

"Nope, Robert," she said. "Always."

"And he really has a—"

"Jaguar," Melissa finished.

"And he's . . . what? A pharmacist, right?"

"Daddy," Melissa said reproachfully. "You know he's a doctor. A pediatrician."

It was Paris's turn to roll his eyes. "Well?" He picked up his sandwich and took a generous mouthful, chewing it slowly, hoping that it would sufficiently mask the anxiety on his face. Here he was, shaking down his daughter for information on his ex-wife's new boyfriend. Some detective. Real hardnose.

"Well, Mom doesn't love him," Melissa said. "He stays over sometimes, but mostly they go out to dinner. Or rent movies and kiss on the couch. But Mom doesn't love him."

Paris wiped his lips, ricocheting between "stays over" and "doesn't love him." Which to hold on to? "I see," he said. "And does he, like, take you places and buy you things and—"

"Oh, Daddy," Melissa said, laughing. "You're *so* jealous." She stopped, tilted her head to one side and called for the check. Then she smiled at him—a huge, confident, grown-up, career-girl smile— and Jack Paris's heart flew into a thousand pieces.

She would be a woman any minute.

Then she would leave.

o   o   o

BEFORE PARIS COULD MAKE IT TO THE OFFICE HE HAD A TWO-THIRTY APPEARance before the grand jury, an obligation he surely would have missed had Melissa not called. It was a case involving the mother of a young Hispanic kid who had been killed in a King-Kennedy Estates drug dispute that had nothing to do with him. About nine months earlier, a few days after the shooting, the kid's mother, it appears, conned one of the gang members responsible onto the roof of number 1728 and threw him off. Seven stories, onto a jungle gym. Some witnesses had contacted Paris a few weeks ago—people who had just remembered that they had seen somebody throw a human being off a roof around that time—and Paris had reluctantly passed the information along to the prosecutor's office. Reluctantly, because he was not looking forward to building a case against the poor woman. The little fucker she tossed had it coming.

But he *was* looking forward to meeting Diana Bennett, the new assistant prosecutor for Cuyahoga County.

Tommy Raposo, he knew, had hit on Diana Bennett a few times, with no evidence of success. But then again Tommy hit on everybody. The word was that she did her homework, always came prepared, but was no immediate threat to Chief Prosecutor Ardella Patterson-Jones for the top spot. Not the overly ambitious type, if he could believe his ears, and that's probably what made her even more appealing to Jack Paris.

He couldn't wait to see what all the fuss was about.

And it was for that reason alone that he stopped back home, showered, shaved and did his very best to wrest the wrinkles from the only suit he had that wasn't at the cleaners.

o   o   o

THE WAITING ROOM FOR THE CUYAHOGA COUNTY GRAND JURY WAS VIRTUALLY deserted when Paris arrived at one-fifty. He imagined that the jurors were already in session and that the couple who had decided to come forward—Lucius and Azalea Quarles—were already on the stand or in the witness room.

Paris saw Rocky Dobson, one of the oldest bailiffs in the entire American justice system, cut quickly across the reception area. Rocky was seventy-five if he was a day, but still managed to outrun Jack Paris after disappearing down a hallway. Paris found him in the small lunchroom reserved for county employees.

"Hey Rocky," Paris said, perhaps louder than he needed to.

"Jack Paris," Rocky said, looking up from his newspaper. "How the hell are ya, buddy?"

Rocky was of an age where words like "buddy," "pal," "mac," "chum," "champ," "chief," "jocko" and the like were automatically attached to the end of every sentence.

"How's everything?" Paris asked.

"Oh, let me tell *you*, bucko," Rocky began, lowering his voice as if he were a Watergate conspirator finally revealing the identity of Deep Throat. "The world's going to hell in a sidecar faster'n Jack got nimble." He smiled and knocked on the worn Formica conference table twice. "You can take that to the bank, my friend. And smoke it."

Paris laughed and drew a cup of coffee from the urn as Rocky continued his diatribe on societal ills and their proper solutions, a monologue that was years running when Jack Paris became a cop and was bound to continue long after he retired.

He leaned against the doorjamb and blew on the hot coffee. When he looked up, over the rim of his Styrofoam cup, there, at the opposite end of the long hallway, stood Diana Bennett. Tommy had described her perfectly.

He watched her walk the entire length of the corridor—desperately, almost comically trying to find a sense of symmetry for her files, folders, attaché case and oversized purse. As she got a little closer Paris could see that she was around thirty years old and very fit. She was five six in her sensible pumps and wore a double-breasted glen plaid blazer with a white rayon blouse and a charcoal wool skirt, cut just below her knees. Her black hair fell to just past her shoulders and she had ice-blue eyes.

Paris was tongue-tied.

"Diana Bennett, prosecutor's office," she said with a disarming smile.

From somewhere amid her cargo of paper, cardboard and leather, she extended her hand. Paris took it as if it were bone china.

He waited a few beats, composing himself. "Jack Paris . . . pleasure . . ."

She certainly was as striking as he had heard, and he knew she was unmarried, but he had reached a point in his forty-two years—forty-three, he corrected himself with a stab of discomfort—where he was certain there was absolutely no point to chasing after women as pretty as Diana Bennett. He was getting old and the last thing he wanted to hear was, "No thanks, *Pop.* I'm busy Friday."

Paris watched her, his feet leaden, as she deposited her parcels on the table and exchanged a quick pleasantry with Rocky Dobson.

"We'll try not to keep you too long this afternoon," she said to Paris as she drew a half-cup of coffee from the huge urn. "You'll be first, in fact."

"Oh . . . uh . . . okay," Paris said. *God,* he sounded stupid. "Are the Quarleses here?"

Diana Bennett peeked around the corner and into the witness room. "Yes," she said. "But they look pretty nervous. Maybe you could . . ."

"Sure," Paris replied, liking the fact that he and Diana Bennett were speaking in a kind of professional shorthand. The ice, he thought, was already breaking. "No problem."

"Great," she said, switching hands with her coffee cup. She extended her hand once more. "Nice to have met you, Detective Paris." They shook. "See you inside."

Paris exchanged a quick look with Rocky, who gave him a wink as if to say "hubba hubba" or whatever guys Rocky's age say when they meet a bona fide babe. Rocky, it seemed, was still looking.

"You got that right," Paris said as he clapped the old-timer gently on the back and walked around the corner to the witness room.

o   o   o

"AND HOW LONG HAVE YOU BEEN A POLICE OFFICER?"

"Seventeen and a half years," Paris said, squinting, feeling the beginnings of a hangover headache. "Eighteen this November."

"And how long have you been a homicide detective?"

"Four years."

"And how many homicides would you say you've investigated in that time?" she continued. "Approximately, of course."

He knew that she was merely trying to establish his competence, validate his instincts, because all the evidence against Marcella Lorca-Vasquez was purely circumstantial. "Oh . . . maybe two hundred fifty. Three hundred, perhaps."

"And what percentage of those were solved? Once again, approximately."

Paris knew exactly. He was at eighty-one percent. He wasn't sure how to say it out loud without sounding like some pompous asshole who would actually sit down and get that specific about it. "About eighty percent, I believe."

Diana Bennett walked beneath one of the hanging fixtures, her silken black hair shimmering momentarily. She stopped a few feet from Paris's chair. "That's a rather remarkable record, Detective Paris."

Paris was a bit surprised. And flattered. "Uh . . . well . . . I suppose it is," he said, trying to sound humble but not having the slightest clue how. Diana Bennett walked over to her table and reached into her briefcase. "But thank you for saying so," he added. "Miss *Bennett.*"

At that moment, he noticed the slightest smile forming at the corners of Diana's mouth. But her professionalism pushed back the smile and she continued. "Please tell us what occurred after you arrived at the King-Kennedy Estates on the evening of June eighth of last year."

After taking a moment to organize the chronology in his mind, Paris related how, when he arrived at the scene, the body of Dennell "Too Bad" Breland, sixteen, was enmeshed in the jungle gym directly below the seventh-floor fire escape at number 1728. Witnesses said that someone definitely threw Too Bad off the roof, but nobody could say just who it was. The fact that Too Bad was a Crip, Paris was assured at the time, had absolutely nothing to do with the mass amnesia that seemed to have descended over King-Kennedy that night.

When Paris made it to the top floor of 1728, the door to Marcella Lorca-Vasquez's stifling apartment was wide open. The fact that Lorca-Vasquez was sitting at the table, handkerchief in hand, weeping, and that she was the mother of eight-year-old Rodolfo Insana, who had been killed in a recent Crip-Blood shoot-out, led Paris, and hence the state, to believe she may have been the one who gave Too Bad Breland the ride of his life.

The fact that she stood five nine and weighed in at about two-sixty told Paris that she was, indeed, capable.

"Detective Paris," Diana Bennett said from just a few feet away, her subtle perfume taunting him mercilessly, "we thank you for your time."

o   o   o

THE HOMICIDE UNIT OCCUPIED THE SIXTH FLOOR OF THE JUSTICE CENTER ON Ontario Street, six floors below the grand jury room, and it was well after four o'clock that afternoon before Paris walked through its doors. The pile of pink and yellow "While you were out" notes nearly obliterated the blotter, and the remains of whatever he had eaten for lunch the previous day were still there, half-wrapped in greasy wax paper and beginning to smell like a landfill. The first waft brought an instant replay of Olive Garden tomato sauce into his gullet.

"You ever going to clean this desk, Jack?" Tommy Raposo asked, setting down one of the two Styrofoam cups of coffee he was carrying in front of him. Along with a fat bear claw, wrapped in a single sheet of bakery wax paper. "I think this might be a little stale, though. I got it, like, this *morning*." Tommy knew how to grind it in. "You look like shit too. Are you aware of that?"

Paris glanced up. "Jesus, anything else?"

Tommy Raposo lifted his hands in mock surrender. "No, no, no . . ."

"Good, then take it around the corner. No mood."

Tommy Raposo was the precinct fashion plate, always dressed to the nines. He had been Paris's partner for only a few months, having transferred from the Akron PD when Paris's partner of three years, the legendary Dom Tomei, had taken his twenty and headed to Florida. Tommy's style, to Paris's taste, was a little too slick, a little too guinea-pimp, but he seemed to be a damn good detective.

This day Tommy wore a navy, double-breasted suit, blinding white shirt and maroon jacquard tie. Shoes so shiny you could shave in them.

"You da man," Tommy said. He smiled, but Paris thought he detected a little hurt, a little surprise beneath the surface. Tommy disappeared around the corner.

Paris felt like a complete asshole for snapping at him. "Hey G," he yelled out the door. They called Tommy Raposo "G" for *GQ*. "*Tommy!*"

Tommy poked his head around the doorjamb. He hadn't moved.

"Thanks for the coffee," Paris said.

"And the . . . uh . . . bear claw?"

"The bear claw you owed me, *paesan*. The first of many. The coffee was, I'm sure, out of the kindness of your heart."

"Of course." Tommy stepped back into Paris's office and picked at a microscopic piece of lint on his forearm. "So how'd it go at the grand jury?" he asked.

"Grand jury's a pain in the ass sometimes," Paris said. "But they should give the woman who threw that little shit off the roof a fucking medal."

"You get Diana?"

"Jesus, Tommy. You ever zip that thing away?"

"Never," he said.

"It's gonna get you in trouble."

"You think it hasn't?"

Paris shook his head. "You cops are incorrigible."

"What was she wearing?"

"She was wearing a bright orange Danskin and black hot pants," Paris said, dumping a spoonful of sugar into his cup. "She also had on these spike black patent leather heels and an ankle bracelet made out of puka shells."

"No hat?"

"Didn't I mention her hat? She had a silver derby on, too."

"C'mon, Jack," Tommy pleaded. "How'd she look?"

Eventually, Paris caved in and told him, which resulted in Tommy saying that he had to take another serious run at Assistant Prosecutor Diana Bennett. As if bedding half the available women in the department and half the working court reporters in town wasn't enough, Tommy now wanted to work his way through the prosecutor's office. Paris felt a strange needle of jealousy—or was it rivalry?—when Tommy mentioned Diana Bennett in those terms. It was as if he had shared something with her already.

Which, of course, was ridiculous.

Tommy walked over to the file cabinets and absently thumbed through the files in the top drawer. "I read the report from last night," he finally said. "Was it as bad as you wrote it up?"

"Worse," Paris confirmed. "You know I'm no good with the gory details."

Tommy started picking at his teeth with a RotaPoint—one of those white plastic things you get from the dentist. Tommy Raposo was always doing something to himself: flossing, whisking, straightening, brushing, combing. "Same MO as . . . uh . . ."

So he *had* put the cases together. "Reinhardt?"

"Yeah," Tommy said. "And Mills?"

"Milius."

"Who caught that case again?"

"Greg."

"Yeah . . . I remember the photographs . . ."

Fuckin' A, Tommy, Paris thought. "Let me make a few calls . . . then we'll go terrorize some citizens, okay?"

Tommy winked at him, straightened his tie, spun in place and strutted down the hall in an exaggerated homeboy roll. "You da man," he repeated. "You fuckin' *it* . . ."

o   o   o

THE MAN WHO STEPPED BETWEEN TOMMY AND PARIS'S DOOR WAS BUILT LIKE A Maytag—five eight, thick-waisted, oak-necked. He looked to be in his early sixties but he still held on to a full head of unruly, cloud-white hair. The man stared at Tommy's back for a few moments, watching him walk down the corridor. Then he said: "You keep usin' that friggin' language and I'm gonna kick your ass . . ."

Tommy stopped and turned slowly around, a broad smile across his face.

"You and who else . . . *Primo Carnera?*"

The two embraced briefly, talked for a few moments, then turned toward Paris's office. Paris got up and walked around his desk, sensing an introduction on the way.

"Jack . . . this is my father, Nick," Tommy said, stopping in the doorway. "Pa . . . this is Jack Paris. Best nose at the Unit."

Nick Raposo stepped forward and held out his hand.

"Nice to meet you," Paris said.

"Likewise," Nick answered. "Heard a lot about you."

"Yeah, but you haven't heard my side of things yet," Paris said.

Nick Raposo laughed.

"So what are you doin' downtown?" Tommy asked Nick, his hand on his father's thick shoulder.

"Taking your Uncle Sal to the VA. Everything's fucked up with him, all the time. He can't eat, he can't piss, he can't fart, he can't get it up. You know how he is . . ."

Tommy and Paris exchanged a glance.

". . . so I tell him, 'Sal, you're eighty years old. You're not *supposed* to get it up.'" Nick shook his head. "And what the hell is he gettin' it up for anyway?"

"Dad . . ."

"The guy's a mess," Nick continued. "All the time."

"Pa," Tommy said. "Jack doesn't need to know *every* detail, you know?"

"You're right. Anyway, I gotta go," Nick said. "Sal's down in the car and he's probably blowing the horn by now, probably hanging out the window, yelling at people."

Nick and Tommy Raposo shrugged in unison, obviously a long-observed routine when it came to family matters.

"I'll walk you down. C'mon," Tommy said.

"Okay," Nick said, holding out his hand for a second time. "Good to meet you, Jack."

"Same here," Paris replied.

They shook again and Nick and Tommy turned and headed down the hall. By the time they got to the end of the hallway, they ran into Greg Ebersole, and the three of them shared something that resulted in Greg stamping his feet and laughing his high-pitched goat-laugh.

o   o   o

PARIS DIALED THE CORONER'S OFFICE, HOPING REUBEN WAS STILL HOME SLEEP-ing and that sweet blond lab tech would pick up. No such luck.

"This is Reuben Ocasio," said Reuben's voice mail. "I'm either away from my desk now, on the phone with one of Cleveland's finest or up to my elbows in somebody's innards. Leave your message when you hear the beep. Adios."

Paris looked skyward. "Reuben, Jack Paris, it's . . . uh"—he looked at his watch—"four-twenty. Call me the minute you have the Schallert preliminary." He moved to hang up. "Oh yeah . . . adios." He hoped the sarcasm dripped through.

He pulled the stack of business cards that were in Karen Schallert's wallet out of its clear plastic envelope and looked at the top card. Arthur Banks. Investment counseling. If only it said Arthur Banks, Psycho Fucker, my job would be a lot easier, Paris thought. He flipped the card over. Blank. He flipped it back.

Did you do it, Artie? Huh? Are you tall and partial to Irish walking hats? Got a mustache? Were you dumb enough to give her your card, wine her and dine her and screw her, then carve her up like an Easter ham?

Are you hung like a Shetland pony, Artie?

Paris got up, tossed the fouling half-sandwich into the wastebasket and pulled the files on Reinhardt and Milius.

It had been five months since the murder of Emily Reinhardt; three since Maryann Milius. Both were career women. Maryann Milius was twenty-two, a short, trim brunette with a three-year-old daughter, Desiree, who was now living with grandparents. She worked as a teller at the Society Bank branch at Euclid and East Ninety-third, which was located only a mile or two from the Red Valley Inn on Superior. Her body was found in an abandoned building on East Fifty-seventh Street, slashed and beaten, a patch of skin removed from her left calf.

Emily Reinhardt was much taller, blond and willowy. She had worked for an accounting firm in the National City building at Ninth and Euclid, and as Paris stared at her picture, he wondered how many times she had been part of that rushing herd: flirtatiously coy, handing out her phone number with cautious optimism, swimming her part in the chicken-wing and kraut-ball feeding frenzy that is the downtown happy hour life. Never suspecting that one night someone would feed upon *her*.

Emily was twenty-four when she was murdered. She was found in a room at the Quality Inn on Euclid Avenue and East Fortieth, her throat cut. She also had a large piece of skin missing, this time from her right shoulder blade.

And now Karen Schallert.

Hers was the first patch of skin that had been recovered.

A rose tattoo.

o   o   o

SIDE BY SIDE, IT WAS OBVIOUS. MARYANN, EMILY, KAREN. SIDE BY SIDE—SIX eyes so full of life, so full of promise—the tableau looked not unlike a page out of a yearbook. And that, of course, is what made the first domino tumble. It *could* have been out of a yearbook. A high school yearbook. Because if there was one thing that leapt out at Paris when the photos sat in a row it was how *young* the three women looked. Reinhardt was twenty-four but she could have passed for eighteen. Maryann Milius looked sixteen, maybe younger. Karen Schallert might have been a varsity cheerleader.

Paris made a note to roust the pedophiles, the teen-baiters.

He also made a note to compile a list of all the tattoo parlors between Toledo and Erie, Pennsylvania.

o   o   o

PARIS WAS JUST ABOUT TO PICK UP THE PHONE WHEN IT RANG.

"Homicide, Paris."

"Hey Jacquito."

"Talk to me, Reuben," Paris said. "Gimme something good."

"Well, I don't have much yet," Ocasio said. "Karen Schallert was drunk. One-five." Paris could hear the shuffling of papers. "Let's see . . ."

"Cause of death?"

"Cause of death? Shit, Jack, she stopped breathing and her fucking brain shut down. It's been twelve hours . . . You think you got the only stiff in town?"

"I thought—"

"I got a drive-by lying here from somewhere on Central this morning. No face. Legs, arms, chest, shoulders, dick, balls, everything else is there. No fucking face. And Medavoy's up my ass for cause of death. Can you believe that? How about 'no face'? He died because he no longer had a fucking face. That's my ruling. Death by lack of face."

Reuben was cooking. Paris tried to jump in. "Okay . . . just give me—"

"To top it off, I got a stack of messages from QB on this Choo Choo asshole that could choke a moose."

Choo Choo Green was a homeless black man who had died while in police custody three weeks earlier. White police custody. QB stood for Queen Bitch: Ardella Patterson-Jones, Cleveland's chief prosecutor. Reuben had deposed that the man had choked on his own vomit, but the perennial cop-haters were out in force on this one and wouldn't let up on the case surrounding the beloved Choo Choo Green. And Patterson-Jones kept whacking the ball back into the coroner's office. Somehow, somebody was supposed to craft the evidence into something that would support a charge of excessive force at the very least, but there was simply nothing there this time.

"So . . . you want cause?" Ocasio continued. "Okay . . . how about death? She fuckin' died. Next case."

"Jesus, Reuben," Paris said. "Ease up on the NyQuil there, pal." He tried to shift gears. "Whenever you get the chance—and there's no *huge* rush on this—I'd like to know about her makeup, too. Especially her lipstick. I want to know if it was applied after she was killed."

"Why does this sound so familiar?" Ocasio asked. "You got something, Jack?"

"Maybe," Paris said. "Check it out and get back to me." He paused, then added, "And I want to know what she ate and when."

"Anything *else?*"

"*Where* she ate would be nice," Paris replied. "Who *with* would help."

"Reinhardt," Ocasio recalled with satisfaction. "And there was another one."

"Milius," Paris said. "Maryann Milius."

"Yeah, yeah, pretty girl. Young." He paused, formulating. "We have a *serial,* Jack?"

"Not sure. But try and keep it quiet for the moment, okay?"

"Shit," Reuben said.

"What?"

"Now I'm interested. Fuck you, Paris."

"Maybe later, Reuben," Paris answered. "But I want dinner and dancing first."

"You're just another *gringa.*"

"Yeah, but I ain't cheap. Call me."

He clicked onto line three and dialed the number.

o   o   o

By the accent he could tell it was Gunther Reinhardt, Emily's father.

"Mr. Reinhardt, this is Detective John Paris with the Cleveland Police Homicide Unit. I'm the officer—"

"I remember you quite well, detective," the man said. "How are you?"

"I'm just fine, sir," Paris said. "I was wondering—"

"Have you caught him?"

Paris had heard the question a thousand times before, but

never, he thought at that moment, quite so clinically put. Gunther Reinhardt was a retired colonel in the Austrian army and, it appeared, offered no quarter to circumstance. "No, I'm afraid not, Mr. Reinhardt. I do have a few more questions for you, though. And I'm afraid they're kind of delicate. You'll forgive me . . ."

"Of course," Reinhardt said.

"Do you know if your daughter had any tattoos?"

"Tattoos?"

"Yes. As you may remember—"

"You're talking about the skin that was missing from my Emily's shoulder, aren't you?" Reinhardt said, betraying his rage. He went silent for a few beats. "What are you saying, detective?"

"Well, we have reason to believe that—"

"Is that why my daughter was murdered, detective? Is that what you're telling me? Because she had a tattoo?"

"I don't think it's quite that simple, sir."

"I disapproved of it, of course. Such things. But you see, when Emily's mother died, I had to raise her myself. Emily was only six. What a job for a soldier to do on his own! She was ordinarily so shy, but sometimes she could be so . . . so *willful*. Tattoos . . ."

"It's just that we believe the party responsible may be singling out women who—"

"It was roses," Reinhardt said quietly.

"Beg your pardon, sir?"

"The tattoo on her shoulder. It was roses."

5

WHEN *HAD* HIS VOYEURISM BEGUN? WATCHING JUDY Minnissale change at the Essex Heights pool? Or was it at sixth-grade camp when he had spied on the girls' cabin and had seen Darcy Adelman taking a shower? Or was it the time he happened upon the couple having sex in the MetroPark; thrashing around in the leaves, all but naked, so fully consumed by their passion that they didn't hear the twelve-year-old Matty Heller nearly fall off his bike and scramble behind the huge boulders that surrounded Squire's Castle?

As he pulled onto I-90 he concluded that the whole thing had been decided for him long before he realized that anyone else had anything different in their diapers than he did.

The fact that he liked to watch strangers was one thing. But when had it begun with Andie? When had he started to think about his wife in those terms? They had been married for five years before it had even crossed his mind, and even then he hadn't dared discuss any of it with her.

Because Andrea Della Croce had been raised a "gooda Catholica girl," as her grandmother would often remind them when they were dating. Which meant, of course, that every chance that Andie got she would screw Matt Heller's eyes out. Over the years, they had tried every position, had played around with a "marital aid" or two, had even made love in their semiprivate backyard in Shaker Heights on some warm summer nights. But for the most part, the kinky things were relegated to the back of Matt Heller's mind.

Yet it wasn't that Andie hadn't acceded to a few of her husband's games.

Andie Heller had her moments.

Twice they had gone grocery shopping, in a manner of speaking, by driving to a west side Heinen's. Andrea wore a short skirt and a very thin tank top, while Matt took a separate cart and walked the store behind her, fielding the looks her perfect legs and soft, pendulous breasts would fetch. Both times, the escapades had heated their sex life for weeks afterward.

Matt was certain that there wasn't one of his male friends—single, married, divorced or otherwise—that didn't envy him, didn't want to do the Sealy samba with his sexy wife.

Andrea Heller was a shade over five four and very well proportioned. She had a tiny waist; her legs were well defined, aerobicized. And although her hands were petite and young-looking, she rarely painted her nails; a cause for great concern for a woman who made her living in the cosmetics business. Her skin was an alabaster white, her hair a charcoal brunette that set off the natural red of her lips.

Andie was twenty-seven pushing seventeen in Matt's eyes and every bit the sexpot he had married. Maybe more so. He, on the other hand, was nearing thirty.

But, Matt thought, it's different for men. Isn't it?

Of the few times they had gone out to play—mostly when they were out of town, mostly nothing more than a casual flirtation in a disco while Matt watched—Andrea's outfits were planned down to the smallest detail. Like what kind of shoes she wore. How short her skirt should be. Would she wear a slip, hoop earrings, nylons, a bra, jewelry.

Matt Heller was a pro. A voyeur's voyeur. In his six years as a civil engineer he had helped design huge, multimillion-dollar municipal projects with less attention to detail than a single Andie Heller outfit. But he wanted more. It was time.

He wanted . . . *what?*

When he rounded the corner and saw his wife standing in the lobby of the Terrace Room Restaurant, wearing a blond wig, he knew.

o   o   o

FOR MATT, OF COURSE, THE FANTASY BEGAN THE MOMENT HE SAW HIS WIFE IN the lobby.

For Andrea, this first time she walked the edge of her *own* fantasies, it began midway through dinner.

Their waiter, an Italian-looking kid about twenty-five, couldn't seem to keep his eyes off Andie. Lots of extra butter for their table. Lots of extra rolls. Gallons of water. Much repartee. Matt could see that the attention was not lost on his wife. Andie seemed to arch her back a little more often when the waiter was around.

Matt waited for him to leave. "Are you flirting to turn me on?" he asked.

"What do *you* think?" Andie replied, raising her wineglass to her lips.

"I'm not sure," Matt said. "I've never had a blond wife before."

"Do you really like it?" Andie asked, sounding genuinely concerned, moving one of the golden curls from her forehead.

"Are you kidding?" Matt whispered. "Did Rose Kennedy have a black dress? Of course I like it. I'm just a little . . ."

"Shocked?"

"Yeah."

"Me too." Andie laughed and threw her head back, knowing that every man in the restaurant wanted to take her to bed; every woman wanted to be like her.

Matt looked at his wife, her red blouse parting slightly, revealing just a hint of cleavage, while Andie looked around the room, running her tongue over her lips—an absolutely transformed, blond sex maniac in his grasp. He could have her, even in the car if he wanted to, and he wouldn't be cheating on Andrea!

No guilt!

"You know, I'd *die* if we ran into someone we know," she said, slightly sullying Matt's illusion.

Matt spoke quickly. No negative thoughts, please. "So, what possessed you to . . . uh . . ."

"Go Monroe?" Andie replied. "I thought you'd like it."

"Oh, I do."

"And besides, I know I've been a real bitch lately."

"Nah," Matt said, hoping she wasn't losing the mood.

She slid around the booth, closer to him. "And I wanted to make it up to you."

"It's working, believe me."

The waiter returned and poured the rest of their wine into their glasses. Andie leaned forward in front of him, her breasts shifting noticeably, purposefully, beneath her blouse.

"Will there be anything else?" the waiter asked, trying not to gawk.

"No," Andie breathed, staring at her husband, slowly uncrossing her legs and slipping her hands under the table. "That will be all."

The kid placed the check on the table, shook his head once and left.

"You're a real piece of work, Della Croce," Matt said, moving closer to her.

"Want me to flirt some more?"

"Well, let's see," Matt said. "Are you going home with me?"

"Mm-hmm," she said. *"Always."* She drained her glass and set it on the table. "But that doesn't mean we can't have a little fun while we're out." It was her third glass of wine and Matt knew that that was prime Andie-buzz level for sex. She ran her finger up and down his leg. "Let's go play," she said.

"Andrea *Heller,*" he scolded. "Now who's the naughty one?" He felt himself start to harden measurably. Something was definitely happening here.

"Me," she said.

"I see," he said, drawing even closer to her. "And where would you like to go?"

"Oh," she began, absently running her hand over his thickening erection, "let's go someplace where nobody knows us." She squeezed him. "I've got this idea." She stuck her tongue in his ear. "Tell me what you think."

o   o   o

HE SAT AT THE BAR, SCANNED THE ROOM. FORTY OR FIFTY PEOPLE. MOSTLY men. Mostly business types.

They had driven thirty miles to the Painesville Sheraton to avoid any possible run-ins with anybody they knew. Between their two jobs, their circle ran rather wide, and Andie Heller in a blond spiral-perm wig on the opposite side of a bar from her husband would en-tail some pretty good tap dancing to explain.

Matt's erection had reached furious proportions before he even made it inside the bar, so he had ducked into the men's room first and hidden out in a stall until it was manageable. All that Andie had said—that is, the new Andie, as Matt was beginning to think of her—was to go in, sit at the bar and she'd be in in ten minutes or so. That was it. Matt had no idea what she was up to, but he was ab-solutely delirious with the possibilities. How far would she take this?

Was she going to pick someone up?

Would she actually *do* that?

And if she did, how would he really feel? He had no idea, but the very notion filled him with an intoxicating mix of arousal, jealousy and an incredibly physical euphoria.

After a few minutes, Andie walked into the bar and sat three empty stools to Matt's left. She crossed her legs and ordered a White Russian, another first.

Before long, one of the business types stepped between them. Blond, medium build, gray suit, thirtyish. Matt heard the man say something about buying her a drink. Andie said something about having one on the way. They chatted for a bit, but Matt could only pick up bits and pieces over the deejay's music. After ten minutes or so, the guy left.

Matt found that his heart had been racing the whole time, and for the first time in his life he was beginning to wonder if he was cut out for the actual fulfilling of his fantasies.

Andie looked over at him and smiled. Matt was just about to slide over and suggest they leave, when another of the business types slipped between them. Taller, much better-dressed, much better-looking. He paid for Andie's drink and said something that made her laugh.

Somehow, for Matt Heller, that wasn't part of the fantasy.

6 HE STARED AT THE BOTTLE. MANFRED STARED AT HIM.
He had walked the dog twice, smoked a pack and a half of Marlboro Lights, eaten an entire package of turkey hot dogs without benefit or comfort of mustard and drunk a six-pack of Diet Pepsi. Everything but clean the tiny apartment. What was left? He looked at his watch. Eleven-oh-five.

Let's see, there was news, more food, another cigarette, another walk . . .

Fuck it.

He grabbed the pint of Windsor, as he had a dozen times already, then put it back. He patted the sofa twice and Manfred leapt to his side. "Are we going for another walk, Manny?" The word put a motor in the Jack Russell terrier's abbreviated tail. "You're gonna be the best-conditioned mutt in Cleveland. Gonna get your own TV series. We'll call it *Manny and Mannix.* I'll executive-produce." Manfred licked his face, clearly pleased with the possible career move.

Paris clicked the remote, turning on Channel 5. Hank Theodore, the never-aging cyborg who anchored the six and eleven o'clock news, was chatting with a citizen in Collinwood who was carrying a picket sign. Paris shook his head. All he ever heard was people bitching all week about the drug problems in their neighborhood and how nobody gives a shit, but come Saturday night when some dealer with a 9mm pistol in his hand gets capped on somebody's front lawn, you can bet they'll be on the streets Sunday carrying signs about how the cops are killing their children. Paris hit the mute button and lit a cigarette.

But before he could blow out the match, the words cut across the screen in eye-popping red, superimposed over the silhouette of a man brandishing a butcher knife. Then came a huge black question mark. "Serial Killer?" Paris's heart sank. He turned on the volume.

"*. . . have a serial killer on our hands? Well, our very own Triple F—Fact Finder Five—has been sniffing out the details. TV Five's Paul Coaklin has more. Paul?*"

The camera cut to a medium shot of the Red Valley Inn. The reporter stood in front of room 127 and began to speak as the camera zoomed slowly in.

"Hank, she was twenty-three years old, single, active in the community, a woman who, according to friends, didn't date much, due to her extraordinarily high standards. A graduate of Cleveland State University, a career woman just trying to make it in the big city.

"So how did Karen Schallert end up here, in a cheap motel, savagely murdered by someone who, in all likelihood, was someone she trusted. Someone to whom she had reached out in love or friendship. Someone who—"

Paris shut it off. He couldn't handle the soap opera bullshit. Next they'd have his boss, Captain Elliott, commenting on how it was too early to tell if there was a connection between the three murders, and yes, it was safe for women to go out of their houses and yes the investigation was continuing and yak, yak, yak.

When he stood up, Manfred dove off the couch and all but slid to the door on the wood flooring. "All walked out, Manny," Paris said. "Going to hit the showers." Paris made his way across the small living room, dodging a minefield of Domino's Pizza boxes, stiff socks and beer cans, and stepped into the equally disarrayed bathroom.

Manfred, banking on the outside chance of an after-shower jog, staked his place by the door.

o   o   o

TAKING A SHOWER AT THE CANDACE APARTMENTS, A TWENTY-SUITE GOTHIC nightmare at the corner of East Eighty-fifth and Carnegie, was a science. Early in the cleansing experience, when the water was hottest, it was also rusty as hell, so unless you wanted to step out of the shower looking like Chief Dan George, you waited. But as the water got clearer, it also got cooler, so there was this window of opportunity no more than two or three minutes long where the water was warm enough and clear enough to take a shower.

When Paris stepped in, the water was still pretty hot. He soaped himself quickly, feeling better by the second. Better about not stopping at the Caprice after his tour. Better about not touching the Windsor. Better about Missy.

He knew that there was a good chance that Elliott would call him in in the morning and give him the job of organizing the task force to catch this psycho. His solve rate was one of the highest in the department and it had been two years since there had been any real movement in his career.

Was he up for it? He knew it would mean less time off, less time with Melissa. Less time at the bars, too, he thought with a curious mixture of emotions. It would also mean that the media would be in his face until it was over. Unless he was going undercover, something he had not done in years.

He thought about Karen Schallert and what a shame it was. She was so pretty. So *fresh*. He thought about her body, the arc of her breasts, the dusty rose of her nipples, the contrast of the black lace camisole against her fair skin, the curve of her hips as she lay, naked and violated, on the carpeting. He closed his eyes and saw Karen Schallert's beguiling face before him. But it wasn't the face so mechanically rendered on her driver's license, or even the twisted death mask in the police photographs that would haunt his desk by morning. Paris instead imagined a more impassioned Karen Schallert: expressive and very alive, moving, smiling, laughing and—

Sweating.

Beneath him.

You wanted to fuck her too.

Paris opened his eyes, surprised at the vividness of his thoughts. He looked down and surprised himself further.

He was hard as a rock.

But soon, a wave of guilt and a burst of cold water took care of that.

7 "PHARAOH KNOWS."

The blond woman rolled over, onto her stomach, and bit her lower lip. Like a child. "Pharaoh *doesn't* know," she said, pouting.

I ran the feather along her spine, over her full hips, around to the side and up along her torso. Her skin was porcelain-white, smooth and supple. She had a few imperfections, a blemish or two on her back, but overall her skin was soft and sweet-smelling. One of the current rage perfumes, I was certain. When I met her at the bar the scent had been a little weaker. She had put on more for me and I appreciated it.

I reached her breasts, which were ample and pressed tightly against the sheet, and drew the feather up and over onto her back. The blonde shivered. "Pharaoh will show you." I climbed on top of her and reached toward the headboard, turning up the volume slightly on the portable CD player. It was a recording by Vangelis, very spacey, very New Age.

I also grabbed a condom.

"Pharaoh has something he knows you're going to like." I reached down between her legs and touched her. She was very wet, very warm. "Pharaoh wants to please you." When I inserted my fingers she let out a little gasp, as if she had not been touched in quite some time. She tried to turn over and face me, but I gently resisted her.

"You have something . . . for . . . me?" the blonde managed, her breath starting to come in shorter and shorter gulps as I stroked her.

I raised my fingers to my lips and tasted her. "*Oh,* yes," I said. I slipped the condom on and flattened myself against her back for a moment. We locked fingers and I drew her hands toward the headboard. Her flesh tasted salty, with a rich, underlying musk that taunted my erection. I nibbled on her ear.

"Fuck me," she whispered.

"No," I said.

"*Fuck* me."

"No."

She writhed her hips beneath me. "Fuck me *now,*" she said, pleading, her breath becoming more labored.

"I said no." I punctuated this by running a sharpened fingernail down the center of her back, raising a welt. The blonde shuddered with delight. She liked a little pain, it seemed. But how much? When would she bid me to stop?

"Let me turn over," she breathed. "I want to watch you fuck me."

"In time," I said. I pulled the handcuffs from beneath the left pillow as I gently spread her thighs and directed my penis between them.

In my periphery, I saw the door to the closet open slightly.

I brought the handcuffs around to the right and began to run them up and down the slicked planes of her back, her shoulder blades, the tops of her arms, all the while toying with her, probing her, drawing her deeper into the game.

"Wha . . . wha . . ." the blonde tried as I gave her an inch, then took it back. She emitted a short sigh.

The closet door opened a little more.

"And what do you want, little kitty?" I licked all the way up her spine.

"Y-you," she said.

"You want me?" I leaned over and kissed the back of her neck, tugging lightly at a wisp of baby-fine hair.

"Mmmmm . . ."

"Why do you want me?" I ran my tongue around the side of her face and when she turned her head I thrust it deep into her mouth.

"Because . . ."

"Because why?"

"Because . . . you're so . . . buh-big."

I teased her as she said the word, moving my whole body forward.

"I knew when we were dancing," the woman said. "I could fuh-feel you. I *knew*."

"And you want all of me?" I let slide another inch or so.

"Mmmmmm . . ."

"You can't handle all of me."

"Try me," she said, breathless now, nearing her orgasm.

I flexed.

"God . . . you . . . I can't . . ."

Another inch, then back.

The blonde groaned. I got the cuff over to her right wrist as I thrust myself halfway inside her, moving her body up toward the headboard, up where I could secure the shackle to the post. The blonde screamed once and tried to get up on all fours, trying to buck me deeper. She was strong and, for a moment, she lifted me high into the air. When we crashed back down to the bed, the handcuffs swung into her face and fell between the headboard and the wall. I reached for them but, in that instant, the blonde made the game. She began to fight me off. "What the hell are you *doing?*" she screamed, struggling to turn over.

I grabbed her arm, trying to get it near the headboard. "It's just a game," I said, but I knew that I had lost her. She was *very* strong.

"I'm not going to let you handcuff me!" She wrestled herself free of my grip and rolled onto her back, then off the bed. "Are you fucking *crazy?*"

"It's okay," I said, trying to calm her. "We don't have to if you don't want to . . ."

But the blonde already had her skirt in her hand and was backing toward the bathroom and the rest of her things. She was nearly hysterical with rage. "I can't believe that I almost . . . that I . . . oh God . . ."

"Look, I'm sorry," I said, stepping off the bed, slipping the small taser unit out from between the mattresses. At 100,000 volts, I just needed to touch her once. "I got a little carried away. We'll forget the kinky stuff, okay?"

"I don't even fucking *know you,*" she spat.

I stepped closer to her, naked, led not by my desire now but rather by my obligation. "If you'd just—"

"Don't come near me," she said as she wiggled into her skirt and pulled her blouse over her head. She reached down and gathered her shoes. She held her hands out in front of her. "Just stay away."

She looked so incredibly beautiful, still flushed with her nearness to orgasm, her golden hair matted with the sweat of our lovemaking. As she turned to put on her shoes, the closet door closed completely and I knew then that the blonde would get away. It was a first.

"No hard feelings?" I dropped the taser into the pile of sheets at the foot of the bed.

"You turned me on, you bastard," she said. "I can't believe

I . . . You . . . *shit!*" She threw open the motel door and the light from a nearby streetlamp washed the room.

And then she was gone.

I walked over to the door and closed it. I smelled my hands: perfume, sweat, the woman's musk. I touched myself with what was left of it. As I walked back to the bed I noticed that the blonde had left her bra and panties. They looked very expensive, but something told me she wouldn't be coming back for them.

I slipped into her panties and pulled the makeup kit from underneath the bed. I set it on the nightstand next to the bottle of Absolut. I lay down on the bed, cuffed myself to the headboard and waited. After a few moments, the closet door swung wide.

I closed my eyes.

And took my punishment.

8 ABOVE THE FOLD YET, PARIS THOUGHT. THIS WAS GOING to be a long one. The *Plain Dealer* had run the three pictures side by side—Maryann Milius, Emily Reinhardt and Karen Schallert. It had been just a few hours since the Schallert investigation began and already the newspaper had more information than the police. The *PD* had managed to fit all three pictures under the headline—set in guaranteed-to-induce-panic 140-point type: *Are these women victims of a serial killer?* The article beneath carried no answers of its own:

Michael A. Cicero
PLAIN DEALER REPORTER   CLEVELAND

As Karen Ann Schallert stepped through the door at Room 127 at the Red Valley Inn on Superior Avenue, she had every intention of leaving in just a few hours. According to Donna Ballou, the woman's sister, Karen Schallert taught a morning reading group at Mayfield Regional Library and this Saturday they were going to read from "Oh the Places You'll Go" by Dr. Seuss.

Her partner had no intention of letting Karen Schallert go anywhere.

Because, according to police reports, sometime early Saturday morning, Karen Schallert, 23, a personnel assistant with the United Way organization, was attacked with a razor and killed in Room 127 at the Red Valley Inn.

A random killing? There are indications that it was not.

On October 21 of last year, the body of Emily Reinhardt, 24, a secretary with the accounting firm of Rolff and Bagdasarian, was discovered in a second-floor room at the Quality Inn on Euclid Avenue. She had also been killed with a razor. On December 23, police say, the body of Maryann Milius, 22, a bank teller living in Bedford Heights, was found in an abandoned warehouse on the city's near east side. Her body had been severely battered, her throat cut.

63

Although Cleveland police have not yet confirmed that they are treating these three murders as the work of a serial killer, according to Captain Randall B. Elliott of the Homicide Unit, the similarities are growing as the investigation continues. Capt. Elliott said that a task force—to be led by Detective John S. Paris—was being formed to catch the killer or killers. The details surrounding the [SEE SERIAL/3B]

And all of it above the fold, section 2.

Paris had found out that he was to lead the task force at five-thirty that morning when Elliott had awakened him and briefed him over the phone, prior to the *Plain Dealer* hitting the stands. It was nice to see it confirmed in print, though, Paris thought—right there on the front page of the Metro section, right over a double order of blueberry pancakes in the back room at Eddie's on Coventry. It seemed his appetite had returned with a vengeance after only one night of not drinking himself into a coma.

He returned to the front page of the section and began to reread the article. He looked at his name in print and wondered if Beth was reading about him at that moment. If she was proud of him. If she was pointing it out to Melissa.

He also wondered if someone else had had the chance to read it. He wondered if the tall man in the Irish walking hat was sitting somewhere at that moment—perhaps in a little Italian bakery on Murray Hill, or in a booth at the Detroiter, or maybe even at the other end of the back room at Eddie's—and perusing the article over his scrambled and sausage.

The *Plain Dealer* was on the story full press, with three writers contributing to the lead story, and a pair of sidebars that jumped to page 9B. There was even a graphic of the city with each of the three crime scenes depicted with a star.

"You're gonna get fat eating that shit."

The voice came from behind him. Paris spun around. It was Tim Murdock, one of the best detectives in Beachwood, ex of the Third District, and Paris's senior by one year at the academy. "Timmy . . ." Paris said. "What's doin', big man? How goes the rat race?"

Murdock had taken a .38-caliber slug in his shoulder three years earlier—a drug shoot-out at the Carver Estates. He had arms the size of a football player's thigh and a complexion like a Maine shrimper, but his grip was weak because of his torn-up shoulder. Paris could never remember if he was supposed to squeeze his hand hard or go easy on it when they shook. He usually opted for both, always waiting for Timmy to double over in pain, clutching his shoulder.

"Fucking rats are still winning, Jackie." Murdock slipped into the booth and tried, unsuccessfully, to get the waitress's attention. "Congratulations on getting lead dog on this task force," Murdock said. "Is Dietricht gonna shit a potato or what?"

Bobby Dietricht was the Homicide Unit comer. He had his gold shield before he was thirty and had designs on captain by forty. It was just this kind of task force that would have saved Bobby Dietricht a year on the ladder. But Captain Elliott didn't care too much for Bobby Dietricht and Paris got the call.

And Jack Paris would lose no sleep either.

"Thanks, Timmy."

"Play this smart, Jack . . ."

Paris smiled. "I got two till my twenty, man," he said. "After that, I'm out."

Murdock laughed and called for the waitress again. "What the hell are you gonna do off the force, Jack? Go security? Go PI? I don't think so, buddy. You're too much like me. Blue all through. Just another fucking lifer." The waitress finally came over, took Murdock's order, grabbed his menu and walked back to the kitchen. Murdock lowered his voice. "So what do you have?"

Paris matched his volume. "I have shit," he said. "Not a print, not a partial, no blood from the killer, no semen. Not a fucking thing. Except three bodies."

"What do you have on the asshole?"

"I got a tall white male, thirties, glasses, mustache and a tweed hat. *Maybe*. And *that's* probably a disguise. Could be you, even. If you had a mustache."

Murdock smiled. "And if I was tall and still in my thirties."

"Right," Paris said. "And we don't even have this guy anywhere near the Milius murder. She leaves work one day, she shows up dead. Boom, boom. Could have been someone else. Except—"

"Except what?"

"It doesn't leave this booth?"

"Hand to God, Jackie."

"I mean it."

"What do I have to say?"

"All three had patches of skin removed. Sliced off like salami." Paris kept the information about the bodies being made up after they were killed to himself. He trusted Tim Murdock as much as any other cop, but some things were better kept inside the investigation for as long as possible.

Murdock didn't press Paris on any other details for the time being. He knew the routine. "How's the hot shot?" Murdock asked.

"Tommy's fine," Paris said. "He's really going to be the lead sniffer on this one, though. Great instincts for a guy his age. He's the real sleeper at the Unit. Everybody's talking Bobby Dietricht and me, but Tommy Raposo might just smoke us both."

"Kid's that good?"

"That good," Paris said. "Personally I don't know too much yet. Never been asked to his place. But give him time."

"But he is one *GQ* dude, isn't he?" Murdock said.

"He's our cover boy," Paris said. "Precinct peacock."

The two caught up quickly on each other's ex-wives and children and Paris rose to leave just as Murdock's breakfast arrived. Paris, whose stomach was legendarily susceptible to any and all sick jokes, knew that Tim Murdock was just as bad, if not worse. As Reuben Ocasio couldn't resist taunting *him,* Paris found that he couldn't resist taunting Murdock. For the first time, Paris thought he understood Reuben.

"I'm telling you, Timmy," Paris began quietly, nonchalantly, laying down a two-dollar tip, "this guy sliced the skin off in a wide strip. And when you look at it like that, it's almost transparent, you know? Like you could read a newspaper through it. Reuben held it up to the light and showed me."

Murdock—whose face was beginning to take on a khaki tinge— looked down at his two pieces of slightly undercooked bacon and called for the waitress.

o   o   o

PARIS DROVE SOUTH ON COVENTRY, NOTING THAT THE DOGWOOD TREES THAT lined Fairmount Boulevard were straining at their buds once again. He had told Beth that he would stop by on his way to the office, knowing that she and Melissa would probably be going to ten o'-clock mass. He needed a built-in excuse for leaving in case his emotions got the best of him, as they seemed to be doing with unnerving regularity of late.

He made a right turn onto Van Aken and headed toward Shaker Square and Beth's apartment. She had sold the house in Lyndhurst after the divorce and taken a huge, three-bedroom place on Shaker overlooking the boulevard out the front windows, and Shaker Lakes out the back. Paris figured her nut, every month—which, in reality, was partly his own—had to be fifteen hundred. Plus.

Paris found a space right in front of Beth's building, got out of the car and raised his collar against the wind.

It may have been Easter Sunday, but it was still March in Cleveland.

o   o   o

BETH WORE A PALE APRICOT DRESS AND MATCHING PUMPS. HER HAIR WAS MUCH shorter than Paris had ever seen it. Lighter too. She seemed to have taken on the look of a woman who was content to move among her new circle of friends: the movers and shakers of Cleveland society. Jack always scanned Mary Strassmeyer's society column in the *Plain Dealer* to see if Beth Shefler-Paris attended this society function or that hospital benefit. He saw her name once in a column about a recent chichi gourmet function called the Five Star Sensation and it made him feel like shit for a week.

But he still found himself looking at *Mary, Mary*'s column every time he picked up a newspaper.

Beth kissed him on the cheek, looking, close up, no more than two thirds of her thirty-six years. She took the half-dozen day lilies he had grossly overpaid for at the last minute, knowing well enough to let him hand Melissa the huge Easter basket himself. "How are you, Jack?" she asked, walking him into the kitchen. "You look . . . *good* . . ."

Even if she hadn't hesitated, Paris knew what she thought. He hadn't been able to get any of his three suits to the cleaners and back in time for Easter, so he had come in just-laundered jeans and a black polo shirt. It was a Sunday and, even though he had to work, he figured that *Beth* would figure he opted against the suit and tie because he was about to go undercover. Which wasn't entirely untrue.

"Oh . . . you know . . . overpaid, underworked, overstaffed," he said. "The usual."

Beth found a vase for the lilies, cut them, filled the vase with water and arranged the flowers on the dining room table. "Read about you in the paper," she said as she poured him a cup of coffee, black, one sugar, without asking. Just like old times. "Does one say 'congratulations' at a moment like this?"

Paris had hoped she would know that. One of the reasons they no longer shared deodorant anymore, he imagined.

"Yeah," he said. "It's a good move."

"Well then . . . *congratulations*."

"Thanks."

She brought his coffee over to him and sat down.

"Melissa said lunch was a lot of fun," Beth said. "She was pretty excited to come home with some change, too. She said you hardly ate a thing."

"Well, I've never been a big lunch eater, you know."

"I know, Jack," Beth said. "It hasn't been that long."

Paris sipped his coffee and put his cup back into the saucer, realizing that he had never seen the china pattern before. Like half the things in the apartment, they were brand-new. And expensive. "Not for you, perhaps," he said, then instantly regretted it. "I mean . . ."

"I know what you mean," Beth said. She reached forward and placed her hand beneath his chin. "Jack . . ."

Just then, Melissa came racing around the corner. She wore a white dress, white shoes and a white ribbon in her hair. But, because she was Jack Paris's daughter, her purse was a shocking lime green. "Happy Easter, Daddy!" She flew across the kitchen and into his arms, knocking him back on his heels. Out of the corner of his eye, Paris saw his wife look away.

"Hi punkin," Paris said. "Let me look at you."

Since she was five or six, that had been her cue to walk around the room like a runway model, spinning, hand on hip, flipping her hair as coquettishly as possible. "Don't *we* look pretty," he added.

"Thanks, Daddy."

"You're welcome."

"*Heee-yah!*" Melissa suddenly shouted, assuming a karate attack position.

"*Heee-yah!*" Paris answered, squaring off, then immediately covering up as his daughter rained pretend karate blows to his sides and shoulders and back.

"I quit!" Paris eventually shouted and Melissa, very solemnly, took a few steps back and bowed.

"Pretty good pepper there, kid," Paris said as Melissa collapsed in laughter.

Paris knew that later that night he would feel a few of those blows. His daughter was getting pretty tough. He retrieved the basket from behind the island.

"Easter bunny left this for you at my . . . uh . . . house." Paris felt strange, in the company of his wife and daughter, talking about *his* house. It had been a long time since they had all lived under one roof as a family, but Paris was still wrestling with geographic demons; those real, and those whose boundaries were etched only on the map of his heart. He was still madly in love with his wife.

"Wow!" Melissa exclaimed, looking through the purple cellophane for her favorite Easter candy, knowing, of course, it would be in there. She spotted them. "Cadbury Creme Eggs!" she said, sounding reasonably surprised. "And Jelly Bellies!"

As anxious as she was to get at all that sugar, she slowly, methodically removed the cellophane and bows, folded them and stacked them on the kitchen counter. A cop's kid at work.

Paris had gone name brand all the way with Melissa's basket, remembering how, when he was a kid, his mother would sometimes have to go with budget candy because times were tough. And some years, there was simply no money at all. Melissa's basket, on the other hand, which also contained a stuffed Opus the Penguin doll and a small plastic Woodstock that you could wind up and watch scoot across the table, had set him back fifty dollars.

Melissa walked over to the dinette table and plucked a hard-boiled egg from the centerpiece: a two-foot-high bunny made out of accordion paper and surrounded by green cellulose and what looked like two dozen brightly painted eggs. She removed a strand of hay and handed Paris the egg. "Easter bunny left this for *you,*" she said. The egg was light blue with dark blue speckles. It had a bright red *Daddy* across one side, and a decal of a duck with a policeman's cap drawn in on the other.

"It's beautiful, Missy," Paris said, choking a bit, glancing at Beth, who was still looking out the window. "Thank you." He kissed her on the top of her head in the instant before she grabbed her basket and raced into the living room, leaving a trail of a dozen or so Jelly Bellies in her wake.

"She worked really hard on that egg," Beth said, crossing the kitchen with the coffeepot. She topped off Paris's cup. "All I got was a plain white egg with a *Mom* sticker on it."

Paris crouched down and began to pick up the jelly beans. "She's getting so big. I nearly walked right by her at the Olive Garden."

"Junior high next year," Beth said wistfully.

The words filled him with disquiet. Junior high. His little angel. Paris stood up and dropped the jelly beans into the wastebasket. "Wasn't it just a few weeks ago she went running up to the glass wall at Sea World yelling 'Samoo, Samoo' and got splashed and screamed her brains out?"

Beth smiled. "Or, remember the time—I think she was about two, maybe two and a half, still in diapers, though—when you told her that airplanes were exactly the same size as they looked in the sky and that they could fly really low and get tangled up in her hair. And then she heard the plane that one day and—"

"She ran out of the house with a saucepan on her head," Jack said.

"I could've killed you for that," Beth said, laughing. "I think she got over that one about a week ago."

They went quiet for a few moments, Jack turning the handle of his coffee cup around and around. They had laughed together and the sound was so foreign to him. Odd, but warming at the same time. Finally, he asked. "So how is she, Beth?"

"She's still adjusting, Jack. She doesn't cry every day anymore and she's doing better in school. Her friends are coming around more now. But she still talks about you all the time. Her daddy, the cop. Even *with* the karate lessons, it's still her most effective playground threat."

Paris smiled. "As long as I don't have to shoot anyone named Skippy or Chip or Scooter," he said.

"Skippy?" Beth said, smiling broadly. "You are so *square*, Jack. Kids haven't been nicknamed Skippy since Bozo went off the air."

"She isn't . . . uh . . . She doesn't have like a . . . boyfriend or anything, does she? Like some kid who walks her home or something? Or some kid she goes to the library with or somewhere?"

"Jack, she's *eleven* years old. You think she's dating?"

"Well," Paris began, feeling a little stupid, "she's going to be twelve and that's one year away from being thirteen and that's a *teenager.* And teenagers *date.*"

Beth threw her head back and laughed. "You are too much, Jack Paris. I'll try to keep the little Lotharios in line for a few more weeks. Keep those raging hormones in check."

Paris screwed up his face. "How can you use that word anywhere near our daughter's name?"

"What word?"

Paris whispered. "Hormones." He tried to keep a straight face, but it was hopeless. They both laughed again.

It didn't last long, though, and soon they were back at their awkward postures. Paris took a big, painful gulp of the hot coffee and stood up. "Gotta run, Beth . . . bad guys are waiting." It was an old line, one that Beth would use to placate the pouting three-year-old Melissa when her father the patrolman had to head off to work second shift. *"Baggize?"* the little girl would ask, quizzically, all brown eyes and curls. Her parents would then dissolve into laughter, and they would all give each other a three-way hug and kiss. A "gang-smooch" they used to called it. Way back in the Stone Age. "Thanks for the coffee."

"Oh . . . you're welcome, Jack," Beth replied. "You don't have to . . ." She trailed off.

They stood face-to-face for a few moments, clumsily out of love. "And . . . uh . . . happy Easter, too." Paris reached out to kiss her, when, on the other side of the huge apartment, a key turned noisily in the lock. He dropped his hands and looked at the floor.

"Bethy?" It was a man's voice. Paris looked up, met his wife's eyes and mouthed the word, a questioning look on his face. She glanced away, suddenly afraid that she would burst out laughing. Paris looked around the corner and saw for the first time the new man in the lives of his wife and daughter.

Paris made Dr. Bob to be about forty, trim and tanned, collegiately handsome, perhaps an inch or two taller than himself. He wore a navy-blue worsted suit with some kind of club tie, and the standard wing tips that befitted a man of his standing.

"You must be Jack," Robert said, his hand leading him the entire thirty or so feet between the front door and the entrance to the kitchen. Paris waited until the man's hand was in the same zip code as his own before reacting.

"Someone has to be," Paris said with a smile. "And I must have lost the coin toss." They shook hands. "And you have to be Robert, right?"

"Yes . . . yes . . ." Robert said, glancing between Paris and Beth, then back again, not really sure how to react to this rumpled ex-husband cop daddy stranger. "Hi hon," he said to Beth, but didn't dare lean across and kiss her.

"Hate to just run off like this but duty calls, I'm afraid," Paris said, immediately thinking that he was starting to sound like Barnaby Jones or something. "Nice to have met you, *Bob*," he added. He exchanged a quick glance with Melissa, who immediately covered her mouth. "Take good care of my girls."

"I'll do my best," Robert said. His frozen grin remained in place and unthawed.

"Or I'll arrest you," Paris added with a wink. He kissed Beth on the cheek, Melissa on top of her head, and shook the rather weak right hand of Dr. Robert Allan Abramson, pediatrician, surrogate daddy and brand-new boyfriend.

o   o   o

PARIS STOPPED AT ARABICA ON THE SQUARE AND PICKED UP A PAIR OF MEGA-muffins and two large coffees for Tommy and himself. The coffee at the Justice Center on Sundays was generally a lot worse than during the week—due to the fact that one of the detectives was responsible for brewing it. In line he had heard two women discussing the morning's *Plain Dealer* cover story about the killings. They seemed to think that the killer was a mother-hater, sadly deprived of affection when he was weaned, someone from whom the legal and psychiatric communities could learn a great deal if they would only see the poor man as a victim, not some sort of devil.

God, he hated the Heights, Paris thought. Deprivation? The only thing he wanted to deprive this sick asshole of was air.

He drove up Fairhill, cut across University Circle and got on Chester Avenue just as the churches let out their nine o'clock Easter masses. Paris noticed the families, mostly black, dressed in their finery: snug little units that sauntered up the avenue, renewed and re-newing. They all looked so happy, so together, so cohesive. Although Paris knew better than to idealize anyone else's situation. He had seen enough of life's underbelly to know that nothing is ever what it seems or, for that matter, as good as it looks.

He pulled into the lot at the Justice Center just as Tommy was getting out of his car, a TransAm. Word had it that somehow Tommy had managed to buy a new Pontiac every two years since high school and each one of them had been some combination of white, black and gray. It was only one of Tommy Raposo's quirks, pulled from his bottomless bag of superstitions. "Hey Jack," Tommy said. He was dressed casually, much the same as Paris—jeans, polo shirt and Timberland deck shoes—but somehow it looked a lot better on him. "See the *Plain Dealer* yet?"

Paris shut off the engine of his Olds and listened to the postignition do its Ginger Baker drum solo for about twenty seconds. "You believe it?" he finally said, stepping out of the car. "Fucking paper's turning into the *Enquirer*, I swear."

"Or *USA Today* . . ."

"You mean the Three-D map?"

"Yeah," Tommy said. Ever since the city's only daily newspaper had gone color, the need to justify the expense manifested itself in a number of pointless ways. Three-dimensional maps of the city were used whenever there were two dog bite victims in a twenty-four-hour period. "What, we gonna have aerial surveillance on this? We need to know distances in case we have to fire a missile?"

Paris laughed. "I need you big-time on this one, *paesan*."

"You own me, Jack," Tommy said, holding open the door to the stairs. "I'm telling you, no pussy, no nightlife, no nothing. I don't eat, I don't sleep, I'm yours twenty-four, seven, three hundred and sixty-five till this fucker's in jail or dead or both."

"Let's hope it ain't three hundred and sixty-five," Paris said.

The two men stepped inside and were met with total chaos.

o   o   o

SUNDAY MORNING IS THE TIME OF THE WEEK—ESPECIALLY IN LAW ENFORCEMENT and emergency room care—when the brilliant ideas of the previous Saturday night cash in their vouchers. Drunk tanks are always full, assault and drug charges always lead the way among complaints. Everybody is bitchy and sleepy and strung out and hung over and not about to recover anytime soon.

"Hey *Serpico . . .*" someone yelled in Paris's direction. "When's the movie coming out?" Paris heard some greasy laughter from the other side of the room. The noise had come from a junkie named Scotty Delfs, whom Paris had used on occasion while working Narcotics.

Paris just sort of nodded his head at Scotty Delfs as he and Tommy quickly wound their way through the crowded booking area, holding their coffee cups high, and ran up the back steps.

On the way up, Paris caught a glimpse of something even more ominous than the milling dregs of Cleveland's underworld. Even though the press conference wasn't scheduled for another six hours, Paris could see the media already setting up.

The sixth floor was a lot quieter, with only two secretaries on duty and a handful of detectives. Paris looked into the common room and saw Greg Ebersole and Bobby Dietrich talking animatedly about something. It was probably Dietrich bitching about the politics of interdepartmental cocksucking that resulted in him—King Collar—not getting this cherry of an assignment. Paris was going to enjoy running Bobby Dietrich ragged.

Paris checked the messages on his desk. Nothing pressing. He started to gather the files on the two cases he was in charge of, when Miriam Bostwick, the secretary whose services he shared with Tommy and Greg Ebersole, poked her head into his office.

"Congratulations," she said in a loud stage whisper. She made a fist and shook it in the direction of Bobby Dietrich's office. "Go *get* him."

"Thanks, Miriam," Paris said softly.

Miriam Bostwick, an old navy pilot's wife, gave him a quick thumbs-up. "I've made five sets of copies of the important files," she said, pointing toward the copier table. "They're ready whenever you are," she added, and walked down the hall.

"I think she digs you, Jack," Tommy said, smiling.

"I'm too old to go for older women, Tommy. You add up the numbers, it's frightening." He gathered the files under his arm, grabbed his coffee and exchanged a woeful glance with his partner.

"This is it, partner," Tommy said. "Start of something big, eh?"

"Start of something," Paris said.

                    o   o   o

THE COMMANDING OFFICER OF THE HOMICIDE UNIT WAS CAPTAIN RANDALL EL-liott, but everyone in the department referred to him as Oscar Meyer. Behind his back, that is. It seems that one night Elliott, in the throes of passion with the missus, in *flagrante delicto,* heard a noise in the kitchen, threw on a pair of pants, surprised the perpetrator and chased him out the back door. After a few seconds, and some hand-to-hand combat, Elliott collared the man and took him into custody as three patrol cars arrived at the scene.

Elliott, fired up from the chase, emboldened by the act of best-ing the intruder, had no idea that a certain part of his anatomy was swinging in the breeze as he dragged the suspect to the patrol car— in plain view of at least thirty neighbors and six cops—his little backup unit dangling freely from his unzipped station door.

The nickname never went away.

But you never said it to his face. Especially on a day like today. This day, Captain Randall Elliott had the look of a man with a ten-ton mayor on his back.

The task force was made up of five detectives, including Paris and Tommy Raposo. There was also Sergeant Greg Ebersole and Sergeant Cynthia Taggart, on loan from the Fourth, and last but not least there was Sergeant Robert Dietricht, who seemed to be taking the news with a surprising amount of tact and team spirit. Paris wondered what he was up to.

But five big-city detectives—when combining their respective Rolodexes of informants, stool pigeons, crackheads and networks of fringe players that a group of veteran cops would acquire over the years—threw a rather wide net, reaching far beyond the city or even the county's borders. In all, it amounted to a few thousand people who, when push came to shove, could be pressed into action.

In this case, push came to shove the moment the razor descended upon Karen Schallert.

"We think we have a psychopath on the loose, people," Elliott said in his slaggy Midwest brogue, bringing the group to order. "Three women, nearly six months, no leads. And we've been averaging a half-dozen calls an hour since the *Plain Dealer* broke the story this morning. How do we tell them it's okay to leave the house? Or that it's okay to stop at the corner tavern for a drink?" He turned and looked at Paris. "What do we have, Jack?"

It was Elliott's awkward way of passing the baton.

Paris rose and opened his portfolio. "Let me first brief you on what we have so far. All three women were white and in their twenties, but, as you'll see, they all looked much younger," he began as he placed the crime scene photos on the trilevel easel at the foot of the table, somewhat surprised at his authoritative tone. "Karen Schallert was twenty-three, Emily Reinhardt was twenty-four, Maryann Milius was twenty-two. They were all working women, no criminal records, except the usual motor vehicle stuff. No drugs, no gang affiliations, no intrigue." Paris placed the last of the photos on the easel and stepped to the side. "Neither Milius nor Reinhardt were seeing anyone special at the times of their death. Maryann Milius had an ex-husband but he has an airtighter in Phoenix the week of her murder. As far as Schallert goes, we haven't interviewed her family yet as to the woman's personal life."

"What about murder weapons?" asked Cyndy Taggart.

"Straight razor," Paris said. "All three had patches of skin removed, but Karen Schallert's was the only one recovered at the scene. On it was a tattoo of a pair of roses. I spoke with Emily Reinhardt's father and he told me she had a rose tattoo on her shoulder, which is consistent with the patch of skin that was missing."

"Were the other two patches of skin ever found?" Bobby Dietrich asked.

"I'm afraid not," Paris said. He picked up a pointer and continued. "What else appears to link these three murders is that the victims were all found with what looks like a professionally applied layer of makeup on their faces—powder, rouge, lipstick, eye shadow, the works. Reuben thinks that in two of the cases for sure the makeup was applied *after* the time of death. Lab's working on a comparison study which we should have by Tuesday or Wednesday morning. But the crime scenes have all been very clean. Not a drop of anything that didn't belong to the victim—no semen, no saliva, no urine in the toilet. If this is in fact the work of a single killer, he is extremely thorough. No prints, no palms, no partials.

"All three women went out to a nightclub alone and were never seen alive again. And we're not talking some rum bucket down by the river. We're talking fern bars, hotel lounges, yuppie watering holes. The Radisson, the Ritz-Carlton, the Marriott."

"Sounds like it's time to dust off my Travolta suit," Greg Eber-sole said, drawing laughs from Tommy and Dietricht. "We're going *under . . .*"

"I'm afraid it's the only way," Paris said. "This psycho is cruising the bars and that means we cruise with him."

Paris placed the sketch of the suspect as described by the night clerk of the Quality Inn onto the easel. The oversized Irish walking hat effectively hid the upper half of the man's face, and the rest was taken up by tinted glasses and a big mustache. The man's nose was straight, his jawline square.

"That's our boy, eh?" Tommy asked.

"Looks like you, Raposo," Greg Ebersole said, drawing chuckles from around the room and a crumpled cup from Tommy.

"That's him," Paris said. "White male, thirty, over six feet. Checked into the rooms at both the Quality Inn and the Red Valley Inn. Paid cash for both, of course." Paris distributed the files to each of the detectives. "Looks like we're going to be spending some time at the yuppie meat markets."

"Could be worse," Tommy said. "I saw *Cruising,* you know."

"What, like heteros don't get vicious?" said the politically correct Bobby Dietricht, a little too loudly.

Tommy turned slowly and glared at Dietricht. The feud between these two was three months running already, and everybody in the room rolled their eyes because they knew exactly what was coming next. "I'm sorry . . . Did you take that *personally,* Bobby? Because if you did, I apologize. I didn't mean to offend you."

"Fuck you, Raposo."

"Right here?" Tommy said, sliding off the desk. "You want me to bend over and drop my pants right here? Is that what you're asking me to do?"

Greg Ebersole placed a hand on Dietricht's arm. "Boys . . . - boys . . ."

"You know . . ." Dietricht began, standing up, shaking his head. "You people and your—"

"What?" Tommy yelled as he walked straight into the chest of Greg Ebersole, who stood about four inches shorter than Tommy's six-two frame. "You *people?*" He didn't fight Ebersole too hard to get by, letting the fact that someone was restraining him dictate the ebb and flow of the argument.

"You're so goddamn typical, Raposo—"

"I'm so—"

"Shut the fuck up!"

The shout came from the back of the room. Tommy and Dietricht jumped a bit at the volume and force of the command. They turned, like two third-graders caught misbehaving on the playground, and looked at Cyndy Taggart.

"Gentlemen," she continued, standing, stirring a cup of coffee with her pen. "We have a job to do, don't we?" She sat down and crossed her legs. "Let's play nice until we catch this crazy son of a bitch, okay?"

o   o   o

BECAUSE OF THE UNDERCOVER ASSIGNMENTS ON THE CASE, RANDALL ELLIOTT conducted the news conference while the five detectives remained out of sight. Paris and Cyndy Taggart, they had determined, would be going undercover on the east side; Tommy, Ebersole and Dietricht would all team up with female vice officers and cover the south side, the west side and downtown, respectively. They would begin the following Wednesday night.

Paris put his homework in his briefcase—including photographs of all three crime scenes and the autopsy protocols for the first two victims—and grabbed his coat. He was wrestling with whether or not to stop at the Caprice for a quick one before heading home, when his phone rang, deciding for him.

"Homicide, Paris."

"Officer Paris?"

It was a woman, maybe in her mid-twenties by the sound of her voice. And she was nervous. "*Detective* Paris," he said, correcting her. "What can I do for you?"

"Um . . . I was calling about the . . . um . . . the story in the *Plain Dealer?*"

She made it sound like a question. They all did. Paris had spoken to thousands of people like her in his seventeen years on the force, people who are afraid to get involved, people who have been fucked over or know someone who has been fucked over, and they figure that if it all sounded like a question, the answer might be: No. No, you aren't going to die. No, you're not going to jail. "This morning's *Plain Dealer?*" he asked.

"Yeah . . . and . . . uh . . . well, you see . . . I met this man . . ." She trailed off.

Paris waited a few beats, then prompted her again. "And?"

Deep breath. "I think he might be the guy you're looking for."

Paris sat up a little straighter. "What makes you think so?"

"Well . . ." the woman began, stressing out by the minute. "I'd . . . I'd rather not talk about it on the phone."

"Were you attacked?"

"Oh *no*," she said. "No, no . . . I'm fine. Nothing like that."

Paris eased up. "Would you like to come down to the station and talk? We're located at the corner of—"

"Uh, could we meet somewhere else?" she asked.

"Sure," Paris said. "Where do you have in mind?"

"How about the lounge at the Radisson?"

"Which one?"

"The Radisson East," she said. "In Beachwood."

"That's fine. What time?"

They made arrangements, but as they did, Paris sensed that he might be losing her, that she might be setting him up for a no-show.

"If you like," Paris continued, "I could bring a female officer along." He caught Cyndy Taggart's eye and waved her into his office. She came in and sat on the edge of his desk. "She's very nice and she's very good at her job. I could even send her alone if you'd like."

The woman hesitated for a few moments, but then said: "No, it's okay. I'll be there. I really will."

"Sure?"

"Yes."

"And how will I know you?" Paris asked.

"Oh, uh, I'll be wearing . . ." She trailed off again, a career woman who didn't know she'd be planning an outfit this late at night. "I'll be wearing an oatmeal skirt and a beige cardigan."

"Fine," Paris said, jotting the information down in his notebook, knowing he would look at the word "oatmeal" somewhere down the line and wonder what the hell it meant.

"And how will I know *you?*" she asked.

"Well . . ." Paris began, hoping to lighten the conversation up a bit, "do you know what Alec Baldwin looks like?"

Cyndy smiled and rolled her eyes.

"Uh, yes," the woman said, a quizzical edge to her voice.

"Me too," he continued. "I'll be wearing a black sportcoat and I'll be sitting as close as I can to the entrance." It was either a really lousy joke or the woman was still way too freaked out to find the humor. Jack Paris opted for the latter explanation.

9

ANDIE HUNG UP THE BEDROOM PHONE AND PEEKED around the corner, looking for Matt. But there was no sign of him. He was still eating dinner. She crossed the bedroom to the bathroom, letting her robe drop to the floor, turned the water on hot and stepped into the shower.

The water soon reached the perfect temperature and Andie turned into it fully, letting it cascade over her breasts, down her abdomen, her legs. She followed the stream with a smooth bar of soap, rounding the curve of her hips, creating a lather slowly, rhythmically.

She knew she had crossed a line the previous night—she was willing to bet that she had crossed nearly all of them, from the look on Matt's face at the end of the evening—but there was something beneath the surface of the game, something that drove her to do what she did, as if she had little or no control of herself. She had wanted to flirt. She had wanted to be wanted. She had wanted . . . *what?*

She still wasn't sure. But she knew enough to know that it wasn't over.

When she had stopped at Ava's HairPort at Seventh and Prospect at around four o'clock that afternoon, she had no idea what she would buy. She had never bought a wig in her life and, although she was bound and determined to finally live out at least the first phase of her fantasy, she wasn't about to drop two hundred dollars on something that, best-case scenario, she might wear a half-dozen times in her life.

"What can I do for *you?*" the saleswoman had asked with that knowing smile that some women, women who are far freer about their sexuality than Andrea Della Croce–Heller on Wheels would ever hope to be, always seem to possess. This time the woman was black, mid-thirties, and she smiled as she looked Andie up and down. She wore a red wig, cut into Prince Valiant bangs in the front and razored straight up into an inverted V in the back. Her fingernails were bright turquoise and sported small opalesque stones in the center of each.

What *am* I up to? Andie thought. What was she doing in a cheap wig store on a sooty downtown street, gearing up, literally, to do

God knows what—with, near or in front of her husband? "Well . . ." she began, "what I'm up to is getting my husband up to—" She stopped, seized by the double entendre of what she had said, and burst into laughter. The saleswoman, whose name was Denisha, joined her.

"I know what *you* need, girlfriend," Denisha said. "It's what all us women of brunette shading must turn to at times." She sashayed down the narrow area behind the counter. "That is, if we want to keep our men up and running, if you know what I mean." Denisha wore a tight red and black pin-dot dress with extraordinarily large capped sleeves and silver drop earrings in the shape of T squares.

Andie followed her, marveling at the array of wigs and hairpieces and color sprays. A person could walk out of this place another woman, she thought, as Denisha reached into the window and pulled out a blond, shoulder-length, spiral-curled wig.

But that *is* what I'm doing here, she thought.

Isn't it?

At first she thought the wig made her look like a streetwalker and, at first, that was a negative. Because Andie Heller always took the traditional road to fashion: Pringle sweaters, Burberry coats, Land's End polos and espadrilles. But when Denisha spun her around in the chair and held a mirror up behind her, and she saw the soft, golden curls splayed out against the black of her blazer, Andie Heller *was* another woman. Even her friends might not have known her from behind.

Even Matt.

There was something about it that seemed to transform her. Perhaps, she thought as Denisha rang up the sale, it had something to do with the fact that although she spent most of her time at the high end of the cosmetics industry—lunching in the best restaurants, cocktailing with the international fashion fops—there was something about *this* end that excited her. Something about the chalky scent of the cheap powders, the look of the outrageously colored eye shadows and the low gloss of the waxy lipsticks.

Andie left the store wearing the wig, her collar up, her huge sunglasses snugly in place, standing guard between her and the daylight world.

o   o   o

ALL THROUGH DINNER MATT HAD STARED AT HER IN SOMETHING THAT AP-
proached wonderment, Andie had thought. Like a kid at his own
birthday party. But she knew that, beneath that boyish fascination
with her admittedly outrageous prank, Matt was very excited. She
knew she was turning him on, and it was fun and she felt as if she
might try anything.

During dessert, when she reached over and felt the measure of
Matt's erection beneath the table, she had her answer.

"I've got this idea," she had said as she tongued his ear. "Tell me
what you think."

They drove to Painesville and she sent Matt into the bar first,
alone. She waited in the car, and even though the alcohol was ham-
mering at her to just do it, to take this all to the next level, she still
had second thoughts.

But when she walked through the lobby of the Painesville Sheraton, and drew the stare of every man between the ages of sixteen
and ninety, she was energized again. And barbarously aroused.

She sat a few stools to the left of her husband, and ordered a
White Russian. A hooker's drink, she thought. She crossed her legs
and wished that she smoked. It would have been a perfect moment
to light a cigarette.

It didn't take long for the men to swoop.

The first man to hit on her was named Geoffrey Faragut, Jr. He
said he was an attorney with Sanders, Felder and Goldstein and that
no, he didn't come to the Painesville Sheraton all that often, but yes,
he sure would like to buy her a drink.

There wasn't anything terribly wrong with Geoffrey Faragut, Jr.,
in Andie's eyes—he was pleasant-looking enough, and he had a certain boyish *joie*—but she met a lot of Geoffreys in her line of work.
Average-looking men. No spark, no flame. And none could hold a
candle to Matt Heller, of course. Andie sighed a few times, and
when the conversation lapsed into a coma, Geoffrey Faragut, Jr., got
the hint and took off.

She had glanced over at Matt as the deejay spun out of a se-
quence of slow songs and into a heavy reggae tune. Matt's face was
a mixture of lust and lost; like he wanted this to go on forever and

he wanted to leave. Andie saw him lean over just as another man stepped between them. He was taller and far handsomer than the first.

The man didn't introduce himself right away, but instead made a comment about the extraordinary resemblance between the recently departed Mr. Faragut, Jr., and one Opie Taylor of Mayberry. Andie laughed, partially because she saw it was true, and partially because she was somewhat overwhelmed by the man's looks.

They chatted for a while, but Andie would later be hard-pressed to say about what. The man asked her to dance as the deejay swung back into a slow number.

She said yes.

She slow-danced with the stranger as Matt moved to the edge of the dance floor and sipped his beer, running his eyes over the two of them, watching her hands, his hands. Andie could not believe that she was in the arms of another man in front of her husband. The thought, as much as the alcohol, had an intoxicating effect.

But she had no idea what to do next, or what Matt wanted her to do next.

So she did nothing.

She thanked the man for the dance, walked briskly past her husband, grabbed her blazer off her stool and walked out of the bar. She was spooked but she was also pretty damned proud of herself. And wet as hell.

They had come in separate cars and they took different routes home, both dallying along the way for their own reasons. After they got home they didn't speak much, and after undressing silently, they climbed into bed. Their lovemaking seemed a bit tentative at first, as if Matt wasn't quite sure how he felt about any of it, even though he had carefully planted the seeds of an evening such as this years earlier. But after a few minutes, they began to pick up steam, as they always did.

Midway, Matt asked Andie to put the wig back on.

She did, and more than once wondered if Matt imagined he was having sex with another woman. If he thought she was—

The shadow nearly made her jump. The water had cooled considerably, and she wondered how long she had been in the shower. But Matt's fleshy, distorted image on the other side of the frosted glass threw a bolt of excitement and fear down her back. In the instant before he pushed the glass door to the side, Andie looked down and was somewhat surprised to find her hand between her legs.

Her husband stepped into the shower. "Hi," he said.

"H-hi."

Matt was already half-erect. He had been watching her. "Need any help with anything here?" He cupped her breasts in his hands, leaned over and lifted one of them to his lips. He ran his tongue around her nipple.

"I might," Andie said, standing on her tiptoes, accommodating him, the excitement starting to build again. She grabbed him and began to stroke his penis, pulling him roughly toward her.

"So do we go out or stay in tonight?" Matt asked with the makings of that lascivious smile.

"Mmmm . . . I have a meeting tonight," she said. "I have to leave in a little bit."

"Again?"

"Sorry, honey," Andie said. "But . . ." she began as she bent forward, kissed Matt deeply and stroked him faster, "we'll go out and play soon, okay?"

"S-soon?" Matt said softly as he closed his eyes, holding on to the top of the tub enclosure.

Andie dropped to her knees. "Soon."

1 0

HER NAME WAS ELEANOR BURCHFIELD AND SHE WAS late.

She had called Paris back almost immediately, probably with the intention of canceling, but Paris had talked her out of it. At least, he hoped he had. In an attempt to explain it all over the phone, she said that she had met the man, they had danced a few dances, tossed a few drinks back, then gone to his motel room in Solon, nearly twenty miles away. Paris asked her if she hadn't thought it strange for the man to have met her at a hotel bar and then to have taken her to a motel. Eleanor Burchfield replied that that was only one of the things she felt pretty damn stupid about regarding that night.

Paris posted himself at the end of the bar, near the entrance to the lounge at the Beachwood Radisson, hoping the woman hadn't been spooked.

The bar was about a third full and the music was basically yuppie-lounge-bar Kenny G in the can with an occasional Phil Collins tune thrown in for good measure. Paris was a Beatles/Stones/Kinks man, but he could usually tolerate anything but rap and opera.

"Can I get you another?" the barmaid asked. She was impossibly young and athletic-looking: huge hair, early twenties, very petite. She wore a tight red vest over a white pirate shirt with a black miniskirt. Seamed stockings.

"Sure," Paris said.

According to her tag, the barmaid's name was Rita, and when she put Paris's beer down in front of him she knocked twice on the bar. "On the house," she said with a smile. "Officer."

They stared at each other for a few seconds, exchanging resolve, until Paris broke away and sipped his beer. "What makes you think I'm a cop?"

"Seriously?" Rita said, giving him the twice-over. She thought for a moment. "It's the jacket. Definitely, the jacket."

Paris had stopped at his apartment and thrown on a suit jacket over his polo shirt and jeans. He thought it made him look pretty nineties—casual and elegant at the same time—but he was about to hear the opposite, he guessed. He was just glad Tommy wasn't with him. He'd never have heard the end of it.

"See, only a cop would think a suit jacket is the same thing as a blazer," she said. "They're not interchangeable, you know. Suit jackets go with a specific pair of pants. For life. One pair of pants per jacket. That's it." She lifted Paris's beer, wiped the bar beneath it, then set it down on a fresh cocktail napkin. "Now a blazer," she continued, leaning forward, "a blazer goes with jeans, with slacks, with corduroys. Blazers are a lot more practical because you can wear them with anything. Blazers are the way to go. Especially for divorced men." She winked at him and placed a small bowl of goldfish crackers on the bar.

"You could tell that, too?" Paris asked.

"Hey, what do you think I do here all night?" She got a call from the other end of the bar. "I watch people," she said, walking away backward. "I *know* people. I could be a *cop*."

That you could, Paris thought.

The hotel bar was starting to fill up, mostly with what looked like graduate students trying to get in that one last cruise before heading back to school after their Easter break. The men still outnumbered the women—at least that much had not changed since Paris had gone wolfing the first time around, nearly twenty years earlier—but he noticed that the young women were a lot more aggressive than he recalled. That was certainly different.

Yet it *had* been the twenty-two-year-old Elizabeth Shefler that had asked *him* to dance that sweltering July night so many years ago. It was a slow dance, he recalled. Slow and sexy. "Reunited" by Peaches and Herb. Paris still played the 45, in all its scratchy splendor, whenever the Windsor Canadian was on all-night duty.

He looked at his waitress, leaning over the opposite side of the bar, her perfect derriere high in the air, and was just about to concede that he had bunions older than Rita the Barmaid when the voice came over his left shoulder.

"Officer Paris?"

Paris turned on his barstool. The woman was in her mid-twenties, strawberry blond, medium build, very pretty. He decided not to correct her on his title. "Yes," he said. "Miss Burchfield?"

She extended her hand. "Call me Ellie," she said.

"Sure," Paris said, shaking her hand. "Jack Paris."

"Sorry I'm late," she said. "Easter and all. I was over the folks and . . ."

"Not a problem. Can I get you something?"

"No thanks," Ellie said. She leaned against the bar. "I had my fill the other night, believe me."

"I understand." The two fell quiet for a few moments, avoiding each other's eyes, looking around the bar.

"I appreciate you meeting me here," she said, "and not making me come downtown."

Paris noticed a slight quiver in her voice. She was scared.

She continued: "I thought that . . . well . . . this is where I met him. And I figured that if you and I met here I might stay pissed off enough to actually go through with this."

Paris had heard it before. The scene keeps you mean. "It's no problem," he said. "If you're not pressing any charges, there was no reason to come down to the station." He was hoping that his point was getting across, but there was no evidence of that happening yet.

Paris showed Ellie the police sketch, but because most of the man's face was obscured, she could not say for sure if it was the same man. They fell silent once again, this time for a few minutes. In that time Rita wiped the bar around them twice, offered up smiles, but remained silent. When Rita returned to the far end of the bar the woman spoke. She told Paris how she had met the man who called himself Pharaoh.

"Do you know how he spells that?"

"No," she said.

"No business card or anything?"

"No. I just assumed it was 'Farrow' as in Mia Farrow, you know? But he never gave me a first name, either. That might have actually *been* his first name. He said it as if he had just the one name. Like Cher or Madonna or something."

Paris wrote 'Farrow' in his book and made a note to check alternate spellings.

"Go on . . ." he said.

Eleanor Burchfield went on to describe her life in brief, skillful sketches. She was twenty-five, a speech pathologist at Lake West, unmarried, not really the nightclub type, in her estimation. But when she did go out out, she rarely went alone. The previous night had been an exception. She told Paris that she had seen the man from across the room and had been immediately taken with him—his looks, his confidence, his impeccable tailoring. Paris decided to wait until she was finished to get the full and detailed facial description of the man.

She described their slow dance, how the man had seduced her, talking her into returning to the Solon Motel with him. Every so often, as she trod lightly over the embarrassing parts, she would look skyward, perhaps for some sort of divine explanation as to why she did what she did.

As if sheer loneliness wasn't good enough, Paris thought.

"Could you ID this man if you saw him again?" Paris asked after he had recorded most of the pertinent details in his notebook. He knew it was a dumb question, having heard how intimate the two had become, but he learned a long time ago to just ask the dumb questions and get them over with.

"Oh yes," Ellie said. "I don't think I'll ever forget this guy."

"What makes you think he had anything to do with these murders?" Paris asked. "Did he strike you, threaten you?"

"No . . . not really," she said. "He was charming as hell in the beginning. Actually . . . right up until I saw the handcuffs. But there was just something about him, you know? Maybe that was part of the attraction for me. You know what I mean? The danger? Most of the men I know are . . . what? . . . I don't know . . . *boring,* I guess." She began to play with her hair. Paris knew that that meant something rather revelatory was forthcoming. He remained absolutely still. "So when he tried to handcuff me to the bed, I wasn't so much surprised as I was frightened. I just got the hell out of there." She sat down on a barstool and crossed her legs. "I feel so *stupid,*" she repeated, as if saying her mantra. "I mean, I'm really not the kind of person to do this . . . to get picked up in a bar and go to a motel room with some guy I don't know. You may not believe me, but I've never done anything like that before."

"Look," Paris began, trying not to sound judgmental, "we're all allowed a few mistakes in life, aren't we? This guy . . . how were you supposed to know?" He finished his beer and pushed the empty glass across the bar. "And on the stupid scale, believe me, you're not even close to the top ten. Stupid is my business. Besides, how are you going to know you're a lady if you don't kiss a few tramps?"

Ellie smiled a little and, for Paris, it lit up her face measurably. She was very charming indeed. "I suppose . . ."

Paris waved to the barmaid, deciding that this one would be coffee. "Would you like to get a booth?" he asked.

"Okay," she replied. "But I'm going to get some cigarettes first. I know it's filthy—please, no lectures. I'll meet you over there."

Paris held his hands up in surrender. "Sure I can't get you something?"

"Uh . . . no thanks," she said.

"Positive?"

"Okay . . . uh . . . Diet Coke's fine," she said. "Be right back."

Paris signaled Rita and watched the woman walk out into the hotel lobby. He could see how what happened to her got started. Eleanor Burchfield was a very attractive woman, very stylish in a *Town & Country* way. And Paris had always gone for the conservative dressers.

He had discreetly looked her over for tattoos, but he hadn't seen any. He would ask.

"Another one?" Rita asked.

"Coffee for me. Black, one sugar," Paris said. "And a Diet Coke."

Rita grabbed a cup, poured the coffee and smiled demurely.

"What?" Paris asked, dropping a twenty on the bar.

"Nothing . . ."

"Rita," Paris said, sounding far more fatherly than he would have liked. "With all we've been through together . . ."

Rita laughed. "It's just that she wasn't drinking Diet Coke last night. But that's none of my business, right?"

"You saw her last night?" Paris asked.

Rita put the mug of coffee in front of him and grabbed the nozzle for the Coke. "*Oh* yeah," she said. "She was with this fucking dreamboat." She looked up quickly, a little embarrassed. "Sorry."

"I've heard the word once or twice," Paris said. He retrieved the police sketch from the adjacent barstool. "Could this be the guy?"

"This could be anybody," Rita said, staring at the sketch. "This could be a million different guys."

"Okay. Go on."

"Anyway, I noticed the guy right away, even though he was hanging around the corner over there," she said, motioning to a dark corner of the bar, across from the entrance. She put the Coke in front of him and grabbed the twenty. "Tall, dark suit, wavy hair. Like a movie star."

Paris took out his notebook. "What color hair?"

"Brown, I think. Like yours, I guess. Maybe darker. There's not a lot of light in here, you know."

"Yes, of course," Paris said. "What's your full name?"

"Shit," Rita said, putting the change on the bar.

"Can you spell that for me please?" Oldest cop joke on record.

"Am I allowed to ask what this is about or no?" Rita asked, smiling, but not laughing.

"Just routine," Paris said. But he already knew Rita well enough to know that that wouldn't be the end of it.

"Um, routine . . . about . . . like . . . *what?*" She made small circular motions with her hands, punctuating each word.

Paris told her. She straightened up immediately, as was befitting the gravity of the circumstance, and did her civic duty, telling him all that she remembered about the night in question. Rita—full name, Rita Constance Weisinger—told him no, she had not seen this man before and yes, believe her, she would have remembered. She also said she thought he was drinking Absolut on the rocks, but couldn't be sure. He was in for about an hour, danced slow once or twice with Eleanor Burchfield, then left. And no, she hadn't seen them leave.

"Would you be willing to talk to a police artist?"

"Sure," Rita said with a slight grimace. "You know, I'm starting to regret buying you that beer."

Paris smiled and put his notebook in his pocket. "Yeah . . . but think of how you'll swell with civic pride when we catch this maniac."

Rita rolled her eyes.

"I'll talk to you when I'm done with this interview," Paris said. He looked at his watch. The Burchfield woman had been gone ten minutes. He grabbed the drinks and motioned toward one of the booths with a nod of his head. "We'll be over here if you remember anything else."

"Yeah, yeah," Rita said, wiping down the bar, finding nothing surprising at all about the fact that the gorgeous ones were always the ones who turned out to be fucking crazy.

o o o

GETTING CHANGE FOR THE CIGARETTE MACHINE HAD BEEN AN UNBELIEVABLE ordeal. The gift shop, where they would have been available over the counter for some outrageous gouge of a markup anyway, had closed at ten. Cigarettes were $2.75 in the machine and, of course, the front desk didn't have enough change, so one of the bellhops had to go into the lounge and get change and bring it back. Then, after running the quarters through the temperamental machine three times, Ellie pulled the handle for Newports, but the machine was out of them. Ditto for Kools. And Salems. In fact, she was to discover, the machine was out of menthol cigarettes in general.

She had thought she had the habit licked, but since her bout with Mr. Handcuffs she had already smoked three packs and didn't seem to be able to talk to anyone for too long without one lit and in her right hand. She finally opted for (yuck) Winston Lights and turned to leave the tiny alcove, when she ran straight into a woman carrying a plastic glass full of cabernet sauvignon. The deep burgundy liquid seemed to hover between them for a moment—apparently deciding who had the more expensive outfit—then proceeded to bounce off Ellie's chest in a splash worthy of the opening credits to *Hawaii Five-O.*

Let's see, Ellie thought in that instant, insult plus injury equals . . . exactly . . . $125 for the cardigan she would soon contribute to the landfill.

"Oh my *God!*" the woman said, covering her mouth in shock. "I am so *sorry.*"

The woman was fiftyish, on the tall side, mousy, dressed in a rather ordinary cotton-print smock, and was carrying an overcoat and an overnight bag in her other hand, the hand not engaged in spilling wine on Ellie Burchfield. She wore very thick glasses, very cheap perfume, and had a beauty mark on her cheek, à la Miss Kitty on *Gunsmoke.*

"Oh . . . it's all *right*," Ellie said, meaning exactly the opposite.

"I can't believe I . . . I am *so* clumsy I . . ."

"Really," Ellie said. "Don't worry about it.

"You know *what*," the woman began, snapping her fingers. "I have a bottle of club soda in my room." She looked at her key. "I'm just around the corner in one-eighteen."

"Well, if it's not too much trouble," Ellie said.

"*Nah*. Not at all. Least I can do. Name's Earline Pender." She stuck out her hand.

Ellie introduced herself.

They rounded the corner and the woman pushed open the door, which was slightly ajar already. She called out to her husband.

"Ben?"

No answer.

"Women on the poop deck, Ben," she said with a brief chuckle. "Stow your anchor."

Ben Pender? Ellie thought. What a curse of a name. But it didn't look like she was about to meet its owner anytime soon.

"Oh well," Earline mumbled. "In the bar'm sure." She tossed her bag on the bed. "Club soda's on the table and the bathroom's over there," she added, heading back out the door. "Be right back. Was going for a pack of smokes myself."

She left the room.

Ellie grabbed the one-liter bottle of Cotton Club club soda, crossed the room to the bathroom, spread the sweater out on the vanity top and poured the carbonated water over the deep red stain.

She decided that she would go back out to the bar and apologize to Detective Paris for wasting his time. Then, of course, she realized that he'd never let her go without asking her a million other questions about Mr. Handcuffs, so she decided to just leave.

Because the man from the other night simply was not the killer he was looking for. Couldn't have been. He was just some dance hall Romeo, a little kinky maybe, but just a gigolo nonetheless. Why would a guy like that have to kill women? He was beautiful. So he liked to tie girls up when he had sex. Big deal. We all have our deviant little ways, don't we?

Sure we do.

o   o   o

ELLIE PAUSED AND LIT A WINSTON LIGHT. THE RED WINE STAIN ON HER sweater was permanent, and that seemed to be that. She had already given up on the notion of having a beige cardigan in her wardrobe, so, unless the clumsy Mrs. Earline Pender was really filthy rich and intended to flip her a pair of hundred-dollar bills for her trouble, the cardigan was heading for the Dumpster.

Without the ivory buttons, though, Ellie thought. No need to make it a total loss.

She drew on the cigarette once, then tossed it into the toilet with a look of disgust. As she flushed the toilet, she thought she heard the door to the hotel room click shut.

Or did she?

"Mrs. Pender?" Ellie said, looking out into the darkened bedroom, her eyes momentarily affronted by the sudden change of light. "I don't think I'm going to get this stain out after all . . ."

Silence.

"*Mr.* Pender?" Ellie tried again, but decided she was mistaken. The noise must have come from the hallway. She felt along the wall for a light switch.

Then came a glimmer from near the bed, just a few feet away. A brief sword of incandescence in the black room.

Ellie stepped forward. "Earline?"

A hand shot out of the darkness. It closed quickly around Ellie's mouth, then slammed her head against the steel doorjamb, stunning her, her mind showing her stars. Ellie began to struggle but there was another hand immediately at her chest. The fingers were powerful, ironlike.

The flat, petroleum smell of the rubber glove filled her nostrils and Ellie saw in an instant that the reflection she had seen had danced off the blade of a straight razor—long, highly polished, pearl-handled. Muscular arms dragged her back into the brightness of the bathroom and tossed her against the wall, pummeling the air from her lungs.

The woman who called herself Earline Pender held Ellie tightly against the cool blue tile. Her breath was hot and sweet with mouthwash.

Ellie glanced down and saw that the woman had changed her shoes. She now wore white stiletto-heeled pumps. Through the opening in her coat, Ellie also saw that the woman was nude.

"I know who you're talking to out there," the woman said. She lifted a solitary finger from Ellie's mouth, daring her to make a sound.

"Whuh . . ." was all Ellie could manage.

The woman increased the pressure, the razor now lying up against the fleshy well at the base of Ellie's throat.

"Don't *fuck* with me, kitty cat," the woman said. She tapped the razor once with her forefinger, as if knocking the ash from a cigarette, drawing a trickle of blood. "I know who he is. It's the cop from the newspaper, right?"

Ellie could see that the woman was younger than she had originally thought. The lines on her face seemed to have been drawn in, the gray streaks in her hair sprayed on. But the beauty mark was real. "Yuh . . . yes . . ." she said.

The woman looked at the ground for a moment, thinking. She brought herself to within an inch or two of Ellie's face. "Where does he think you are right now?"

"Guh-getting cigarettes," she said, her eyes beginning to glisten with tears. The woman looked at her curiously for a moment, flicked her tongue out, waiting, it seemed, for one of the tears to fall. Then, as a tear gathered at the corner of Ellie's eye, the woman watched it for a moment, then caught it on her tongue and ran it around her lips.

"And what were you going to tell him?"

"I—" Ellie said.

"Were you going to tell him all about last night?"

"I—I—" The tears began to flow freely now.

"Were you going to tell him about how you're a fucking whore?" The woman ran her hand around the back of Ellie's neck, grabbing onto a fistful of hair, pulling her down to her knees. She threw her leg over Ellie's head and sat down on the toilet behind her in one perfect, fluid motion.

"I don't . . . What do you w-want from m-me?" Ellie sobbed.

"I saw you, you know," the woman said, suddenly distant. "I saw what you did with him." She extended her legs and gathered Ellie closer to her, locking her ankles around Ellie's chest. "Just tell me that you realize that you made a mistake, and I won't hurt you." The woman eased the pressure on the razor. "Tell me you're sorry."

"I—" Ellie began, fully prepared to say anything that this woman wanted. But the woman interrupted.

"Because, you know what we do to scheming little cunts?" She brought the razor to rest at a ninety-degree angle to Ellie's throat and reached into her overnight bag. She pulled out what looked like a stack of Polaroids and thrust one of them into Ellie's face. It was a medium shot of the man she had gone to the Solon Motel with. He was standing in the very same motel room, near the foot of the bed. Even considering the horror of her situation, Ellie was still taken with the man's physical beauty; the marble hardness of his chest and abdomen, the aristocratic line of his jaw.

He was naked and fully erect.

"Look familiar?" the woman asked. Playful now. *Girlfriends*. She brought out another picture of the man, this one a side view. "Rather impressive, isn't it?"

The woman then fanned three more photographs. The first picture, farthest to the left, was a close-up of a woman with a thin red scarf draped loosely around her shoulders. The woman was nude from at least the waist up and was lying across a bed, staring vacantly at the ceiling. "How about these?" the woman said. "You recognize these gals, don't you? Sure you do. You read the papers . . ."

The picture of Maryann Milius that Ellie had seen in the *Plain Dealer* had been cropped from what might have been an Olan Mills–type portrait. Ellie had thought the young woman pretty at the time.

But the image of Maryann Milius in front of her now—the likeness that soon told Ellie it was not a scarf at all but rather a broad swirl of blood from the gaping wound in her neck—was hideous beyond belief. She opened her mouth to scream, but the sound that came forth instead was small and thin.

A doll's scream.

Earline Pender wrapped one leg around the base of the toilet for leverage and bore down with all her strength.

At the moment the steel slid silently across Ellie's throat, exposing her trachea to the cornflower-blue bathroom in room 118 at the Radisson East, Eleanor Catherine Burchfield looked at her shoes and thought about the day she had bought them. Eighty dollars on sale. Nona's at La Place. They went with her Donna Karan, too.

Funny, Ellie thought, to think such a thing at such a moment as this.

A few moments later, when the black wind blew, she thought nothing at all.

11

SAILA GOT BACK INTO THE CAR AND I KNEW IMMEDIATELY that she had been bad. Her lips were slicked with saliva, her breasts heaved, her eyes were rimmed with red and full of fire. Before I could shift into reverse and pull out of the space, she placed her hand on my forearm, and from the strength of her grip, I could tell she was wired. She pulled the release on the side of her seat and slid back, falling into a reclining position, spreading her legs. Her thighs were perfect in the light that dripped in from the parking lot, her calves looked smooth and well defined. I shut off the engine as Saila ran her left index finger slowly down her outer thigh, then back up.

She told me the details of what she had done.

o   o   o

When she was finished I moved closer. Saila placed her right foot on the dashboard and, with the draining hull of a woman she had cut with a razor lying no more than a hundred feet from where we sat, she took my head in her hands and directed it down between her legs.

She stroked my hair as I did her bidding, my erection starting to amass.

Hers.

Again.

Soon, beneath her soft moaning, she began to hum a tune, one to which she had been a slave all evening for some reason.

A song by Peaches and Herb.

1 2

PARIS ASKED THE FIRST WOMAN HE SAW. BLACK WOMAN, well dressed, early fifties.

"Excuse me," he began. "I was wondering if you could help me. My cousin Eleanor left the bar about a half-hour ago, and I thought perhaps you could pop into the ladies' room here and see if she might be in there, see if she's all right . . ."

"Sure," the woman said, pushing open the door. "You say her name's Eleanor?"

"Yes," Paris answered. "Ellie, actually. About this tall, blondish, wearing a light brown cardigan."

"Hang on," the woman said, and disappeared into the ladies' room.

Paris leaned up against the wall and looked both ways down the hallway. Empty and clueless. The front-desk clerk had told him that Eleanor Burchfield had gotten change and, he presumed, gone off to use the cigarette machine in what he referred to as the "convenience lobby." The small alcove, which contained a Coke machine, an ice machine, a cigarette machine and a candy machine, was empty when Paris glanced in. His heart had leapt when he saw the deep red stain on the carpeting, but after scolding himself severely for his reaction, he knelt down and rather rapidly ascertained that someone had spilled some wine. No bogeyman, no razors, no blood.

But no Eleanor Burchfield, either.

The door to the ladies' room opened and the woman came out, shrugging her shoulders. "Sorry," she said. "It's empty. I even looked in the stalls."

"Okay . . . thanks very much."

"You're quite welcome," the woman said, and walked toward the lobby.

Paris made a once-around the first floor, listening at the doors of some of the guest rooms, looking into the pool room and the arcade. She was gone.

She had seen a real-life cop with a badge and a gun and a notebook and realized that she'd still got her health and the whole thing just wasn't worth it.

Fuck the next victim, right?

Right, Paris thought as he sauntered back into the lounge, which was now reduced to a handful of only the most desperate of Sunday night yuppie-bar holdouts. There were two women in their early forties sitting in one of the booths by the dance floor. One of them kept looking over at Paris every time she used her hands to make a point to her girlfriend. Paris wanted to be interested, but he just wasn't.

Now Rita, on the other hand . . .

She waved Paris over to the bar.

"I remembered something else," she said, her face grown serious.

"Lay it on me," Paris said, retrieving his notebook.

"I seem to recall this guy talking to another woman. Over there." She gestured to a darkened corner to the right of the dance floor. "Not for long, though. But I'm pretty sure it was before he and your friend got together."

"Did they look like they were a couple?"

"I don't know. Maybe. They *did* look like people who've . . . you know . . . had *sex,* I'd say. Like they were intimate without touching each other?"

Paris nodded. "Can you describe her?"

"Not really." Rita said. "Young and pretty. Like everyone else. Kind of on the tall side, I think. Although, when you're five two, everyone's on the tall side." Rita curled a fingerful of hair. "But that's about all I remember. It's dark in here. Couldn't even tell you her hair color, which for me is pretty rare." She poured an inch of coffee into Paris's cup, then hesitated. "Let me think about it. I don't know why, but I seem to think he may have even come in with this woman. Let me think about it, okay?" She topped off his cup.

"Sure," Paris said, closing his notebook.

"Speaking of the other woman . . ." Rita said. "Did your friend take a powder?"

"Take a powder? *Take a powder?*" Paris asked, disbelieving. "Where the hell did you hear that? That one's older than *me.*"

Rita laughed. "So's Shakespeare," she said. "Heard of him?"

"He play for the Indians?"

"Second base," Rita said.

"Okay. I keep underestimating you."

"You do," Rita said. "So . . . did she book?"

"Yep," Paris answered, resignedly, tapping his index finger on the edge of the cup. Rita, the veteran barkeep, reached behind her, grabbed a bottle of Crown Royal and slid a California shot in the side door of his coffee. She looked up and winked.

"You know," Paris said, tilting the coffee cup to his lips, "you are damn good at what you do, you know that?"

"Of course I know that," she said, smiling, exhibiting the slightest hint of a sexy little gap between her front teeth. "Tips don't always show it though."

Paris sipped his coffee and glanced at her left hand, which sported rings on every finger but her ring finger. "Someone should just take you out and marry you."

"*Marry* me?" She laughed. "Hell . . . I'd settle for a movie and something from column B at Chung Wah's."

Paris laughed with her. "Maybe someone should take you up on that."

"Oh yeah?" she said, wiping down the bar in front of him, showing the palest insinuation of a blush. "Well . . . maybe someone *should.*"

So she *was* flirting with him.

But she was young and it was late and if he stayed he would get drunk. He dropped a five and his card on the bar. "If you think of anything, you give me a call." He pushed himself away from the bar. "Either way, stop down at the station when you have time and we'll hook you up with the police artist."

"Okay, officer," Rita said, saluting. She put Paris's card down the front of her blouse, teasing him. "And hey," she said, borrowing a line from *Hill Street Blues,* a show she was probably too young to have caught the first time around, "let's be *careful* out there." She smiled and put her hands on her hips.

"Oh, I will," Paris said as he walked out, waving, already thinking that Rita Constance Weisinger could probably be a lot more dangerous to his health than a trainload of serial killers.

o   o   o

HE FOUND HIS OLDSMOBILE IN ROUGHLY THE AREA HE REMEMBERED LEAVING it, the last shot of Crown having pushed him one step closer to Stupid Heights than he wanted to come. But he had had tougher assignments, so, after a short bout with the door lock, he fell into the car, still fully confident in his abilities.

As he pulled out onto Chagrin Boulevard, he was functioning on autopilot, and all of his thoughts were where they belonged: on Rita the Barmaid's extraordinary tush.

When he turned right onto Lee Road, he didn't notice the white BMW that made the turn behind him.

o   o   o

PARIS AWOKE AT SEVEN, PUT ON HIS SWEATS AND JOGGED MANNY OVER TO BOLland's Famous Bagels on Euclid and Seventieth. He jogged back (a rarity after slam-dunking two of Bolland's Famous Bialys and a large chocolate phosphate), showered, made all the lights and was in the office by eight-thirty. He dialed Eleanor Burchfield's number at eight forty-five but there was no answer. Nor was there an answering machine. He thought it odd that a telephone belonging to a woman as sophisticated as Eleanor Burchfield seemed to be would just ring and ring and ring.

He and Tommy spent the early part of the morning interviewing Karen Schallert's co-workers and acquaintances at United Way. It seemed that she had never had an office romance in her two years at the agency, that she lunched with only two or three of her co-workers and rarely hit the downtown bars after work. By most accounts, Karen Schallert was considered to be a shy, retiring young woman, but always ready to lend a hand.

Before they left the agency Paris saw Tommy pocket a pair of business cards from two of the more attractive volunteers he had interviewed.

o   o   o

THE STOREFRONT WINDOW AT 1190 EAST 185TH STREET HELD A STRANGE WEB of neon lighting which, from the other side of the street, and only from the other side of the street, could be deciphered as the slogan for the Ultimate Line Tattoo Company, Inc. *From Roses to Dragons!* it proclaimed in hot-pink and carbon-blue tubing. Then, below: *Old Tattoos Reworked!* The cardboard signs in the window hawked other services: *Oriental, Tribal and Celtic Styles! Hundreds of State of the Art Colors! Ear & Exotic Body Piercing!*

The counter area was small and dank, crammed even tighter

with wobbly plastic chairs and charity gumball machines. The man who stepped through the soiled red curtains separating the reception area from the parlors was forty, garbed in standard beard and black biker drag. He sported surprisingly few tattoos on his arms, considering his profession, and brought with him a faint scent of marijuana.

"My name is Detective Raposo. This is Detective Paris. We're with the Cleveland Police Homicide Unit," Tommy said, flashing his shield.

"Homicide," the man said, a little surprised. "What can I do for you, gentlemen?"

"And what's *your* name?" Tommy asked.

"Chuck. Chuck Vasko," he answered. He spelled it.

"Mr. Vasko," Tommy continued, "we'd like to ask you a few questions in regards to a homicide we're investigating." He placed the suspect sketch on the countertop. "Do you recognize this man?"

"That's the guy from the newspaper," Vasko said. "This is the guy who's killing those women, right?"

Paris saw a thin, paste-white woman of maybe twenty-five peer out from between the curtains. She was holding an infant in her arms.

"Do you *recognize* him, Mr. Vasko?"

"Only from the newspaper. I mean, he's not a customer, if that's what you're asking," Vasko said. "Why? Does he have a tattoo?"

Paris stepped forward. "If you don't mind, do you think you could let Detective Raposo ask the questions for the time being?"

"Sure. Sorry. No problem, boss man."

He's done some time, Paris thought. "Thank you."

"Do you do a lot of rose tattooing. Mr. Vasko?" Tommy asked.

"Oh yeah. Very popular," Vasko said. "In fact, our motto is—"

"Yeah, we caught it on the way in," Tommy said. "Mr. Vasko, what kind of people get rose tattoos?"

"Well . . . women, of course."

"Young women?" Paris asked.

"Absolutely. Teenagers too," Vasko said. "Then of course, there's your occasional, you know, *freak.*"

"Freak?" Tommy said.

"Yeah, you know, guy comes in, a little pervy-lookin', wants a tattoo of a rose on his dick, his ass, his balls. I do 'em. Can't say I enjoy 'em, but I do 'em. On the other hand, I sure as hell ain't gonna let my wife handle it." Chuck Vasko let out a loud snort of laughter and uncovered a thick row of uneven yellow teeth.

"Do you keep records of everyone who gets a tattoo here?" Paris asked, once the man had composed himself.

"Some," Vasko said. "But this is mostly a cash business, as you might imagine. Tattoos are a strange thing, gentlemen. People get 'em, but then they don't want anyone to know they have 'em."

"Who has access to your customer list?" Tommy asked.

"Just me and my wife," Vasko said. "Me 'n' Dottie."

Paris looked at the skinny woman and the fat baby in the doorway and tugged once on Tommy's coatsleeve.

They were wasting their time with the Vaskos.

o   o   o

THE TWO DETECTIVES SPENT THE REMAINDER OF THE MORNING TALKING TO Karen Schallert's mother, Delores, in the woman's tidy two-bedroom ranch in Parma Heights. They learned that Karen had had a five-year relationship with a man named Joseph Turek, an airline mechanic, but the affair had ended nearly two years earlier over a slight difference of opinion regarding Mr. Turek's avocation of hydroponic pot growing. A quick check revealed that Joseph Turek had died in an automobile crash in Solon in January.

Karen, Delores Schallert told them, had been a lot more involved in community work in recent days than she had been with men. But she also said that once in a while, maybe four or five times a year, Karen would let her hair down and go out to bars with one of her girlfriends. Or sometimes, over the strenuous objections of her widowed mother, on her own.

Delores Schallert gave them a recent photograph of Karen, the same one that had run in the *Plain Dealer,* and as they rose to leave, Paris scanned the panorama of framed pictures on the wall over the couch. There, above the cream and brown afghan, were photographs of the toothless, baby Karen Schallert, the high school Karen, the college Karen, the career-girl Karen, all grown up now, handing an oversized check to a gray-haired man in front of the United Way building.

As he stepped into the bright sunlight and raised his sunglasses to the assault, Paris thought of the pictures over his own couch.

o   o   o

THEY GRABBED A COFFEE AT THE CUP ON BROOKPARK, AND PARIS TRIED ONCE again to contact Eleanor Burchfield, with no success. He also had her paged at Lake West Hospital, but was told she wasn't answering. Thanks to the thousands of orange barrels that made four lanes magically turn into one on I-480, Paris didn't arrive at his desk until noon.

As soon as he sat down—a pile of message slips on his desk, the java starting its march uphill—the phone rang. He debated on whether or not to let his voice mail get it, but he remembered that he was in demand now. He was management. He picked it up on the third ring.

"Homicide."

"Detective Paris?"

He couldn't believe it. It sounded like Diana Bennett. "As charged," he said, wincing, instantly regretting it.

"This is Diana Bennett. How are you?"

Paris felt like he had a water balloon between his neck and his collar. "I'm just fine, thanks," he managed.

"I just wanted to let you know that the grand jury voted not to indict Marcella Lorca-Vasquez."

"No kidding?" Paris said, trying to mask the pleasure in his voice. "Something I said?"

Diana laughed. "Maybe . . . You were *awfully* persuasive."

"Yeah, but I was the one supposedly bringing evidence against her."

"Albeit reluctantly."

She had him pegged. "That obvious, huh?"

"I can always spot a softie. Especially when I get him on the stand."

Was she flirting with him? Amazing! And Rita the Barmaid from last night too? Maybe turning forty-three wasn't so bad after all. "She probably did it, you know," Paris said.

"I'd hate to think so, detective," Diana replied, her tongue planted firmly in her cheek. "That would mean that neither of us did our job properly. And *that* would mean that we're taking our money under false pretenses."

"Speaking of false pretenses . . ." Paris began, feeling a little of the old Paris charm returning to his red blood cells, ". . . would it be terribly out of line if I asked you to have lunch with me today?" He closed his eyes and waited for the bullet.

"Lunch would be lovely," she said.

"Really?" He opened his eyes.

"Really," she echoed.

"Okay . . . uh . . . am I supposed to pick the restaurant?"

"Let's see," Diana began. "What decade are we in?"

"Nineties," Paris said.

"Hang on, I'll look it up," she said, rustling some papers. "Yep, here it is, you pick the restaurant and I pay. For dinner it's exactly the opposite. Of course, if one of us cooks, it complicates matters geometrically. Wine, flowers, dessert—stuff like that."

"Okay, how about John Q's?" It was a steak house near Public Square.

"John Q's is fine," Diana said. "One o'clock?"

"Who says you get to be in charge of the time?"

Diana laughed. "See you at one, Detective Paris."

"Bye."

"Bye."

Diana Bennett. Tommy was going to fucking *kill* him.

And he would love every minute of it.

o   o   o

SHE WAS ALREADY AT A TABLE AND CRUISING A MENU WHEN PARIS ARRIVED. HE was ten minutes late.

"Miss Bennett," he said awkwardly, extending his hand. "Nice to see you again." They shook and Paris immediately noticed how smooth her hands were. And strong. "Sorry I'm late."

Diana Bennett wore a navy-blue belted dress with a white collar and spectator pumps. Her hair was pulled back and held by a white bow with navy pin dots. She wore no jewelry. "I'm on the same clock, Detective Paris," she said with a knowing smile. "I know how it goes."

"Okay then," Paris began, seating himself opposite her and placing the emerald-green linen napkin on his lap, "should I say it or do you want to?"

"You," she said.

"Okay." He cleared his throat and sat up straight. "Please, call me Jack."

"Diana."

"Good," Paris said. "I'm glad we got that out of the way." He opened his menu. "And . . . in the words of Woody Allen—"

" 'Now we can digest our food,' " Diana said, offering the rest of the line from *Annie Hall,* Paris's favorite movie of all time. In fact, the cassette was at his apartment, in his VCR, at that very moment. He was thoroughly impressed.

Their waiter—Viktor with a *k,* a Russian waiter whom Paris had seen at at least five other restaurants in downtown Cleveland in the past two years—took their order with precision and quiet flair. He disappeared for a moment but quickly returned with a basket of rolls.

They sat mute for a few minutes, buttering their bread, sipping water, straightening themselves in their chairs, sensing each other's sexual presence. Finally, Paris spoke. "So you think I soft-pedaled my testimony?" he asked, not really knowing what else to talk about.

"Well . . . let me put it this way," Diana said. "No one's going to accuse you of trying to lynch Mrs. Lorca-Vasquez."

"That's the last thing I wanted to do, believe me."

Diana leaned forward and fixed Paris with a slight arch of an eyebrow. He noticed that her eyes were no longer the snow blue of the other day, but now a deep forest green. The magic of contact lenses, Paris marveled.

"Can you keep a secret?" she asked, almost whispering.

"I'm a cop," Paris said. "So I guess the answer would be no."

"I didn't press too hard on this one myself."

Paris smiled, wondering just how brushed his teeth were. "And you think that's a secret?"

"That obvious, huh?" she said, mimicking him. She leaned back as Viktor brought their plates. When he left she said, "I just don't know how much the world is supposed to mourn the loss of one more gang-banger, you know?"

"Amen," Paris replied.

The conversation flowed easily as they ate their lunch. Caesar salad for her, burger with bleu cheese for him. By the time they were served their coffee, Paris had learned Diana's story: thirty-two, never married, no children, born in Norwalk, Ohio, where her mother still lived. An only child. She had been with the prosecutor's office for six months; before that, three years with the Summit County office. There was no current boyfriend because she had had her fill of lawyers, and that's about all she ever met anymore. Except for criminals.

And, she confessed, the line was getting increasingly blurred between the two. So she had decided to drop out for a while.

"And what about you?" Diana asked, stirring a dollop of cream into her coffee.

"Not much to tell, I'm afraid," Paris said.

"Tell me anyway," she said, smiling. "I'm a prosecutor. We need all the evidence we can get."

Paris gave Diana the *Cliff's Notes* version of his life. Born and raised on the near west side of Cleveland, graduated St. Ed's, four years at John Carroll University. Father passed away when he was sixteen. Cop, married, divorced, one incredible daughter: his life.

Diana seemed genuinely interested. "Do you have a picture?" she asked.

"You want to see a picture of my ex-wife?"

"Smartass," she said. "*Melissa.*"

"You kidding?" Paris said, producing Melissa's sixth-grade school picture in less than three seconds.

"She's beautiful, Jack." She studied the photograph intently before handing it back.

"Thanks." It sounded like she really meant it, and Paris liked that. "So," he began, replacing Missy's picture in his wallet, wondering if he was about to blow it, "what made you say yes to lunch with an old flatfoot like me?"

"Oh," Diana said, "I figured you were going to ask me out the day of the grand jury. But no such luck." She smiled again and it threw a warm quiver up Paris's back. "So a girl's gotta do what a girl's gotta do, right?" She picked at imaginary lint on her dress. "Besides . . . you're going to be famous when you catch this psycho-gigolo lunatic." She sipped her coffee. "I wanted to be able to say I knew you when."

Paris ran his big hands through his hair like he always did when a woman gave him a compliment. "Uh . . . well . . . it's going to be a team effort, I assure you," he said, taking a stab at, and missing, humility.

"Wouldn't mind making the team myself."

"Beg your pardon?"

"I mean I would *love* to prosecute this guy. Everybody in the office is drooling over it. It's all that anybody's talked about for the last three days."

"We have to catch him first."

"Oh, I have no doubt that you will." She looked at Paris with . . . what? Admiration? *Adoration?* "The man who put Cyrus Webber on death row can catch a little old serial killer."

Paris was shaken for a moment. The Webber killings were more than four years old. "How do you know about Cyrus Webber? You weren't even in Cleveland then, were you?"

"Cops aren't the only ones with computers, you know." She finished her coffee, her blue-turned-green eyes rimming the cup.

Paris tried to shift the conversation back to Diana. He was always a little uncomfortable talking about his accomplishments. Especially with pretty women. "So what's so appealing about a case like this?" he asked, suddenly on his toes. "The chance to put a big-time wacko away?"

"That, and the chance to smash the insanity defense we all know will come when you catch him. It's what we prosecutors live for, you know. Taking on some pervert who thinks he can go around doing what he wants." She crossed her legs beneath the table, accidentally brushing up against Paris's leg. He jumped a foot. "But personally, I'm not all that interested in the fame," she said, pretending not to have noticed. "I *am* interested in clout, however. Clout trades higher."

She was a little more ambitious than Paris had thought, but it was sexy-ambitious. It was a kind of single-mindedness that Paris liked to see in himself, in his fellow cops. Goal without greed. He was enchanted.

The maître d' approached their table. "Are you Detective Paris?"

"Yes."

"There's a phone call for you, sir."

"Oh . . . uh . . . thanks," Paris said, silently berating himself for turning off his beeper. He hoped this wasn't an emergency. He stood and looked at Diana. "Excuse me."

"Certainly," Diana said.

Paris followed the maître d' to his station, thanked him again and picked up the phone.

"This is Jack Paris."

"Jack, it's Tim Murdock."

"*Timmy* . . . twice in twenty-four hours. You must need some serious bailing. Lay it on me, babe."

"Got a stiff at the Radisson East you might be interested in."

Paris's heart plummeted. For a moment, his skin broke out in stiff gooseflesh. *"What?"*

"Female white, early to mid twenties," Murdock said.

Paris felt the bile start to rise. "Pretty blonde?"

Murdock exhaled quickly and Paris had his answer. "No . . . I'm afraid not, buddy. Not anymore." Paris heard some rustling papers. "Victim's name is . . . let's see here . . . one Eleanor Catherine Burchfield, age twenty-five. Weapon was probably a knife. Razor maybe. It's a pretty bad scene though, Jack. Hacked up in the bathroom of one of the empty suites. One of the cleaning crew found her early this morning. Thought it might dovetail with the psycho you're looking for, you know?"

Paris was speechless for a moment, his mind reeling, his heart thrumming a little too quickly, a little too loudly in his chest. He took a deep breath. "Is the *Plain Dealer* on it yet?"

"Cicero's around here somewhere. His photographer, too."

"What about TV?" Paris asked.

"Nah," Murdock said. "But any minute . . . you know."

Paris had to tell him. "It gets better, Timmy."

"What do you mean?"

"I was with her last night."

Murdock went silent for a few moments. "What the fuck are you talking about, Jack?"

"I saw her last night."

"What? *Where?*"

"There," Paris said. "At the Radisson."

"You knew her?"

"Yes," Paris said. "I mean no. I mean . . . I just met her last night.

I met her at the Radisson to interview her about the multiple. She was a little hesitant at first. She thought she had met our boy and she was too scared to come in. So I met her out there."

"And . . ."

"And we did part of the interview; she went to get cigarettes and she never came back. I just figured she bailed on the whole thing." Paris flashed on the woman's face, the way she flicked her hair from around her ear. He had known the woman less than fifteen minutes and he was mourning her little ways.

"What time was this?" Murdock asked.

"I don't know exactly," Paris answered. "Why? You have a time of *death* already, Timmy?"

"Oldest known method," Murdock said. "Smashed watch. Looks like ten thirty-five."

"Fuck."

"What?"

"I was with her right around that time."

Murdock waited a few beats, out of respect for the twenty years they'd known each other, and said, placidly, "Get down here, Jack. Room one-eighteen."

o   o   o

THE LOBBY LOOKED MUCH DIFFERENT IN THE DAYLIGHT. GRAY-SUITED MEN, blue-suited women, all name-tagged, all hustling, all doing some sort of commerce with one another. A suburban hotel in its midday swing. Conferences, meetings, luncheons. Paris wondered how many of these people were aware of the fact that a woman had been sliced up in one of those tastefully appointed guest rooms. He also wondered if it would matter one bit. As long as all the widgets get sold, why should anyone give a shit?

When Paris cut short their lunch, he had told Diana Bennett merely that duty had called, no details, knowing full well that she would learn of this homicide by the end of the day herself. They had exchanged home phone numbers, much to Paris's relief, and made the usual promises.

Tim Murdock stood on the opposite end of the lobby, folding over his notebook, wrapping up an interview with one of the housekeepers. He noticed Paris with his cop's third eye and walked leisurely across the quiet carpeting. "What a fuckin' world, eh Jack?"

he said softly. Murdock smelled like onions, Ben-Gay and cigar smoke.

"Getting worse, too," Paris replied, as if by rote.

"By the minute."

Murdock flipped to a clean page of his notebook and the two policemen fell into a very familiar routine.

"What happened, Jack?"

Paris explained what had happened the previous night, about his involvement, reliving the chronology as he remembered it. And even though he anticipated each and every one of the detective's questions, he let Murdock ask them anyway. It just went a lot more smoothly that way.

"And you left the bar when?"

"Elevenish, I guess."

"With anybody?"

"Timmy . . ."

"I'm asking."

"I can't do that anymore. I'm an old man. Who the fuck's going to go home with me anyway?"

"Uh, if you're old, Jack, what the hell am I?"

"You're a perennial, Murdock," Paris said. "It's better than being young. But to answer your question, I left alone and I went right home. Thanks for the thought though."

"All right," Murdock said, putting his notebook away. "Let's go in."

o   o   o

THE ARTERIAL SPRAY THAT HAD RESULTED FROM THE WOMAN'S THROAT BEING cut had decorated the shower curtain in the bathroom of room 118 to look like a Kmart version of a Japanese mountain scene. Red, snowcapped peaks against a light blue sky. Distant gulls.

The body had already been taken to the morgue on Adelbert Road and Paris was somewhat relieved to see only the taped outline remaining on the floor, sharp and angular at the base of the toilet bowl. He had not been looking forward to seeing Eleanor Burchfield's torn flesh scattered about the room after having sat and laughed with the woman twenty-four hours earlier.

The blood on the floor had spread to a tortured circle about four feet in diameter and was already brown and sticky. A huge Rorschach on the smooth tile.

The room, Paris learned, had been vacant, and Nels Morrison had already determined that the lock had been picked. And very professionally, at that. No shavings. Only very minute telltale nicks.

Murdock and Paris agreed that whoever had carved up Eleanor Burchfield either was a professional thief or had been partnered with one. They also agreed that the new wrinkle narrowed the investigation considerably. Serial killers rarely came from the ranks of second-story men. And they almost always acted alone.

I think he may have come in with this woman. . . .

"So is this where you tell me not to leave town?" Paris asked as he and Murdock stood in the doorway.

"Get the fuck outta here," Murdock answered, edgy but still confident in their friendship.

"I'm serious, Timmy. I know how this looks and I appreciate the fact—"

"You're not a fucking *suspect,* Jack," Murdock replied, a little more soberly than Paris would have liked. He lowered his voice. "Jesus Christ . . . you're heading the task force. This is probably going to be on *your* desk in twelve hours."

1 3

THEY DIDN'T TALK ABOUT THEIR ESCAPADE ALL WEEK. Nor did the Dolly Parton Special make another appearance. Andie had put the wig in an empty hatbox on the top shelf of the linen closet and that's where it stayed.

But they did agree that the murders made what they were doing more exciting somehow. Sexier. Certainly more dangerous.

Saturday night it had been clear that they were still running on Friday night's leftover animal energy. Sunday afternoon found them on the floor in front of the Kemper Open on NBC, screwing like college students. Andie had put on her cheerleading outfit. It was a little tighter than it had been at Normandy High, but that was just fine with Matt Heller.

Monday took Matt to Buffalo and a project he was working on for their Port Authority. He spent the night at a TraveLodge and made a cursory, hands-in-pockets stroll around the parking lot at two in the morning, glancing at the few windows that were still lit.

Nothing exciting.

When he made last call at the hotel's small lounge, all he could think about was his wife on one of the stools, her blond hair splayed along her smooth shoulders. He went back to his room a little bit buzzed and chock full of lead.

Wednesday morning, back home, as he absently buttered his English muffin, Andie was already dressed and on the phone to her sister Celeste. She sat on the counter letting her skirt ride up her thigh as she talked, the lace edge of her slip peeking ever so coyly from beneath the hem, taunting him.

To his dismay, by the time Matt stepped out of the shower, Andie had already left for work. But she had left him a small billet-doux to tide him over until that evening.

There, on her dressing table, perched on a velvet rostrum, sat the blond wig. Beneath it sat a white tea rose, a lone petal pierced with a ruby earring.

Enthralled, en*gorged,* Matt Heller turned on his heels and walked back into the bathroom.

1 4 BY EIGHT O'CLOCK WEDNESDAY MORNING THERE HAD been a half-dozen confessions to the killings, spurred on, no doubt, by the *Plain Dealer* headline that screamed *FOURTH VICTIM?* next to a rather unflattering picture of Eleanor Burchfield. The usual group of nuthouse Napoleons had come in and spilled their guts, but none of them had known enough of the specific details to warrant the task force following up.

The truth was, every alley Paris and the task force had ventured up in the past seventy-two hours—the friends, family, co-workers, acquaintances and casual contacts of the victims—was blind. And for a string of homicides that had produced such copious amounts of human liquid, and thus the potential for a forensic field day, there was nothing.

And the weight of nothing was becoming unbearable around the sixth floor of the Justice Center.

∘   ∘   ∘

AT EIGHT FORTY-FIVE, PARIS'S PHONE RANG AGAIN.

"Homicide, Paris."

"I know where to find them," a woman's voice said.

Paris knew right away that the woman on the phone was using a voice-altering device of some sort. It had a soulless sound, flat and electronic. He had become very familiar with such devices when Cyrus Webber, a twenty-eight-year-old Wadsworth, Ohio, schoolteacher responsible for the death of five young girls, had used a small digital processor to make his voice sound younger when he telephoned his victims, claiming to be from their school, asking to meet them at the playground. Paris himself had once used a voicebox as part of a drug sting.

"What do you mean?" Paris asked, wondering what this woman had to hide.

Silence for a few moments, then: "Look in the backyard. Next to the sandbox. What do you see?"

Paris should have known. "Well, I'm not sure *what* I see," he said, rapidly losing interest. "I don't have my glasses with me. Why don't you tell me what I'm supposed to see?"

"Four girls gone," the woman said, her voice changing pitch, up and down, as the synthesizer cycled.

"Right. Okay," Paris said. "Thanks." He absently made a note about backyards.

"Four roses cut and laid to rest in long, white boxes."

The word sat him upright. The rose tattoo information had not been made public. "What about the roses?" he asked, pressing the record buttons on the tape machine connected to his phone via an in-line microphone.

First came the loud hiss of the woman's voice device, followed by a low, warbling sound. Finally, she said, "The one you seek is like the rose of Jericho, Detective Paris."

"Uh, why don't you let me have your name and phone number and I'll call you back in a little bit," Paris said, but even before he had finished the sentence, he knew the woman had hung up.

o   o   o

REUBEN CALLED AT NINE-TEN. "I GOT GOOD NEWS, I GOT BETTER NEWS, I GOT great news," he said. "How do you want it?"

"Ascending, Reuben," Paris said. "Always ascending."

"The good news is that Eleanor Burchfield had a large piece of skin missing. Of course, that isn't good news for *her,* but damned if the pattern of the rectangular cut isn't the same as the other three. I'm positive this is the same cutter, Jack."

"Do you have the skin?"

"No. It wasn't found at the scene."

"Where was it?" Paris asked. "I mean, where was it cut from?"

"Let's see . . . It was about two inches wide by four and a half inches long and it came from . . . the back of her neck."

Paris had looked for a tattoo on Eleanor Burchfield, but of course, he hadn't looked at the back of her neck. Maybe her hair had been pinned up with barrettes the night she met the killer, he thought. Maybe she had a rose tattoo there.

"What else have you got?" Paris asked.

"We have a match on the face powder for the first three. Haven't gotten to Burchfield yet," Reuben said. "Brand called Chaligne. An import of Cinq, Limited."

"Who?"

"*Cinq.*"

"How do you spell that?"

"It's French for the number five, Jack." Reuben spelled it for him as Paris erased what he had originally written on his pad: S-o-n-k. Eventually he would also revise his spelling of S-h-a-l-e-e-n for the face powder.

"It's very expensive powder," Reuben continued. "But the other stuff is cheap. The lipstick and blush and mascara. Strictly bargain basement shit, so it's going to take a while to pin down the formula. Need the feds for that one, though. Anyway, Cinq has a field office in Cleveland, if you want to talk to them or get a client list. Over at Tower City. . . . But there's no doubt about it. All of these women were made up postmortem."

"You're positive on that?"

Silence.

"Reuben?"

Nothing.

"Okay," Paris said, moving on, remembering that silence was one of the many endearing ways Reuben Ocasio had of saying, "Fuck you . . . I can do *my* job . . . can you do *yours?*"

"I also found something else on two of the victims' upper lips that I guarantee they didn't put on before leaving the house," Reuben said, letting Paris off the hook for the moment.

"Lay it on me, babe."

"Spirit gum."

"Lay it on me again, babe."

"Jac*quito,*" Reuben said. "You are so uncultured."

"What the hell are you talking about?" Paris said. "I watch PBS."

"The main use of spirit gum is in the theater, Jack. It's used to keep on beards and eyebrows and sideburns and birthmarks and—"

"Mustaches," Paris said, smiling.

"Yep."

"You *have* something for me, don't you, Reuben?"

"Unless Maryann Milius and Karen Schallert were making out with Emmett Kelly, I would say that we've got a psycho in disguise out there. Your boy's mustache is a phony."

"I *knew* it," Paris said. "Anything available in there?"

"In the spirit gum?" Reuben asked, incredulous. "This ain't fucking *Star Trek* yet, Jack." Ever since DNA testing had begun, cops expected MEs to find it in the strangest places. Reuben then hesitated a few moments for dramatic effect. This was the best part of his job.

"But we still may be able to get something anyway."

"You're kidding. How?"

Reuben was going to play him for a while, but he couldn't stand it. "Got the mustache, Jack."

"Say *what?*"

"It was tangled up in Karen Schallert's hair. Nobody saw it until last night. We'll have to send it out, but I think there may be something we can use on the backing."

"I love you, Reuben," Paris said, standing up at his desk.

"Oh yeah? Does this mean I should start shopping for a dress?"

"Charge it to me." Paris looked through his doorway, into the common room, and caught Greg Ebersole's attention. He waved him into his office.

"I'll call you as soon as I have brand names on the other cosmetics and the details on the mustache," Reuben said, clearly pleased with himself. "In the meantime, tell your partner that he has won, hands down, the Cocksman of the Year award."

"Huh?"

"He didn't tell you yet?"

"Tell me what?"

"Connie Maitland—you know Connie, right?"

"Do I know Connie . . ."

"Yeah . . . stupid question," Reuben said, considering the fact that Connie Maitland, one of the assistant MEs, looked exactly like Darryl Hannah. Everybody in the department wanted to jump her bones, so, for Tommy Raposo, it was like a mission. "Anyway, Connie's on third shift last night and she's walking through the fridge and she sees a light on. She opens the door and there's Tommy Raposo nosing around a couple of stiffs."

"What do you mean 'nosing'?"

"I guess he had a couple drawers open or something," Reuben said.

"Okay . . ."

"So anyway he tells her that he dropped something at a scene, that he's working a case, he tells her yak, yak, yak—the next thing you know, Connie comes in this morning walking like a penguin and speaking Italian. Kenny Mertenson saw them leave together last night."

"You're telling me Tommy bagged Connie Maitland?"

"That's the way it looks, amigo. The Formaldehyde Princess herself."

"Unbelievable," Paris said.

"I've seen men go to great lengths," Reuben said. "I've gone to a few myself. But over a fucking stiff?"

"We're going to have to give him a plaque before this is all over," Paris said.

"Maybe a statue."

Paris said goodbye and hung up, thoroughly envious, once again, of Tommy Raposo's astounding prowess with women.

o   o   o

IT WAS THAT QUIET TIME OF THE AFTERNOON, THAT BRIEF CORRIDOR BETWEEN lunch and dinner when the calm before the deluge flattens out into silence on the sixth floor of the Justice Center.

By noon Paris had talked to every major wig and barber-products distributor in the Northeast. He was told time and again that mustaches—high-quality, professionally woven, real-hair mustaches—had not been in demand for about fifteen years, since the height of the disco era. The cheaper ones were available locally at Cleveland Costume and a few other theatrical supply houses, but the type of mustache found in Karen Schallert's hair, he was told by virtually all of the firms, was not even being manufactured anymore. The most recent wholesale shipping record anyone was able to fax him was from a decade ago. And that was to a wig supply house in Dayton.

Blind alleys. Dead ends.

"Who the hell you gotta know to get arrested around here?"

Paris, who had been daydreaming at his desk about slamming the iron door shut behind his clean-shaven psychopath and receiving a ticker-tape parade held by all the women in Cleveland, looked at his watch—already three o'clock—then looked up to see the owner of the surprisingly sweet voice.

It was Rita the Barmaid.

"Hi," Paris said as cheerfully as possible, suddenly acutely aware of the stain on his tie, the shine on his trousers and the quality of his breath. "Come on in." She looked even younger than she did at the bar. She wore faded denim jeans, white Reeboks and a short leather jacket. Her wild brunette hair was pulled back into a ponytail, secured by a huge, black leather bow, and she wore very little makeup. Her skin was criminally clear.

She took off her jacket to reveal a white T-shirt with the logo for Coco Ribe emblazoned across the front.

"I just got done with the sketch artist, but I don't know how much good it did. I never really got that close to the guy and it's pretty dark in there. Plus, I never wear my glasses at work." She tapped her forehead. "It's just that I know a hunk when I see one. Radar, I think." She helped herself to a handful of Karamel Korn from the bag on Paris's desk. "But I had no idea it was all done with computers these days, you know?"

"Yeah, well, we're real modern up here in the big city," Paris said.

"I thought it was gonna be one of those charcoal sketch guys. Like at Cedar Point? The ones who make everybody they draw look like Helen Reddy?"

She helped herself to a sip of his Coke.

"Can I *get* you something?" Paris asked, more than a little charmed by Rita's forthright, familiar manner. And the way she made everything sound like a question.

"Why? You wanna *wait* on me, Detective Paris?" she said, leaning over his desk, smiling broadly. "Is that it?"

Paris felt himself going red. Real tough guy. Zoomed by a ninety-eight-pound waitress. "Let's just say . . . I owe you one. I appreciate you getting involved. And if you want something to eat—"

"No . . . I'm fine."

Paris shifted gears. "Let me ask you something, Rita. Did you notice anyone suspicious hanging around the bar, either before or after I was there that night?" Paris asked. "Like, somebody watching me or maybe someone who might have followed Eleanor out of the bar?"

"Sorry," Rita said. "There wasn't much of a crowd, as you know. When it isn't busy I tend to zone out. I just remember a couple of the regulars and a busload of little old ladies with cheap raincoats. Grain-and-feed convention or something."

"Did you remember anything else about the first woman?" Paris asked. "The one our boy may have come in with that first night?"

"No. Sorry. I see a hell of a lot of people, though." Rita's smile disappeared in a flash and she narrowed her brow. She looked out into the hallway, then closed the door to the office. "You know, that other cop was asking about you."

Tim Murdock, Paris thought. "What cop?"

"Big guy? Smells like a warm day at the animal shelter?"

"Murdock."

"Right. He asked me a lot of questions about you."

"Yeah, well, it's just routine, Rita," Paris said. "There *was* a murder after all and I *was* there. He's just doing his job."

"Well, I had to tell him the truth, you know? Like how you were in the bar with her, then she left, then you left for a while, then you came back, but she didn't. Doesn't *look* good for you. But I still don't think you did it."

"Gee thanks," Paris said, hoping she was just kidding.

"But it freaks me completely the hell out to think that this woman got . . . you know . . . And at the fucking *Radisson*." She brought her hand up to her mouth. "Sorry. I keep swearing around you. Not very ladylike."

"It's okay. This is a police station, it's mandatory to say that word a hundred times a day here or we all lose our jobs. Even for the female officers."

"But I mean, I've never even seen a *fistfight* at the place. Two years," she said with a nervous flip of her hair. "Cheese Louise. It could've been *me*."

"I don't want to alarm you, but I would keep an extra cautious eye out until we catch this guy," Paris said. "I mean, if he saw me talking to her, he saw me talking to you. Now if you like, I can have a patrol car drive by your place every few hours."

"I'm on the twentieth floor at Fenton Place on Lakeshore," Rita said. "Unless they drove down the hallway, I don't think it would help."

Paris smiled. "I just think it—"

"Look . . . Jack . . . if I may call you Jack—"

"Sure."

"I grew up with five brothers, Jack. I've kicked *much* ass in my life," she said with a good measure of confidence. She put her jacket on, rescued her hair from beneath the collar, opened the door and stepped into the hall. "So I can take care of myself, eh?" She blew him a kiss. "But thanks for worrying about me. It's sweet, you know?" She flashed her biggest, high-school-yearbook smile. Paris was right about the sexy gap.

"No charge," Paris said. "Let me ask you one more thing."

"Sure."

"Have you ever heard of something called the rose of Jericho?"

"Rose of Jericho . . ." she said, thinking. "Sounds like an old-ladies' perfume or something. Like Jungle Gardenia. Is it?"

"I have no idea what it is," Paris said, having run it through the computers and come up empty.

"Sorry. Doesn't ring a bell. Is it important?"

"I don't know," Paris answered. "I'm not sure yet."

"Well . . . don't be a stranger, okay?" Rita said, shaking a finger at him. "Remember? Chung Wah's? Column B?"

"I remember," Paris said.

"Gotta run. See you." She turned on her heels and was gone.

"Hey . . ." Paris said.

Rita looked back around the corner.

"Let's be *careful* out there," he added.

As she headed down the hall, she got the *Hill Street Blues* reference from the other night and laughed.

And as Paris listened to that sunny sound float by his door—the laughter of a young woman as yet untouched by life's shambling array of horrors—it blanketed him with a wave of sadness.

Or perhaps it was just nostalgia.

She sounded a lot like Beth had at her age, and it made Jack Paris miss his family all the more.

o   o   o

"What can I tell you, Jack? It was a profoundly moving experience."

"For who?" Paris replied.

"For her," Tommy said. "For me it was just another mission, of course."

"Gonna give me details later?"

"Only if you can stand them."

Paris looked at the doodle he had unconsciously been drawing for the past ten minutes. Considering his lack of sleep and level of frustration, he was not at all surprised to see that he had rendered a fairly passable sketch of an Irish walking hat on his paper blotter. "Where are you?" Paris asked.

"Across the bridge. West Side Market," Tommy said.

"Listen, two things," Paris began. "One, we're probably going to have a better sketch by the end of the day. The barmaid from the Radisson just left."

"Weissman?"

"Weisinger," Paris said. "Rita Weisinger."

"Weisinger . . ." Tommy echoed. "What'd she say?"

"Said she didn't get that close to him, but maybe she was able to fill in a feature or two, you know? The two desk clerks never saw his eyes or his hair because of the hat and glasses."

"Think she could ID him?"

"Yeah, I think in person she could. Put him in the dark and in a suit and I think she could pick out anyone."

Paris heard an RTA bus passing Tommy's pay phone. He heard Tommy draw heavily on a cigarette.

"And there's even better news from Reuben," Paris said.

"What's that?"

"He found our boy's phony mustache."

"What?"

"It was tangled up in Karen Schallert's hair. Can you believe it? Reuben says there may be something we can work with on the mesh backing."

Tommy hit his cigarette again. "Fuckin' Reuben, huh?"

"Why don't you follow up the two west side guys from Karen Schallert's wallet," Paris said. "And I'll take the guys in the Heights. The doctor and the other one."

Silence.

"Tommy?"

"Okay . . ."

"And if you want we can—"

". . . kick *yat*."

"Huh?"

Another bus passed.

"Said I'll see you later," Tommy replied.

"I didn't—" Paris began, but he already had a dial tone.

1 5

SAMANTHA HAD SEEN THE MAN IN THE STORE THREE OR four times in the past year, but she had never had the courage to try to wait on him. Mr. Hendershott had always taken care of him while she straightened merchandise on the other side of the room, peeking around the rows of aerosol cans and plastic tubs of blue and pink and yellow gel. She never seemed to be able to muster the necessary fortitude to walk across the store and actually speak to him.

Although she *had* wanted to.

Because he was one of the handsomest men she had ever seen.

Every other Wednesday Mr. Hendershott took a three-hour lunch so he could see his acupuncturist about his back pains, and Samantha was left alone to hold down the fort at Allied Salon Products on West Forty-fourth Street. This had been the routine for eleven years. So, on this particular Wednesday, when the bell on the door jingled and Samantha looked up, she nearly fainted.

"Hello," the man said. He wore a dark overcoat and a tweed hat.

Samantha clutched the hem of her dress as the man smiled, doubling her anxiety, and walked to the other side of the store. He stopped by the color rinses.

Samantha swallowed once, brushed her hair from her forehead and charged across the store.

o   o   o

"HOWEVER, IF IT'S IMPORTANT THAT IT WASHES RIGHT OUT, YOU WANT THE EZ Color line," Samantha said for what she was hoping was no more than the fifth or sixth time. "Otherwise it takes two or three weeks of washing your hair to get it out."

"This *is* kind of a community theater group," the man said, holding a pair of EZ Color boxes with "deep chestnut" written on the side. "Almost all of us have day jobs and it's important that we all show up for work looking like we did the day before, if you know what I mean."

"What play are you putting on?"

"We're doing *Guys and Dolls* this year."

"That's one of my *favorites!*" Samantha said, a little too loudly. She had seen the revival twice when the touring company had stopped at the Palace Theater the previous winter. "Who do you play?"

"Why, Sky Masterson, ma'am," he said with a slight Brooklyn accent, a touch of his brim and a smile.

"I *knew* it," she said, giddily. "Well . . . uh . . . will there be anything else?"

"Mr. Hendershott showed me something once . . . I believe it was a display rack called . . . the, uh . . . *Penrod Collection,* I believe. I didn't see it out here so I—"

"The Penrod Collection . . ." Samantha mused, trying to put a product to the name.

"Yes, it was in the men's grooming section and it was a display of—"

"Mustaches!" Samantha said with the zeal of an amateur sleuth finding the key clue to an unsolved murder. "Of course. For the *play!*" She walked behind the counter, through the curtains and into the back room and emerged with a dusty, two-foot-by-two-foot display card of real-hair mustaches on fine mesh backing. Mr. Hendershott kept them around mostly for their gay clientele who, Samantha guessed, liked to go incognito at times. But her handsome actor wanted one for his play. Because, with a little spirit gum, they looked exactly like the real thing.

Samantha knew the mustaches were priced at fifty dollars, but they had been lying around the store for so long that she felt it would be ridiculous to charge such a sum. Impulsively, amazed at her temerity, she said, "Pick any one you want. On the house."

"Oh I couldn't," the man said.

"I insist," Samantha said, not really knowing what had come over her, or what she'd tell Mr. Hendershott if he ever found out. "Special for our good customers."

The man, who had lost the last mustache he had purchased at Allied somewhere in room 127 of the Red Valley Inn on Superior Avenue, unbeknownst to *his* boss, decided he would take Samantha up on her most gracious offer. But only if she agreed to have lunch with him sometime in the near future.

After ringing up the purchase, Samantha scrawled her name, address and home phone number on the back of an Allied card in a sort of fugue state. All she would remember later that night was the man's smile. And his movie star eyes.

16

WHEN PARIS WALKED INTO THE MOUNTAIN JACK'S OFF Chagrin Boulevard and saw her sitting in the reception area with her legs crossed, her auburn hair down around her shoulders and a Virginia Slim in her hand, he almost didn't recognize her.

Those *legs*.

Cyndy Taggart's dress was spectacularly short.

"You look great," Paris said.

"In this old thing?" she replied, smiling. "I just throw this on when I couldn't less care less *what* I look like." Her dress was a black knit and she wore a small silver crucifix on a chain around her neck. She had on dark, seamless stockings.

Cyndy stood up and straightened her hem—which seemed determined to stay about midthigh no matter what she did—and in her high black heels she was nearly as tall as Paris, who strained to make five eleven on a good day. She butted out her cigarette.

"Where to first?"

There were five hotels close to I-271 and the dozens of corporate headquarters that line Chagrin Boulevard. Four had cocktail lounges.

"Let's go to the Impulse," Paris said.

"Oooh, the *Impulse*," Cyndy said playfully. "Just don't know what a girl might do at a place like that. I may not be responsible for my actions, Detective Paris." She walked ahead of Paris, out the door and across the parking lot, purposefully swinging her hips in a wide arc, her strong legs causing her spike heels to click loudly on the asphalt. She stopped, opened Paris's car door, turned and said, "Too much caboose?"

"Not for me," Paris replied, laughing. "Not for me."

o   o   o

THE IMPULSE WAS THE LOUNGE IN THE EMBASSY SUITES HOTEL ON MISSION Parkway, one of the commercial-park ingress routes. It was decorated in an art deco style with a lot of high banquette tables, stained glass, indirect pink and white lighting and an elevated dance floor against the back wall of the huge rectangular room. There were two bars. The music was mostly techno-pop dance music, provided by a deejay who was ensconced in a raised, smoked-glass cubicle behind the back bar.

According to the placard in the lobby, Wednesday night was Ladies' Night at the Impulse and, at ten-thirty, the place was hopping.

Cyndy had gone in first, and as Paris leaned against one of the brass railings, next to a long line of waist-high banquette tables, he scanned the room and saw her sitting at the front bar, lighting a cigarette, stirring what looked like a screwdriver but, Paris figured, was really just orange juice. They made eye contact, setting their positions.

Although Cyndy was an attractive woman, from that distance, Paris thought, in those clothes, she looked like a knockout. He began to rummage his mind as to what he could remember about Cyndy Taggart's marital status.

"Can I get you something?" one of the barmaids yelled to him over the music. She was tall and spidery, and sported a black vest, white shirt and lemon-yellow bow tie. She also wore at least an inch of makeup.

"Yeah . . . uh . . ." He had never had to come up with a nonalcoholic choice in a bar before. For a few moments, his mind went blank. He couldn't even recall what he liked. Root beer? Sprite? Yoo-Hoo? "Do you have ice tea?"

"Long Island ice tea?"

"No . . . like . . . *regular* ice tea."

"I don't think so . . ."

"Let me have a Coke then. With a swizzle stick."

"Pepsi all right?"

"Pepsi's fine," Paris said. "But hold the syringe, okay?"

"What?" she said, all but screaming in his face.

"Nothing," Paris yelled back.

She rolled her eyes, wrote down his order and began to weave her way toward the bar.

Paris smoothed the sleeves of his blazer, an unconstructed, deep blue wool jacket he had borrowed from Tommy a few months earlier when they had hit the yuppie bars one night for real. The sleeves were too long but Tommy had told him to push them up, as in, that's how you wear unconstructed jackets.

Whatever the fuck that meant.

Regardless, Paris felt like he was wearing something about the size and shape of the tarp they throw over the field at Municipal Stadium when it rains. He looked like an asshole.

No—worse, he decided. He looked like an *old* asshole.

"Nice jacket."

It sure didn't sound like Cyndy. He turned around and found that it wasn't. The compliment came from a shapely, well-dressed woman in her mid to late twenties. She had wild, curly blond hair, full red lips, and was leaning against a banquette, holding a drink that may have been a brandy Alexander.

Her smile gave way to dimples at either end.

"Oh, uh, thanks," Paris said, sounding way too much like Richie Cunningham for his liking. He glanced over at Cyndy. She was talking to a short black man in a white three-piece suit. Paris turned his attention back to the blonde, already wishing he had a cold Budweiser in his hand at the very least. "But I must confess, I borrowed it for the evening."

The blonde nodded in understanding and sipped her drink through the straw; a woman who obviously had borrowed an outfit or two in her time. "Well . . . it looks good on you," she said.

"You really think so?" Paris said, standing up a little straighter, throwing his shoulders slightly back.

"Oh absolutely," the woman said. She gave him the twice-over. "Turn around for me."

Paris turned around slowly, feeling a little stupid. By the time he had turned 360, the woman was smiling broadly.

"Definitely *GQ*," she said. "Maybe even *Uomo*."

Paris smiled, although he was pretty sure she had just called him a homo. He was about to ask her about that when the deejay kicked into an oldie: "When Doves Cry" by Prince.

"You dance?" the woman asked, already swaying to the beat.

Paris's heart immediately doubled its rate. "To *this?*" he replied. He hadn't been to a bar where there was dancing in so long that he had forgotten the abject horror lodged in the notion of fast-dancing in front of people. Sober, no less. In his time as a patrolman, he once stared down a gang-banger who was jacked up on PCP and twirling a Mauser .380 on his index finger, but fast-dancing in front of total strangers scared the shit out of him. "I . . . uh . . . if I could . . . I don't . . ." Now he was Ralph Kramden. "Maybe the next one . . ."

The blonde smiled and stepped closer. "Not a dancer?" she asked.

Her perfume was deliriously sexy. "I'm more of a . . . um . . . slow dancer, I guess," Paris said.

"My favorite kind." She stepped even closer, and as she did, she looked to her left for what Paris imagined to be the third or fourth time. After a few moments, Paris looked in that direction and caught the glance of a man standing near one of the emergency exits. The man was about thirty, brown hair, conservatively dressed. Handsome in a yuppified way. He held a beer in one hand and an unlit cigarette in the other.

When Paris made eye contact, the man looked away.

"Next slow dance, maybe you could show me a few moves," the blond woman added.

"It's a date," Paris said, wondering about the man's connection to this scene.

"By the way, my name's Abigail."

"Jack . . . uh . . . Jack Partridge." What the *hell* was he thinking about? Jack *Partridge?*

They shook hands briefly and Paris could not help but notice the shift of the woman's breasts beneath her white silk blouse. He looked back into her eyes, which were a warm cocoa brown.

She had caught him looking. She smiled.

Paris thought: What am I, Mel Gibson, these days? He decided to look into this high-fashion thing, just as a slow song started. Something by Whitney Houston. There was no avoiding Abigail's face, which, of course, was very pretty to begin with. She arched one eyebrow, as if to ask . . . *well?*

Paris decided to give the lady a whirl around the dance floor. All in the line of duty, of course. He could get a better view of the room from the elevated dance floor, he told himself.

He glanced over at the bar.

Cyndy was gone.

They had agreed that neither of them would make any moves without giving the other a high sign. And now he didn't see her.

"Shit!" Paris vaulted the brass railing and slammed into the crowd, jostling elbows and arms, spilling a few drinks in the process. He unsnapped his shoulder holster. He knew he was over-reacting, that Cyndy could take care of herself. He knew that just

because she wasn't in her seat didn't mean a thing. She was a cop, she was armed, she had experience, so there had to be a really good reason . . .

He knew and he charged ahead anyway.

Halfway to the door one of the larger lounge monkeys—big blond kid, muscular, maybe twenty-four—tried to detain him, something about an apology from Paris for bumping into a girl the kid had known probably all of ten minutes. When Paris opened his coat sufficiently to show him the butt of his weapon, the kid backed off and let him pass.

But the exchange delayed him, eating seconds. It took him a full minute to bull his way to the front. When he arrived he found Cyndy's seat in the possession of an obese Hispanic man with a pair of margaritas already on call in front of him.

Paris looked left and right; into the angled mirrors above. He turned toward the room and scanned the crowd, the women on the dance floor. There was no sign of her. And all the other women were all too . . . *something:* Asian, blond, young, short, black, old, butch.

The deejay mixed into another slow song as Paris found himself momentarily hemmed in by what had to be three or four of the Cleveland Cavaliers. He fingered the badge attached to his belt, considered using it to clear a path, but managed to push his way to the lobby door without it.

He looked through the etched glass. A few couples scattered around the brightly lit foyer. A priest and a little girl. A handful of hotel maids on break, smoking cigarettes.

No Cyndy.

Paris exited the lounge and crossed the lobby, the silence briefly affronting his ears. He waited near the rest rooms for a few minutes and witnessed a parade of rather extraordinary-looking young women. None of them police officers.

He moved down the main corridor, toward the convenience lobbies, the pool, the banquet facilities. He peeked into one of the huge meeting rooms. Nothing moving.

Paris stood in the doorway, watching and listening, sensing people nearby but not being able to pin them down. Muted conversation floated by, a man and a woman, rapid-fire talk.

Paris stepped into the hall and tilted his head to the sound.

And that's when he heard Cyndy scream.

o   o   o

AT FIRST, PARIS COULDN'T TELL IF IT WAS A SHRIEK OF PAIN OR DELIGHT, DANGER or pleasure. It may have even been laughter, but the sound remained in the air, chilling him. He drew his weapon and held it tightly to his side. Flat against the wall, he rounded the corner and found more alcoves for service and housekeeping functions. The passageway was quiet, empty.

At the end of the hall Paris noticed an oversized swing door bearing a *Hotel Employees Only* plate. Through the small, frosted-glass panel he could see movement. Light, dark, light, dark. More voices, closer now. Paris strode silently to the door, crouched, edged it open.

Cyndy Taggart was up against the wall at the far end of the long service corridor, partially obscured by a tall man in front of her and to her right. The man was lean, but broad-shouldered. He held a black overcoat in his left hand.

Before Paris could react, the man raised his right hand high over Cyndy's head and the track lighting above him caught a reflection off his . . . watch? Bracelet? Keys? *Razor?*

"Police!" Paris yelled.

He sprinted the length of the hallway, taking the distance between them in eight or nine long strides, and blindsided the man at full speed. He heard the air rush out of the man's lungs as they locked arms momentarily and slammed into the cigarette machine. Somebody's knee smashed the glass into a thousand sparkling pieces.

For a moment, the edge of Paris's world went brown as the right side of his face, in direct contrast, went blue-hot. He recovered from the impact first, righted himself and kicked the man's feet out from under him. Although he was already breathless, courtesy of twenty-eight years of Marlboros, Paris's upper-body strength prevailed. He wrestled the bigger man to the ground and managed to get one arm behind him in the process.

"Jack!" Cyndy screamed, for what was probably the third time.

Paris dropped his knee into the middle of the man's back and leaned forward, sucking for air. He looked down at the man's profile and immediately recognized the cheekbones, the hair, the earring.

It was Danny Lawrence. Danny lived in the city, but sometimes stayed with his brother in Beachwood. The yuppie bars on Chagrin were his natural hunting grounds.

"Aw fuck me to *tears,*" Paris said.

He had tackled a fellow police officer in what would certainly become "the middle-of-a-hotel lobby" when this story started to make the rounds in about an hour. And according to the blood that was coming from somewhere, he had probably fucked him up too. This was going to dog Jack Paris for as long as he knew cops.

Maybe longer.

"*Shit,* man," Paris said, catching his breath. "I'm sorry, Danny." He rolled off, onto his side, every muscle in his body now starting to howl in response to such rapid and unexpected abuse. To add salt, he barked his elbow on the edge of the Coke machine.

"It's . . . okay, Jack," Danny replied, unconvinced. He stood up and straightened his clothes, gathering his breath as he did. A thin trickle of blood ran from his nose to his lower lip, then onto his shirt. "It's our fault, man. We weren't thinking . . ."

"I thought you were going to be talking to that blonde for a while, Jack," Cyndy said disconsolately, helping Paris to his feet. "I needed cigarettes. I was just going to be gone a couple of minutes."

"*Jesus,* Cyndy," Paris managed, brushing bits of broken glass from his pantleg. "We're on the fucking *job.*"

Paris turned, remembering where they were. The door to the hallway was wide open and a crowd had begun to gather. He flashed his badge and asked them kindly to disperse, effectively blowing his cover at the Impulse Lounge for the rest of the evening.

Probably, he thought, for the rest of the detail.

o   o   o

HIS FACE WAS KILLING HIM. PARIS FIGURED THAT HE HAD HIT HIS RIGHT CHEEK on the top edge of the cigarette machine when he slammed into Danny. But nothing seemed broken. He hoped.

He held the kitchen towel with the ice in it up against his face, pushed the play button on his remote and put his feet on the coffee table. He had left the movie cued up where he always had, right before the scene in which Woody Allen's character, Alvy Singer, visits Annie's parents. Whenever Paris saw the cutaway shot of Woody dressed up like a rabbi he all but died laughing. *Annie Hall* was one of the first videos he and Beth had rented as a married couple. They had seen it at least a half-dozen times since.

But when he saw the FBI warning flash across the screen, followed by some coming attractions, he realized that the tape had been rewound.

And that was impossible.

Someone had been in his apartment.

Paris jumped to his feet. A quick glance around the room, and the fact that he was sitting there watching television at all, told him that his valuables, what few there were, were still on the premises. He bounded over to the bedroom—wedding ring, a pair of cheap watches, his Saint Christopher medal. All intact. What else was there?

Nothing.

He checked the windows, the back door into his apartment. No signs of entry, no nicks around the door locks. He walked back to the living room and stared blankly at the simple black-and-white credits to *Annie Hall* rolling by.

But he hadn't rewound the tape. He never rewound *anything*. The only reason the video stores didn't charge him an extra two dollars every time he brought his tapes back was because he was a cop.

Yet everything in the apartment was where it was supposed to be. And besides—

Wait.

Had he seen Manfred on the way in? Of *course* he had. Manny was always at the door. What dog doesn't run to the door when his master gets home?

He couldn't remember.

He panicked.

"Manny!"

The dog, who had been bunched up on the La-Z-Boy just a few feet from his master's booming shout, snoozing beneath a pair of marvelously pungent flannel shirts, levitated briefly before crashing back down onto the chair. In a moment, he shook the dream from his head, leapt onto the couch, over the top and into Paris's arms.

"Oh *man*," Paris said, barely catching the dog. "You had me going for a second there, Manny." The dog licked his face with sloppy abandon. "Don't know what I'd do if something happened to you."

Manny stuck his nose inside Paris's shirt pocket, instantly snapping in two the solitary cigarette his master had allowed himself to bring home from the bar.

"By the way, champ," Paris said, holding the dog's head between his hands and staring into Manny's lively brown eyes. "Was somebody here today?"

Manfred, in lieu of an explanation, let out a hearty woof.

o   o   o

HE DREAMED HE WAS IN A PORNO THEATER. SWEATY PURPLE WALLS, DAMP seats, the smell of fortified wine and urine and come and mildewed plaster.

Paris knew that the pain in his face had something to do with his presence on West Twenty-fifth Street. Payment for something, penance for something. His head throbbed. Felt oversized.

There were three or four other afternooners in the theater with him; slicked-back humps in the darkness. Paris found a seat in the back row.

He sat down, drew deeply on his pint of Crown Royal and unzipped his pants.

The movie that was unreeling was standard fare, a couple in the missionary position on a royal-blue bedspread, the camera beginning on the image of their feet entwined at the foot of the bed, then moving up . . . ankles, calves . . . up . . . up to their knees, their thighs. The film was a soft-core edit, so the camera cut away quickly when it reached the couple's nasty parts, yet in that moment when the camera jumped to their faces, Paris could see that the woman was blond and pretty; the man, in profile, Euro-swarthy. Handsome. Paris only saw them for a moment before the camera returned to their bodies, but they looked familiar, as if this was some sort of home movie footage he himself had shot years ago.

The thought made him hard. He freed himself.

The camera returned to their glistening bodies, poring over the man's hips, tanned and muscular, silhouetted against the whiteness of the woman's thighs, gyrating, grinding. The woman's breasts rippled from side to side with each thrust; her sighing became more pronounced, more guttural, with each successive parry.

As their lovemaking grew to a frenzy, Paris finally recognized the woman's hands, the manicured fingernails that dug into the man's back, the very rhythm of her breathing.

And as the man brought the woman to a deep, shuddering orgasm, Paris *knew,* and the knowledge filled him with rage and dark excitement.

Tommy Raposo.

The woman, Paris acknowledged as he reached his own climax, was Beth.

17

KAREN SCHALLERT'S BUSINESS CARDS PRODUCED NOTH-ing in the way of leads, nor had Wednesday night's undercover dry run yielded anything useful. Except, of course, the fable of Jack Paris's now legendary blindsiding of Danny Lawrence. There was already a photocopy circulating the Justice Center that showed a team photo of the Browns with Paris's head stuck onto one of the linebackers' bodies.

Funny, funny shit.

Paris picked up the phone and called the Fourth District desk. He asked for Officer Daniel Lawrence.

A minute later: "This is Officer Lawrence."

"Danny, Jack Paris."

"Hey killer."

"How's the face?"

"It's okay," Danny said. "A little sore, maybe. But not too bad, considering the fact that I got blitzed by a strong safety on a dead run last night."

"Tell me that fucking team picture of the Browns is over there already."

"Ever hear of a fax machine, Jack?"

Paris shook his head. "Anyway . . . I just wanted to apologize again, Danny."

"Don't worry about it. I'd have done the same thing," Danny said. "Cyndy Taggart's worth saving, you know?"

"Got that right."

"But you're going to be a legend around here for a while, I'm afraid."

"What can I do to make it up to you?" Paris asked.

"Buy me a scotch and something someday and we'll call it over. Maybe I'll see you at the Caprice later."

"You got it."

"Listen, I got to hit the street. I'll talk to you."

"Okay, Danny," Paris said, and hung up, the pain beneath his bandages beginning to swell with its own remembrance of the previous night's acrobatics.

o   o   o

By Friday morning, the trail had come full circle. With a ton of pressure from city hall, the files on all known sex offenders began to circulate the Unit for the second time in a week, even though there wasn't a cop in Cleveland who had ever run into a pervert like the one they were looking for.

Paris was willing to bet that there weren't too many cops anywhere who had.

The *Plain Dealer,* at least, had taken the story of the murders off the front page and put it in the Metro section, but still they persisted in running something about it every day, bold and detailed. The phone had not stopped ringing since the Burchfield murder Sunday night and all the major tabloids were beginning to set up shop at the downtown hotels.

A short item had already run on page 3 of the *Inquisitor.*

o   o   o

The entrance to Cinq, Limited, was impressive—dove-gray marble, plush charcoal carpeting, brushed-chrome appointments—and behind the posh retail storefront that graced the upper level at Tower City sat the quiet wealth of a successful international concern. Paris was met by an immaculately groomed woman of fifty or so named Rhonda Salinger. She was tall and slender and had soft white hair that fell to her shoulders. He showed her his detective's shield and asked to speak to whoever was in charge of local distribution of Cinq, Limited, products.

"That would be Andrea Heller. She's our regional sales representative," Rhonda Salinger said. "If you'll have a seat, I'll see if she's available."

Paris sat in one of the dozen or so black leather chairs that were carefully arranged around the dimly lit reception area. Instinctively, he picked up a magazine, one he would have certainly been willing to read had it not been written in Italian.

Instead, he looked at pictures of suits that would cost him a month's wages, and of women who, were they available, would probably cost even more.

o   o   o

"What can I do for you, detective?"

They locked eyes, and in that instant, they both knew. It was the blonde from Wednesday night. The one who had tried to pick him

137

up at the Impulse. But her hair was now a reddish brown and she wore far less makeup.

As a detective, Jack Paris had a failing in that he really wasn't all that good with people's faces. Never had been. He was far more adept at reading behavior, body language. So, at first, he was only seventy-five percent sure about the woman; then they shook hands and Paris saw it in her eyes.

The rabbit look. Scared beneath the cool.

He glanced at the woman's left hand, saw her wedding ring and decided to keep the obvious questions to himself until they were alone.

"This way, please." She led him silently down a series of gray corridors whose walls were decorated with large, rear-lit slides of lips and eyes and cheeks and every other body part to which one might apply cosmetics. And each photograph bore the distinctive Cinq, Limited, logo of a 5 that turns into a white bird, wrapped in a circle.

"Abigail, isn't it?" Paris said, once they were well ensconced in her spare but tastefully outfitted office. There were five windows and a spectacular view of the river.

"Andrea," the woman said. "Andrea Heller." She sat behind her desk and beckoned Paris to sit in the chair opposite her.

"It's not Abigail?"

"I think you have me mixed up with someone else, detective." The woman reached into her purse and took out a pair of glasses. She put them on and looked back up at Paris, as if they might hide a significant portion of her face and therefore obscure her real identity. "My name is Andrea."

"You weren't at the Impulse Lounge Wednesday night?"

"Uh, no," she said, pausing for a moment as if trying to remember. "I was home that night. With my husband. I've never even heard of the—what did you say the name was?"

"The Impulse Lounge. The bar at the Embassy Suites Beachwood."

"No," she repeated, perceptibly calmed. "I'm sure I've never even heard of it. I played Scrabble that night with my husband," she said, committing the cardinal sin of offering up too much information without being asked.

Paris figured that the operative word here was "husband," so he decided not to press her on this point. So she was out partying in a blond wig. Different strokes, eh?

Besides, at the time, hadn't he been a designer suit–wearing fraud named Jack Partridge himself?

"Well," Paris began, "in the course of a homicide investigation we are conducting, we've run across a product of yours that was used by more than one of the victims. What I need is a customer list. Where the product is available retail in this area."

"What product is that, Detective Paris?"

She was back in control, Paris thought. She's a pro. Kinky, but a pro. "A face powder called Chaligne."

Andie reacted as if pricked with a needle. "I know it well," she said. "I'm wearing it now."

"Is that right?" Paris asked, sounding intentionally suspicious, although he wasn't sure why. Because as he looked at Andrea Heller in her career-woman suit and Naturalizer pumps, he found himself wishing they could pick up where they had left off on Wednesday. But she was married and that was that.

"It's our top-of-the-line powder," she said.

"Well," Paris began, knowing full well that the next thing to come out of his mouth was going to be monumentally stupid, but not having the slightest clue as to how he might head it off at the pass, "it looks . . . you know . . . *good* on you."

Andie blushed slightly. "I'll get you a copy of the list, detective." She rose from her desk and crossed the room. "There's coffee on the credenza," she said. "Help yourself."

Paris poured himself a cup and did a casual nosing around of the office. Scandesign, high-tech furniture: gray and white. The ever-present silk plant. A quick glance at the photo on the desk neither confirmed nor denied the fact that the man in the picture was the guy hanging around the perimeter of the Impulse Lounge. The man was tall and lean, about thirty. He had a long, straight nose and wavy hair. Paris studied it. Could have been the guy.

Which led Paris to two questions.

One: What kind of sex game were these people playing?

And two: If it had nothing to do with the murder investigation— which he was certain it had not—why the *hell* was he so interested?

"Here we go," Andrea said, striding silently into the office and handing Paris a short stack of photocopies. "I gave you all of Ohio. I wasn't sure how far you wanted me to go."

"Ohio is just fine," Paris said. "And I really do appreciate your time."

"That's quite all right."

Paris stood up. "By the way, how much does this particular powder retail for?"

Andie sat on the edge of her desk, her skirt riding far above her knees. Paris noted that she immediately made an effort to pull it down; a huge contrast to her actions at the Impulse Lounge. "Chaligne retails for anywhere from seventy to eighty dollars, depending on the store," she said. "Around seventy-five dollars on average, I'd say."

"Is that a lot?"

"It's high-end, yes," she said. "But we're in a lot of places, too. Over fifty stores and catalog outlets in northern Ohio."

"Is *that* a lot?"

"Yes, it is," she said, smiling. "We have a very aggressive sales force."

Paris saw a flash of the man-eater she had seemed to be when she tried to pick him up at the Impulse.

Back, he thought as he stood to leave, when she was a blond.

o   o   o

PARIS PULLED THE CAR OVER AT THE CORNER OF WEST THIRTY-FIFTH AND Franklin just as the rain began to come down in sheets. Tommy, who had been standing in the doorway to Minerva Beauty Care, made a dash for it with a newspaper over his head, cursing each drop of deep gray water that hit his Hardy Amies worsted suit.

"*Fuck* this weather," Tommy shouted as he slammed the car door behind him.

"We've got two left," Paris said, ignoring him. Chaligne was available at nine Cleveland locations in all. They had visited seven. "Allied Salon Products on West Forty-fourth, and DeQuincey's on Clark and Fiftieth. We could almost walk." Paris handed Tommy the list and looked over his shoulder at the traffic. "I'll tell you what . . . I'll drop you off at Allied and swing by to pick you up when I'm done with the other place."

"No," Tommy said.

"Huh?"

"I'll take DeQuincey's."

"What's the difference?" Paris asked, pulling out into traffic.

"I want to hit Clark News. It's two doors down from there and I want to pick up a *Racing Form*."

"I'll get it, Tommy."

"Jack . . . I owe Benny DeMarco for like six months of forms. Gotta be up to a hundred-fifty bucks by now," Tommy said. "I was gonna take care of him today, but if you want to pay him for me . . ."

"Fuck no," Paris said.

"A'ight, then," Tommy said, doing his wiseguy thing, shooting the monogrammed cuffs of his shirt like a mobster. "Drop me off close, though. I'm not walking in this shit."

o   o   o

PARIS OPENED THE BELL-CLAD DOOR TO ALLIED SALON PRODUCTS AND IMMEDI-ately noticed a rather plain-looking woman in her late thirties running a feather duster over a long row of aerosol cans. She had dishwater-blond hair that drooped into her face and she wore a pale lavender cotton print dress and tan Rockport walkers.

"Hi," Paris said, shaking off the rain.

The woman looked at the floor, as if he had shouted at her. Her name tag said *Sam*.

"Hello," she said softly.

"I was wondering if—"

"Can *I* help you?"

The man appeared to Paris's left. He was loud and fragrant, overdressed for the warehouse ambience of his showroom. He was fiftyish and balding, but impeccably groomed. Accessorized. His tag said *Mr. Hendershott*.

Paris turned open the wallet bearing his shield and got right to business. "Do you carry a product called Chaligne?" he asked.

"Of course," Hendershott offered, snapping to attention, energized by the intrigue of having a policeman in the store.

"Would you have a recent customer list handy?"

"It's all on the computer," Hendershott said. "Right this way."

Hendershott moved with a feminine grace through the labyrinth of shelving. He reached the back counter and tapped a few numbers into his computer terminal. He brought his bifocals to his face and grimaced. "Just six this month. Not good."

"All to one person?"

"No, no, no. Six separate sales," Hendershott said. "Chaligne is expensive."

"Can you tell me who bought them?"

"Well . . . there's one, two, three . . ." He drifted off. "Five of them are cash sales. No record of their names, I'm afraid. One's a credit card sale, but she's a regular customer."

"Her name?" Paris held his pen expectantly over his pad.

Hendershott frowned, but after a few moments, reluctantly gave in. "Dorothea-with-an-*e-a* Burlingame. But Miss Burlingame has got to be eighty-five years old if she's a day."

"That's okay," Paris said. "You never know where a lead is going to come from." He replaced his notebook and handed Hendershott a card. "If you think of anything . . ."

"Certainly," Hendershott replied.

Paris turned to leave—the weight of having to ask the same questions a thousand times suddenly draining him of all energy—and smiled perfunctorily at Sam. He placed his hand on the worn brass knob, but before he could turn it, it registered.

It had been propped against the top of a wooden bin full of Aqua Velva quarter-ounce samplers, directly behind Mr. Hendershott, the entire time, daring him to notice, mocking him like the old arcade steam-shovel games that never gave you a really good grip on that pack of Luckies with the lighter strapped to it:

The Penrod Collection, it read in faded blue and red type.

Mustaches of Distinction for Men of Action.

Freddie Mercury, Paris thought as he walked back to the counter. The man in the Penrod Collection logo looked just like the late, great Freddie Mercury.

o   o   o

"LET ME SEE," HENDERSHOTT SAID. HE KEYED SOMETHING INTO HIS COMputer, scrolling through screen after screen. "Nope, haven't sold one of these mustaches in . . . uh . . . Well, I haven't sold one this year. Last year either. Not a one." He looked over at the display card, wrinkling his nose. "Nobody really wants them anymore, you see. I think it was a seventies-disco kind of thing in the first place. In fact,

I don't even know why they're out here. I haven't seen the Penrod Collection in a very long time." He shot a reproachful look at Samantha, who reacted by lowering her eyes and dusting a little faster.

"Could one of these mustaches have been sold recently without having been recorded on your register?" Paris asked.

"Absolutely *not,*" Hendershott said, somewhat indignantly. "Everything is rung up."

"I'll need to take two of them with me. I'll sign a receipt, of course."

Hendershott rolled his eyes, as if he had been asked to donate a few thousand gallons of Chanel No. 5 to an old hookers' charity.

"Will the department reimburse me if something happens to them?" Hendershott asked as he reached beneath the counter and retrieved a narrow plastic box with a thin block of Styrofoam along the bottom. He put the mustaches inside and clicked the box shut.

"Of course," Paris answered. He signed the receipt, took the box, dropped it into his pocket and headed once more for the door.

"They're fifty dollars, you know . . ." Hendershott added, wistfully, hopefully. *"Each."*

Paris turned in the doorway and glanced skyward, as if he were thinking. Then he said, "You know . . . I'm going to go way out on a limb here and suggest that maybe that's why you haven't sold one in a few years, Mr. Hendershott." He winked at Samantha, who immediately flushed beet-red. "Just something to think about," Paris added, and stepped out into the rain.

18

UNTIL THE RED LANTERN, I HADN'T BEEN COMPLETELY sure.

We had dared the semipublic venue on a few occasions. Like the time she sat on my lap, wearing a full peasant skirt, sans lingerie, on the crowded RTA. During the twenty-minute ride I was able to work myself out of my zipper and deep into Saila. As we sat in the corner fold-down seat—lost in a forest of overcoats, elbows, umbrellas and briefcases—the rhythm of the train and the nearness of those sweaty strangers brought us both to a silent, blazing orgasm as the car roared through the East Fifty-fifth Street station, the lights dimming and flashing and strobing above us.

But that night at the Red Lantern was the first time she ever went violent.

She wore a lemon silk dress.

o   o   o

WE HAD EATEN ONLY APPETIZERS, SO WE WERE STILL RATHER FRISKY, NOT TOO weighed down by the food. Friskier than usual perhaps because of the bottle of Wan Fu wine we had polished off and the half-joint of *sensimilla* we had smoked on the way to the restaurant.

"Fuck me in the bathroom," I said.

Her voice dropped a half-octave. "Bad little *tomcat*."

I moved closer. I ran my eyes over her chest, her shoulders, up to her mouth.

"Go into the bathroom," I said. "Take off everything under your dress and walk back to the table. I want to watch every man in here get hot."

I glanced at the *Rest Rooms* sign at the back of the restaurant and then at Saila, who was beginning to color. I moved my hand between her legs and squeezed gently. Saila responded with a short gasp and a slight arch of her back, thrusting her breasts up against me. She clamped her thighs around my hand and smiled.

"What do I get out of this?" she asked.

I grabbed her hand and brought it under the table. I moved it a few inches down my leg.

"And what about later?"

A few more.

"I think I'm going to order us a brandy," I said. "This is a brandy caper, don't you think?"

She looked at me, her green eyes full of a thousand mischiefs, and said: "Make mine a double." Then she slid out of the booth, grabbed her shoulder bag and started toward the back of the restaurant.

A full five minutes passed.

Then, a glimpse of silken hair in the dim light of the hallway told me that Saila was coming. The sexy, confident click of her heels on the floorboards kept time with my accelerating pulse.

Ten minutes later, in the car, she placed a perfect leg over the front seat and whispered my name. But before we could consummate our passions, we saw Emily Reinhardt walk across the parking lot.

And everything changed forever.

○　　○　　○

IF THERE WAS A MAJOR KICK TO IT ALL, BESIDES THE OBVIOUS, IT WAS GETTING ready to go out. Because, in spite of the danger, in spite of the unflinching *forever* of it all, that was my end of things and I could never get enough.

It may have been too early in the season but I selected a cream-colored ventless linen sportcoat by Calvin Klein and pleated black linen trousers. My shirt was straight-collared white silk and I wore no tie. My shoes were leather and linen.

Friday.

Saila had said look smart on the phone, and in British vernacular, one of her favorites, that meant *dress*.

1 9 AT EXACTLY 12:40 A.M. SATURDAY MORNING, WHILE JACK Paris stood at the bar at the Emerald Lounge on Euclid Avenue, dressed in his borrowed, blue tarp-jacket, chatting with a short, thrice-divorced woman named Laurel Bettancourt, the man and woman responsible for the recent wave of killings in Cleveland, the ones who called themselves Saila and Pharaoh, but only after sundown, figured out precisely what they had to do. They knew how risky it was, of course, but they agreed, without discourse, that they had no choice.

Soon.

They would take out the cop.

Part Two

Tantrum

2 0

PARIS WANTED MELISSA TO GIVE THE WOMAN THE BENEFIT of the doubt. But, like all young girls of her age (almost twelve), and her delicate position (child of divorce), Paris knew that she lived for the day her parents would come to their senses and realize that they just couldn't live without each other, that they had made a huge and terrible mistake and that from there on in, the divorce would be over and every Easter and Christmas and Halloween and Thanksgiving and birthday would be spent together, cross-legged, in their pajamas, on the living room floor, like families are supposed to. And they'd take a lot of pictures and laugh themselves silly at something Daddy did. And they'd have their old house back.

Jack and Beth and Melissa Paris.

Maybe a brother for her to pick on.

But until then, if she had to put up with the Dr. Bobs of this world, Paris hoped she would warm to the women her father brought around too.

Paris swung into a parking space and stepped out of the car, straightening the front of his brand-new sweater. His casual-date sweater. Sixty bucks he didn't have. He started anxiously toward the door to the theater.

"Wait for me, Dad," Melissa said.

She called him "Dad." It sounded so . . . *teenaged* to him. He was counting on "Daddy" for at least a few more years. "Sorry . . ."

They grabbed each other's hands, instinctively, as they had in every parking lot since Melissa had taken her first rambling steps out of the stroller. Paris wondered if his daughter was embarrassed yet. Most teenagers would rather be eaten by sharks than even be *seen* with their parents, let alone *touch* them.

But neither of them let go.

Not yet.

o   o   o

AS THEY APPROACHED THE FRESH-FACED WOMAN IN THE FADED GUESS JEANS and white L.A. Gear high-tops leaning against the counter at Malley's Chocolates, right next to the Cineplex, Melissa's first thought was that she approved of the woman's style.

She looked okay, in fact.

Actually, she looked kind of *cool*.

○   ○   ○

AT LEAST THREE TIMES DURING THE MOVIE THERE WAS SOME KIND OF SEXUAL reference that made Paris squirm. He couldn't believe what was passing for PG-13 these days. He'd picked the movie because it was Neil Simon and therefore supposedly safe, and what wasn't safe would most likely be over Melissa's head.

But about every twenty minutes or so there was some kind of sex thing.

He was dying.

To make him even more uncomfortable, each of those times, as if on cue, Melissa and Diana glanced at each other and giggled. They seemed to be sharing "girl" moments, and the thought both scared and intrigued him. He wanted Melissa to like Diana, but he didn't want to feel excluded.

Later, as they sat in the Food Court finishing their Cinnabon pastries, Paris couldn't get a word in edgewise. But it wasn't as if he had anything to contribute anyway. The talk between Diana and Melissa ricocheted from boys to clothes to music to boys to school to boys to movies to martial arts to *colleges*. None of the topics were a part of Paris's knowledge base. Except college, perhaps. When he joined the force nearly eighteen years earlier, he had been one of only a handful of four-year college graduates—most of the recruits then had high school or two-year degrees—but now you were considered a slacker if you weren't working on a master's. But Missy? College? That was still years and years and years away.

Please God, let it be years away, Paris thought.

He watched the two of them chatter away as he sipped his coffee, and wondered if he was doing the right thing.

When he heard them making a tentative date for the Home and Flower Show in a few weeks' time—plans that didn't seem to include him—Paris almost said something.

But, for reasons unknown to him, at least at that moment, he kept silent.

○   ○   ○

A SWATH OF EARLY HYACINTH BORDERED SHAKER SQUARE: A SOFT, LAVENDER quilt straining for the sun. The air was fat with their bouquet.

Beth sat at one of the dozen or so tables on the patio in front of the Yours Truly Cafe on the Square, scanning a *USA Today,* nursing a cappuccino. She wore sunglasses with burgundy frames and lipstick that matched.

Paris wondered: Had she requested that he drop Missy off across from her building to save him the agonies of seeing Dr. Bob again?

Or had *she* wanted to see *him* alone?

"So how was the movie?" Beth asked, holding out her hands to Melissa but directing a concerned look at the bandage on Paris's cheek.

Missy ran across the sidewalk and gave her a hug. "It was good." She sat down. "Daddy got a little embarrassed at some of the sex stuff, but otherwise it was okay. We had Cinnabons."

Paris looked at Beth and smiled nervously, shrugging his shoulders. How had Missy known that he was embarrassed? *God,* he was an open book.

He sat down across from Beth, her perfume finding him in an instant. "You look really good," he said.

"Why thank you, Patrolman Paris," Beth replied with a genuine blush. She had called him "patrolman" when they were courting. It was a long-shelved term of endearment that, from the look on Beth's face, had just slipped out. Perhaps it had something to do with the fact that the first day of spring was near.

Missy, having witnessed the exchange with a look of measured hope, slipped a dollar bill off the table and skipped over to the pharmacy.

"What happened to your face, Jack?"

Paris fingered the gauze. "Bad guy threw a cigarette machine at me."

Beth shook her head, remembering living with it day in and day out. "Stitches?"

"Nope," Paris said. "Not this time." He snapped off a corner of her raspberry scone. "So how's . . . uh . . . business, Beth?" It sounded so strange when he said it out loud, but he was determined to change the subject.

"Business," Beth replied, sipping her cappuccino, "is *fantastic.*" She had gotten her real estate license the year she met Jack Paris, but had put it on hold when Melissa came along. In the time they had been separated Beth had gone back to work and risen to the number two slot at Hall-Merryman, Cleveland's largest realtor. "Closed on a house Friday in Rocky River. Iranian engineer and his wife. *Cash,* Jack. Can you believe it?"

He couldn't.

"I can," Paris said. "Who can resist you?"

They went quiet for a few moments, looking around the square, feeling the sun on their faces, sensing the impending change of seasons in the air. When Jack looked back at Beth, she was smiling at him.

"What?" he asked.

"Nothing . . ."

"Oh yeah," Paris said. "Right. You look like the Cheshire cat."

Beth caved in with no further prodding. "I saw you the other night, you know."

"What?" The words sounded like another language for a moment. He felt oddly violated but, ever the law enforcement professional, managed to calmly ask the next logical question. "Where?"

"The bar in the Embassy Suites in Beachwood."

"You *saw* me?" He really hoped she wasn't talking about his tackling of Danny Lawrence.

"Uh-huh . . ."

It was that playfully accusatory tone that only two people with a deep sexual history could recognize in each other. She even sounded a little jealous.

Paris smiled, felt himself redden a bit. "What was I doing?" He crossed mental fingers.

"Forget *doing.* Let's talk about what you were *wearing.*"

Tommy's jacket, Paris thought. Here we go. "What about it?"

"Well . . . you looked really handsome, Jack."

"I did?"

"Oh *please,*" Beth said. "You had to know that you looked good."

"Well . . ."

"It's just that I don't remember you ever looking so *GQ* when we were married."

He debated about whether or not he should tell her that he was undercover, but, seeing as Beth hadn't brought up the task force, neither would he.

"So how'd you do with that blonde?" she asked.

Paris was stunned at Beth's bluntness. It was one thing to be divorced and not know what your ex was up to. But here she was asking about his sex life. Something was definitely afoot. He felt a hopeful stirring deep inside.

"How'd I *do?*" Paris replied. "I . . . uh . . . did okay I guess." He went a shade redder. Forty-three and he was blushing. Real Dirty Harry. Then it dawned on him that he had a big fat nosy, diversionary, yeah-we're-unbridled-but-what's-up-with-this-shit question of his own. "And what brought *you* to the Impulse Lounge, if I may be so bold as to inquire?"

Beth recognized the tone and smiled. "Just stopped in for a drink. Business."

"Oh . . . so we're doing business in discotheques now, are we?"

"I have to go where the *clients* are, Jack," she said. "Just like you have to go where the bad guys are."

"Okay," he said.

"Get it, big guy?"

"Touché, already."

Beth recrossed her legs. "Are you going to see her again?" She didn't wait for him to answer. "You should. She was very pretty."

"Well . . . I . . ." he began. "I'm afraid I had to leave in a bit of a hurry. I didn't get her phone number."

"Oh," Beth said. "Maybe you'll run into her again. Y'never know."

"Maybe . . ."

Silence for a few beats. Uneasy, but not unnatural.

"You know . . . Missy's going to tell me all about her," Beth finally said.

"Who?"

"The one you bought the new sweater for. The one you took to the movies today."

"Really?"

"*Oh* yeah," Beth said. "Girl code and all."

"Is that right?" Paris hoped she was just kidding. He didn't ever want to do battle for Melissa's loyalty.

"So why don't *you* tell me about her . . ."

Paris gave Beth a basic description of Diana, downplaying Diana's looks a bit. He still knew what he was doing, it seemed.

"Is it serious?" Beth asked.

"I don't know," Paris replied. "How are you supposed to know?"

"Well, you just left her, right?"

"Yeah . . ."

"Are you still thinking about her?"

Paris found that he was. He told the truth.

"Then it's serious," Beth replied with what Paris read as a forced smile. She *was* a little jealous, after all.

"Well, it looks like you're going to get a chance to assess her for yourself," Paris said. "She and Missy made plans to go to the Home and Flower Show. Without Daddy, I think."

"I'll be gentle with her, Jack. I promise. I won't tell her how you use toothpicks and leave them lying around the house."

"I never did that."

"Or how you can't light a barbecue to save your life."

"Who can't?"

"Or how you'll wear a pair of sweatpants until they drag themselves to the washer."

"Hey . . ."

"But I appreciate the mini-profile. Every little bit helps," Beth said. "The serious stuff, though—like how she *really* looks—I'll hear that in about thirty seconds."

"From Missy?"

"Yep," Beth said as she arose from the table abruptly and straightened her skirt. "We'll be gossiping like fishwives before we hit the lobby. I'll get the lowdown on what she wore, how much jewelry and makeup she had on, if she colors her hair. Standard dossier stuff."

Paris hung his head, clearly outgunned.

"You can't escape the scrutiny of two nosy women," she added with a smile. "Don't even try."

"She doesn't tell me all that much about Dr. Bob, you know."

"I rest my case," Beth said.

Paris swung his legs out to the side, and when he stood up he found himself inches from Beth's face. Her heels, and his Top-Siders, brought them close to the same height.

"Do you really have to go?" he asked.

She nodded. "Got some work to do. I'll talk to you next week."

Beth leaned over and Paris turned his cheek, as was their perfunctory custom. Instead, this time, she grabbed him beneath the chin, turned his head back and kissed him gently, soulfully, on the lips, the first time in more than two years.

"See you," she said, and walked toward the Shaker Square Pharmacy.

Jack Paris could only stand mute.

21

SHE WAS ASHAMED OF HERSELF. SHE KNEW IT WAS wrong. It had haunted her all weekend and she was *going* to do something about it in very short order.

But, she had to admit, there was something about the whole matter that was kind of exciting, too. Sexy, in a perverted kind of way.

Morbidly fascinating.

Yet when the policeman came into the store that day, she looked at him and just *knew* what he wanted, what he was going to ask about. It all made sense somehow, although she really didn't want to believe in the sense that it made. The rinses, the Irish walking hat, the mustache. The sketch she had seen in the *Plain Dealer* didn't show much of the man's face but it was enough. She would have known him from behind.

Because for more than a year, in her dreams, she had touched every centimeter of the man's face—had kissed his forehead, his lips, the small, almost-cleft in his chin. And in her dreams she had looked like Michelle Pfeiffer, her soft blond hair cast so seductively over one eye, pinning the object of her desires so helplessly to the bed.

Her Mr. Faroh. Or Farrow. Or Pharaoh. She didn't know how he spelled it.

When the policeman asked Mr. Hendershott about the mustache, though, Samantha knew that she would have to tell the truth. And soon. As much as she would hate to have anything happen to him, there were all those other women to think about, women he might just want to do those things to over and over and over . . .

But how could it be? How could her Mr. Faroh be the man who killed all those women? No. His eyes were *kind*. Cultured. He was an actor, for heaven's sake. An artiste.

She knew that sooner or later the police were going to catch this killer, and if they found out that he got his phony mustache for free at Allied Salon Products . . .

Something would most assuredly happen, Samantha thought. Something bad.

She picked up the phone, looked at it, as if expecting it to dial itself, then replaced it onto its cradle. All for the fiftieth time. She stroked her tomcat, Cosmo, debating.

But it wasn't *really* a debate at all. Because . . . who was she kidding? Did she really think that a man like her Mr. Faroh would ever call her? Would ever date a woman like her? With her plain face and mousy hair and flat chest and knobby knees and crooked front tooth.

Fat chance, Sammy, she thought. The only reason he wanted your name was because you had to be so stupid as to give him that mustache. And then, for him, there was no turning back. He wanted to know where you lived. *Had* to know. Just in case.

He's a clever one, that Mr. Faroh.

She ran a tub, scorchingly hot. She dropped her robe to the floor and stared at herself for a few resolute moments in the bathroom mirror: droopy and lined and puffy in the harsh light thrown by the single bulb hanging from the ceiling.

Thirty-seven, Sammy. Thirty-eight in three days.

She settled into the steaming tub, coming alive, feeling rejuvenated and aroused, hoping that this would be the very last time she would ever fantasize about him.

She grabbed the worn, plastic shampoo bottle, and closed her eyes.

o   o   o

"HI . . . THIS IS DETECTIVE JOHN PARIS. YOU KNOW WHAT TO DO AND YOU *know when to do it* . . ."

Beep.

"Uh . . . hi . . . uh . . . my name is Samantha Jaeger and I work at Allied Salon Products on West Forty-fourth Street and you were in the other day and you were asking about mustaches and Mr. Hendershott said that we hadn't sold one in a really long time and while that is in fact true it is not exactly what you might call the truth. Call me . . ."

She left her number, hung up and grabbed a full breath, exhaling slowly. It had been relatively painless, she thought, this "notifying the proper authorities."

"See, Cosmo?" she said to the cat. "If you just *do* things, it's so much easier than stewin' and stewin' and stewin' about them until your stomach gets all edgy and you can't eat anything." She gently shook the rather portly cat. "Which has never been *our* problem, has it, kitty cat?"

She put the policeman's card on the coffee table, walked over to the kitchen and scanned the contents of her refrigerator. The same as yesterday, save for one less Diet Coke. She absently checked the cupboards, even though she knew there were no two things in the apartment that could be combined to make anything resembling a meal. Cocoa Puffs and evaporated milk. Hamburger Helper with absolutely nothing in the freezer to help. She ambled back to the living room, muted the goofy voice of Mr. Bob Saget and his silly TV show and dialed Domino's Pizza, her third time in three days.

Which is one of the reasons why, when the buzzer rang about twenty-five minutes later, she didn't ask who it was.

2 2 SERGEANT ROBERT DIETRICHT AND SERGEANT THOMAS
Raposo were late for their 7:45 A.M. Monday
briefing. The task force started without them.

"We've run the name Farrow through the computers, spelled just about every imaginable way.
There's sixteen Farrows in Cleveland. Ten Farohs.
Three Faros," Paris said to the handful of detectives scattered around
the common room, including Tim Murdock, who was now on shared
duty with the task force, and an attractive woman Paris hadn't met yet
but who looked a lot like a shrink. She had the posture, the confident
bearing of education. "We have paper on six of them," he continued,
writing the names on the chalkboard. "Nothing bigger than a B and
E, though. The rest are mostly traffic. No violence."

"Eleanor Burchfield told me she had not asked the man about
his name, having assumed it was spelled F-a-r-r-o-w. It didn't occur
to her that it may been Pharaoh, with a *P-h*. Regardless, there's no
'Pharaoh' in the databases. The FBI is currently running it through
VICAP to see if there are any serial wackos out there with an Egyptian bent. On the other hand, he said his name as if it were just one
word. I'm inclined toward 'Pharaoh.' "

"What about the makeup?" asked Greg Ebersole, who looked to
Paris about as alert on a Monday morning as he could remember
seeing him. His unruly red hair was moussed and combed, his suit
pressed. He looked like a cop for a change. "Did we get any matching MOs on any earlier victims being made up postmortem?"

"Nothing yet. Or nothing that hasn't been closed, I should say.
As for fingerprints, we've got everybody accounted for at the four
scenes. The few errants that were picked up belonged to police officers. Carl McCracken, a rookie from the Fourth, dropped one at
the Red Valley Inn. This is a rubber-glover at all times, folks. Every
other surface was wiped hospital-clean." He scanned their faces for
more questions, found none. "Cyndy?"

Cyndy Taggart stood up and flipped open her notebook. "No
connection yet between Reinhardt, Milius and Karen Schallert," she
said. "They went to different high schools, different colleges,
worked at different ends of town, they even banked with three different banks. Different health clubs, different gynecologists, different social circles. These three women did not know each other."

"What about boyfriends? Exes?" Paris asked, finding it hard, after seeing Cyndy all dolled up the previous Wednesday night, not to look at her legs. Today she was wearing *very* tight jeans, making it even more difficult for him. "Any crossover?"

Cyndy shook her head. "Phoenix PD comes up negative on Milius's ex-husband. No record. Burchfield had been seeing a guy named"—she flipped a few pages—"Peter Heraghty. But he was in New Orleans. Got his signature on a VISA receipt the day of the murder. The other two were real loners, I'm afraid. No steadies." Cyndy shrugged, wishing she could add more.

Paris nodded at Greg Ebersole, who stood up, cleared his throat.

"All the women followed the same routine, including Eleanor Burchfield. They all went solo to a discotheque after work, had maybe one too many Wallbangers and ended up leaving with our boy. All blood-alcohol levels were high, indicating that they probably had been drinking for at least a few hours."

"Is there any evidence that they hit more than one bar on the evening of the murder, that they may have met someone and gone barhopping?" Elliott asked.

"Well, no one has ID'd them at any other bars in the area. None of them smoked, so we didn't find matches or anything. No numbers on wet cocktail napkins . . ."

Greg Ebersole sat down beneath the approving glance of Jack Paris.

Captain Elliott stepped forward and introduced the woman. "Everyone . . . this is Dr. Gayle Wheaton, Associate Chief of Psychiatry at Johns Hopkins. We're *extremely* fortunate to have her, but just for the week, I'm afraid," Elliott said, shooting a reproachful glare at Paris. "Dr. Wheaton?"

"Good morning all," she said.

Paris immediately noted a slight British accent. Dr. Wheaton looked to be in her late thirties, brunette, tall and statuesque. She wore a charcoal and white chalk-stripe suit.

"I'm not here to subject you to Serial Murder One-oh-one," she continued. "I'm sure you've all seen *The Silence of the Lambs.*"

Polite laughter.

"And I'm sure you've all been well briefed on the basics of the deviant sexual mind. The reason I *am* here is to fill in a few gaps in the recent research."

In spite of her promise, Dr. Wheaton proceeded to explain the very cardinal elements of the serial murderer's MO. Shrinks always have to start at the beginning, Paris thought. That way they can bill a few more hours. He listened to her explain how there is always a pattern, each murder followed by a cooling-off period. How the killer usually takes a memento from the victim or the scene. How they almost always act alone.

Paris knew the rudiments. He took the opportunity to slip away and check his voice mail.

And find Tommy.

o   o   o

ELEVEN MESSAGES!

Message one was from six-thirty Sunday evening. Stan Azzarello of the *Midnight Beacon,* perhaps the trashiest of the tabloids. If such measurements could be made. Paris often thought that making such comparisons was like trying to judge which piece of dog shit smelled the best.

Message two was from the woman who worked at Allied Salon Products. Something about the mustache. Paris jotted down her number and made a note to call Reuben to see if FBI Hair and Fiber had gotten back to him about the mustache found in Karen Schallert's hair.

Messages three through nine were all from either tabloid reporters or the regular group of sleazebags. The calls had come in all night. Out of habit, Paris copied these numbers down as well.

Number ten was from Melissa, who had called him at 7:05 A.M., before she left for school, to remind him about her upcoming play.

Message eleven was a hang-up.

Paris glanced at his watch and determined that it probably would not be too early to return Samantha Jaeger's call, seeing as she was a nine-to-fiver. He dialed the number, noting absently that she lived in Lakewood. He got her machine, left a message.

Ditto for Tommy.

He then dialed Kasimir's on Lorain, where Tommy had breakfast three or four mornings a week, but neither Kas Jaroz nor his wife, Bette, had seen him. Paris retrieved the Allied Salon Products card from his folder and was just about to dial when he noted that the shop was closed Mondays. He called anyway, but there was no answer, no machine.

Four for four, he thought.

With practiced ease he stood up, tossed the reporters' phone numbers into the wastebasket and rejoined the meeting.

o   o   o

". . . IS THE SORT OF MAN WE'RE LOOKING FOR," DR. WHEATON SAID. "THE makeup, the mutilation caused by the removing of the tattoos . . ."

"So what does it all mean?" asked Cyndy Taggart. "I mean, they're dead, why the lipstick and rouge and mascara? The reports say there's no intercourse taking place after death. What's the . . . uh . . . I don't know . . . *attraction?*"

"Well, the killer seems to be obsessed with the application and removal of adornments," said Dr. Wheaton. "These are, of course, generally thought of as games young girls play. Dress-up, putting makeup on dolls, that sort of thing. I'd say there's a good possibility that he was raised in an all-female home."

"What about an only child, raised by his mother?" Cyndy asked.

"Certainly possible."

The question had been bothering Paris since Rita the Barmaid had raised the possibility the previous week. He asked while the asking was free. "What are the chances that we're looking for a woman? I mean, that this guy is partnered with a woman? As in, he's luring them to the motels and she's killing them and putting on the makeup. What are the chances we're looking for a couple?"

Greg Ebersole and Randall Elliott glanced at each other, exchanging incredulous looks, but remained silent.

"According to FBI stats, about nil," Dr. Wheaton answered. "Less than one percent of criminals designated as serial murderers are female."

"I'll bite," Paris said, instantly regretting his choice of verbs. "Why?"

"We're not quite sure. The prevailing theories tend to lean toward the maternal instincts. Women tend to kill out of passion, not obsession. Men still commit most of the homicides in this country."

Paris glanced over at Cyndy Taggart, who stuck her tongue out at him as punishment for asking such a sexist question.

"But don't think women can't be just as sadistic as men," added Dr. Wheaton. Paris returned Cyndy's sneer. "The Aileen Wuornos case in Florida is an all too graphic reminder of the growing incidence of female serial murder."

Paris knew very well about Aileen Carol Wuornos, the roadhouse prostitute who was thought to have committed a string of murders along Florida's I-95. Sunday afternoon he had visited Cleveland Public Library and photocopied clips about the case from *Time, Newsweek* and *Vanity Fair.*

He had also looked up rose of Jericho.

The rose of Jericho was a Middle Eastern flower that had a strange tendency to roll up when dry, then once again expand to full bloom when moistened. The Syrians and Egyptians had another name for it, Paris discovered, an ancient name he hoped would not be a portentous sign.

They called it the resurrection flower.

o o o

THE EMS UNIT WAS PARKED DIRECTLY IN FRONT OF 11606 CLIFTON BOULEvard. The arched door that was the front entrance to the twenty-four-suite apartment building was propped open with a stone pot bearing a few sadly neglected twigs, hollow stalks begging skyward.

The inner door was held open too—this one with a triangular wooden block—and as Paris scanned the mailboxes, found Samantha Jaeger's name and apartment number and began to mount the stairs, he found himself tempted to look into whatever it was that had drawn the paramedics to 11606. Besides being a detective, he was a terrible snoop. Born to nose.

But instead he focused on his duties, grateful to be pursuing something that had even a nodding acquaintance with a lead in this case.

The hallway on the second floor was narrow and medicinally clean. The wood floor beneath the carpet runner had been painted a dark brown enamel and it looked like it had been buffed about once a week for years. The occasional sconces, and the floral wallpaper, gave the corridor a 1930s-hotel look. Warm and inviting. Paris wondered about the rent.

Maybe, he thought morbidly, the presence of the EMS boys meant there was going to be an opening.

He shook his head, amazed at the perverse nature of his thoughts sometimes, and knocked on the door to number 206.

○   ○   ○

"ARE YOU WITH THE POLICE?" THE VOICE WAS NICOTINE-RASPY, FRIGHTENED.

Having given up on Samantha Jaeger ever answering his knock, Paris was nearly through the doorway to the stairwell when the woman opened her door and spoke. He spun around to see a short, frail woman in her seventies, bunching the top of her robe together at her throat. She held a rhinestone-encrusted cigarette holder in the other hand.

"Yes ma'am," Paris said, producing his shield. "What can I do for you?"

"There were two of them, you know," she said soberly, as if passing along a government secret.

Paris walked toward the woman, who took a cautious step backward as he approached.

"Two of who?" he asked, stopping short, not wanting to spook her. "Two of what?"

"Two people, of course. A man and a woman."

Paris could see a half-dozen cats perched in various positions through the slightly ajar door to the woman's apartment. He smelled the aroma of simmering onions and tomatoes.

"What two people would that be?" Paris asked, patronizing the woman, sensing a crackpot answer coming. Benson and Hedges, maybe. Bausch and Lomb. Ben and Jerry.

"Two of them," she repeated. "They came for her last night."

"Who?"

"And now they've found her at the bottom of the basement steps, her neck snapped in two."

"*Who?*" Paris said, straining to keep his temper in check.

"Why, Sam, of course," the woman said matter-of-factly. "Sammy Jaeger. She's dead, you know."

The words were like a roundhouse blow to Paris's gut. He heard *dead*. He heard *a man and a woman*. He turned on his heel and headed for the stairwell, hoping to catch the paramedics before they moved the body. He glanced over his shoulder. "I'll be back up here in a few minutes," he said, feeling winded, shaken. "Please don't go anywhere, Mrs. . . . uh . . . Mrs. . . . uh . . ."

She wasn't getting it.

"What's your *name?*"

"Estelle," she said softly, seeming to snap out of some mild trance. "Estelle Estabrook."

"Please don't leave the building, Estelle," Paris said, feeling lousy about barking at an elderly woman. His father, rest his soul, would have gone upside his head.

"Yes sir, sergeant," she answered, saluting.

Paris headed down the steps toward the basement, wondering how much of what Estelle Estabrook had told him, or would tell him, was born of this planet.

As for Samantha Jaeger, and *her* relationship to this life, he would soon find out.

o   o   o

SAMANTHA JAEGER'S APARTMENT WAS SMALL AND UNCLUTTERED, HAPHAZARDLY furnished with a worn camelback sofa of indefinable color and a matching overstuffed chair. The chair was draped with a green and white afghan and sported a sleepy, long-haired cat. The other pieces of furniture in the living room—a wobbly blond coffee table, a thread-bare ottoman, a braided oval rug—were all Salvation Army specials.

The only warm touch in the room—indeed the only real clue that any human lived there, besides the stack of Domino's Pizza boxes—were the bookshelves that contained row after row of brightly hued paperbacks.

Paris flipped through the collection: Barbara Cartland. Barbara Taylor Bradford. Marylyle Rogers. Jennifer Blake. All romances, all dog-eared, many boasting covers with windblown muscular men and busty, raven-haired women. There had to have been hundreds, Paris thought.

He sat down at a small, short-legged desk by the front door and surveyed the room. A woman's place, but only barely and then, per-haps, by default. The faded green chintz curtains did only cursory battle with the afternoon sunlight, the few scrawny plants on the windowsill were badly in need of water. The room had a palpable scent of loneliness.

Had she entertained men in this room? Paris wondered. Had she had parties and Christmas gatherings and birthdays and baby show-ers with her friends and family?

Paris thought about his own small apartment across town, with its mismatched furniture and its noisome smells of disinfectant and long-boiled coffee. Is this how his life would look to someone else? If he was taken out on the job one day, not given the chance to clean up the detritus of his existence, would some cop sit at his dining table and pity him like this?

Estelle Estabrook had told Paris that a man and woman had knocked on Samantha's door at exactly 7:30 P.M. the previous night. She told him that she knew the precise time because it was just at that commercial break after *America's Funniest Home Videos.*

And no, she added, she didn't actually see the couple. But after forty-four years in the same apartment, she confessed, her ears had become rather highly attuned to the comings and goings and family disputes and midnight lamentations of the people in 206 and the people in 210, the apartments with which she shared walls.

She was certain there were three distinct voices. Samantha's, a voice she'd know anywhere. A man, whose baritone was deep and spooky. And another woman, who more than once had shouted something unintelligible at Sam.

Something, Estelle Estabrook believed in her Christian soul, that contained the *f* word.

Paris rose, kicked absently at the stained cotton throw rug and tried to plug Samantha Jaeger into this picture. She certainly wasn't the attractive career woman who fit the killer's profile. But she *had* called and left a message on his voice mail. What had she wanted to tell him about the mustache? On the other hand, maybe the man and woman had nothing to do with anything. Maybe they were bill collectors. Maybe it *was* simply an accident. Happened all the time. He decided to head back into town, maybe send a lab team to work the hallway and the basement stairwell.

But what he saw when he glanced into the apartment's tiny bedroom nearly took his legs away.

Samantha Jaeger had built a shrine to a madman.

23 ANDIE DIDN'T TELL MATT ABOUT THE COP. SHE KNEW that the very idea of police and courts and the very suggestion of trouble would have spooked her husband, and she wasn't done playing yet. After all, the detective's questions had nothing to do with their little game, right? *They* weren't involved with the murders, were they? So why rock the boat?

Matt wouldn't have liked the idea of her being questioned by the police, so he didn't have to know. She didn't like lying to him, but it was the only way she could think of to maintain the status quo.

The cop who called himself Jack Partridge, then Jack Paris, had looked a lot more ordinary at her office than he had at the bar, but he was still rather sexy in a rumpled kind of way. A little rough around the edges, maybe, but he had great hair, big hands. Wise, confident eyes.

Matt was out of town for two days. Ashland Oil had him on the road, a scenario that seemed to be unfolding more and more frequently at this point in their marriage. Their *childless* marriage, Andie amended, a little annoyed at her husband but not knowing why. He *was* working hard, wasn't he? So that they could live in Shaker and maintain their one luxury car and their one all-American tin box.

She was just about to open a bottle of Chardonnay, put her feet up and see what was on HBO, when the phone rang.

"Hello . . ."

"Hi . . ."

"Hello?" Andie asked again. "Who is this?"

"Who *is* this? You know who this is . . ."

"No I don't. This is why I asked, see? It's what we in the profession call a *question*."

"Don't play games."

"I'm playing games?"

"Yes."

"Five . . . four . . . three . . . two . . ."

"Don't hang up, either."

She was sure that she didn't know the voice. Clearly it was a man, and it wasn't Matt. Unless of course Matt had a bad cold and had put a pair of Huggies over the mouthpiece. The voice had a strange, electronic sound to it.

"Last chance, Sparky . . ." she said, her finger hovering over the button.

Silence. Light breathing.

"Bye."

She hung up the phone.

○   ○   ○

THE MOVIE WASN'T VERY GOOD, SOMETHING WITH VAN DAMME. BUT SHE actually sat and watched two thirds of it. Matt would have been proud of her.

She missed him, thought about calling him in Ashland, but it was late.

She left a few lights on downstairs, brushed her teeth and was halfway under the covers when the phone rang again. "Hello?" Andie said, fully expecting to hear Matt's voice.

It was the breather. She had almost forgotten.

"Oh it's *you* . . ." she said, mocking him. "How've you been?"

"Why do you show me this disrespect?"

The voice was clearer than before. Softer, somehow. Friendlier. It actually *could* have been Matt. There was some hissing behind the voice. It sounded like long-distance static.

Softly: "Matt?"

"I saw you at the nightclub."

Andie wasn't sure, but she decided to play along for a little while, not wanting to kill the game if it was Matt, but not wanting to play along with some pervert, either. The Chardonnay was on duty, though, and it voted for the game.

"Yeah?" she said. "Which one?"

"The yuppie bar," he answered after a moment's hesitation. "Beachwood."

It had to be Matt, she thought. Who else knew?

"Is that right? And what was I wearing?"

"You looked like a vixen. Tight career-girl suit, gray. White rayon underneath. Underneath *that* . . . God only knows."

"God and me," Andie said, starting to sound a bit too eager.

"I can imagine though."

Andie heard something in the man's voice that told her it wasn't Matt. The voice was too deep and authoritative. Then again, Matt Heller was always the one at the party who did the impressions, told the dialect jokes. The idea that it might *not* be her husband both excited and frightened her. A bit.

But not enough to make her hang up, she discovered.

"Can you?" Andie untied her robe, flicked off the table lamp on the nightstand and lay back on the bed.

"Umm-hmm."

"And what do you imagine?"

"I imagine silk," the man said. "I imagine the feel of the silk against your breasts, against your nipples."

"Yeah?"

"That's why you wear it, isn't it?"

"Maybe."

"Don't play with me."

The voice commanded the truth.

"Yes," Andie said. She pulled open her robe and ran her hand over her inner thighs. She had just shaved her legs, and her skin was supple and smoothed with oil.

"Does it happen often?" the man asked.

"What?"

"Your nipples, standing erect. Does it happen on the elevators at work?"

"Sometimes . . ." she answered.

"Say it," the man said.

"Sometimes my . . . uh . . ."

"Say it."

"Sometimes my nipples get hard while I'm at work."

The man humphed, pleased with the fact that he had gotten her to talk dirty to him.

"Do you think the men notice?" he asked, whispering now.

Andie licked the tips of her fingers. "Oh, I'm certain they do . . ."

"Do you think they want you? Want to fuck you?"

"Yes, I think they do."

"Think?"

"I know they do."

"How does it make you feel?"

"Good," Andie whispered, her breath coming in shorter and shorter waves.

"I know *I* do . . ."

"You do what?"

"Want to fuck you."

Andie liked the way the man said the word. "Yeah?"

"Umm-hmm."

"Tell me," Andie said.

"Tell you what?"

"Tell me what you want to do to me . . ."

o   o   o

AFTER ANDIE WAS CERTAIN THAT THE MAN HAD COME, THAT HER *HUSBAND* had come, she fell silent; hushed in this strange afterglow of telephone sex.

Finally, he spoke.

"I have to go," he said.

He sounded small, spent.

"Okay," Andie replied, surprised at the weakness in her own voice.

"I have work to do."

"At this hour?"

"Yes," he said. "Before I leave you, let me ask you something."

"Yes?"

"When you see me, will you know me?"

Andie thought for a moment.

But before she could answer, the man chuckled softly, as if the question was rhetorical, and hung up the phone.

2 4

LET ME TELL YOU ABOUT WOMEN. I KNOW THEM, LOVE them, adore them, couldn't imagine myself living without them for one day, one hour, one minute, one second. It is the pursuit of women that makes life endurable.

I say this because I have always been good with women. "Good" in the seduction sense. If ever you've spent any time in a nightclub, and watched a guy talking to a beautiful woman and her no-slouch friend, making them laugh, getting them to slow-dance, walking out of the club for a round of sex or drugs or both, that was me.

And it's not just about looks, see, it's not just about clothes—although I think I might be dead myself without them—it's about *style.* And confidence. If you give a beautiful woman the impression that you couldn't care less if you got between her legs, you'll drive her crazy with desire. How *dare* you not fall over yourself to pursue me? she thinks. How *dare* you not call? Who do you think you *are?*

I'll tell you who I am. I am a most prolific lover of women; the bane of every working husband. Yet, when I give myself over to one woman, I am just another slave.

Just like every other man.

And I trust my woman with my life.

2 5

THE HOLE IN THE CENTER OF HIS FOREHEAD WAS LESS than a half-inch in diameter. Clean around the edges, except for the ash white of the powder, the deep violet streak of the burn.

The back of his head told another story altogether.

A story punctuated by the dried clumps of pink and gray tissue that clung to the lampshade and stereo receiver behind the chair.

The .38 Smith and Wesson Police Special was taped to his hand and wrist with a huge ball of silver duct tape, lest there be any frantic searching for the weapon when the team arrived, lest there be any spasming that might have flung the revolver out the window. At his feet lay an empty fifth of Absolut Citron Vodka and a pair of Perry Ellis leather slippers, neatly tucked under the base of the couch.

But there was no note.

No confession.

It was Tuesday morning and Reuben was positive, going on smell alone, that the corpse was at least seventy-two hours ripe. Which made it Friday night. Which made sense, if everything was as it appeared to be.

And Paris was far from convinced of that.

Yet the shock of the scene was still enormous, even to the so-called grizzled veteran. Cops say they get used to it after a while, but there are some things you never get used to. Dead kids. Maimed kids. Mutilated bodies. *Brains.*

You can't be grizzled enough for this, Paris decided as they zipped the plastic body bag around the man's broad shoulders.

The police officers walked silently around the living room for the next forty-five minutes, doing their respective duties, sidestepping each other, averting eyes, trying to deflect the anger and guilt they all felt, the sense of shame at not having been able to prevent this.

Paris knew he was putting it off.

He walked slowly into the bedroom and began the ritual scavenging of the dead man's treasures.

o   o   o

THE BEDROOM FURNITURE WAS JAPANESE IN DESIGN: BLACK LACQUER FINISH, red-tasseled nylon sash cords, silver hardware. The bed was huge, easily a king-size, probably a special-order job that looked as if it could sleep six across. To the right of the bed stood a tall dresser bearing a large collection of expensive colognes, cut-crystal sentries standing guard on a carved wooden tray. Presents mostly, Paris suspected. Women who don't know you well give you cologne. Minotaure, Kouros, Quorum, Lagerfeld. Paris remembered when there were only three colognes to choose from: Jade East, Canoe and Old Spice. This was all so foreign to him. Another world, really.

He pushed the bottles around, from side to side.

At the back he found a small vial of spirit gum.

o   o   o

THE BATHROOM WAS SPOTLESS AND FRAGRANT, HARDLY A BACHELOR'S STRONG suit, Paris thought as he pushed open the door. Gray curtain, black carpet, white fixtures. He rummaged the drawers and cabinets and found just what he expected to find, the usual minutiae of an unmarried man: nail clippers, Bic razors, airline soaps, mint-flavored floss. He looked into the wicker wastebasket. A couple of used Band-Aids they would bag for blood type. A pair of greatly reduced soap bars. There was also a brightly colored box bearing the words *EZ Color Fashion Rinse*.

o   o   o

THE CLOSET. TWO DOZEN SUITS, AS MANY BRILLIANT WHITE SHIRTS, ALL CARRYing names Paris knew only from the magazines. Armani, Gianfranco Ferre, Willi Smith, Gianni Versace. There were a dozen pairs of shoes all filled to their welts with carved mahogany shoe trees, all reflecting back a funhouse-mirror face at Paris. At least a hundred ties, thirty or so belts.

Paris stepped back, stood on his tiptoes and, within a few moments, found what he was looking for.

On the uppermost shelf, perched atop a quartet of meticulously folded Ralph Lauren and Alexander Julian sweaters, sat an Irish walking hat.

Paris knew where he would find the patches of skin.

The rose tattoos.

He just didn't feel like opening the freezer quite yet.

2 6

WHEN THE BUZZER RANG AT ONE O'CLOCK IN THE MORN-
ing at the Candace Apartments, it was never
good news. Pick one: some crazyass, some
drunk crazyass, or one of Jack Paris's deep list of
junkies in need of a cure.

He was a third of the way inside his own evening's
whore, a fifth of Jameson's Irish, when he finally marched over to
the intercom. He shushed Manny and pressed the button, expecting
any manner of lowlife to respond.

The last person he expected was Diana.

○   ○   ○

"I HEARD, JACK," SHE SAID SOFTLY. "I'M SORRY."

She took off her coat. She was wearing an oversized white shirt
tucked into a denim skirt cut just above her knees.

"I . . . uh . . ." Paris didn't know what to say. He was so full of
rage and sadness. Impotence. He felt the same debilitating weari-
ness he had felt the moment he knew his marriage was over.

Diana took the cue and pulled him to her. She grabbed the bottle from his hand, placed it on the end table and held him close.

Within a few moments, she drew his lips to hers for the very
first time.

○   ○   ○

"CINDY CRAWFORD."

"Okay," Paris said. "Good one." He looked at the ceiling, lost in
thought. "Okay, how about . . . um . . . Honey West?"

"Who?"

"Honey West. Blond PI. Used to wear leotards all the time."

"Never heard of her. Take a drink."

"She's for *real,* I'm telling you. Hers is right where yours is. On
the cheek. Ask anybody."

"And I'm telling *you* I never heard of her. Take a drink."

Paris obeyed, tilting his head back in deference to the bottle of
smooth Irish whiskey. They were sitting on the couch, facing each
other, their hands from time to time finding each other's knees and
thighs and shoulders as they told their stories. They had talked for
what seemed to be hours—about the case, about themselves, about
the nature of life and death. Somehow, they had drifted into this
drinking game. They were about two inches from the bottom of the

bottle of Irish, but that was okay. Paris had another.

"Honey West . . ." Paris repeated, trailing off. "You're too damn young is the problem." He swigged again, his face now beyond reacting to the liquor. "That's what's happening here."

"Can't blame everything on my innocence," Diana said.

"Innocent. Right, counselor. Your turn."

"Easy," she said. "Madonna."

"Madonna?" Paris pleaded. *"Where?"* He asked, even though he had seen her *Sex* book and knew precisely where each and every one was located.

With a wave of her hand Diana gestured toward the bottle, confirming what he already knew.

He swigged.

It was getting to be a very loopy game.

o   o   o

SHE WAVED IT PLAYFULLY IN FRONT OF HIS EYES, THEN TOSSED IT TO HIM. A LA-tex condom. "Don't even *say* it," Diana warned, laughing a bit nervously as the color began to rise in her cheeks.

"What?" Paris said, finding a brief smile somewhere within him. He flopped onto the couch, flipping the condom between his fingers. "What was I going to say?"

"Oh, some kind of Girl Scout joke, I'm sure." She stood up, unzipped her skirt and stepped out of it. "Something about being prepared."

She sat on the coffee table in front of him, the tails of her big white shirt between her thighs. Paris looked down and saw that her toenails were painted a blood red. She reached into her shirt pocket and produced a perfectly rolled joint.

"Miss *Bennett* . . ." Paris said, surprised but not shocked.

"Yes, detective?" She batted her eyes demurely, licked the end of the joint and lit it.

"Are you aware of the fact that you are endeavoring to use a controlled substance in the presence of a police officer?"

"Well . . . *yes,*" she said, releasing the smoke slowly. "But it's just that I'm trying to get control *of* the police officer."

"Is that right?"

"It is."

She leaned forward and put the joint to Paris's lips. He drew on it deeply. Immediately the pot found the booze in his system and put an entirely new, euphoric perspective on the evening. He let the smoke leak out of the corners of his mouth in thin gray ribbons, then took another leisurely hit. It had been ages. When he looked up, through the haze, he found Diana staring at him, smiling, cataloging his features.

She sat back and unbuttoned two more buttons on her blouse, the tops of her breasts now visible through the folds of white cotton. She ran her hands slowly up his thighs. Back down.

"I'm afraid I'm going to have to place you under arrest," Paris said, slurring the word "place" so that it sounded like "plaish."

"I don't see that you have any choice," Diana answered, hitting the joint again and passing it back to Paris. "I'm completely incorrigible. Irredeemable in the eyes of this court."

Paris took another drag, nearly coughing it out.

"You have the right to remain sexy . . ." he said.

"Uh-huh."

She slid to the floor, catlike, fluid.

"Anything you hold against me," Paris continued, "will be held against *you* . . ."

"Fair enough." She finished unbuttoning her shirt and pulled it down over her shoulders, letting it drop to the floor as she worked her way between his legs.

Paris drew on the joint again. "You have the right to be an attorney . . ."

She unbuttoned his shirt and kissed her way down his face, his neck, his chest. She kissed his stomach and pulled open his cop-issue black leather belt.

"And . . . and . . ."

Finally she worked his pants open and started running her tongue around the tip of his penis, that inch or so that had begun to brave the room above the waistband of his underwear. She slid up—the brief rush of her breasts against his skin maddening his erection—and buried her tongue in his mouth. She sat back on her heels.

"Jack . . ."

"Mmmm . . ."

"Tell me about the first time you saw me."

"What do you mean?"

"The first time you saw me. What did you think? Did you want me?"

"*Oh* yeah." *God*, he wished he wasn't so drunk. So . . . *slow.*

"When I questioned you on the stand. Were you thinking about it then?"

"Yes . . ."

She drizzled her way back down the length of his body, this time taking him fully in her mouth. Up and down quickly, but only for a few seconds.

"Tell me what you want, Jack," she whispered.

She flicked her tongue out once, twice.

"I . . ."

She remained on her knees as she pulled him to his feet and steadied him at the foot of the couch. She reached behind her and lifted the venetian blind to the top of the window, displaying the two of them dimly to the night, to the parking lot that faced Eighty-fifth Street and the handful of cars that grew out of the darkness there.

"Say my name . . ." she said softly.

A whisper from . . . where? Paris thought, digging at his memory, his pants down around his shoes, his legs ninth-inning weak. He watched Diana's shoulders move up and down, side to side, circular now, smooth and marbleized in the faint green light thrown by the stereo receiver. Her luxuriant black hair buffeted his thighs.

The next thing Paris knew, he was on his back and Diana was on top of him. He was deep within her. He grabbed the cool flesh of Diana's hips and pulled her down onto him harder, probing her as deeply as the angle allowed. She brought her mouth to his and kissed him, tensing her muscles. She began to whisper.

Jack . . .

To Paris, her voice was thin, floating somewhere between the scratchy jazz rock coming from the radio and the traffic noise below. A voice from his past . . . a hooker in the back seat of his cruiser, maybe . . . too drunk for his tour . . . Patches of sound. The room decided to spin again.

She leaned forward now, her nipples brushing his chest, her lips close to his ear.

Do you still think about her, Jack?

Was that *her?* Paris thought. Was he imagining it? Think about *who?*

Moments later, Diana shrieked once as she reached her orgasm, but it was loud enough to be heard by half the people on the third floor of the building.

Although, at the Candace, it was just another scream in the middle of the night.

o   o   o

TOO MUCH BOOZE. FOUR-OH-FIVE, ACCORDING TO THE BRIGHT GREEN NUMbers on the VCR.

She was leaving.

"Don't go . . ." Paris managed.

He wanted her to stay, to be there in the morning. Because this time it felt different. Of the handful of times he had had sex in the past two years he had not wanted any of them to stay. One-nighters from the Caprice. Hookers from the precinct. He wanted to sleep with his arm around this woman, but as he reached out his hand, the room began to wobble again.

His body was deserting him, but his mind was working overtime.

Tommy.

Diana stood at the foot of the bed for a while, darkly silhouetted against the now drawn blinds. Her breasts looked smooth and full in the buffed white light.

"Why don't you lie down . . ." she prodded him gently, her voice calming, her hand now so familiar on his thigh. She zipped her skirt and put on her shoes. "Come on. I'll help you." She lifted the covers and pulled Paris's feet toward the foot of the bed, covered him and sat down. "I have to go, baby." She wiped his brow with the top of the sheet.

Paris rose unsteadily onto one elbow.

Diana laughed at his failed attempt at coordination, but two words snatched her laughter unceremoniously from the air.

Tommy. Dead.

"No . . ."

Paris flopped onto his side.

Moments later, when the door closed behind her, he rolled onto his back, sated and drunk, his body flat against a wall of fatigue, his mind a dark deadfall of questions.

Part Three

Furor

27

IN THE PHOTOGRAPH, HER MOTHER WORE A SHORT suede skirt and turquoise platform shoes, one of her many watershed statements of seventies fashion. Her legs looked perfect in the early-morning sunlight, her hair, a symphony of reds and browns and rusts and silvers. Hairdresser hair. But then again, she was only twenty-eight years old at the time the photograph was taken, brash and still adolescently defiant, her rose tattoo so brazenly exposed on her stomach, just below her spangled midriff shirt.

And why shouldn't she look good?

Why shouldn't she look like a movie star?

She was standing in the doorway to their apartment at Holly Knoll, the ever-present menthol cigarette growing out of the yellowed V between her painted fingernails, the ever-present purple bruises mottling her thighs and arms. She was off to work at some beauty parlor or another, the longest stint being the one she'd had at the Hair Force on Victorville Road, next to the Cork and Bottle.

And although she had long ago completed her two-year course in cosmetology, and had the most extraordinary cheekbones this side of Faye Dunaway, she'd never quite gotten the hang of putting on rouge. At the distance from which the photo was taken, her cheeks appeared to be slashed with a thick streak of crimson, giving her the painted look of a warrior-squaw.

o   o   o

LOIS BENTIVEGNA LIKED TO DANCE NAKED FOR HER BOYFRIENDS, AND SHE DID so, with a remarkable amount of vigor, right up until the cancer got her at thirty-four. She never danced professionally in any sense—her Christian upbringing would have squarely prevented that—but once in a while, on a Friday or Saturday night, after she'd had a few tumblers of Jack Daniel's, she would put on an old, scratchy Average White Band album and strut around the apartment, Styrofoam cup in hand. She'd usually make a sexy outfit out of whatever she had available, whatever was clean and wasn't too elastic-worn, but once she'd sent away mail order and gotten a garter belt from Frederick's of Hollywood.

And all the while she believed her daughter to be safely stashed away in her room with a pizza, along with her own black-and-white

TV and her very own Princess phone. Sometimes she'd let her daughter have a friend stay overnight and the two girls would covertly slip out of the bedroom window and sneak around the apartment, peeking through the living room window, hiding in the hedges, at once repulsed and deliriously stirred by the acts unfolding in front of them.

Then, one day, came the blood.

And there was change.

Because it was Lois at the door to her daughter's room that very first time, just a few years after the photograph was taken, the same year the cancer began to nibble at her lungs. It was Lois, unexpectedly home early from her station at the second chair at René and Julian's Hair Port at Burton Center, stepping lightly, the sounds of sex drawing her silently toward the door, the unmaskable sighing of a young woman, inexperienced to the touch and rhythm of a man, drawing her closer, closer.

Lois Bentivegna didn't throw a tantrum like other mothers might have. Lois didn't burst into the bedroom that day, or any day thereafter, seething with righteous middle-class parental indignation, threatening years of groundings and the absolute denial of junior prom tickets.

Lois watched. Lois crept up to the slightly open bedroom door, her eye to the jamb, and watched her daughter take this young man into her hands, her mouth, her body. A fifteen-year-old girl and her sixteen-year-old lover.

Lois stood by, her own hand so violently between her legs, a woman of barely thirty-one years herself, and thought of the afternoons, not all that long ago, when she had entertained a series of inexhaustible sixteen-year-olds of her own.

28 NICHOLAS RAPOSO LIVED IN A THREE-BEDROOM BUNGA-
low in Garwood Gardens, a pre–World War II
residential development in Garfield Heights, on
Cleveland's southeast side. There were no gardens to speak of, no greenery rimming the fifty-
foot lots as the northern end of the street, once a part
of the MetroPark system, now gave way to I-480. It was a gray,
working-class street. On an even grayer day.

Paris had only met the man twice, once at the Justice Center
and once at Tommy's service, three weeks ago. He knew that Nick
Raposo had been a cement worker most of his life, and his hands
proved it—rough planks of flesh that seemed to swallow Paris's
hand when they shook.

"Nice to see you again," Nick said, a red sadness limning his
eyes. Paris knew the man had lost his wife a dozen years earlier,
and now, his only son. The grief hung upon his shoulders like an
old, tattered cardigan.

"Nice to see you too, Nick."

"Come on in . . ."

Paris stepped into the small, fastidious living room. The walls
bore the odd grouping of religious pictures and the occasional
gold-framed photographs of Tommy and his sister, Gina. The worn
sofa boasted an orange and brown afghan—Cleveland Browns colors—and a disheveled pile of *Time* and *Sports Illustrated* magazines.
Paris instantly smelled the rich aroma of Italian staples: Romano
cheese, basil, garlic. Nick Raposo was making sauce.

"Coffee, Jack?"

"Only if it's already on," Paris said. "Don't go out of your way."

"I make the espresso," Nick answered. "It's no problem, eh?"

Paris held up his hands as if to say yes.

"Come on in the kitchen."

Paris followed him into the kitchen, and although he thought
Nick Raposo was still a physically powerful man, he looked small at
that moment, a brittle sketch of the man he was before death
stalked his family.

o   o   o

PARIS SIPPED THE HOT, SWEET COFFEE. IT WARMED HIM. THE HOUSE, THE
kitchen, the way the small Formica table butted on the wall beneath

the window, the way the dish towels cascaded over the handle on the oven door—these things warmed him even more. Unlike his apartment, with its deep smells of transience, this was a *home*. He noticed a row of plants sitting on the windowsill over the sink, patiently waiting for spring: parsley, oregano, tarragon, chive. Things move on, Paris thought. Things grow back.

"You get Tommy's belongings from the station all right?" Paris asked, even though he knew the answer.

"Oh yeah . . . yeah," Nick replied, waving his leathered hand absently in the air.

"The stuff from his apartment too?"

Nick Raposo just nodded. The two of them fell silent for a while, the sound of the kitchen clock the only thing between their breathing and the constant drone of the freeway two blocks away. Finally, Nick spoke.

"Tommy didn't do it, Jack," he said. "You know that, don't you?"

Paris didn't know what to say. "Well, I—"

"I'm not going to tell you he was clean," Nick continued deliberately, as if he had rehearsed this speech a few hundred times. "I . . . I think you know better than that. Jesus, you worked with him on and off for three months. I mean . . . I don't have that thirty-two-inch TV in the other room or that big Chrysler in the drive because of my IRAs, eh? He took care of me, Jack. He took care of his sister."

"I know, Nick," Paris said. "But it's—"

"But what? That's just money, no? What they said he did to those girls. He wouldn't . . ."

Paris met Nick Raposo's eyes and found a deeply wounded man there. "The case is closed, Nick. I'm afraid everybody wants it that way."

"Not everyone . . ."

"You know what I mean."

"But you can do something about it, no? You can still ask questions, can't you? You can still ask around."

Paris realized then that he was talking to a man who still believed in a fundamental order to things. A man who still clung to the notion that if you play fair you always win. But Paris also knew that the reason he was in Nick Raposo's house in the first place was because he also knew something was wrong. He simply couldn't shake the notion that the Pharaoh case—as it had come to be known—had closed a little too quickly.

"Everything I do I gotta do on my own," Paris said. "After hours, off the meter. You know that, right? I push too hard somewhere, hit the wrong buttons, I'm back handing out parking tickets in Hough."

Nick nodded in understanding. Then he looked deeply into Paris's eyes and said softly: "Clear my son, Jack."

o   o   o

THE BASEMENT WAS COOL AND ORDERLY, TILED, A TRADESMAN'S REFUGE. THERE was a wall of tools at one end, along with an embattled workbench, smooth and worn and black with years of spilled 3 in 1 oil, blue with carpenter's chalk. Down here the religious pictures gave way to Ridgid tool calendars and *Penthouse* centerfolds, but none of them offered anything too racy, nothing the late Bernadette Raposo would have objected to having in her house.

The opposite wall reflected the habits of the son, who also, it appeared, had learned the virtues of order. The boxes were stacked floor to ceiling, wall to wall. They were mostly the kind in which people store legal papers and they were all dutifully marked in green block letters. It did not take Paris long to find the box containing Tommy's personal papers.

On top was a stack of *Playbills,* mostly from the Palace or State theaters, mostly musicals: *Les Misérables, The Fantasticks, Fiddler on the Roof, Cats, Guys and Dolls.* Beneath them were postcards from what had to be a hundred different women. Crystal and Denise, Jackie, Barbara, Peggy, Lydia, Sarah, Junie and Annette. At least a dozen were signed, simply, "me." All, Paris noted, in different handwritings.

He picked up a plain white business envelope, open at the top, jammed full of photographs of various sizes and vintages. There was a pair of Tommy and his sister in Atlantic City, a few with his mother and father at his police academy graduation, Tommy with girl after girl after girl. There was Tommy with cops, Tommy with citizens, Tommy with crooks.

Next there was a layer of softbound books, textbooks from the feel of them. Paris lifted out three or four. *Leisures and Pleasures of*

Roman Egypt. A Handbook of the Ancients. Arabian Nights. They looked like they had been opened, but not necessarily pored over for any great length of time.

At the very bottom of the box were a series of maps and travel brochures, along with a nine-by-twelve-inch brown kraft envelope that was clasped and sealed. Paris flipped it over and saw the familiar rooster scrawl of Tommy's signature over the seal. It appeared that Tommy had signed the envelope in black ink, right over the flap, so that if anyone ever tried to steam it open and then reclose it he would know. It took Paris all of five seconds to decide to tear off the top. He coughed as he did it to mask the sound of ripping paper, lest Nick think he was doing exactly what he *was* doing: destroying evidence. If evidence is what it turned out to be. He folded the pieces of the envelope into quarters, placed the pieces in his pockets and looked at the contents.

The only thing in the large envelope was a stack of photographs—Polaroids, maybe a dozen—held shut by a pair of crisscrossing rubber bands. On both ends of the stack the photographs faced inward.

The appearance of the envelope and the feel of the photographs filled Paris with a mixture of apprehension and excitement. What didn't Tommy want him to see? What secrets? What was he going to find on the other side of these seemingly benign white cardboard rectangles?

And yet, Paris thought, if Tommy knew he was going to swallow the barrel, why didn't he just destroy them?

Paris glanced around the corner, up the yellow-and-gray-linoleum-clad steps. He could hear Nick making kitchen sounds, preparing another espresso for them.

"You need any help up there, Nick?"

"Hah?"

"I asked if you needed any help with anything up there . . ."

"No," Nick said. "I'm okay."

"You sure?"

"I can still make a cup of coffee, eh?"

Paris walked to the far end of the workshop and stood directly beneath the fluorescent swag lamp. He removed the rubber bands from the stack, and as soon as he flipped over the top photo, he realized that his vigilance had been warranted after all.

The top photograph was of a woman in S&M leather drag, her back to the camera, kneeling at the foot of a bed. It was taken in a standard motel room, a Best Western or perhaps a Budgetel, with no regional clues in the decor. The bedspread looked to be dark green or dark blue. The woman's body was perfect, her waist was thin, her hips rounded and smooth. Her leather bustier crossed her back in a spiderweb of thin lines that seemed to cut deeply into her flesh. Her hair was soft brown, blond maybe, falling to her shoulders.

The second photograph showed a side shot of the woman from the waist up. She had the flushed look of a woman fresh with sex, but her face was once again turned away. Of the ten photographs, only one showed any degree of the woman's face, but even that shot was a profile, and she wore a thin, black lace mask over her eyes.

There was one photograph taken outdoors, in a wooded area, a side shot of the woman with her white camisole pulled to her waist, her hands bound to a tree with what looked like electrical cord.

Tommy was not to be found in any of the pictures.

Paris turned the photographs over, one by one, looking for any writing that might have been on the backs. There was a faint pencil mark on one, something like a check mark, but nothing decipherable. He was about to flip two at a time when something caught his eye, and he had to go back a few. There, written in pencil at the bottom right-hand corner, printed in a rather childlike manner, were three words. It looked like: "SAILA DOES QUALIFY."

Saila does qualify? What the hell did *that* mean?

Paris looked around for some sort of magnifying glass and was gratified to find that Nick had a lit, swing-arm magnifier attached to a small table against the wall. He switched on the light and ran the photograph beneath the glass.

"Saila does *quality*," he corrected himself immediately. And who the hell is Saila? And quality what?

He turned over the photo with the writing and found that it was the one picture that didn't seem to be of anyone or anything in particular. It was a photograph of a slightly opened closet door, with just the hint of something that looked like a white shoe—a white high-heeled shoe, maybe—visible at the bottom.

Paris placed the photos into his pocket, not really knowing why, and searched the remaining boxes, finding little else he could use. Certainly nothing to match the impact of the photographs. There were, to Paris's surprise and dismay, no financial records of any kind.

"You want this down there?" Nick asked, calling from the top of the steps.

"No, I'm coming up," Paris said, a little startled, feeling suddenly like a teenager caught with a *Hustler* magazine. "I'm finished."

"Okay," he said. "Don't forget to close the light."

Close the light, Paris thought, smiling. Was it just Italians, or did all ethnic types say *close* the light? His own grandfather, Angelo Parisi, who had somehow managed to lose the *i* in the noise and confusion of Ellis Island, had said close the light.

So, mounting the steps, as if the directive had come from Grampa Angelo himself, Paris did just that.

o   o   o

ALTHOUGH IT WAS PAST THE MIDDLE OF APRIL, WINTER STILL ROAMED THE streets of Cleveland. When Paris drove to Garfield Heights, the sky had dusted the city with a light powdering of snow. Now there was blinding sunlight. Paris headed into town up I-77, getting off at the Broadway exit. He came to a stop at a red light, directly in front of the entrance to the old McCrory's five-and-dime.

Saila does quality.

He held the photograph up to the sunlight. It had been perched on the front seat beside him since he left Nick's house, taunting him, begging his glance at every stop light. This one was a low-angle, dominatrix-type shot of the woman.

Saila does . . . quality.

I'll bet she does, thought Paris, wondering about the where, the who, the what, the why and the when of it all. Who *was* this woman? Where did she come from? Why did he have a nude photograph of her in his hand? When did she—

The man who suddenly appeared at his window and the sound of the car horn from behind him registered at the same instant. But it was the hulking gray shadow to his immediate left that unnerved him more.

Paris turned quickly and saw that it was a homeless man, part of the Broadway squeegee brigade. It looked as if he had come over to approach Paris about a quick wipe job, but he must have seen the photograph and decided to just enjoy the view. As Paris pulled away he looked in the side mirror and saw the man shake a finger at him and display a wide, toothless smile.

o   o   o

QUALITY, HE THOUGHT AS HE CUT THE ENGINE.

How about "quality" as in Quality *Inn?* Maybe the inscription on the back of the photograph meant that Saila does *Quality* like Debbie does *Dallas.*

Emily Reinhardt had been killed at the Quality Inn on Euclid.

o   o   o

"SORRY ABOUT YOUR FRIEND," SHE SAID.

"Thanks," Paris replied. "But it's not like . . . I don't know . . . It's not like I can say I *knew* him now, you know? It's still pretty hard to believe." Paris sipped his Harp's Lager, the first alcoholic beverage he had had at lunch in two months. "My *friend . . .*"

Otto Moser's was jammed with the usual lunch crowd, the impending spring giving license to everyone to speak a little more loudly, a little more animatedly than they had all winter. On this day, for Jack Paris, it was just an annoying wall of noise.

But Rita the Barmaid had left a rather urgent-sounding message on his voice mail and said that she would be at *this* table, at *this* restaurant, at *this* time and if he wanted to . . .

He knew exactly what was on her mind.

"I'm afraid I was as fooled as everyone else," he continued.

"You don't sound too convinced, if you ask me." Rita gave her hair a quick toss over her shoulder and bit into her turkey club sandwich. As she continued to speak, Paris noticed a drop of mayonnaise that had made its way onto her chin. He was going to point it out to her but he already knew enough about Rita Weisinger to wait until she had made her point. "I guess what I'm trying to say is . . . that's not the guy. The guy in the picture that was in the newspaper and on TV? The cop they say did it? Tommy . . ."

"Raposo," Paris said softly.

"Raposo," she said, rolling the *r* briefly. "Anyway, I don't know how to put this . . . It's not the guy I saw at the Radisson with the Burchfield woman." She paused, placing her sandwich on her plate, and took a swift, silent breath for maximum effect, waiting for Paris's reaction to this case-breaking bit of evidence.

"I know," Paris said. He absently waved his finger near his mouth, hoping Rita would catch the vibe and wipe her chin. After a few beats of stunned silence, she did.

"You *know?*"

"Yes."

"How?"

"I'm a cop," Paris said.

"Yeah . . . *and . . .*"

"Well, number one, why else would you ask an old flatfoot like me out to lunch unless you had something you wanted to add to the Pharaoh case. And two, if you look at it with any objectivity, the sketch doesn't really look like Tommy. It could be him, but it could also be a thousand other guys in this city."

"Exactly."

"But the bad news is that all the evidence was there, Rita. It was way too pat for me but it was still a grand jury's wet dream," Paris said. "The hat had bloodstains tied to two of the victims. The makeup kit was found in the trunk of his car. And the patches of skin, for God's sake." He poked at his sandwich, a shaved ham on rye, suddenly disinterested.

Rita paused, studying Paris's face. "I don't know, Jack . . . it just . . . It just isn't in your friend's *eyes,* you know?" she said, crunching a potato chip for punctuation. "I mean, I can tell a lot from looking into a man's eyes. And even in that shitty photo they published in the newspaper, I could tell. Your friend Tommy was no killer. Arrogant maybe. A ladies' man, yes. But . . ."

"But?"

"But not a psycho."

"How do you know that?" Paris asked.

"Because he was way too cute, number one . . ."

"And number two?"

"That's number two, also. Way too cute."

"I see."

"I think cute might actually cover one through four."

"Is that right?"

"You should know, Detective Paris," Rita added with a smile.

She kept catching him off guard with this stuff. Zoomed again. He started talking before his face could begin to color. "Yeah, well, the point is that this case is frozen shut, Rita. Captain Elliott is happy. The prosecutor's office is happy. Tommy Raposo was this unknown, up from Summit County four months ago, nobody really knew him well. A real department outsider. The shingles just fell into place."

Rita shook her head, new to the machinations of institutional politics. She asked a few more why-not and how-come-there-isn't type questions as they finished their lunch. Halfway through coffee, Rita waved for the check.

"What are you going to do?" she asked, lighting a More menthol cigarette. Paris drew one from the pack and joined her.

"Now? Well, I'm going to go back to work, Rita. I've got three unsolveds on my plate and I have no partner," Paris said. "Anything I do about the Pharaoh case is going to be off the meter. And probably very stupid. Not to mention a huge waste of time."

She looked at her watch and stood up to leave. "Well, if you need any help with any after-hours sleuthing, you let me know. I'm the Terminator when it comes to these sorts of things." She reached into her purse and dropped a twenty on the table. Then, anticipating his reaction, held up a hand to deflect Paris's protest about her paying the check. "Oh . . . by the way . . . this is the last time I'm going to fling myself at you like a wanton woman. Ball's in your court, officer." She swung her bag over her shoulder, the early-afternoon sunlight rushing through the windows, painting her hair with highlights of gold.

"And me with this *wicked* forehand," Paris replied, surprised at his burst of wit, his sports metaphor. He had never played a game of tennis in his life.

"Promises, promises . . ." She leaned forward, kissed him on the cheek, then smiled as she thumbed away the lipstick. "Call me."

Rita turned her extraordinary derriere toward him and left the restaurant, trailing a long wake of rubbernecking men—young, old, and those of Jack Paris's rather ill-defined vintage: somewhere in between.

o   o   o

THE HOMICIDE UNIT WAS BEGINNING TO RECOVER FROM THE MEDIA BLITZKRIEG that began about twenty minutes after Tommy's body hit the freezer and didn't even begin to abate until three weeks later. But now, in spite of the best efforts of the tabloids, the cop-haters and the loyal political opposition, the story was being eclipsed by other, more pressing problems facing the Best Location in the Nation. The Unit averaged about eighteen homicides per month and usually maintained no more than twenty detectives at any given time. So, given the average daily shitfall in a city like Cleveland, the shitstorm eventually passed.

And then there was a threatened garbage strike which, in a purely sensory capacity, eclipsed everything.

Yet any time a police officer is directly involved in a big-time felony, or some kind of sex crime, it is always a huge embarrassment for the department. When you combine the two, the fallout is devastating and, considering the longevity that sex gossip usually has, politically far-reaching.

After a few thousand Scuds from all corners, the department's new whiz-kid spin doctor, a PR flack named Teddy Dahlhausen, had somehow managed to put the Pharaoh case into manageable media blocks. The grand jury was satisfied with the evidence that linked Sergeant Thomas Anthony Raposo to the deaths of Emily Reinhardt, Maryann Milius, Karen Schallert and Eleanor Burchfield, and that seemed to be that.

But, Paris thought, then there was Nick Raposo.

And his sad, rheumy eyes.

He reached his desk and was relieved to find only three messages waiting for him: Diana, Cyndy Taggart and Beth.

Three women. Could be much, much, much, much worse, he thought as picked up the phone and pecked out his wife's number. Could have easily been three guys named Rasheed, Nunzio and Hector.

Beth either wasn't home, wasn't answering, or was already on the phone with some millionaire Libyan tractor manufacturer. He left a message and dialed Cyndy's number.

o   o   o

"GOT SOME STUFF OF YOURS," SHE SAID. "YOU MUST HAVE LEFT IT IN MY CAR that day we staked out the Versailles."

Paris hadn't touched base with Cyndy Taggart since the debriefing. Cyndy worked out of the Fourth.

"Thanks, I'll pick it up at the station."

"You all right?"

"Yeah," Paris answered. "Barely . . ."

"If you say so, Jack. Anyway, maybe I'll drop it all off to you tomorrow. I'll be up around Eight-five and Carnegie after dinner."

"Okay," Paris said, distracted.

He decided to trust her.

"Hang on, Cyndy." He looked into the common room and into the adjacent offices. The floor was very light with detectives and other personnel. Greg Ebersole was in his office with his feet up, sawing logs. Paris closed his door.

"You know I'm not happy with . . . you know . . ." he began softly.

"I know."

"Well, I'm going through Tommy's things at his father's house the other day and I found some photographs. Polaroids."

"Of . . ."

"Of a woman. And it's wild stuff."

"What do you mean?"

"Well, it's sadomasochism drag. Costume stuff. Really kinky."

"Tommy in them?"

"No."

"Can you identify the woman?"

"No. Can't see her face in any of them. But believe me, you sure can see everything else."

"And why do you think this woman is tied to the murders?" Cyndy asked.

Paris really didn't know. "The sex aspect, I guess."

"Tommy *did* get around, you know."

"Yeah, but there wasn't any S and M stuff in his belongings. No magazines, videos, books. No whips and chains. Certainly nothing like this."

"I don't know," Cyndy said. "I mean, us gals on the job heard some pretty interesting things about Tommy."

"Yeah? Like what?"

"Oh," she said, "the kind of things girls are interested in. The kind of things men generally lie about. Or exaggerate about."

"And?"

"And word has it that Tommy Raposo wasn't exaggerating."

"Jesus . . ."

"We're talking .*357*, here."

"You women are unbelievable."

"Guilty, Your Honor."

"Women really talk about this stuff?" Paris asked.

"You're kidding, right?"

Paris fell silent for a few beats. "So tell me, Cyndy. Why can't I shake the idea that there is a woman involved?"

"Because now you can see her. You've got photographs."

"I suppose . . ."

"Okay, Jack," Cyndy said. "I've got a few minutes. Gimme the list."

"Okay. One, the makeup kit. Just doesn't fit with Tommy Raposo, does it? He's cutting up women, wiping their faces clean and putting makeup on like he works a cosmetic counter at Kauffman's? Make sense to you?"

"Nope. Next."

"Samantha Jaeger."

"What about her?"

Paris hadn't told anyone about the Jaeger woman's bedroom. He wasn't going to now, either. "I know her death was ruled accidental, but the woman next door said she heard a man *and* a woman arguing with her the night Samantha took the fall. I don't know. There's a woman around here somewhere, Cyndy."

"Hmmm . . ."

Paris told her about the "SAILA DOES QUALITY" message on one of the photographs. Cyndy said that the name held no significance for her, either, but was much quicker to pick up on "QUALITY" as meaning a possible location.

"You think 'Saila' is the woman's name?" Cyndy asked.

"Don't know," Paris said. "But I'm going to run it through the computers, just in case."

"Okay. Anything else?"

"Well . . . last but not least, of course, is the fact that we have no razor. Even if someone was setting Tommy up, why not leave the murder weapon? I mean, with all that neatly placed evidence in Tommy's apartment, why not give us the weapon? You can pick up a straight razor for twenty-five bucks. Why not leave it?"

"Unless . . ."

"Unless you weren't done with it."

"So . . ." Cyndy asked, knowing full well the answer, but playing the game all detectives played: Saying It Out Loud. "What's the next step?"

"Next step of course is to revisit the Quality Inn and see if the photo matches up with the guest room where Emily Reinhardt bought it," Paris said. "If we get a match there, I think we can get Elliott to reopen. We've got an accomplice."

"Makes sense, Jack . . ."

The two police officers fell silent for a few moments, assimilating the information.

"We'll . . . uh . . . We'll talk later," Paris said as Bobby Dietricht knocked on his door and then entered anyway.

"All right," Cyndy said. "But now you've got me thinking."

"Good," Paris said.

"I'll stop by with your stuff tomorrow."

"Thanks."

"Maybe I'll go with you to the Quality."

"Even better," Paris said, and hung up the phone.

o o o

THIRD WAS DIANA.

"So . . . are you going to make it to the Home and Flower Show with us?"

"Us," Paris repeated. "By the use of the word 'us' you of course mean . . ."

"Melissa and I are going tomorrow?" she continued, reading his silence, letting him off the hook. "Remember? We talked about it?"

"Yeah, sure," Paris said. "I remember. I just don't think I can go, Diana. I'm buried down here."

"You sure this is going to be okay with Beth? This strange woman doing something like this on a Saturday afternoon with her only daughter. Some women are pretty protective, Jack. It's primal."

"Believe me, if you're okay with me, you're okay with Beth. I'm a cop, remember?"

"You're right. I just get a little paranoid. There's three people I want to like me now and it's too much."

"You'll wow her," Paris said.

"Kowloon Garden afterward? On me?"

"I'll do my best . . ."

Paris hung up the phone, awash with a wave of standard Dad-guilt. He hadn't seen Melissa for more than a few minutes in the past two weeks, although it was certainly understandable in light of the Pharaoh case aftermath. He had caught the last five minutes of Missy's play—a strange hybrid called *The Easter Bunny and the Three Scrooges*—but his daughter hadn't seen him until he came backstage. He wasn't able to fool her into thinking he had seen the whole thing. If pressed, she would have asked him specifics anyway, and he would have caved.

But Missy was a very bright girl, very worldly for her age. She read the newspapers and she watched the local news and she knew full well what had happened where her father worked. She knew that the man who had killed those women had worked with her father.

The information, unfortunately, was not lost on some of Melissa's schoolmates, either. "M.P. is a pervert" showed up written on the blackboard in her homeroom one morning. Another creative young artist had ripped an illustration of an Egyptian mummy out of a school encyclopedia and drawn a rather obscene appendage between the figure's legs, then taped it to Missy's gym locker. The "Pharaoh" aspect of the case had been well publicized.

Paris put his feet up and attempted to catch a nap.

He tried to remember if there really *was* a time when art class meant white paste, construction paper and safety scissors.

2 9

IT WAS FRIDAY AND THIS GLORIOUS STRANGER STOOD A few fragrant inches away from me. We were in a quiet, multiroomed nightclub called Whitney's.

Saila and I knew that we shouldn't have been out playing so soon, but spring was in the air, I guess.

I used my flawless Brit.

"You look like a very young Jeanne Moreau," I said. "Around the time she made *Five Branded Women,* I'm thinking."

The edges of her mouth turned up slightly, but she wasn't quite ready to release the smile just yet. Her eyes betrayed her, telling me that my reference was not lost on her. Nor were my looks. She was dressed conservatively in a burgundy tailored suit, cream blouse and navy pumps, yet there was no concealing the fullness of her breasts, the firmness of her upper thighs. She was a working woman, a citizen, and the very idea sent my blood to steam.

The fact that Saila was standing right behind me, sipping her drink at the bar, made the moment all but unbearable.

"Do I?" she answered.

"*Oh* yes. But sexier," I replied softly, moving very close to her. She didn't flinch or pull away in the slightest. "Jeanne Moreau was so . . . how should I say . . . two-*dimensional.*" My knee touched hers, a delicious shiver. "You, on the other hand, you are made of flesh and blood."

Her hand trembled a bit as she reached for her nearly empty glass, giving her pause, betraying her resolve to remain in complete control of the situation. I was intimidating her somewhat and, as always, that pleased me.

I imagined her to be about twenty-six or so, probably married, probably a suburban mommy type, although she wore no wedding ring. Her blond, permed hair was obviously a wig, but perhaps that was part of her appeal for me. She was out to play. She fancied herself the conquering bitch, and for the moment, I let her believe it.

She called herself Abby.

o   o   o

AFTER A VERY EROTIC SLOW DANCE, WE RETURNED TO THE BAR. SAILA WAS ON the loose. I didn't see her.

"Can I get you something?"

"White Russian," she said.

I motioned, ordered. Out of the corner of my eye I could see her looking me up and down, further cruising my wares, as it were. She was very well accessorized herself, tasteful, with moderate-to-expensive jewelry, just a few show pieces. A very pretty Piaget watch. Her makeup was flawless.

She was also petite in just the proper, most appealing ways: small hands and feet, a tiny, turned-up nose, a narrow waist.

Our drinks arrived. I clasped mine, an Absolut straight, with my cocktail napkin—in case a quick departure was forthcoming—and raised the glass heavenward.

I recited: *"Hold fast thy secret, and to none unfold. Lost is a secret when that secret's told."*

We touched glasses and sipped.

"What does that mean exactly?" she asked.

"It's a caveat. It's from the *Arabian Nights.*"

"Funny . . ."

"What?" I said.

"You don't *look* Arabian."

"I know," I said. "I'm very aware of my appearance."

"I'll bet you are," the woman said, fashioning her mouth first into a smile, then around her straw. Her lips were full, scarlet in color. I imagined them doing all sorts of things.

"So . . . what's an intelligent, cultured woman such as yourself doing in a common roadhouse such as this?" I asked. "And why on earth would you entertain a villainous lout like me?"

"Oh," the woman said, searching for a morsel of wit. "You could say I'm slumming, I suppose." Her smile betrayed the outrage of her insinuation.

"Really?" I asked. I put my hand upon her leg. She tensed the slightest bit but did not resist me. Instead, her eyelids fluttered once and I knew that she was mine. "And just what is it that you're used to?" I moved closer.

"I'm used to the best."

"The best."

She looked at my lips. "Yes . . ."

"And what if I told you that you had never once *had* the best?"

"I'd say . . ." she began, her hands finding my waist, giving in to me. "I'd say *show* me."

She leaned forward, ran the tip of her tongue over my lips, then pulled away.

God, I loved a challenge. "Come with me," I said.

"No."

"Come with me now. Just for an hour."

"No."

"You're going to play with me, aren't you?"

"Uh-huh. Long as I can."

"I think your time is running out, kitty cat," I said.

Without further talk the blond woman in the expensive Anne Klein suit and the hooker's wig took me by the hand and led me toward the lobby, full of sass and womanly self-possession.

I knew we were being watched, of course.

My only hope was that, for everyone's sake, he was part of the game.

3 0

HE SMOOTHED THE MUSTACHE WITH ONE INDEX FINGER, caressed the rim of his shot glass with the other. The conversation around him was quiet, piano bar talk, cool and important: Land Rovers, stocks and bonds, the films of Gus Van Sant, smart drugs.

He picked up a cigarette and began to turn it over and over, end behind end, as if it might spontaneously combust, as if it might flame to life and he would have to smoke it. He called for the bartender and the look on his face must have communicated to him that it was, in fact, time. The man traversed the length of the bar, led by a large, fully fueled Zippo with an embossed set of stainless-steel bowling pins on one side and the name "Del" engraved in Old English script on the other. The bluish-yellow flame danced to life and the scent of burning tobacco filled Jack Paris's nostrils, pleasing him, calming him.

Nonsmokers would never know the soul-rattling beauty of such a moment, Paris thought.

o   o   o

SO MANY THINGS DIDN'T FIT. FOR INSTANCE, THE TIME OF TOMMY'S CALL THE night of the Schallert murder. Tommy had taken the call at 1:12 A.M. Saturday, and beeped Paris at the Caprice Lounge at 1:18. Tommy had indeed called from Berea.

The coroner's office was able to do a liver temperature reading on the body and the reading put the time of Karen Schallert's death at very close to twelve-thirty, which made it at least *possible* for Tommy to have driven the twenty-five miles from the Red Valley Inn—through the ever-present construction that is endemic to the geography in Cuyahoga County—all the way out to Berea. Possible, but not likely, considering traffic and the fact that every Clevelander knows that there are only two seasons in this town: winter and construction.

The woman Tommy was with that night—one Arlene Pankow— said Tommy had gotten to her place around a quarter to one, maybe one o'clock. Paris had never met her before but she had told him, through a fully soaked handkerchief, that she had known Tommy less than a month but had seen him three or four times.

And then there was the fact that Tommy's hair was dark brown, so why on earth would he *dye* it dark brown? Yet, the lab had found traces of the EZ Color "Deep Chestnut" in Tommy's hair.

And then, of course, there was the matter of Samantha Jaeger's bedroom. A sick little ditty known only to Jack Paris and Mr. Larry Goldblatt, the super at 11606 Clifton Boulevard.

Paris conceded that he might never understand the significance.

Because, of the hundred and forty photocopies Samantha Jaeger had tacked to her bedroom walls—photocopies of the killer's sketch that had run in the *Plain Dealer,* blown up to an eight-by-ten size—fifteen of them had been drawn upon. She had smeared lipstick on the man's lips, rouge in the hollow beneath his cheekbones. The lenses of his glasses were colored yellow and orange and amber, some gradient. The rest of the black-and-white images were untouched, showing the same idiot repetition of the grayed-out tweed of the man's Irish walking hat, the same slashed cleft in his chin. Paris imagined the woman furtively visiting a Kinko's Copy Center at three in the morning with her *Plain Dealer,* running off all those copies of the composite sketch, taking them home, mounting them carefully on the walls, drawing on them and then . . . what?

Something twisted, he was sure.

Something far more perverse than his own little games.

The bottom line was that the department had lacquered the case shut the moment the story had moved to the Metro page, in spite of the fact that there was probably going to be a movie of the week. A book for sure. The killer-cop angle and all.

He caught a glimpse of himself in the mirror behind the bar. Kind of dashing, he thought, sitting there in the wash of the red and blue and green lights from the dance floor. The mustache—the extra one he had gotten from Mr. Hendershott the day he visited Allied Salon Products, the mustache he had *known* he didn't need for the investigation—had been an afterthought. It had sat in his dresser since that day, clipped securely inside its clear plastic case, teasing him every time he went for a pair of dress socks.

The spirit gum he had purchased at Mark's House of Fun on East 152nd Street was another story altogether. Because, as it turned out, there *was* a maximum that one could apply before the mustache became almost permanently attached to one's face.

Paris had seen Diana three times in the previous weeks, but it had never matched the first night. Or maybe it was just the stress of the case that made him think so. Maybe it wasn't just the physical, although the physical *was* rather awesome.

Then why was he so worried about having it *become* something?

He dropped a twenty on the bar, made his way to the men's room, did his business. He stepped out of the bathroom and was just about to cross the lobby when he saw her. He knew who it was, even before she turned and showed him her profile.

It was Andrea Heller.

And she was once again decked out in her B-girl blond regalia. *Abigail.*

Paris stepped back into the men's room, his heart pounding, his body filled with an adolescent flood of sexual excitement. He looked at himself in the mirror and frowned at his deception, the mustache sitting atop his lip like a bushy trained caterpillar.

He thought: If she sees me, will she know me?

The killer's phony mustache had figured prominently in all accounts of the story; it had even made it onto *Hard Copy.* If she spotted him, and made him in his "disguise," he was going to look like a real pervert. Which was exactly the way he was beginning to feel. He pushed the door open slightly and peeked out. Andrea Heller was standing in front of the hotel, her arms crossed, shivering in the chilly night air. Finally, a white BMW pulled up and she got in.

Paris negotiated the lobby quickly and dashed across the parking lot.

He was less than three car lengths behind them before they pulled out onto Auburn Road.

3 1 Matt Heller thought: What the hell am I doing? None of this had been planned to his satisfaction. Not really. Control was a very important part of his fantasy life and Andrea, it was clear, had just decided to wrest it away from him. Part of it was very exciting. Part of it scared the crap out of him.

She had leapt up from her stool and walked out of the bar with this *very* attractive man, without even giving him a high sign of any sort. What if he hadn't been watching them at that precise second? What if he didn't think it was such a good idea? What if the car hadn't been able to start? What if . . .

What if Andrea was a lot more involved in this game than he had ever known?

Regardless, there he was, following his wife and another man to God knows where, to watch them do God knows what. He had always wondered what Andrea would be wearing when this finally happened; what he would finally, after all these years, see some other man unsnap, unzip, unhook, unfurl, undo.

Matt Heller had also thought that what was about to happen to him would happen just once in his life. Just one, hopelessly erotic time, and then they would go back to their marriage as if it had never happened. Each to their own private fantasies. And although he had planned it a thousand times over, now, now that it was unfolding in front of him like some steamy off-off-Broadway show, now as he drove four car lengths behind his wife and another man, now that he was so furiously aroused, he wasn't at all certain he could go through with it.

Because, besides being the most outrageous thing he had ever concocted, wasn't this also the most dangerous? Didn't that psychocop prove that you can never tell about people?

Matt followed the white BMW from a safe distance, not knowing that yet a third car was a few lengths behind *him,* heading to the same destination.

Matt thought: Why does it have to be a fucking *Beamer* on top of it? Couldn't he look like that and drive a Lumina or something? Or a Fiesta?

He would call it off. The minute he found out where they were headed, he would find a way to call it off. Say he was Andrea's brother or something. In from Waukeegan. With the sad news that Uncle Conway had died and that his six Akita pups needed a home.

Fantasies, unlike reality, Matt Heller thought as he rounded the Bainbridge exit ramp, are a lot more manageable.

And probably, he imagined, a whole lot safer, too.

3 2   PARIS PARKED ON THE BERM OF THE ROAD AND WALKED back the quarter-mile to the single-story, rust-red building that formed the L-shaped Motel Riverview in Bainbridge, about twenty-five miles east of Cleveland. It was a mostly rural area, and while the motel had a small neon sign on Townshend Road, it was virtually hidden from the highway, set back a few hundred yards and bordered on three sides by a gravel parking lot that quickly gave way to the woods.

From his position behind the first layer of second growth, Paris found himself completely hidden from view, yet no more than twenty feet from the building. The two windows to the right were dark, but the third window, the window that corresponded to the BMW parked on the other side, was slightly illuminated, perhaps by a light left on in the bathroom. The glow gave the impression of a diaphanous curtain, drawn on a tiny stage.

So, moments later, when a woman's hand flipped on the light in the main room and Paris saw that the shades were in fact up, he nearly jumped. The bright rectangle of color in the darkness dazzled him. It looked like a film unreeling, or perhaps some big-screen television that somehow managed to be placed in the middle of the forest. Yet the clarity, the heightened reality of what was about to happen, the *presence* was . . . what?

Exhilarating, Paris confessed. Very erotic and highly exhilarating.

He could see the torso but not the head of the man as he stood against the far wall and removed his jacket, then his shirt. His abdomen was hard and rippled, his arms muscular. He wore black pleated trousers and a thin belt. Paris occasionally caught a glimpse of Andrea Heller's profile, she being by far the shorter of the two, but he had not had an opportunity to see the man's face.

Paris argued that part of him was there, hiding in the woods like a Peeping Tom, because he felt in his heart that the Pharaoh case was not closed, and that this somehow would give him insight. He argued back that there was something about the prospect of watching this woman have sex that was driving him mad . . .

Hadn't he thought about Andrea Heller a number of times since they had met at the Impulse Lounge that night? Hadn't he fantasized about her body, her eyes, her lips against his own? Hadn't he wondered what sort of game she was playing? What sort of lover she would be?

Now, it appeared, he was going to get the opportunity to find out. He felt himself harden as he watched the man remove her blouse and unzip her skirt, letting it slide to the floor. She wore a wine-colored lace teddy.

The man disappeared and then the lights dimmed again. Now Paris strained to penetrate the diaphanous curtain, seeking out shapes, assessing movements. Finally, his eyes adjusted enough and he could see them, or at least their forms.

They kissed for a while, caressed for a while, kneading, probing. Then, in one powerful movement, the man lifted Andrea Heller high into the air and put her roughly onto the bed.

As they made love, Paris could only discern the back of the man's head, his dark, matted hair and the sinewy tiers of his back and broad shoulders. His face never really came into view. As Paris stood up and tried to achieve a better vantage point, he realized that his left leg had fallen asleep. He immediately fell backward into a tree trunk, which, mercifully, was substantial enough to hold him. As he righted himself and turned back to the room, the man pulled back far enough for Paris to see his—

The explosion—a huge barrage of fireworks that Paris figured was located about an inch or so behind his eyes—beckoned to him in that instant in bright orange bursts which, were it not for the pain at the base of his skull, would have been tolerable.

Perhaps even enjoyable.

Then everything went dark, and the universe swam away.

o   o   o

WHOEVER HAD SAPPED HIM FROM BEHIND HAD BEEN EITHER A REAL PROFESsional or a real amateur. Paris had not "seen the lightning" in a few years and he had forgotten how much he hated getting hit in the head. The one who had belted him had either clipped him just right, so he'd be out for only an hour or two, or else had tried to kill him and missed completely.

But there was little doubt in Paris's mind as to who had hit him. He figured it was the guy he had seen hanging around the edges of the Impulse Lounge that night, the one he'd pegged as Andrea Heller's husband.

Either way, all things considered—the fact that it was four-something in the morning; the fact that he was lying facedown in a gravel parking lot in Bainbridge, Ohio; the fact that he probably had it coming for being such a pervert—he *had* felt worse.

Paris sat up and focused on his watch, the ache sitting at the base of his neck like a full hod of bricks. His hands then instinctively tapped where his gun and shield should have been, and he was very pleased to find them in place. Then he tapped his jacket pocket and that mildly gratifying sense of satisfaction left him just as quickly.

The photographs he had found in Tommy's belongings were gone.

Saila does Quality.

Shit. He should have stashed them away somewhere.

The light in window number three was off now, as were all the other lights in the motel. A check of the parking lot in front showed Paris that the white BMW was gone too.

He found his legs, then his car, then his car keys.

The next thing he knew, he was throwing up in his kitchen sink.

○   ○   ○

FIVE HOURS AND FIFTEEN ASPIRIN LATER HE FELT NEARLY HUMAN. HE SCRAMbled a half-dozen eggs, along with a questionable hot dog chopped up and fried to the point of discouraging any and all potential bacteria from even *thinking* about fucking with him.

He wolfed down the food and went back to bed.

At two-thirty he got up and went to open his door for his newspaper. He found a yellow Post-it note stuck to the inside doorframe, and his paper lying on a nearby table. He brought the note over to the window, trying his best to focus. He didn't immediately recognize the handwriting. It read:

> *Stopped by, came in, decided not to wake you. (Why were these doors unlocked, detective ??!!) Off to pick up Melissa for the Home & Flower Show. Hope Beth doesn't hate me (nervous). Had to change on the fly so please mind my overnight bag. Hope you can meet us at the restaurant as planned . . .*
>
> *Diana*

Paris looked at the couch and saw the Louis Vuitton bag. It looked new, expensive. The desire to peek inside was overwhelming, but Paris bullied it back for the time being.

He reached around the door and discovered that it was, indeed, locked. But, he conceded, Diana might have locked it on her way out. He sprinted down to the lobby door and found it closed and locked securely as well. Usually, when there's a cop in the building, the locks are pretty good. Everything seemed to be in order. Then Paris ran back up, suddenly aware that he was running around the Candace in his boxer shorts. Paisley ones, at that.

He had no idea what time it had happened, but he did recall hearing Manny let out with a few barks sometime early that afternoon. He had shushed him, and the dog, not exactly Conan the Terrier anyway, had curled back up on the bed. That must have been when Diana had stopped by, he decided.

He poured a second cup of coffee and flipped open the paper. It was the first day since Tommy's death that the story wasn't mentioned, even in a short item.

Hallelujah, Paris thought, as he gulped his coffee and headed for another scintillating adventure in urban bathing—a cold, brown shower at the Candace—a session during which he would, unknowingly, wash off all traces of the blood on his hands.

o   o   o

AT FIVE-THIRTY, THE BUZZER SOUNDED. IT WAS NICK RAPOSO. HE WAS CARRYing with him a bulging plastic garment bag.

"Nick . . . what a surprise," Paris said. "What brings you here?"

"Got a few things," Nick said, puffing from the four flights of stairs, handing Paris his hat and coat. "Thought you might like to take a look at them."

Nick caught his breath while Paris hung his coat up and poured him a cup of coffee.

Paris explained to Nick that there were no leads yet, nothing to deflect Tommy's guilt in the Pharaoh killings, but that he had a few ideas he was going to follow up on. For the time being, Nick Raposo seemed satisfied.

"My brother's a tailor, Jack," Nick said, crossing the room and grabbing the large garment bag. "Fuckin' genius at it, too. Always was. You 'magine an Italian kid on the Hill in the forties who could *sew?* Jeezez. I had to rescue his ass three times a week."

"I'll bet," Paris said.

"Anyway, I figured you to be a forty-two long. Here. Try this on." He held up the suit coat.

Paris slipped on the deep charcoal Joseph Abboud jacket and it was a perfect fit. Flawless, right down to the sleeve length. Even the feel of the lining against his skin told him that he'd never had on anything like this in his life. He buttoned the double-breasted jacket and the transformation was complete. He looked like a million bucks.

"The pants," Nick continued, "the pants we work on later."

"Nick, I don't think I—"

"Hey, don't worry about this stuff being Tommy's. It's just things, you know. No soul, no heart, you know? Why waste them? I sure as hell can't use them . . ."

"I don't know what to say, Nick."

Nick held up his hands. "My pleasure. I got a box of stuff in the car, too. Books and tapes and other things I want you to have. Jazz and some other crap. R and B. Whatever the fuck that is. On the other hand, if it ain't Frank or Tony Bennett, I'm kind of lost, you know?"

"I hear you," Paris said.

"The rest of the stuff I already gave to St. Vincent de Paul. I just don't want it around. I mean, I've got a few pictures, I've got memories . . ."

"Thanks, Nick."

"Not a problem," Nick replied. "Now get your ass downstairs and get the box out of my car. I'm too fucking old to be hauling shit that heavy up four flights of stairs because you can't live in a building with an elevator."

o   o   o

AFTER NICK LEFT, PARIS FOUND A BOBBY DARIN TAPE IN ONE OF THE TWO large boxes. He popped it into his mini–boom box, and within minutes had completely forgotten his headache and was heard belting "Beyond the Sea" three apartments away.

o   o   o

IN THE LARGER OF THE TWO BOXES PARIS FOUND SOME OF THE BOOKS HE HAD seen when he went through Tommy's things in Nick's basement. He flipped open one book, *A Handbook of the Ancients*. It was inscribed: "Happy Birthday from Marta, Danny, Chauncey and the rest of the crime-slaves at the Fourth." Paris knew them all. Marta was Marta Perez, the bombshell dispatcher. Danny was Danny Lawrence. Chauncey was Ed Chance, a lifer with a job-related limp and a laugh like Art Carney's.

Next was a stack of 45rpm records inside a pile of T-shirts from every major airport in America. Underneath was a small leatherette photo album, one he had not seen before.

The first photo in the book was Tommy sitting on a concrete bench at Sea World or Geauga Lake or King's Island, holding a plump little girl about two years old on his lap. The girl, who had curly blond hair and wore a shocking-orange sun bonnet, didn't look anything like Tommy, so Paris figured she wasn't his child or even his niece. But, Paris marveled, it wasn't as if there weren't enough single women in Cleveland. Tommy found a way to date women with two-year-old kids.

The second photograph in the book was of Tommy in a cream-colored suit, his arm around the waist of yet another gorgeous woman. It was taken at what looked to be the lobby bar at Stouffer's Tower City. The woman had soft-looking hair and long, shapely legs. She wore a short aqua dress, shaped like a toga, along with a gold rope belt and matching gold pumps. The moment Paris was able to tear himself away from the woman's legs and breasts and hair and shoes, he noticed something else about her.

The woman was Diana Bennett.

o o o

MIDWAY THROUGH DIANA'S OVERNIGHT BAG, PARIS GOT PISSED OFF. PISSED AT the world, pissed at his stupid fucking life, pissed that he had allowed himself to tumble even an inch for this woman, pissed that he was, at that moment, rifling her bag, for the childish reason of finding not only more evidence that she had slept with Tommy Raposo—which was none of his goddamn business anyway—but evidence that she was tied to a series of homicides.

There had been nothing remotely kinky about the photo of Tommy and Diana. Nothing perverse at all. It was just a party shot of sorts; a posed picture, snapped through a boozy haze. All potentially explainable. He was a cop, she was a prosecutor. Cops and lawyers hung out from time to time, got invited to the same parties sometimes.

But regardless of how innocent it might have all been, it was as if that first night with Diana was tainted in some way now. He had been hoping that it was love that he had made to Diana Bennett, but now he wasn't so sure. And although he had just as many doubts about Tommy's guilt, the knowledge that Tommy had probably been with Diana before him simply pissed him the fuck off.

But, in an instant, the heat of his anger turned to a cold knot of fear.

He reached deeper into Diana's bag and pulled out a short black slip and bra. Next he retrieved a much dog-eared paperback copy of *Sphinx* by Robin Cook, bookmarked with a register receipt from Heinen's.

Then, even as his hand closed around it in the darkness of the bag, he *knew* what it was. He pulled out the Polaroid camera. Then two packages of unexposed film.

In the large pocket at the side was a zippered, clear plastic makeup kit, the same size and type as the makeup kit found in the trunk of Tommy Raposo's TransAm. Paris dumped the contents onto the dining room table and his eyes were immediately drawn to a familiar size and shape. A powder compact. He picked it up, turned it over and, with it, flipped his heart. Engraved in silver atop the slim ebony case was the tastefully small logo of a bird morphing into the number 5. Beneath it, a silver, engraved word:

Chaligne.

Was he being paranoid?

It didn't matter.

He dialed the phone anyway.

o o o

"I HAVE TO SAY, I'M A LITTLE JEALOUS, JACK," BETH SAID. "I DIDN'T THINK she'd be so . . . I don't know . . . what's the word I'm looking for here . . . beautiful? I guess that *would* be the proper one. If you like perfect looks, that is . . ."

"Beth . . ."

"Actually, now that I think about it, I'm a lot jealous."

"Are they back yet?" Paris asked, trying his best to mask any hint of anxiety in his voice.

"I mean, what is she, a size *five* for God's sake?"

"Are they back yet, Beth?"

"No . . . not yet." Her voice shifted, the playfulness gone. She had made him. She knew him way too well. "Why? Is something wrong?"

"No," Paris said, sounding far more convinced than he felt. "No . . . of course not. We were all supposed to hook up for Chinese food later and I, um, don't remember if it was the Golden Dragon or Silver Pagoda. Some precious metal as I recall."

"Jack . . ."

"I'm telling you, nothing's wrong. Listen, I gotta run, so I'll either meet up with them, if I can figure the restaurant out—"

"Kowloon Garden, Jack."

"Thank you, and more than likely Diana will be dropping Missy off in the next few hours."

"You sure everything's all right?"

"Yes."

"Okay, then . . ."

She didn't sound convinced. "There's no intrigue. I mean it," Paris offered.

"Okay, detective," Beth said. "See you . . ."

o   o   o

He rounded the corner and nearly knocked over Cyndy Taggart. She was still in uniform.

"As promised," she said, regaining her balance. She held forth a pair of gloves and sunglasses, task force leftovers that Paris, in keeping with most of his adult life, figured he had donated to the Land of the Lost Father's Day Gifts, along with the umbrellas, lighters and scarves. "Dig those Ray Bans, though," she added. "Almost kept them, except they were a little too big for me."

"Knockoffs," Paris said. "Got them on Prospect somewhere. You of all people should know that I can't afford Ray Bans." He turned on his heels. "Come on up for a second."

"So, what's goin' on, Jack? You don't look too good," Cyndy said, mounting the steps.

"It's nothing," Paris replied. He opened his door and they stepped into his apartment. Paris winced at its state of disarray. "I'm okay. It's just a little—"

"No sale, Jack"

"Really. I don't—"

"*Jack* . . ."

She gave him that fellow officer/mom look that told him he should have his head examined rather than try and lie to another cop. He caved.

"You know Diana Bennett?"

"Sure," Cyndy said, sitting on the arm of the couch. "I mean, I've met her at the grand jury when I've testified. She's questioned me. Why?"

Paris told her the barest details of his past three weeks with Diana and how, without thinking about it too much, he had let her take Melissa to the Home and Flower Show and how he was probably just being paranoid about the whole thing but . . .

He told her about the Chaligne compact in Diana's overnight bag, as well as the photograph of her and Tommy.

"Well, number one, the Chaligne doesn't mean anything. I use it too. In fact . . ." Cyndy began rooting through her purse. She held up the black and silver compact. "See?"

"Okay, but that just means—" Paris began.

"And number two, there's all kinds of Polaroid-type film. How do you know they match?"

"I haven't had the chance to make any comparisons."

"Do you have the Polaroids you found at Tommy's father's house?" Cyndy asked.

"Uh . . . no," Paris said, hoping Cyndy would buy it. "They're downtown."

"Exactly how kinky are they?"

"Nothing really hard-core. But I have the feeling these weren't the first pictures of that type she's ever had taken."

"That's a long way from serial murder, Jack."

"What I'm saying is—"

"What you're saying is that you somehow think this 'Saila' might be Diana Bennett."

Boy, did it sound stupid when she said it out loud, Paris thought. "I don't know what I'm trying to say."

"I think you're losing a little perspective here, detective. I mean . . . let's see . . . how do I put this delicately? You've been *with* Diana. In the biblical sense. Don't you—"

"Recognize her body in the photographs?"

"Yeah."

"No. I'm afraid it was dark and I was drunk and there isn't quite enough in the pictures to rule her completely in or completely out."

"You men are unbelievable. We do this long, complicated dance for you, we finally give it up and you get so drunk you miss it."

"What can I say?"

"So where are you heading?"

"I guess I was going to stop at the Home and Flower Show and peek in at them. Just take a look from the upper deck at Public Hall and prove to myself that I'm a paranoid asshole. If I didn't see them, I was going to go to Kowloon Garden. Then I was going to head out to the Quality Inn."

"I'll go with you," she said.

"No, Cyndy," Paris replied, locking his door, heading toward the stairs. "I can't ask you to give up your Saturday evening."

"It's no problem. Personally, I think you're blowing this way out of proportion, but I understand your concern."

"You sure? I mean, I feel pretty stupid already and we're not even there yet."

"Don't worry about it," Cyndy said. "Besides, we don't have any tickets to the Home and Flower Show and the way you look you won't be able to bull your way in with a *badge*."

"Thanks," Paris said, unfortunately seeing her point and agreeing with her.

"Just want to stop at my place and get out of my blues. Why don't you just follow me there—then we'll take one car into town."

"Is this little excursion going to remain between you and me?" Paris asked.

"You mean like me deserting my post at the Impulse that night?"

"Exactly," he said. He held open the door at the top of the steps.

"You're my kind of man, Jack Paris," Cyndy said, and ducked under his arm.

o o o

"How long have you lived here?"

"Almost two years," Cyndy called from the other room. "Two years this July."

"Nice," Paris said, running his hand over the cherry credenza in the dining area, holding a fat but well-groomed Persian cat in the other hand. Like everything else in Cyndy's tastefully appointed apartment at the Terrace View Towers on Cedar Hill, the cat looked European somehow. It smelled of fresh lemons. "I never knew you were such a . . . you know . . . *decorator*."

"Well, let me put it this way—my ex is doing pretty well."

Cyndy swung out of the bedroom buttoning her short denim jacket, carrying an oversized shoulder bag. Once again, Paris was disarmed by her out-of-uniform looks; her toned and muscled body carried her with a lithe grace across the living room. Her black jeans were snug in all the right places.

Cyndy checked the action on a small, nickel-plated .25 semiautomatic pistol, snapped in a clip and put it in her purse just as Paris's beeper went off.

"Shit." He checked the number and walked over to Cyndy's phone. He punched in the number. "This is Jack Paris. Uh-huh . . . yeah. . . . S.I.U. there yet? . . . Is the building secured? . . .Okay, give me fifteen. . . . Okay then, call me here as soon as you know." He gave the dispatcher Cyndy's number and hung up. "*Fuck.*"

"What's up?" Cyndy asked.

"Got a warm one at King-Kennedy. And I'm up, damnit."

"Sorry, Jack. I mean, you know that I'd take it if I *could*," Cyndy said with a fair dose of sarcasm.

"Yeah. Right. Real glamour case."

"Listen, none of this Diana business is going to amount to anything anyway. You're just being paranoid."

"You're probably right."

"But if you like, I'll go meet up with them. I've met Diana, she knows me. I'll pick Melissa up and take her wherever you want. I'll say you decided to take Melissa to a movie, and it starts at whatever time et cetera, et cetera . . ."

"I guess that sounds okay . . ."

"Then you and I will go to the Quality Inn," Cyndy said.

Paris knew he was overreacting, but he decided to take Cyndy up on her offer. "Okay. Check the show, check Kowloon Garden. If you catch up with them, just bring Missy to my place and I'll stop there as soon as I can, all right?"

"You got it."

"Thanks, Cyndy," Paris said. "Ring the super at my place and show him your shield. Name's Jimmy DeBellis. He'll let you in."

"No problem," she replied, opening the door. "And relax. Everything's just like it's supposed to be. Wait for your call. Just close the door when you leave. It's already locked."

"Anything comes up, page me," Paris said.

"We'll be fine, Jack."

"I owe you, Cyndy. Big-time."

"Believe it," she said with a smile, and left her apartment.

o   o   o

ON ONE WALL OF CYNDY TAGGART'S DINING ROOM WAS A HUGE GEORGIA O'-Keeffe reproduction, expensively framed. The floor was highly polished and the wall coverings were very subdued, very tasteful. Lots of beige and brown and brass and antique-type things. Paris flipped through her CDs and tapes. Oldies, jazz-fusion, show tunes.

He found the remote and clicked on the TV. He surfed the channels for a while, landing on the Cavs-Knicks game on ESPN. But he found himself glancing at his watch far too often to concentrate on what the Knicks were doing to his beloved Cleveland Cadaver-liers.

Ten minutes later, his callback came.

o   o   o

THE KING-KENNEDY HOMICIDE WAS A FIFTEEN-YEAR-OLD DEALER NAMED RAmon Jackson. He had been shot point-blank in the back of the head, twice, Scarface-style, and he still had more than two thousand dollars in his pockets. This was clearly no robbery. There wasn't much left of Ramon's face, but one of his cousins identified him to police based on the Raiders jacket he wore with the embroidered *RJ* along the waistband.

The interviewing went surprisingly quickly—Paris suspected that no one had seen a thing, or would admit to it, and he was right—and he was in and out of the scene in less than an hour. He stopped home, found no one there, then drove back to the Justice Center.

o   o   o

PARIS PAGED CYNDY AND DREW A CUP OF COFFEE. AFTER FILING THE REPORT on the King-Kennedy shooting, he laid out the pictures of the four serial victims on his desk and realized immediately how ludicrous it was to think that Diana was in any way involved in this. What was wrong with him? Was he *that* pissed off that she had taken a fucking picture with Tommy Raposo?

Maybe that sap to the back of the head last night was worse than he thought.

The truth of the matter, Paris conceded, was that he was overworked. The truth of the matter was that he was never going to be comfortable with the idea that Tommy was solely guilty, or even guilty at all of the Pharaoh murders, and it was that feeling, combined with the lack of sleep, that was making him stupid. The truth of the matter was that Diana, Cyndy and Melissa were probably, at that very moment, sitting at Kowloon Garden with a puu-puu platter and three bowls of wonton soup in front of them, trashing the hell out of one John Salvatore Paris, Paranoid Supreme.

That was the truth of the matter. Still, even though he believed all of the above:

He dialed the Kowloon Garden and got a busy signal.

He dialed Diana's number and got her machine.

He dialed Beth's number and got her voice mail.

He paged Cyndy again.

He waited.

o   o   o

THE KID HAD THE STRINGY BLOND HAIR AND MULTICOLORED BICYCLE SHORTS that identified him as an urban surfer. As he approached, Paris saw that under his arm was a zippered nylon courier pouch, thus explaining his presence on the sixth floor.

"Are you Detective Paris?" the kid asked.

"Yeah. What's up?"

"Sign here, please." He held forth a clipboard and a ballpoint pen.

"What, you guys are seven days a week now?" Paris asked.

"Yes sir. Twenty-four hours a day, too. Since Feb. one." The kid absently checked his beeper, retrieved his clipboard and handed Paris the package.

Paris flipped him a pair of dollar bills and examined the outside of the cardboard envelope. Beneath the FleetGram logo it read, simply: "Det. Jack Paris."

"Have a good one," the courier said, and loped toward the stairs.

"Yeah . . . you too." Paris was just about to open the envelope when Brian Sands, one of the desk cops on duty, came lumbering up the steps, papers in hand.

"Message for you, Jack," Sands said, clearly out of shape and out of breath. He put his hands on his knees for a few moments. When he recovered sufficiently, he said, "Cyndy Taggart from over at the Fourth called and said to tell you she didn't see anyone at Public Hall. Said she's heading over to the Chinese place."

"She called the desk?" Paris asked.

"Yep."

"Why didn't she just page me?"

Sands just stared at him, as if the question could be anything but rhetorical. Brian Sands was fifty-seven years old, impatient by nature and tired as hell. "I don't know, Jack. We didn't discuss it. But I'm going to go ahead and guess that it's because there was nowhere for you to call her back, seeing as she's on the road in her own car."

Of course, Paris thought. "When did she call?"

"Ten, fifteen minutes ago, maybe." Sands stood in the doorway and arched a single eyebrow, waiting.

"Oh, uh, thanks," Paris said absently.

"Betcha," Sands said, and headed down the hall.

Paris sat for a few moments and wondered if Diana and Melissa were already en route to Beth's place, or if Cyndy was going to catch them at the restaurant. Then he remembered the package on his lap.

He tore open the top of the package and pulled out an envelope, white, unmarked. Inside that was a three-by-five index card with some typing on it. There was also a Polaroid. When Paris pulled out the picture and turned it over, he felt his breath suddenly lunge through his chest.

The photograph was of himself.

It was outdoors, at night, and he was propped against a tree with what looked to be a pearl-handled straight razor in his right hand. Over his left shoulder was the neon Motel Riverview sign. He appeared to be just resting against the tree, as if he were looking down at the razor, but Paris knew for a fact that he was out cold.

On the index card, the message was also quite clear:

> Go to Shaker Square. Park directly in front of Booksellers.
> Bring all P files and this material. Speak to no one.

The *Hellers?* He was being set up by the fucking *Hellers?*

He didn't buy it for a minute. Andrea Heller might be a little kinky, her husband might be the kind of guy who drilled holes in the girls' shower wall when he was in junior high school, but they were no psycho killers.

But if not them, who the hell else was out there in the woods with him that night?

Paris looked at the typeface. It was a standard Times Roman 12-point. Common to just about every word-processing program out there. He found the number for Fleet Courier Services on the outside of the envelope and dialed it.

"Fleet."

"This is Detective John Paris with the Cleveland Police Homicide Unit. I just received a package a few minutes ago and I'd like to ask you a few questions about it."

"Sure thing," the man replied. "Let me get it up on the computer here . . ."

Paris heard the plastic click of the keys and a loud burst of laughter in the background. Outside his own window, a cruiser went by at full speed and full siren. Finally the man said, "Yep. Have it right here. Detective Paris at the Justice Center. What can I tell you about it?"

"I need to know who sent it."

"I'm afraid I don't know that, sir."

"You don't have a record of who sent the package?"

"Well, it's not required. I mean, if someone is paying cash, as they did in this case, we don't require a sender's name or address. We ask, but we don't demand. The important part is where the package is going."

"Where and when was it picked up?"

Paris heard a few more key clicks.

"It was picked it up at six-fifty this evening."

"Where?"

"Six floors beneath you," the man said. "In the lobby of the Justice Center."

o   o   o

THE FILE BOXES FOR THE PHARAOH CASE TOOK UP THE ENTIRE FRONT AND back seats of Paris's Olds. In all, it amounted to a cargo of nine legal-size storage containers. The boxes were empty of course, but Paris had to play the game, had to maintain appearances until he clamped the irons on this motherfucker. The complications of actually *bringing* the files with him—legal, ethical, logistical—were enormous, so that was never an option.

Besides, this operation wasn't going to take anywhere near that long or get anywhere near that far.

o   o   o

PARIS FOUND A SPACE DIRECTLY IN FRONT OF BOOKSELLERS AND CUT THE ENgine. It had rained briefly and gotten completely dark during the ride out to the square, and except for a few window-shoppers and late RTA commuters, the area was relatively empty of activity. He positioned his rearview mirror and side mirrors to his best advantage and slumped down in the seat.

Soon, a woman approached the window at Booksellers. She wore an oversized tam-o'-shanter and an overcoat that looked to Paris to be a bit bulky for the fifty-degree evening. She perused the display of New Age titles for a few moments, hesitated, looking left and right, then moved on to the video store. She rounded the corner onto South Moreland and disappeared.

Five minutes later, just as his unease began to set in, Paris noticed a white rectangle stuck into the hedges directly in front of the hood of his car. It briefly fluttered into view, then out. It looked like it might have been an envelope, but it was partially hidden in the dark recesses of the hedge. Paris got out, retrieved it and found that it was, in fact, an envelope, sealed, bearing the initials JP. Inside was another typed three-by-five card, which read:

> *Leave car unlocked and walk across the square.*
> *Stand in front of the Colony Theater. Will flash headlights*
> *when done.*

Shit.

Paris looked around the quadrant, at the scores of shops, office buildings and apartment complexes. He was one hundred percent positive he was being observed, so he shifted to plan B. He gently closed the car door and walked the two hundred or so yards to the far side of Shaker Square, crossing South Moreland against the light, counting his steps, calculating how long it might take him to sprint back across. He stood directly under the brilliant marquee of the Colony Theater and felt the temperature around him increase a degree or two.

After a few minutes a figure approached his car, but due to the distance and the darkness, Paris couldn't tell if it was a man or a woman. The door swung open and the figure entered the driver's side. Paris moved to the edge of the sidewalk. He could see a flashlight moving around inside the Olds, its beam playing off the white interior ceiling, off the collection of empty two-liter bottles that rattled against his rear window. He stepped out onto Shaker Boulevard and waited for the traffic to pass, hoping he could take advantage of that small window of opportunity between the time his suspect saw the boxes were empty and the time his suspect turned to bolt.

Paris drew his weapon and ran.

But before he had taken three steps, the car door slammed hard and the figure ran through the breezeway between the shops, toward the parking lot on Drexmore.

Paris gave chase, racing across the square at full speed, nearly slipping twice on the rain-slicked RTA tracks in the process. By the time he reached the parking lot it was dark and empty. Just a few cars scattered around. Nothing moving.

He caught his breath slowly, painfully. When he was satisfied that he had fucked up the one and only lead he was ever going to get in this case—a case that was officially closed—he walked back to his car and looked inside. A few of the cardboard boxes were slashed, as was the upholstery on both the front and back seats. Paris got in and pounded his fists against the steering wheel.

And that's when he saw the third white envelope on the dashboard. He opened it. Inside was another Polaroid, a photograph that told Jack Paris that nothing was closed.

Nothing at all.

3 3

"Hi, how was the show?"

Beth found it hard to believe that she was sitting there chatting on the telephone with her husband's new girlfriend. What a difference a few years can make, she thought. At one point in their relationship she and Jack had even resorted to eavesdropping on each other's telephone conversations because of their petty jealousies, and here they were schmoozing with each other's significant others. As soon as Beth heard the woman's voice on the phone, with its take-charge aplomb, any and all doubts she'd had about the woman disappeared.

"It was wonderful. I think Missy has permanently moved into the model home they've built down here. You should see the little-girls' room."

"Michael Bolton posters and lots of ruffles?" Beth asked.

"Yep."

"Every entertainment device in the Sharper Image catalog?"

"You've got it,"

Beth laughed. "Did she behave herself?"

"Oh my, yes. You're raising a very polite and intelligent little girl here."

"Oh . . . uh . . . well," Beth said, a little flustered, "thank you very much."

"Did you know she had an interest in pyramids? There's a huge one here and Missy did five minutes on the history of the pyramid. I was *very* impressed."

"I had no idea," Beth said, not at all sure how she felt about her daughter moving from "Melissa" to "Missy" in two short afternoons. "But, I have to say, she's been curious her whole life. Her father's a detective, after all." Beth was *so* thrilled that she had brought Jack up at that moment. She flashed to the two of them in bed.

"I'm afraid we've cooked up a few more outings in the near future. I hope I'm not overstepping any boundaries."

"No," Beth said, lying through her teeth. "Not at all."

"Well . . . the reason I'm calling is that I'm afraid I won't be able to drop her off as planned. I just got paged and I'm afraid I have to rush back to work tonight. We're just about finished eating and I was wondering if it would be okay if I dropped her off at Jack's. I'm only a few blocks away."

"Sure," Beth said. "I do appreciate you calling, though. Just tell Jack to give me a ring when he's ready to drop her off."

"Not a problem. I know how mothers can worry. I also wanted to say thanks for a lovely afternoon with Melissa."

"Anytime," Beth answered, only half meaning it.

Beth decided that she would sort out her feelings later, but for now, as she hung up the phone, she had to admit that she felt a little jealous and a lot surprised that Jack Paris—he of the endless trail of short con games—would end up with someone quite this nice.

3 4

PARIS'S HANDS TREMBLED AS HE TURNED THE PHOTO-graph over and over in the red light thrown from the traffic signal. The image was of a girl—bound with rope, hand and foot—lying in the trunk of a car. A white car, by the look of the trim.

As Paris stared at the picture, even though the girl's face was turned away from the lens, it didn't take long for him to identify the red cardigan sweater and plaid kilt.

It was Melissa.

On the back was a message:

"Saila does Chinatown."

Beneath that, an address he did not recognize.

3 5

SAILA HUNG UP THE PHONE, A MUCH-GRAFFITIED PAY STA-
tion at the top of Coventry Road, near the Cen-
trum. Jack Paris's ex-wife was as gullible as she
had hoped and it had given her more time with
Melissa, more time to work Jack.

Because, you see, Jack Paris had fucked her at Shaker
Square. Jack Paris had bent her over and fucked her like a common
harlot.

And now it was time to pay the whore.

○   ○   ○

THE WOMAN MAKING THE WOUNDED-ANIMAL SOUNDS FROM THE TRUNK OF THE
BMW was beginning to wear down. Thank God. The little girl was
now sitting in the front seat of the car, perfectly calm, burning holes
in her with her fiercely defiant brown eyes. What a *beauty* she
was . . .

Saila dropped another quarter.

"Hello?" the man's voice answered.

"Guess who?"

"I *know* who."

"How is my Pharaoh?" Saila asked.

"I miss your cunt," he said.

"Bad little *tom*," she replied. "My cunt misses *you*."

"Yeah?"

"My tail is *so* high . . ."

"When and where?"

"It's why I called," Saila said. "Not tonight."

"But I—"

"What?"

"Sorry . . ."

Saila slammed down the phone. There was something funda-
mentally wrong with the deductive processes of a certain type of
man, she thought.

She'd see about Paris.

3 6 THE HEADWAITER AT KOWLOON GARDEN, A SLIGHT, animated man named Anton Fong, said he had seated a girl and a woman matching Diana's and Melissa's general descriptions earlier in the evening, but he also remembered clearly that they weren't alone, that he had seen a man and a woman sitting with them, but only from the back. Then, Fong said, he went into the kitchen. When he returned to the dining room, ten minutes later, they were all gone and a twenty-dollar bill was tented on the table.

"Twenty dollar," Fong said. "Can you imagine? Twenty dollar for water and *tea.*"

None of the other five waiters were able to say for sure that they had seen the foursome actually leave the restaurant.

Paris headed down Chester Avenue to East Fifty-fifth Street. Then he turned south, toward Carnegie and University Circle.

o   o   o

TARLETON STREET WAS AN ODD ENCLAVE OF TWENTY OR SO THREE-ROOM COTtages that sat atop University Hill, surrounded by scores of dormitories, classrooom buildings and high-rise residences for the students and faculty of Case Western Reserve University. The cottages were built in the early thirties to accommodate visiting physicians to Cleveland Clinic, which at that time was a small gray building at Ninetythird and Euclid. Yet, in spite of the ethereal orange glow from the nearby RTA stop, the street had a pretty active crime element, consisting mostly of burglaries and reports of radios being stolen from the cars that were forced to park on the street.There had once been a series of rapes in the long tunnel leading to the RTA stop. Paris had been in on that collar as a rookie.

But this night, the incandescence from the train platforms didn't even make it up the hill. At least half the lamps were out and the remainder of the light seemed to be swallowed by the hedges and trees. Tarleton Street was bathed in darkness.

The address on the back of the photograph was 15203.

Paris found the house, third from last on the dead-end street, cut the headlights and the engine, then rolled quietly to a stop. He checked his weapon and got out of the car.

o   o   o

THE FRONT DOOR TO THE COTTAGE WAS UNLOCKED AND SLIGHTLY AJAR. PARIS pushed it open with the barrel of his weapon and felt along the wall for a light switch. Within moments he found one and flipped it on. A table lamp, set on the floor directly beneath the switch, blazed to life, showing him that the front room was empty. He stepped inside.

o   o   o

THE LIVING ROOM HAD A WORN, TRANSIENT LOOK TO IT. THE FURNITURE CONsisted of a stained maroon futon against one wall, a coffee table, a small desk with a fax machine, a crate with a TV. There was also a broken-down hutch at the other side of the L-shaped dining room.

As Paris drew closer to the dining area, his weapon raised, he noticed that the coffee table was sixties vintage, covered with ashtrays and magazines, a few condom wrappers, a tipped wineglass. He also noticed a pair of half-smoked joints sticking out of the forest of filters in one tray. To the left of the living room was the kitchen, small and filthy, also empty. Straight ahead Paris could see what looked to be a bedroom. He sidled up to the doorway, reached around the jamb and found another switch.

The bedroom was long and narrow. It had obviously been two rooms at one time. At one end was a double mattress on the floor; next to it sat a video camera on a tripod. At the foot of the bed was a small pile of women's lingerie and nightclothes. The other side of the room looked like a smaller version of a Gold's Gym, boasting a Schwinn Air-Dyne exercise bicycle, a rower, a lat machine, a Bow-Flex, a large set of free weights.

But the display in the bedroom didn't come close to the display inside the crudely crafted walk-in closet. Inside was an extensive pegboard array of oils and perfumes, handcuffs and leather restraints, whips and dog collars, a wall of hoods and masks and leashes and headpieces. One side held virtually every sex toy that Paris had ever encountered in his life, as well as a good many he had not. Another wall held an elaborate collection of wigs and leather clothing: skirts, vests, chaps, thigh-high boots.

On the floor were two large cardboard boxes of video and audio tapes; some prerecorded, but most, Paris noted with a stab of fear, apparently homemade. *The A Train* was the title on one of the video tapes. Another, *East Side Mothers*.

In one of the cardboard boxes that held the audio tapes Paris found a variety of electronic equipment used for the covert taping of conversations. There was also a selection of portable, battery-operated voice-altering devices.

Beneath the box of tapes Paris found a thin, flat box full of photos. Most were standard bondage fare, not much different from the "Saila does Quality" photo. Women in leather restraints. Men in rubber suits, clamped into a bizarre collection of devices. Most wore leather masks, and for that reason, no one was immediately identifiable. As Paris began to flip through the pile, he found the photos near the bottom to be increasingly more graphic and violent, more sadistic. Some were close-ups of lacerations and cuts; some, pictures of dark purple welts against soft white flesh, wounds most likely caused by a whip.

But it was one of the last photos in his hand that stopped him cold. Suddenly, in the midst of all this madness, Paris saw a room he recognized. It was the bathroom of room 118 at the Radisson. The photograph showed Eleanor Burchfield curled up on the tile floor, fetal, her throat laid wide open, a shiny pool of blood gathering beneath her head.

And although Paris had seen hundreds and hundreds of crime scene photographs in his career, thousands of color and black-and-white images of carnage and violence and mayhem, the fact that Melissa was in the hands of a monster at that moment, a monster to which he could not put a face, made all the difference in the world.

He barely made it to the sink.

o   o   o

THREE MINUTES LATER, THE PHONE RANG. THE ANSWERING MACHINE GOT TO IT before Paris did.

"Hi . . . If you're sending a fax, send it now. If you'd like to leave a voice message, wait for the beep. Thanks . . ."

"Pick it up," came the voice from the speaker. Cold, even, distant.

Paris lifted the phone in a blind fury. "Who the *fuck* is this?"

"Are you on the fax phone?"

Paris instantly recognized the flat, nasal sound of a voice scrambler. It was a woman, but Paris could not identify the voice. It sounded like computer speech.

"Diana?"

Silence.

"Saila?"

Silence.

"Answer me," Paris said. "Who *is* this?"

After a few moments, the woman said, "I'm going to hang up."

"No!" Paris shouted.

He waited. The electronic hiss gave him hope that she was still on the line.

"Are you still there?" Paris asked.

Flatly: "Yes."

"Is Melissa all right?"

"Of course."

There was a maddening tease of recognition beneath the changing pitch of her voice. "Put her on," Paris said, trying to concentrate on the woman's sibilance. "Let me speak to her."

"Right away, detective. Listen—"

"No, *you* listen. You're going to tell me where my daughter is, and I'm going to come down there and get her. One scenario, that's it."

The woman laughed darkly. "Don't insult me."

There was something grave about her tone that gave Paris pause. He remained silent for the moment.

"I'm not going to hurt your daughter, detective," the woman continued. "Because there's still a way out of this. It involves the destruction of evidence, though. I hope you don't have a problem with that."

"Not when it comes to my daughter," Paris said.

"Good," she answered, the sound echoing slightly. "And by the way, how *did* I look to you in those pictures?"

"You, uh, looked *good*," Paris said, hoping he wasn't sounding too patronizing. "Really good." He listened intently to the background noise: faint traffic sounds, a light wind. She was outdoors, or, perhaps, standing by an open window.

"Did you want to fuck me when you saw them?"

"Yes . . ."

"Did you get hard?"

"Yes." Paris heard her breathe in and out once, very deliberately. He wondered what she was doing with her hands.

"You said the right thing, detective."

Paris heard a car pass loudly by the woman's location. She was outside. The sound reverberated slightly too, so chances were good that she was at a drive-up phone.

"Speaking of Polaroids," she continued, "I'll prove to you that Melissa is fine. You see that table by the front door?"

Paris gripped the phone a little more tightly. "Yes."

"Open the drawer."

Paris found that the phone cord nearly reached the table. He leaned over and opened the drawer. On top was a photograph, a Polaroid. When he flipped it over, a river of bile unleashed itself into his stomach.

It was a color picture of Melissa sitting on the futon, not five feet from where he stood. His daughter looked about eighteen in the photograph, her thick makeup and teased hair having transformed her into a woman. She wore an oversized white terry-cloth robe.

"You sick *fuck*," Paris spat into the telephone. He forced himself to look back at the picture.

"She looks really good there," the woman said.

"My hand to God, I will hunt you down. You touch her and you don't *see* a fucking courtroom. You hear me?"

"Like a little lady . . ."

"She's eleven years old!"

"She told me that she's nearly twelve. That's almost a teenager. Something tells me that you're not going to cope too well with the hormone years."

Paris took a deep, calming breath. It had absolutely no effect upon him whatsoever. "Do you have any idea what I'd like to do to you right now?" he said.

"Girls just wanna have fun, Jack."

"Who the fuck is this?" Paris screamed.

"Don't ever ask me that question again," the woman said serenely. "*Ever.* Do you understand?"

Paris tried again to calm himself. Finally he offered, "Yes."

"Then back to business. I am going to say these things once. I want you to listen, do precisely what I tell you to do, and not to speak, not even one word. Can you hear me, detective?"

Silence.

"Good boy. But you may answer me this one time."

"Yes, I can hear you."

"Good. And please don't think that I can't see you. I can see everything you're doing. Nod if you understand."

Paris scanned the night-black windows of the kitchen, living room and dining room, confirming that every light in the house was on and all the window shades were up. She could have been in any one of ten different buildings. He did as he was told.

"I want you to hold up all the photographs and all the notes you've received this evening," the woman said. "I want to see them."

Paris reached into his pocket and retrieved the three-by-five cards and the photographs. He held them high in the air.

"Tear them into very small pieces and drop the pieces on the table."

Paris obeyed.

"Do the same thing with Melissa's photo."

Paris had no problem destroying the picture. He let the jagged pieces fall to the table.

"Now, obviously, I can never set foot in that house again, right? On the coffee table you'll find two or three small oil candles. I want you to get them and bring them back to the phone. You have ten seconds. No tricks. Go now."

Paris put the phone down, crossed the living room and did as he was instructed to do, a million bytes of departmental procedure flashing through his mind, an avalanche of rage in his gut. The candles were the size and shape of small apples, very light, probably made of a heavy-gauge foil. Each had an open well that was filled with two or three ounces of scented oil, and over the top a curved handle that held the wick. Paris picked up the phone and listened for further instructions.

"Light the candles and place them on the table in front of you, near the base of the fax machine, where the paper comes out."

Paris found a match in his pants pocket and lit the candles. Before he could stop himself, he said: "Done."

She whispered: "I told you not to speak."

"I—"

"You say one more word and I cut little Lois here in half. *Capeesh*, Detective *Parisi?*"

Paris shut his eyes tightly and bore the next fifteen seconds in complete silence, the image of Karen Schallert's three-inch-deep neck wound flooding his mind, the scent of burning strawberry oil filling his nostrils.

Finally she spoke, jump-starting his heart once again.

"Go into the kitchen, under the table, and bring back the throw rug. Place it on the floor beneath the fax machine. Make it look like it belongs there. Ten seconds. Go now."

Paris sprinted to the kitchen. He peered under the table but there was no rug, just a pair of Totes and a small, telescoping umbrella. He looked frantically around the kitchen and was just about to grab a dish towel and go back out and say that he had the rug, when he spotted it, bunched up against the baseboard near the sink. He ran back to the phone, picked it up and breathed heavily into the mouthpiece, announcing his return.

"If everything is in place, say the word 'yes.' "

"Yes."

"Good. Just one more thing to do. I want you to pull that bar cart next to the phone. Position it very close. Five seconds this time. Go."

Paris found the bar cart just around the corner in the living room and did as the woman had instructed. He could smell the sour, grainy scent of rum coming from one of the uncapped bottles and, for a moment, it tore him in twelve different directions. He'd never once in his life wanted a drink half this badly, but when he once again glanced at the torn pieces of the Polaroid scattered on the table, he knew he had higher priorities than his own failings.

He breathed into the phone.

"Move the oil candles to the edge of the table," the woman said. "Like someone put them there at a party."

Paris did as he was told, making sure the candles would fall as planned. He figured there was no point in trying to sabotage this. The last thing he wanted to do right now was disappoint this woman. He knew what this setup was about: destroying the evidence, collecting the insurance and beating the arson investigators, who were easily the savviest people in all of law enforcement. She would say that she'd had a get-together, she left the house with the candles still lit, she got a fax while she was out and the next thing anybody knew—

He had to hand it to her, it was clever.

"Grunt if it's done," she said.

On the other hand, what he wouldn't give to have this bitch in the room with him for five minutes. He grunted.

"Now, you know and I know that we can't have you walking out of there with anything, so what I want, right now, is for you to strip to the waist. Everything off. Do it."

Paris decided that he couldn't take the chance that she was bluffing about being able to see him. He dropped the phone and pulled his shirt, jacket, tie and undershirt over his head as one unit. Unfortunately, his shoulder holster and weapon came with it. He picked up the phone again.

She continued: "When I see you run out of the house I want to see your hands empty and your pockets turned inside out. Front and back. If you understand, say so."

"I understand."

"I'm going to give you exactly ten seconds from the moment I say go to reach your car. I can see it very clearly and I have a very good watch. If it takes you one second longer, bad things happen. Understand?"

Silence.

"Saila says talk."

"I understand," Paris said.

"Oh . . . and there are two things you should know about me, Jack. One, I don't hurt children. And two, I'm no *fanatic* about that." She paused, with Paris stretched nearly halfway to the door, trying to get a jump on her command. "If I'm satisfied," she continued, "we'll proceed to step two in our game. I will call the Homicide Unit and page you twice in rapid succession, so you'll know that it's me. But when I beep you the second time, you're only going to have thirty seconds to call me back and then I'm gone. We're not going to give anyone time to locate the number. Are you ready, officer?"

Paris nearly answered.

Saila laughed. "Oh, just *go*," she said.

He made the trip in less than eight seconds.

THE COLD NIGHT AIR ASSAULTED PARIS AS HE STEPPED, SWEATING AND SHIRT-less, onto the porch. And although he was certain that the cottage was empty, he still backed away from the house, down the walkway, across the sidewalk and onto the street.

About halfway to his car, Paris panicked for a moment, thinking that he had left his keys in his jacket pocket, inside a house that was set, at any moment, to catch fire. Then he remembered that he had stashed them under the passenger seat. He hadn't known what to expect when he went inside 15203 Tarleton Street, and because he had more than once physically engaged a criminal only to find that after the dust settled, things like keys and wallets and watches and rings and lighters had been flung into oblivion, he had decided to leave his keys in the Olds.

He reached his car, well within the time limit the woman had given him.

And that's when he heard the voice.

"Don't move," it said, a calm, reasonable request that came from behind Paris and to his left, just on the other side of the car.

Paris froze.

"Put your hands on top of your head and interlock your fingers."

Paris did as he was told, a wave of relief instantly washing over him. It was a cop. He waited for the next instruction, even though he knew what it was going to be.

"Now turn around, slowly, and face me."

Paris spun slowly to his right. About halfway, he knew.

"*Jack,*" Danny Lawrence said. "Jesus *Christ,* Jack." There was a measure of relief in Danny's voice, but there was also, Paris noticed, still a measure of suspicion. Paris knew what this must look like. Yet in spite of the fact that everybody knew everybody, he kept his hands on top of his head.

It took Danny a moment to realize that he still had his weapon pointed at a superior officer. "Oh, uh, put your hands down, Jack." He holstered his weapon, apparently a little flustered at the turn of events.

Paris took the opportunity to glance at the house. No flames yet.

"Sorry, Danny," Paris said, trying to formulate his story on the fly. "I hope I didn't . . . you know . . . get the adrenaline pumping *too* hard there . . ."

"What's going on, Jack?"

"Actually, I was going to ask you the same thing," Paris said, smiling, hoping his gold shield would carry the moment. It did.

"Well, what *I'm* doing here is that I caught a call on this street. Report of a burglary in progress—15203 Tarleton. This *is* my district, after all. I *am* a cop."

Danny had given Paris his out. He went for it.

"Uh, I heard it too," Paris said. "I was dropping someone off at the RTA and I heard the call. So I swung the car up here and took a look. I've got a scanner in the Olds." Paris stole another glance at the house. Nothing yet. He had to get rid of Danny or this story was going to be continued down at the Fourth District Headquarters. "Nothing going on. False alarm."

"You're a *detective,* Jack," Danny said. "Why on earth would you handle a burglary call?"

"Not sure, Danny," Paris said. "Reflex, I guess. I was here."

"Is there anybody in the house?" Danny asked.

"No," Paris said. "I checked all the doors and windows. Looked in with the flashlight. Nothing. False alarm."

"Well, maybe I should—"

"Danny. It's handled. It's done."

Danny looked at him, a little more skeptically than Paris would have liked. "You'll call it in? You'll clear it?" he asked, turning his flashlight toward the house. He scanned the eaves, the porch, the bushes.

"Absolutely," Paris said. He reached down and quickly turned his pockets back in.

"Well . . ." Danny began, now directing the flashlight toward Paris, "o*kay,* I guess." He finally produced a smile and, with it, all the tension immediately dissolved. "You think you'll ever tell me why you don't have a fucking shirt on at this moment?"

Paris thought about it. "Yes, Danny. I will. I promise." He smiled back.

Danny Lawrence did a few more takes on Jack and the house. Then he clicked off his flashlight, turned toward his cruiser and said, "Have a good night, detective."

"You too, Danny," Paris said. "And thanks."

Paris wasn't sure why he had thanked him, except maybe that it was rooted in the feeling all police officers have after having a gun pointed at them and not getting shot.

The moment Danny's patrol car passed him, Paris reached into his own car, grabbed a quarter out of the change well and ran toward the RTA stop, where he hoped there would be at least one working pay phone.

37

THE WOMAN WAS VERY SEXY, FOR AN OLDER GAL. KIND of curvy but still muscular and fit. Jeff liked them fit. He also knew that a lot of the housewives that came into the Lee Road Dairy Barn didn't give him a second look because of his complexion and all, but this woman had actually *smiled* at him.

"Not sure how it works either, ma'am. Kind of a techno-dunce m'self," he said, knowing that just the opposite was true. But still he winced when he heard himself say the word "ma'am." He had a sneaking suspicion that women of a certain age just didn't want to be called that. He was pretty sure that they preferred "miss" whether they were still a miss or not. "That's a local phone number, right?"

"Oh, yes," she said, handing him three pieces of eight-and-a-half-by-eleven paper. "The number's at the top."

"Do you need a cover page?"

"No thank you," she said.

"Doesn't cost any extra," Jeff said with his winningest eighteen-year-old smile. "And we've got lots of interesting designs."

"Just what I gave you is fine," she answered, sounding very authoritative, and suddenly very much like one of his *teachers*. He took the pages over to the fax machine, right next to the meat slicer, a kid being sent on an errand by a beautiful woman.

So what was new?

He dialed the number.

"Hi . . . If you're sending a fax, send it now. If you'd like to leave a voice message, wait for the beep. Thanks . . ."

Jeff, rather the office professional when it came to combination fax machine/answering machine telecommunication subtleties, pressed the send button with consummate skill. After the pages made their rotation, he breathed deeply and turned back to the woman, hoping he had exhausted his cache of really stupid moves.

He hadn't.

"Will that be all . . . uh . . . miss?"

She smiled. "Yes, that's it. *Jeff.*"

"A d-dollar seven," Jeff said. She had seen his tag and called him by *name*. She handed him the correct change and stared deep into his eyes as if waiting for something.

"What?" he said.

"The original?"

"The original . . . um . . . *what?*"

"The three-page document. The one you just faxed for me?"

"Oh, how stupid." Jeff Trimble turned a bright and remarkably even shade of red. It seemed to devour him. He handed the woman her papers. "Suh-sorry."

"It's quite all right, young man. You have a nice evening."

She turned and left the store, and as Jeff watched her walk to her car, a white BMW, he thought she was one of the most beautiful women he had ever seen in his life.

He could even tell that her daughter, sitting out in the car, was going to be a knockout one day too.

38

PARIS WAITED UNTIL HE SAW THE FIRE BEFORE HE DIALED the phone. Danny Lawrence had barely turned the corner onto East 115th Street before the first flames began to appear. Paris knew that if he had called it in immediately after getting out of the cottage and the fire hadn't broken out for another ten minutes, he would have had a very hard time explaining it. He imagined that the woman had gone somewhere where there was a fax machine and called, sending a couple of pages down the wire and out of her machine, sending the oil candles onto the rug.

He didn't know if the woman was still in the area, still watching him, so he remained on the RTA platform across the street, out of sight. Paris hoped that she hadn't seen him talking to Danny Lawrence, or, if she had, that she had given him credit for enough sense to have kept his mouth shut around a cop.

Besides, he wasn't all that anxious to run into a burning building anyway. He would simply have to hope that the CFD would arrive in time to save some key piece of evidence to link her to the Pharaoh murders.

But as he heard the muffled pop of the liquor bottles exploding, and watched the fire jump up the windows, he knew it would all go up by the time the first engine company arrived. Within minutes, the roof and eaves were spewing fat orange flames high into the night.

Paris also knew that there would soon be a lot of cellular communication taking place in the area and he didn't want to miss her page.

He sprinted back to his car, opened the trunk, retrieved a damp, pungent sweatshirt out of his gym bag and pulled it over his head. He also pulled out his backup weapon, along with a spare holster and a box of rounds. Although he had been forced to give up his revolver inside the cottage, he had, luckily, managed to get his shield and ID out of his pocket and down the front of his pants before running out of the house. He got in the car, turned over the engine, cranked the heat up to high and turned north on Murray Hill, not having the slightest clue as to why he was heading in that particular direction.

o   o   o

THE COFFEE AT BENGAL'S WAS RARELY FRESH, BUT IT WAS ALWAYS STRONG AND hot. Bengal's was a soul food place on Carnegie, about halfway between his apartment and the Innerbelt. He didn't know if he'd have to go east or west when he got the call, but he wanted to be near a pay phone when it came, and the one at the back corner of the Bengal's parking lot was as good as any.

He got out, checked the phone for a dial tone and, having gotten one, got back in his car. He sipped from the Styrofoam cup and tried to put this nightmare in order.

Who the fuck was doing this to him? Was it Diana? And if it was, how could he have been so wrong? Was it the Hellers? He still found that hard to believe.

And where the hell was Cyndy?

And where the hell was Beth?

He fingered the weapon in his shoulder holster and watched the slow, sparkling parade of hookers as they walked up Carnegie, swinging their purses like world-weary schoolgirls.

o   o   o

SAILA CALLED AT NINE-FIFTEEN.

Paris looked at the pager and, for a moment, thought he was misreading the green and gray LCD display. He flipped on the interior light and found that he had been right in the first place.

It was his home phone number.

By the time the second page came over the airwaves, a few seconds later, Paris had the quarter in the phone.

o   o   o

"I FEEL AS IF SOMEONE HAS STOLEN ALL MY DOLLS, JACK. I FEEL CLEAN, BUT also, I don't know, *violated,* I guess."

"Then just leave my apartment," Paris said, trying to build some momentum. "We're even. Leave Melissa there, take off, and we never did this, okay?"

The silence that greeted his seemingly reasonable suggestion was deafening.

"You really are a shitty housekeeper, Jack."

The woman's voice was still synthesized, but it sounded as if the batteries were fading. At times Paris was positive that he knew the voice, that he was no more than one inflection away from total recognition. At other times the sound flattened out into a dissonance not unlike the voiceboxes used by people who've had their larynx removed. "I know, I know," Paris answered. "But let's—"

"I mean . . . you're a very attractive man, Detective Paris, but this place is not going to get the job done. You know what I mean?"

"Saila . . ."

"And what have we *here?*"

Paris heard the sound of rustling papers and then, mercifully, a brief *woof* from Manny. At least *he* was okay and at the right place. The room then went quiet for what seemed to Paris like a full minute but in reality was no more than fifteen or twenty seconds.

"Some interesting reading material here . . . What is this?"

What the hell is she talking about? Paris thought.

"Aileen Wuornos?" she said. "That roadhouse pig? You were actually reading up on this?"

"I was—"

"You actually thought that there were similarities in these cases? What an insult."

Paris could feel the conversation slipping away from him. He could hear something primal and ugly churning beneath the woman's conversational tone.

"Well . . . that's what they pay me for, you know?" Paris said, reaching.

"Don't patronize me," she said.

"I'm not trying to—"

"What else do you have?"

"Nothing. Not a thing, I swear."

"You fucked me over at Shaker Square. Why should I believe you now?"

"You think this job means more to me than my *daughter?* There was nothing in my car because there isn't any evidence. The prosecutor's happy with Tommy Raposo and that's that. The case is closed."

"Then why won't *you* give it up?"

"I'm done," Paris said. "I'm off it."

The woman went silent for a few beats, the digital processor filling the void with a thin, hissing sound. Then she said, "Maybe I'll just walk into the kitchen, Jack. Maybe I'll just stroll into the kitchen and carefully pick up one of your sharper knives—one just loaded with your fingerprints—and stick it into Melissa's chest. How would that be? Leave her right in the middle of your living room floor in a big, dark pool of blood. Then it's bye-bye Daddy. Bye-bye anchor around my fucking neck."

"Don't . . ."

"Or maybe I'll just take this straight razor and send it off to the authorities. Anonymously, of course. Because, I'm pretty sure that the Bainbridge police are going to be very interested in it, considering the fact that there's the body of a Peeping Tom pushing up lilacs in the woods near the Motel Riverview."

Paris's skin crawled. She was talking about Andrea Heller's husband. "What do you mean?"

"I'm not sure how it happened, but your fingerprints are on one end of the razor and this dead pervert's blood is on the other. Can you believe it?"

"You can't possibly be *serious.*"

"And if that wasn't enough, detective," she continued, her voice dropping to a deep, almost manly whisper, "how do you intend to explain away the woman you barbecued tonight on Tarleton Street?"

Paris felt his stomach rebel with a wave of nausea. He gripped the side of the phone booth and took a deep breath. *"What?"*

"The exhibitionist. The Peeper's wife."

"She was—"

"She was *alive,* Jack. That's what she was. Tied up and pretty well chloroformed, but alive. Up in the attic."

"You *mother*fucker," Paris shouted. He slammed a fist against the side of the phone booth, shattering the clear plastic panel.

"The heat probably brought her to before she went up in flames though, seeing as she was covered in kindling and newspapers. Some oily rags too. I really can't see anyone sleeping through something like that, can you?"

Paris shifted into high gear. The horrors were piling up faster than he could sort through them. He had to think, had to find her weakness. He went for the obvious.

"Look," Paris said, "I've got some cash, poker cash, it's stashed in the basement of the building. It's yours. Maybe five, six grand. C'mon . . ."

"You men are so predictable," she said, her altered voice suddenly taking a sinister turn that chilled Paris. "You think everything in this world revolves around your cocks or your cash flow, don't you. You amuse me so . . ."

It sounded to Paris like she might be ready to hang up. "Don't—"

"But, on the other hand, I *will* take the money. Where is it?"

Paris described the location in the basement.

"Hang on," she said.

Paris heard the phone strike something soft, then fall silent. He heard the door to his apartment open, its familiar creak filling him with a rush of fear. When he figured she had begun her way down the stairs, he spoke.

"Missy . . . can you hear me?" he asked in a gruff whisper.

Silence.

"Missy . . . if you can hear me . . . make some kind of sound."

Nothing. Paris looked out at the street, at Carnegie Avenue, and calculated that he was twenty blocks from his apartment. He'd never make it.

Paris heard a quick snort of breath into the mouthpiece of the phone, then the rustling of . . . material? Clothing? Paper? Was someone listening?

He was just about to call out again when he realized that it was Manny, trying to figure out why his master was inside the telephone.

"Manny . . ."

The dog barked once, but the electronic voicebox changed it into something birdlike. Then Paris heard the door creak again. Then, quick footsteps toward the phone and Manny's nails scampering away on the hardwood floor.

"There's no way this is six thousand dollars."

"Well . . . give or take, no?"

"Anyway, I've decided that I don't believe you about the evidence."

"But—"

"I've got to get going," she said. "I usually go out on Friday, but Saturday's okay too, I suppose. Especially now that I have a new partner. Right, Melissa?"

Paris's heart stopped. He didn't hear his daughter's voice.

"Oh, she'll come around," she said, the electronic version of her voice suddenly grown loud and distorted. It sounded as if the woman had changed the batteries on the fly. "But she has a hell of a lot to learn, I think. On the other hand, who better to teach her than me?"

"Just let me talk to Melissa for five seconds. Just let me know that she's all right."

"I don't think so, Jack. No time," she said, the volume returning to normal, the timbre of her voice slipping up a notch on the synthesizer. She sounded younger, more like a teenager. "We're going out. It's girls' night out."

"Wait . . . Where are you going?"

"Wherever. Around. You could try looking in the backyard, next to the sandbox. Maybe we'll page you later," she said. "On the other hand, maybe we won't. Maybe we'll hit the kiddie bars. Maybe we'll pick up a couple of sailors and head off to Atlantic City."

The woman laughed and the sound frightened Paris to the bottom of his soul.

"Don't hang up," he said.

"Use your head, Jack. I want everything you have on the Pharaoh case. And if you bring anyone in on this, if you talk to one other cop, I'll hurt you for the rest of your life."

"But there isn't—"

"Everything."

Paris opened his mouth to speak but was met instead with a brief, antiseptic click.

Then, the coldest dial tone he had ever heard in his life.

o   o   o

HOW WAS HE GOING TO TELL BETH? HE DECIDED HE WOULDN'T, HE COULDN'T. He decided he would call her, take the heat over being so late and tell her that Missy was going to stay at his place.

He was lucky. Beth was either on the phone or not home when he called, and he got her voice mail. He left what he thought was a fairly convincing message and, just before he hung up, added that he and Missy were heading out for ice cream (yes, he *knew* it was late), so if she wanted to call right back they wouldn't be there.

Who the hell was on his team? he wondered. He tapped the receiver against his hand and thought about it.

Tim Murdock was out of the question. Way too blue. Greg Ebersole would help him and keep his mouth shut about it, but Greg was probably two sheets to the wind by this time of night on a Saturday. Bobby Dietrich was far too ambitious to ask for this huge a favor. He would never be able to pay it off completely.

No. Paris knew he couldn't take a chance on another cop, not as long as this psycho had Missy.

He put a quarter in the phone and called one of the few people on the planet he felt he could trust.

o o o

"I HAVE TO TELL YOU HOW THRILLED I AM THAT YOU KNOW I HAVE ABSOLUTELY nothing to do on a Saturday night," Rita said. "I mean . . . that there was a *reasonable* chance that you could call me and I'd be here. Jeez. What a life."

"Actually—"

"I'm usually working on Saturday, you know. It's not like I can't get a date or anything. Most of the guys I know are aware of that particular . . . you know . . . *fact* about me and they don't . . . you know . . . *call* . . ."

Paris let her trail off. "*Actually* . . ." he began, making sure she was finished, "I figured that there was no *way* you'd be there. I was ninety-nine percent sure that I would have to leave a message." Paris hoped there was some degree of charm in his voice.

"Nice try, Jack. Thanks anyway," she said resignedly. "So what's up?"

"Well, I've got problems, Rita. Big-time. I could really use your help."

"On-the-phone help or in-person-and-I-might-have-to-leave-the-house help?"

"Leave-the-house help," Paris replied.

"Okay," Rita said. "But there's no way I'm doing this with dirty hair. Give me twenty minutes. I'm at 2018 Fenton Place."

o o o

RITA WEISINGER'S APARTMENT WAS TIDILY FUNKY. INEXPENSIVE BUT FUNCTIONAL furniture, with a few fairly interesting reproductions on the walls. On one wall was a bookshelf that held nearly as many romance paperbacks as Paris had found at Samantha Jaeger's flat. Rita may have had the same tastes in literature but, thankfully, was a lot more in touch with terra firma than the very spooky Miss Jaeger had turned out to be.

"Before you fill me in, is this a drink-mission or a coffee-mission?" Rita asked.

"Coffee," Paris said.

"Black, one sugar, right?"

"You're amazing."

"It's a gift," Rita said. She poured him a cup, placed it on the coffee table and sat down. As she listened, she ran a wide-tooth comb through her slightly damp hair. "I'm all eyes," she added with a wink.

Paris began the story by relating the events of October 21 of the previous year, the night he had gotten the call to investigate a suspicious death. A woman named Emily Reinhardt.

He ended the story by placing a photograph of Missy on the table in front of Rita. He had told her everything.

"Plus, I can't get ahold of Cyndy. I can't get ahold of Diana. I can't even get ahold of my ex-wife," Paris said. "What the hell is happening here, Rita?"

Rita put the comb down on the coffee table and stood up. She reached out her hand to Paris.

"Let's do it," she said.

39

EVERY LARGE CITY HAS ITS SEXUAL UNDERGROUND, ITS network of gender misfits, tomcats, he/shes, pedophiles and assorted other deviants—people who, for the most part, don't function very well in the sunlight. Paris was well aware of the fact that Cleveland, even with its high-profile escort services and suburban sex clubs, was essentially a blue-collar town. And that meant that while some of the games played may have lacked the imagination, the élan of a New York or Los Angeles club, they always seemed to make up for it with the sheer depth of their depravity.

Paris stopped at his apartment and changed clothes while Rita waited in the idling car. As expected, every drawer and closet had been turned inside out, every bit of research he had done on the Pharaoh case was gone. Manny was fine, but seemed to be wandering around in a fog, wondering why every smell in his entire world had been relocated.

The tape of *Annie Hall* was running on the VCR.

When Paris saw the loop of twine wrapped around the legs of one of the wooden chairs pulled up to his dining room table, his heart trip-hammered in his chest. Had Missy been tied up at his table? Would she, could she, ever get over something like that?

He sponged himself off quickly and put on one of Tommy's Armani blazers, a black woolen jacket with peaked lapels. He ran a comb through his hair.

Rita, who was young-looking for her age anyway, had understood completely what they had to do, as well as the very nature of the danger they were about to court. She wore a short red-and-white-checked gingham dress and a matching ribbon in her hair. She wore white anklets and flat shoes. Considering the inevitably subdued lighting in the places they were heading, she could easily pass for sixteen.

Because, Paris thought, if this psycho was planning a run around town, trying to pass a twelve-year-old girl off as eighteen, he knew there would be only so many places she could go. She had to be at one of only two or three kiddie bars around the city. As far as Paris knew, they were all within a few miles of Public Square, but they always kept moving, for obvious reasons.

Paris phoned Dave Drotos in the vice unit. Drotos told him that there were two bars of this type operating somewhere between the Forties and Sixties off St. Clair, but he wasn't sure where exactly. Drotos of course asked if he could help, but when Paris declined, he asked for no further details.

o   o   o

THEY STARTED WITH THE LEATHER CLUBS, A SERIES OF BLANK-DOORED WARE-houses around the Fifties off St. Clair and south toward Superior.

The first few bars were just getting rolling, with a handful of desperadoes staking out their territories for the evening. It wasn't yet eleven o'clock and the A-list players, it seemed, were still underground, still primping, still piercing something. Mostly they saw the younger hustlers, already pumped and primed and muscled up to the bar. The black-T-shirt boys.

There were places they visited where Paris got all the looks—no doubt, he figured, because of Tommy's thousand-dollar jacket, a dead man's blazer he had so cavalierly thrown over his shoulders—and there were those where Rita drew all the attention.

The fifth bar they hit was a place called Insatiable on East Fifty-seventh. It was mostly a transvestite hangout, but it had different specialty nights now and then, and it was more or less known to draw all sorts of people who could be loosely referred to as having an alternative lifestyle. The music was canned and loud and raunchy and seemed to Paris to be the same five notes repeated over and over and over again with somebody grunting in the background.

At least three times, as they cruised the huge room—sometimes with Rita on Paris's arm, sometimes with Rita out front, on point—Paris looked over at the U-shaped bar and caught a Hispanic kid watching his every move. The kid was maybe twenty-one or twenty-two, tough-posing, decked out in the standard barrio uniform. He sported a blue flannel shirt buttoned to the top, baggy chinos and a pencil mustache. Big arms.

Had they crossed paths before? Paris wondered. Had he busted him, rousted him? He couldn't remember, but the kid seemed to be burning a hole in him. And Rita.

Real Che complex, Paris thought. He kept one eye on him.

Rita ran into some friends, hairdressers and manicurists mostly, plus a couple of people she knew from work. One, Paris overheard, was a tall blond kid named Vasily. They all disappeared for a few minutes, running up the steps to the upper level with a vigor Paris envied.

He scanned the bar and caught one more glance from Che, who looked away immediately.

Paris decided that his proximity to the large, ululating speaker to his immediate left was merely compounding his already splitting headache. But before he could plot his course across the room to the stairs, he saw Rita weaving her way back through the crowd. She arrived nearly out of breath.

"My friend Robin from Mark Drury's Salon introduced me to this guy upstairs named Perko or Burko or something. Really freakin' scary-looking, let me tell you. Big head, nose like a busted anchor . . ." She was yelling into Paris's ear now, inches away. "Anyway, we start talking and I ask him about after-hours-type specialty places, and at first he resists me, then he dials in on the way I'm dressed and he starts babbling on and on about these kiddie bars. I think he liked me, Jack. Or it might have had something to do with the two Johnny Walker Reds I had to buy him."

"I'll take care of it," Paris said.

"Anyway, he said the woman to talk to is named Alida Witherspoon. He told me that she kind of holds court at this diner around the corner. The Good Egg or something."

"Yeah, I know the place," Paris said.

"He said she'd probably be there now."

"Who's she supposed to be?"

"Some kind of pervert social director, I think. I guess she knows all, sees all." Rita reached into her purse and retrieved a cigarette. She offered the pack to Paris but he resisted. "This Burko guy said that if someone as young as Melissa showed up at the kiddie bars— even if it was just a couple of hours ago, even if it was across town—Alida Witherspoon would know about it."

"Jesus Christ," Paris said. "Let's go."

o   o   o

ALIDA WITHERSPOON WAS A GOOD DEAL OF WOMAN, TAKING UP ABOUT TWO thirds of her side of the booth at the Good Egg, a twenty-four-hour greasy spoon on St. Clair and East Sixtieth. The way things were arranged around her, it was easy to tell that she fancied herself to be

Queen Alida, a subterranean sex maven of sorts. Paris thought that, at some point, she may have even been an attractive woman, but years of cheap food and pills and booze had taken their toll. Her whiskey-stippled face, broad shoulders and brittle, straw-colored hair gave her the appearance of one of those women who play the hardened prison guards in the "chained heat" movies.

As Paris and Rita approached her, Alida Witherspoon somehow reckoned that they had business with her and raised a solitary index finger, freezing them in their tracks. She looked up. Her eyes were small and wizened, the color of wet sand. She pointed at Rita and beckoned her forward with one long red-and-white-enameled fingernail. Paris slid into a booth facing them.

After a few moments, Rita reached into her bag and produced Melissa's picture, a photograph Paris had taken of his daughter in front of the Rainforest building at the MetroPark Zoo the previous summer. The two women talked for a while, and when they leaned forward to whisper, Paris knew they were digging in. He ordered coffee and something he theorized had passed for a plain doughnut at some point within the past seventy-two hours.

Ten minutes later, Alida Witherspoon extracted herself from the booth, with no small measure of difficulty, and began walking toward the front of the restaurant. Rita followed her. The big woman did not even glance at Paris as they passed his booth, but Rita leaned over and whispered, "Wait for me outside. I think she has something for us."

Paris waited until they were in the ladies' room. He stood up, dropped a five-dollar bill on the counter and—considering the larcenous motif to the tableau of shady citizens populating the restaurant—made sure the waitress saw him do it. He walked out the door, hung a quick left, turned his collar to the night and marched a few feet up the alley. He stamped his feet to the cold, then felt for his pager for what had to be the three-hundredth time in the last hour or so.

o   o   o

JACK PARIS STOOD IN THE DARKNESS, LEANED AGAINST THE MOSSY BRICK WALL and listened to the night sounds: the traffic on St. Clair, the heavy bass of a rap song coming from somewhere above him and to his left, a parking lot argument under way within a block or two.

Missy, he thought.

Please God.

No.

He decided he would pray, formally, the first time in years, the first time since Melissa was born. He would pray with all the "thous" and "thees" intact, like a Catholic, like he was raised. He would make his deal with God and agree to whatever terms were necessary in a situation like this.

He began with Hail Marys as he walked around the alley for warmth.

o   o   o

Rita had been gone for nearly twenty minutes and Paris was beginning to worry. What had he gotten her into? Sure she was pretty damned savvy for her age, but he was using her to bait a psychopath. What had he been thinking?

Melissa, is what he'd been thinking.

He peeked back into the Good Egg, but neither Rita nor the corpulent Ms. Witherspoon was anywhere to be seen. He walked to the far end of the alleyway and found a tiny, pitted asphalt-and-gravel parking lot stashed between the buildings. There were five or six cars. One of them, a white BMW, looked like the car that had picked up Andrea Heller at Whitney's.

The car, he now knew, that had taken her to her death.

Paris moved quickly across the lot and put his ear to the trunk. He heard nothing. He looked onto the passenger seat. It was empty. He looked into the back seat. There was a pile of papers, balanced somewhat precariously on the edge of the seat. On top was a copy of the *Free Times,* Cleveland's alternative-press newspaper. Beneath it Paris could see junk mail: catalogs, grocery store fliers, insurance company come-ons. He could also see the edge of a huge envelope, a clearinghouse sweepstakes package. The address was in gigantic letters, but all he could read was the very end of the top line. The letter *t* but no more. The person's last name on the big beige envelope from Ed McMahon ended in a *t.*

Paris began to rock the left rear fender, jostling the papers and the envelopes around, sliding them toward the edge of the seat, revealing the address bit by bit. After a few moments, he bounced the fender a little too hard, and the pile of papers fell, facedown, onto the floor. "God*damnit*," he said in a loud whisper. "Why does it—"

A door opened behind him.

A shrieking, rusty hinge, just a few feet away.

Paris spun around quickly, his hand on his weapon, but the shadows were upon him in an instant.

It was Che. And a big friend.

The two sandwiched him with such exactness, such mechanical ease that it appeared they knew he was going to be standing in that precise spot at that precise moment in history and they were just making their appointed rounds. Natural-born predators. The kid flashed a knife, and before Paris could react, the blade was at his stomach.

"What d'fuck you *doin'* here, man?" the kid said, bringing his wine-sour breath within inches of Paris's face. "You way d'fuck outside Pepper Pike, eh?"

"What do you want?" Paris asked.

"*I* do the talking, homes."

"I'm a cop."

"*Hah!* I don't give a fuck if you eff-bee-eye," Che said. "What . . . like . . . that's supposed to *mean* something to me, man? I'm supposed to be scared? Makes me wanna cut you even more."

His partner, who wore a red bandanna and black wraparound sunglasses, found immense humor in the sentiment.

"So wutchoo lookin' for, man? Maybe I can help, you know? You lookin' for black girls? Is that wutchoo doin' down here? Or maybe boys, eh? You like boys, man?"

The kid rubbed his knee against Paris's leg. He licked his lips.

"Or maybe you lookin' for a baby," he continued. "Maybe you like them *real* young, eh *padrone?*"

More laughter from Sunglasses.

"B'cause that girl you was with looked pretty young for you, man," the kid said, shaking a finger at Paris in an accusatory manner. "That your daughter?"

"No . . ."

"Niece?"

Paris just glared at him.

"So . . . where she at right now, man? I got somethin' for her myself, I think." Che reached down to his crotch and gave it a quick squeeze. "She look *good.*"

"She went home," Paris said wistfully, watching a black-and-white patrol car cruise past the other end of the alley.

"I don't think so. I think she talkin' to Alida, you know? I think you all gonna go somewhere and party and me and my homeboy Ottavio are gonna be left out. We don't like that, man."

"Just take the money," Paris said. "I got two, three hundred dollars on me. It's yours."

"I don't need your per*mission,* motherfucker." Che leaned forward, putting a slight pressure on the knife tip. Paris could feel the trickle of blood over his stomach. He could smell the acrid stench of crack smoke in the kid's hair, his clothing. "Besides . . . I'm gonna take your money, your gun *and* your fuckin' shield. Wutchoo think of that? How's it gonna look at the station house . . . a gang-banger takin' your *balls* . . ."

"Look . . ." Paris began. "I'm on the job, man. We're stinging this place around the corner and there's maybe ten, twelve cops right around this area somewhere. Maybe there's one on the rooftop right above us, right now, dialing you into the crosshairs of his rifle. Do yourself a favor. Take the money and run or you're going to be looking up some big fucking barrels in about twenty sec—"

From over his left shoulder, Paris saw the nose of a rusted .45 automatic suddenly, silently appear. The weapon looked to be around World War II issue, and it was pointed directly at the kid's head. Then he heard the cold, measured voice of a man who had probably scared the crap out of a *hell* of a lot of people in his life. A voice Paris found vaguely familiar.

"Get outta here, shitbag," the voice said. "Take your boyfriend with you."

Paris didn't move. Che eased the pressure on the knife, but didn't give any indication that he was getting ready to release him. The kid's eyes flicked between them rapidly, calculating the odds, the percentages, trying to gauge the availability of his own crack-slowed reflexes.

"Looks like we got us a Messican stalemate here, eh, homes?" Che said with a nervous laugh. "Looks like we got us a wash . . ."

"We don't have shit," said the voice. "But I *will* tell you what happens next. I count to three, pull the trigger and detach you from your fucking head."

The kid got the message, withdrew the knife slowly and began to back down the alley, his hands out to his sides, his partner behind him. They both stared, unblinkingly, over Paris's left shoulder.

"Hold it," Paris said, still not turning around.

The kid stopped.

"You got any cigarettes on you?"

Che looked astonished. "What?"

"Did I stutter or something?" Paris asked.

"You shakin' *me* down now?"

"Yeah, I guess I am," Paris said. "Drop down."

"I don't give you *shit,* motherfucker."

Paris heard the hammer being pulled back on the .45. The sound seemed to echo between the buildings before disappearing into the clear black sky.

As if suddenly activated by electricity, the kid mechanically reached into his shirt pocket and tossed a full pack of Newports and a hot-pink Bic mini-lighter through the air. They landed at Paris's feet.

"Menthol?" Paris asked, just to rub in the humiliation.

"You real *lucky,* man," Che said, backing up again, trying to wrest a modicum of machismo from this defeat. He spit on the ground directly in front of him. "Next time we meet, it's gonna be a l'il dif'rent, you know? Next *time,* homes . . ." The kid flashed a gang hand signal.

"Yeah . . . and next time I pay your sister *fifty* cents for a blow job," came the voice from over Paris's shoulder. "Now, get the fuck outta here, *homes.*"

Paris remained still until the two disadvantaged youths had turned the corner onto St. Clair and disappeared. He spun around to meet his savior, his knight in shining armor, his cavalry, only to find that it wasn't John Wayne or Norman Schwarzkopf or Dirty Harry after all.

It was Nick Raposo.

o   o   o

"ONE MORE TIME, NICK," PARIS SAID, LIGHTING A CIGARETTE.

"Like I told you, I've been following you around, on and off, for three days," Nick said. "Almost lost you again tonight, though. Over at Fenton Place."

"You followed me last night, too?"

"Yep. 'Cept last night I lost you around South Russell or Bainbridge somewhere. Then I went home. I don't think I'm cut out for this private eye shit."

"How'd you get so good at sneaking up on people?" Paris asked, feeling some measure of relief that Nick didn't see him do the Peeping Tom bit at the Motel Riverview. He didn't need an eyewitness putting him at the scene. The fact that Nick Raposo knew he was in Bainbridge at all that night—combined with the Polaroid of him at the Motel Riverview with a razor in his hand—would probably burn him to the ground one day anyway.

"Eighteen months in Korea. Saw more than my share at Inchon."

Paris was impressed. He went silent for a few beats, the realization that he had very nearly been stabbed to death in an alleyway near Sixtieth and St. Clair starting to sink in. He finally asked the question, although he had a pretty good idea what the answer would be. "Why are you doing this, Nick?"

Nick Raposo shuffled his feet for a few moments, formulating his plea. "I know you gotta go by the book, Jack. I respect that. But the point is, *I don't,* see? I mean . . . you find the asshole who framed Tommy, you point to him, go home, and I fuck him up. Boom, boom, boom. Done."

"I can't let you do it, though, Nick." He placed his hand on Nick's thick shoulder. "Jesus, man, there isn't anything out here for you. Let me take care of things. Go home and I'll call you, I swear."

Just then Rita came around the corner with a girl who looked to be about fifteen. The girl had on very high heels and a green sequined dress that was far too tight, even for her thin, wiry frame. Her blond hair was set in pigtails. She had her arms crossed over her chest and she was shivering in the cold.

Nick looked at Paris, raised his eyebrows, and Paris knew then that he would have to explain everything, and that Nick Raposo was going to be in this for the duration.

"This is the guy I was telling you about," Rita said. "Tell him what you told me."

"*Could* be her," the girl said.

This close, Paris could tell that the girl was a little older than he had originally thought. She looked to be around eighteen or so.

"I'm not sure," she continued. "I mean, she looks like a little *girl* in this picture you have."

"She *is* a little girl," Paris said.

"Right. Whatever." The girl snapped her gum twice. "Anyway . . . she was with this woman, real looker, late twenties, early thirties maybe. Weird setup if you ask me."

"When did you see her?" Paris asked.

"Twenty minutes ago."

"Where?"

"Up the street," the girl said, looking at Paris's hands to see if he was going to make a move to fork over a ten or a twenty for the information. When she realized that the move was not forthcoming, she sighed and spilled it anyway. "Place called the Swing Set. It's a kiddie bar. Go right on St. Clair and down a block. Brick building with a black door. Door's got a silver rose in the upper right-hand corner. The guy's name is Sandy. Tell him Angel sent you over."

"Thanks, Angel," Paris said, the name of the kiddie bar immediately triggering a recollection.

The Swing Set.

Look in the backyard. Next to the sandbox, the woman on the phone had said. The woman with the distorted voice.

"You're not *cops,* are you?" Angel asked.

"Not tonight," Paris said, and tossed her the twenty she had earned.

o   o   o

SANDY WAS HUGE, STANDING ABOUT SIX SIX, WEIGHING AT LEAST TWO-EIGHTY; bald and black and full of attitude for old white fucks who like to get drunk and play with little girls, or women who dress like little girls. Sandy knew why they all came—welders, politicians, bankers, lawyers, cooks, teachers, businessmen of all sorts. The guy who owns the Quik Print franchise up the street. The guy who drives your children around in the morning. The guy who stands around the mall, outside the Merry-Go-Round store, sunglasses so casually deployed, his hands in his pockets.

They all come to hit the kiddie club jackpot.

But Sandy St. Cyr also knew who was in charge. He looked at Paris and Nick, then, very carefully, very thoroughly, at Rita. He smirked and shook his head, as if he'd seen the act a thousand times before. "Fifty dollars," Sandy said solemnly, batting his long, mascara-caked eyelashes. "Each."

He stared at Paris, who returned his gaze with a cool vengeance, but still reached into his pocket for the cash. Paris felt Nick idling roughly behind him, itching to get into it. He leaned back slightly and Nick got the message.

"Downstairs, to the right, gentlemen," Sandy said, standing out of the way, placing the money in his pocket. "And *lady*." He reached down, lifted the ruffled edge of Rita's dress and ran his hand over her thigh as she passed him, all the while staring Paris down, defying him to react.

Instead, Rita reacted for both of them, swinging around in one fluid motion, positioning a small, razor-sharp hunting knife between the man's legs. Sandy pulled his hand away very slowly. "Keep your fucking hands to yourself, Chewbacca," Rita said with the supreme confidence of a Mafia hit man. "Unless you want to sing with the Vienna Boys' Choir. You hear me?"

Incredibly, the moment Rita put the knife back into her purse, Sandy broke out laughing and stamping his feet, clearly enjoying this start to another Saturday night at the Swing Set on St. Clair.

4 0

THE VOLUME OF THE MUSIC SEEMED TO INCREASE GEO-metrically as they descended the steps to the Swing Set. Oddly enough, it had been barely audible in the vestibule where Sandy had given them such a big, warm, friendly greeting.

About halfway down the stairs, the bass line became thunderous and the drums seemed to shake the sparsely plastered walls around them, as Rita informed Paris that she thought she might recognize the mix.

"The what?" Paris asked, shouting to be heard.

"The mix," Rita said, yelling into his ear. "All the best deejays have a certain style, a certain way they mix the songs together. A lot of them sample other people's stuff, make their own house music."

"Okay . . ."

"I know most of the deejays around town. This sounds like it could be this guy Faustino, old friend of mine. Real twisto, though."

"Probably explains what he's doing here," Paris said.

"He's probably not real big on cops. In fact, I would almost guarantee it, seeing as how he's a Brazilian illegal," Rita said. "He likes *me,* though. If it turns out that it *is* him, let me handle it, okay?"

"Sure," Paris said, realizing that he had made the absolute right choice in trusting Rita Weisinger.

"I don't want to spook him . . ."

"Okay, Rita."

"Do you think he might help us?" Nick asked, looking more and more uncomfortable by the step, but the volume of the music had gotten to the point where it just made more sense for Rita to shrug her shoulders.

Paris placed his pager on the setting for vibration alarm, put it in his shirt pocket and opened the door to the Swing Set.

And although he didn't realize it, was simply not prepared to absorb what he encountered, the first person he saw was Melissa.

o   o   o

JACK PARIS HAD WORKED WITHIN THE CLEVELAND POLICE DEPARTMENT'S VICE UNIT a dozen years earlier. He had handled any number of cases ranging from prostitution stings to busting up child pornography distribution to going on shared duty and shutting down swingers' clubs in the Heights. He had heard about kiddie bars—after-hours, unlicensed establishments whose main attraction was their promise of girls and women who ranged in age from eighteen to their mid-twenties but could still pass for young teenagers. Although he'd never busted one, he knew enough to know that any night of the week, if you flipped the lights on in any of these clubs, you'd find a half-dozen girls under the age of eighteen, and always one or two that were as young as twelve or thirteen.

But when Jack Paris looked into his daughter's face for that brief, smoke-hazed instant—her hair piled so high on her head, her lips painted a deep red, her eyes lost behind a pair of huge, heart-shaped sunglasses—he hadn't known her. He had seen her for a fleeting moment, then someone had stepped between them and blocked his view.

Weeks later he would realize that had he been a little bit better at his job, at his duty as a father, had he recognized *his own daughter* at that moment, the nightmare of what happened next might have been avoided.

o   o   o

THE SWING SET WAS A LARGE, SQUARE ROOM, LOW-CEILINGED. THE SMOKE seemed to hang halfway to the floor like a thin blue parachute. The walls were covered with a cheap paneling that boasted decor that was supposed to resemble a teenaged girl's bedroom: hastily hung posters of teen idols and fuzzy, big-eyed kittens that seemed, Paris noticed, to cover a number of different musical eras. There were two or three posters of the New Kids on the Block. One of Bobby Brown. A few of Marky Mark. But there were also posters of the Stray Cats and one, incredibly, of Shaun Cassidy. There were even a few brightly ballooned squares devoted to Ziggy and the Care Bears.

The handful of Swing Set waitresses were all dressed like little girls too. One, a petite, athletic-looking brunette, wore a very short plaid skirt, white cardigan and saddle shoes. Another was dressed like a junior high school cheerleader. Yet another like a Campfire Girl.

"I can't believe that they do exactly what I do for a living," Rita said. "I mean . . . I could never work in a place like this. How do they . . ." She just shook her head and let her thoughts drift into the loud music.

Paris searched the dance floor. There were eight or ten couples, mostly fat and balding white men, wild-eyed, dancing with girls and women whose outfits were alive with pigtails and barrettes and hair ribbons and knee socks.

One of the Swing Set denizens—an obese, acne-scarred kid about twenty-five or so—asked Rita to dance. She pointed to Paris and Nick, and the kid decided, at least for the time being, not to be contentious about it. Paris was relieved. After Che and his pal, he was ready to shoot the first asshole that looked at him wrong.

And while there was no denying that Jack Paris had encountered more than his fair share of degenerates in his life, and that Rita Weisinger, even for her short years, had seen plenty of life's less than savory underside, nothing in his experience had prepared Nick Raposo for the Swing Set. He looked sucker-punched to Paris, drained, like a man on the verge of imploding with disgust.

"I'm going to cruise," Rita said.

"All right," Paris said. "Five minutes max, right here."

"You got it. If something comes up, I'll buzz you." She tapped her purse and Paris gave her a quick thumbs-up, in lieu of shouting at the top of his lungs.

Rita slid off her stool, took two steps and was immediately swallowed by the crowd.

"Can I get you something, Daddy?"

Nick and Paris turned and saw that it was a barmaid, the one in the white cardigan. This close, Paris could see that she was in her early twenties. Nick looked at Paris, then back at the waitress. "Let me ask you something," Nick said. "Do your parents know that you—"

"We're fine for right now," Paris said, clamping an iron hand onto Nick's shoulder. "We'll give you a shout if we need anything."

"There's a two-drink minimum, you know," she said. "Drinks are ten bucks. Each."

Paris reached into his pocket and pulled out his dwindling roll. He dropped three twenties onto the barmaid's tray. "That should cover the three of us, right?"

The girl looked at her tray, then back at Paris, with eyes like a lost fawn. It was easy to see how, in that outfit and with the baby browns, she'd clean up. Paris looked at the right side of her neck and saw that she had a small rose tattoo there.

He dropped another twenty on the tray and the barmaid smiled at him.

"Name's Gwen," she said. "Call me when you need me. *Daddy.*"

She turned and walked the length of the bar as the word "daddy," as it was meant at that moment, dropped another rock into Paris's roiling stomach.

41

SAILA HAD SEEN JACK PARIS IMMEDIATELY. MELISSA HAD not.

Saila knew that she couldn't take the chance of bringing Melissa into the Swing Set in any type of restraint—a girl Melissa's age was going to draw all the attention in the place anyway—so she had simply informed the young lady that her father would suffer a *most* horrible death if she didn't do *precisely* as she was told.

So far, she had.

The second she saw Paris, Saila grabbed Melissa by the wrist and said, "We're going to the bathroom, little Lois. Spruce you up some. Let's go."

She stood Melissa up, took her by the arm and wove her way to the rest room.

The door was marked with a paper cutout of Dorothy from *The Wizard of Oz*.

4 2

RITA, HAVING BEEN ALL BUT MOBBED BY EVERY MAN IN the bar, had walked quickly, purposefully, across the room, seeking some sort of refuge.

Within minutes, she found the ladies' room.

Dorothy in Oz, she thought with amusement as she pushed open the door. Yeah, *this* place is over the friggin' rainbow all right.

○   ○   ○

THE BATHROOM WAS FILTHY AND DANK, FULL OF GRAFFITI, BUT IT HAD THREE stalls and three large mirrors with lightbulbs arranged around them.

Surprisingly, the room was empty.

Rita—relieved to be alone, at least for the moment—ran her fingers through her hair, reached into her purse and retrieved what was, to her dismay, her last cigarette. She lit it and turned around, resting up against the sink, drawing deeply.

She thought she had seen it all in her day, but, she had to admit, this place definitely took it. She had absolutely no idea that there were clubs like this in Cleveland. Were some of the girls out there really as young as Jack's daughter? She decided that she would finish her cigarette—she was quitting anyway, it was good that it was the last one in the pack—find the deejay booth, talk to Faustino; then she would get back to the bar and Nick and Jack as fast as her five-foot-two frame could carry her. She would—

Suddenly she realized she was not alone.

There was someone in the last stall on the right.

Someone whispering.

Someone . . . *crying?*

Rita cocked her head to the sound, then quickly, noiselessly, stepped into the middle stall and latched the door. She could tell that it was a woman talking in the next stall now, but the voice was muffled, as if her hand was cupped around her mouth. Rita glanced down and saw that the woman was in a crouched position, her black high-heeled shoe curling under the partition that separated them. The woman also wore a thin ankle bracelet from which dangled a tiny pendant: a small silver cat with a solitary emerald eye.

○   ○   ○

RITA FINGERED THE EDGE OF THE TWO-WAY RADIO. PARIS HAD SHOWN HER THE basics of the two-way on the way into town, and having always been a quick study on virtually everything, she remembered to turn it off before walking into the ladies' room. The crackle of an incoming transmission would have been loud as hell in the confines of the bathroom.

She took a deep breath, opened the stall door and stepped back to the mirrors.

Moments later, the door to the last stall opened. The woman who sidled up next to Rita Weisinger was absolutely stunning. Perfect skin, high cheekbones. A beauty mark. Rita would have killed for the woman's lower lip and half her lashes.

"Hi," Rita said, looking at the woman in the mirror.

The woman met her gaze. Her eyes were a deep, penetrating aquamarine. "Hi," she answered. Then she said, "You look very nice. Like a little girl."

"Thanks," Rita answered, her knees betraying the serenity in her voice. "Thanks very much."

"How old are you really? If you don't mind my asking, that is."

Rita Weisinger, already accustomed to creative accounting when it came to calculating her age, even at twenty-four, said: "I'm . . . uh . . . nineteen."

"You look even younger."

"Thank you."

Rita opened her purse and retrieved her brush, being careful not to reveal the black and chrome edge of the two-way radio. She glanced over her shoulder briefly, but the door to the stall from which the woman had emerged was closed. She could not see inside and there were no feet visible under the door.

"You're not here by yourself, certainly," the woman said as she began to gloss her lips.

Rita sensed a dangerous, sexual energy around this woman.

"Actually I am," Rita replied. "I'm waiting for a friend."

"Is that right?" the woman said, pausing, clearly disbelieving her. "Sandy doesn't generally let in unescorted ladies who are . . . how shall I put this . . . *independent* accounts."

"Oh . . . uh . . . Sandy and I go way back, though," Rita replied shakily, certain that the waver in her voice was obvious to this woman. "Way back."

"Really . . ." the woman said, turning to face her fully. "Way back to where?" She stepped closer. "And I mean *exactly* where."

"Well I—"

"Don't lie to me," the woman said, nearly whispering now. "If you lie to me, I'll hurt you."

Rita took a step backward, but remained silent.

"Because I *know* who you are," the woman continued, moving forward. "You're the little bitch from the Radisson. The barmaid with the big fucking mouth."

Rita's heart sank. She could feel the moment slipping away. She reached quickly for her purse but, in her haste, she knocked it over, spilling everything into the sink.

o   o   o

PARIS BARELY HEARD THE CRACKLE OF THE TWO-WAY RADIO THAT SIGNIFIED that someone was on the channel. He ducked into a hallway and put the speaker to his ear, but Faustino Nava's music was still deafening.

He signaled to Nick Raposo and the two of them bulled their way to the front of the club and up the steps. Sandy, who was speaking to a tall Asian woman, didn't give them a second look. They stepped into the night and Paris brought the radio to his ear. It sounded weak, feeble, as if the batteries were winding down.

"Rita," Paris said, whispering into the radio. "Rita, what's up?"

Paris heard the channel open and close. Then . . . nothing.

"Rita . . ."

A short blast of static.

"Rita . . . can you hear me?" Paris asked.

Then: "Jag . . . Jag . . . *goneer.*"

"What?"

". . . *yov goneer* . . ."

Nick and Paris exchanged a glance and a quick shrug of their shoulders.

"Say again, Rita,"

Silence.

"Where are you?" Paris asked.

Another burst of static, then: ". . . dun *steers* . . ."

"What?"

"Wade . . . minna . . ."

The radio fell silent, save for a thin veneer of electronic noise.

Paris began to pace quickly, walking off the twenty-four steps necessary to traverse the frontage of the four-story brick building that housed the Swing Set. He could hear the music now, layered into the traffic noise from Superior Avenue, a few blocks away.

"Come *on,* come *on,* come *on . . .*" Paris said, tapping the abbreviated antenna against his thigh. Nick leaned against the building, his hands in his pockets, his eyes on the sidewalk, waiting.

Then it came. Clear as a bell.

"Meet me out front. I have Melissa. I've got her. Everything's okay . . ."

Paris hit the button and positioned his mouth an inch from the microphone. "You've *got* her?"

"I've got her. She's fine." The words were whispered now. "Meet me out front of the Swing Set."

Nick and Paris exchanged a quick, but still cautious, high five, and walked over to the entrance. Paris put the radio into his pocket and stepped back into the vestibule, freezing Big Sandy to his stool with a flash of his badge. He waited for Rita and Melissa to come around the corner at the bottom of the stairs.

Nick stood out front.

o　　o　　o

MINUTES LATER, AS PARIS RAN DOWN ST. CLAIR AVENUE AT FULL SPEED, TOward the alley next to the Good Egg, two thoughts came to him like a crystalline bullet between the eyes.

One: There hadn't been any music in the background. Whoever had talked to him on the radio could not possibly have been *inside* the Swing Set.

Two: *Saila* was *Alias* backward. It had been there the whole time, taunting him, a rookie's ruse dressed up like a clue.

Saila. Only one type of person would be that fucking bold.

o　　o　　o

NICK RAPOSO, LAGGING WELL BEHIND PARIS, WENT LEFT, UP EAST SIXTIETH Street. He turned the corner and cut across the vacant lot, where he found a dark alcove set into the building that overlooked the alley, a perfect vantage point from which he could see the parking lot and the BMW.

He caught his breath and hunkered down in the darkness.

Moments later, the darkness put a police-issue 9mm handgun to his head.

4 3 RITA WEISINGER HAD ALWAYS PRIDED HERSELF ON HER ability to adapt to any situation. You date a country boy, you wear your Levi's and chambray shirts. You date a doctor, it's Anne Klein and pearls. Easy. Snow tires, reversible belts, wet-dry vacuum cleaners, she was good at it.

And she had a mouth. She could *talk*. Hers was the highest-grossing hotel bar in the state for one reason and one reason only. Rita Weisinger could schmooze the gilt off a gold card.

But when the woman saw the cop-issue two-way radio lying in the sink, next to the Buck knife, all of Rita's systems had shut down. She found herself in a phone booth with a monster and there was nothing she could do or say.

And God knows she tried.

With a force Rita thought reserved only for linebackers and dockworkers, the woman lifted her high into the air and threw her, head first, into the middle stall. She hit the door hard and it flew open with enough force to smash into the partition, shattering its lock. Rita tried to get up but the room was spinning out of control now, the floor was slick with urine. By the time she was able to right herself, the woman had put her spiked heel gently up against Rita's chest and thudded her back down to the floor.

The last thing Rita saw, before she fell unconscious, was the up-side-down face of Melissa Adelaide Paris, staring out from under the partition, surrounded by a cartoon world of stars.

44

SAILA HAD JUST GOTTEN HER KEY INTO THE BMW'S door. Her other hand held Melissa firmly by the wrist. They had both heard Paris's footsteps in the alley before they actually saw him, but it was enough time for Saila to walk Melissa to the center of the parking lot and put the barrel of the .25 semi-automatic pistol to the girl's temple.

Melissa closed her eyes and waited for the pain.

4 5

WHEN PARIS SAW THE TWO OF THEM—PERFECTLY POSED, oddly familiar statuary under the lone streetlamp—he pulled up in his tracks and held his hands out to his sides.

He was twenty-five feet away.

"Hello, detective," Cyndy said. "Good work."

"Cyndy, please . . ."

"Pull it out, left hand, and drop it," Cyndy said calmly, as if by rote. "You know the drill, Jack. Nice and easy."

"Are you okay, Missy?" His daughter remained silent, but Paris could see in her eyes that she had not been harmed. If anything, at that moment, she looked simply exhausted. She wore a short black dress and earrings in the shape of red cherries.

"*Now*, detective."

"Okay, Cyndy, okay. Just . . . Jesus . . . just be careful." Paris reached gingerly inside his jacket and extracted his Colt with two fingers. He dropped the gun to the ground and kicked it along the asphalt, under the green Buick parked next to Cyndy's BMW.

Cyndy eased the pressure of the gun to Melissa's head.

"Talk to me, Cyndy . . ."

She raised her nose to the air. "What do you want me to say?"

"I want to know how we get out of this with no one getting hurt."

Cyndy firmed her grip on Melissa. "What do you have for me?"

"What do you want, Cyndy? My hand to God, if I can get it, I go get it right now and I lay it at your feet. Tell me."

"You know what I want. Everything you have on Pharaoh."

"You've got it all, Cyndy. I mean . . . think about it . . . without those Polaroids, they're never going to reopen the case." Paris tried to remember something, anything, from his three hours of hostage-negotiation training. Of course, it was never supposed to be your own daughter. "The house on Tarleton Street is history. Everything *in* it is history. You get to keep the straight razor with my prints on it. You can set me up three years from now if you feel like it. What more do you want?"

Cyndy looked from Melissa to Paris, then back at the car, calculating the odds. "*She's* not going to shut up about this," Cyndy said, nodding toward the trunk of the car. "Neither is little Lois here." She squeezed Melissa once and began moving her finger, absently, *sensually,* up and down the curve of the trigger.

"Let me handle it," Paris said, the motion not lost on him. His experience was that it meant that the shooter was getting ready to shoot. "Diana'll be pissed off, sure. But I'll take care of it. If you didn't hurt her, she won't press charges. I promise."

Cyndy laughed darkly. "You don't know the first thing about women, Jack. If I gave her a fucking *runner* she's going to press charges. Give me some credit here."

Then came a sound, a steel-on-steel sound, echoing from an alcove immediately to Paris's left. Although the alcove was engulfed in darkness, Paris figured it was Nick Raposo, trying, and failing, to arrive quietly at the scene. The sound instantly drew Cyndy's attention, causing her to relax her grip, her guard, for the briefest of moments.

But the moment was long enough.

Melissa, sensing the opportunity, shifted her weight, lifted her right foot high into the air and brought it down hard on the top of Cyndy's right foot.

"*Heee-yah!*" Melissa shouted.

"*No!*" Paris screamed. "*Missy . . . God . . . no!*"

Melissa turned and ran toward her father as fast as she could.

o o o

IN THAT MOMENT, IN THAT BRIEF INSTANT THAT JACK PARIS SAW HIS DAUGHTER running toward him—her long hair swirling fiercely about her face and neck and shoulders—he noticed, with curiosity, that she had Beth's face. Beth's wise, motherly, made-up, adult face on Melissa's gangling figure, the figure of a still-growing girl, a girl destined to become a tall, graceful woman.

But Paris also knew, in that moment, in his shattering heart, that everything he had ever feared for his daughter was happening all at once: crib death, undertow, scarlet fever, cocaine, the pervert in the car parked near the school.

In that moment, Jack Paris knew that his daughter had lived her whole life.

And that he had killed her.

o o o

IN THAT MOMENT, IN THAT BRIEF INSTANT, CYNDY TAGGART HESITATED, HER right instep afire, her two lives colliding in a mélange of procedure and pain and sexual disgrace. Her arms felt leaden and weak, her body seemed loath to respond to her immediate demands.

Then, just as quickly, she recoiled and sprang.

She raised her weapon into the air, took careful aim at the center of Melissa's back and pulled the trigger.

o   o   o

IN THAT MOMENT, IN THAT BRIEF INSTANT THAT JACK PARIS SAW A MAD-EYED woman fire a small handgun at his daughter, a much larger 9mm bullet, fired from the alcove, tore into the right side of Cyndy Taggart's chest, then exited her shoulder blade in a brief but furious gush of red and white and gray tissue. The bullet clanked against the steel fender of a GMC truck halfway across the parking lot, then skittered onto the asphalt.

Sergeant Cynthia Jean Taggart stood for a few moments, rusted in time, poised to make one final appeal, then followed the warm lead slug to the frozen ground.

4 6

MELISSA SCREAMED ONCE AND STUMBLED FORWARD THE last few steps, slamming into her father's chest. Paris scooped her into his arms, turned on his heels and sprinted back down the alley, head down, not knowing for certain who had fired the other shot or where it had come from, not knowing if Missy had been hit. He felt along his daughter's back as they ran, confused by the dampness he found there, horrified at the possibilities it raised, possibilities that doubled his fear with every labored stride.

They rounded the corner and burst into the shocking fluorescent brightness of the Good Egg Restaurant. Paris ran the length of the black and white diner and lifted Melissa into the last booth, far away from the windows. He shielded her from the street.

"Are you okay, baby?" Paris dropped to his knees and frantically checked her back, her arms, her legs, her face, hoping, *praying,* that his fingers would not come back coated with red. *"Did she hurt you, baby?"*

"No, Daddy," Melissa said, shivering now, nearing her ballast of tears. "I-I'm okay."

"I'm so sorry, baby . . ." Paris held her tightly. "I'm so sorry . . ."

He pulled back and took another long, careful inventory of Melissa's well-being. Cyndy had missed her completely, it appeared. Paris grabbed a napkin and began dabbing Melissa's tears, wincing, finally, at the thick makeup that was beginning to streak down his daughter's impossibly young, impossibly innocent face.

"I'll take it off, Daddy," Melissa said with a twisted half-smile. "I'll take it off . . ."

It was a statement made in the precise, measured tone of voice that they both knew Melissa reserved for those times when she had done something extremely bullheaded or stupid. Like when she was four and filled in the white spots of the neighbor's Border collie one day with a can of black spray paint. Or the time she had, in the course of her potty training, gotten away from her mother, only to be found ten minutes later, dutifully sitting on a toilet in the middle of a display at Sears.

Paris, having caught his breath, touched his daughter's face one more time, arose and turned back to the diner. The restaurant's five or six patrons were watching his every move in a state of near-catatonic silence, their sandwiches and eggs and Danish pastries poised halfway to their mouths. He asked of them all: "Who's the owner?"

A pair of elderly rock-and-rollers in studded denim, sitting at the counter, pointed to a man restocking a potato chip rack near the front. Paris vaulted the counter and approached him.

"What's your name?" Paris asked, flashing his shield.

"Akim," the man said, his hands locked around five or six bags of chips each, his huge brown eyes nearly vibrating with alarm. He had heard the shots in the alley and now this man had run into his place of business with a little girl made up to look like a harlot. And a badge. What was coming *next?*

"This is your place?" Paris asked.

The man nodded, the dryness in his mouth stealing his speech.

"Akim . . . listen to me," Paris said. He put his hand onto the shoulder of the short, solid man in the greasy blue apron, and explained himself quietly, calmly. "I'm a police officer, and this is my daughter." Paris gestured to the last booth at the back of the restaurant where Melissa sat, so small and so garishly adorned. Then he gestured toward the alley. "This thing may not be over out here, I'm afraid. I have to leave for a while and I want her to stay right in that booth. I'm going to leave her in your care. Let *nothing* happen to her. Do you understand me?"

Akim Shalhoub had dealt with many police officers—first in Beirut, then in New York City, and now at the Good Egg in Cleveland—and he knew exactly what this particular brand of *Do you understand me?* meant. He dropped the chips.

"She will be safe," Akim said. He was a family man too. He looked sharply into the back room, snapped his fingers twice and shouted something in Arabic. Almost immediately his wife appeared, a stout, broad-shouldered woman of fifty who plopped down next to Melissa and thrust her big legs threateningly into the aisle.

Paris stopped at the front door and turned back to Akim Shalhoub. "Call nine-one-one. Tell them shots were fired in this alley. Tell them a woman has been shot. Tell them to send an ambulance."

Akim snapped his fingers, sending his oldest son scurrying to the phone next to the register.

Paris left the restaurant and stepped, haltingly, weaponless, into the blackness of the alley.

The whole transaction had taken less than two minutes, yet Paris felt years older.

47 CYNDY HAD LOST A LOT OF BLOOD. HER BODY HAD THE twisted, tangled look of someone just pulled from a hellacious high-speed crash. Her face bore a milk-blue pallor.

Paris had come around the corner and immediately found his Colt Python where he had kicked it. He checked the cylinder and found that it was still fully loaded. He had called Nick's name a few times, but, Paris figured, after firing the shot that dropped Cyndy, Nick had probably come looking for him.

Paris simply followed the trail of blood around the green Buick parked next to Cyndy's car. When he skirted the trunk, and saw Cyndy's condition, his heart nearly went out to her.

Nearly.

Then he remembered Eleanor Burchfield's throat.

Cyndy was propped against the rear fender of the BMW. From the right side of her chest grew a short, purplish sprout of viscera, but she was alive, and she had the barrel of her pistol pressed tightly against the car's gas tank.

o   o   o

"DON'T COME ANY CLOSER, JACK," CYNDY SAID. "GOT YOUR GIRLFRIEND IN the trunk, see . . ." She tapped the back fender with the gun. "Half a tank of gas, too." She looked skyward for a moment, calculating something, then back at Paris. "Five bullets." She managed a crooked grin, then placed the barrel of the gun back up against the tank.

Cyndy winced in agony and Paris took a small, covert step forward.

"Where's Rita?" he asked.

"Who?"

"Rita," Paris said. "The one you took the two-way radio from?"

"Oh . . . *her,*" Cyndy replied. "Taking a nap on the ladies' room floor. Probably having the time of her life, too, considering the way you dressed her for the evening." Cyndy smiled, her teeth red and glistening in the light thrown from the nearby streetlamp. "You sick *fuck.*" She coughed briefly, painfully, eyes shut.

Another step.

"Cyndy . . ."

"So . . . what do you think, Jack . . . we're both pretty good shots, right? Which do you think will happen first? Me hitting the gas tank just right or you hitting a vital organ?"

"Cyndy . . . come on . . . it's over." Paris moved another vigilant step forward. He was five feet away from her now. "You know there's no way out of this. EMS is already on the way. You've got to let me get you to a hospital."

Paris attempted another small step, but the blast from Cyndy's weapon—the muzzle flash startling him more than the loud pop—shoved him back on his heels, his hands instinctively to his chest. Cyndy had aimed, without taking her eyes off him, and blown out the side light on the rear fender of the Buick. Another eighteen inches to the left and she would have shot Paris in the stomach.

Paris then heard Diana's muffled screams coming from inside the BMW's trunk.

"Okay . . . okay . . ." he said, backing up.

"Four bullets now." She struggled to sit upright. Paris could see the pink-foamed saliva coming from the corners of her mouth. She put the gun back up to the gas tank. "Let's deal, Jack."

"Okay. Talk to me, Cyndy."

"But let me ask you something first . . ." she began, very conversational now. "Why do you think women become cops, Jack?"

"Jesus, Cyndy. Is this what—"

"Answer the question."

"But why do we have to talk about—"

"Answer . . . the fucking . . . *question.*"

Her tone was flat, commanding. In deference to Diana, Paris pushed the anger back for the moment. "I . . . I don't know. Same reason as men, I suppose."

"Only partially, Jack. With women, it's not just about control, you see, it's about control over *men.* The ability and the authority to tell men what to do, when to sit, where to stand. To handcuff them whenever we want. Fuck them up when we want. Jesus . . . to shoot one once in a while. It's not just a job, Jack. It's an adventure."

"Why the women, Cyndy? Why the innocent women?"

"Not sure, really. I mean, I know you'd like to pin some deep psychological reason on all this antisocial behavior and put some closure to this case, but I'm really not sure. And don't be so quick to assume they were innocent. *Nobody's* innocent. But I can't really answer your question just yet. Maybe it's a mom thing, eh? Call Rasmussen."

Cyndy laughed, and had the situation not been so horrifying, Paris would have laughed with her. Ronald Rasmussen was once a departmental shrink who ended up doing ten to fifteen for stalking his own mother while dressed like a woman. It had provided at least three years of Norman Bates joke fodder at the Homicide Unit.

It was a judgment call, but Paris decided to push it a little, to keep her talking. "Why'd you kill Tommy?" he asked.

"Well, I was kind of hoping that that would be the end of things, Jack," she said. "See, I don't *have* to do what I do. It's not a drug, not really. And believe it or not, I didn't really have any plans to do it again. No Son of Saila conversations with my cat, I'm afraid."

"Was Tommy Pharaoh?"

"What do *you* think? You're the detective." She shifted her weight and her face trenched with pain. Paris took a deep breath and let it out slowly, hoping to suddenly be blessed with an idea. He knew that the longer she kept talking, the more energy she would expend.

"I couldn't let you get to the Quality Inn, Jack," Cyndy continued. "Elliott would've surely reopened the case. You know that. The 'Saila does Quality' photo you found was a mistake. It wasn't supposed to be in with the others. And once the case was reopened . . . well . . . who *knows?* You can understand why I had to make my move, can't you?"

Paris tried to remain calm, but the anger and rage continued to mount within him. He spoke slowly. "Please, Cyndy . . . cop to cop . . . anything, okay? Absolutely *anything* I have is yours. Let's end this."

"Because you've got nothing here, you know. Reckless endangerment, maybe. Kidnapping, worst case. I'm a decorated cop, Jack. Job stress just got to me. My mother abused me. The usual shit."

"And that's precisely the reason why you should—"

"You've got nothing to tie me to Pharaoh. *Nothing . . .*"

"You're right," Paris said. "You're absolutely right. So let me have the gun, okay?"

It was then that Cyndy heard the first wail of a police siren in the distance, and because she was a cop, because she had shaken down her fair share of beauties and beasts in her days behind a badge, she knew that it meant that the game was *truly* over. Black-and-whites were rolling. She closed her eyes and let the .25 semiautomatic pistol ring her finger. She dropped the gun to the ground. "Just don't let that bitch in the trunk prosecute the case," she said wetly, resignedly. "I think she'll puh-probably come into the court-room with an attitude . . ."

Paris stepped forward and picked up Cyndy's gun.

"Three to five . . . max . . ." Cyndy said, drifting off. "You'll see. Three to five . . . max . . ."

Paris thought about how easy it would be at that moment to just lean over and step on Cyndy's chest. To put all of his weight on her widening wound, grinding in the filth of a thousand infections. Or to simply wind up and stomp her heart right out through the carnage that was her back. Send her to hell in a red fucking dress.

But no, Paris thought. He had other plans. "I don't think so, Cyndy," he said.

Paris switched hands with his weapon and reached into his pocket. He held up the slender silver machine, the microcassette recorder Melissa had given him for his birthday. He rewound the tape.

"What . . ." Cyndy replied.

"Listen to this," Paris said. *"Kitty cat."*

He stuck the recorder near Cyndy's ear and pressed play.

". . . kill Tommy?" Paris's voice asked from the tiny speaker.

He raised the volume.

Then came Cyndy's soft, eerie alto: *"Well, I was kind of hoping that that would be the end of things, Jack. See, I don't have to do what I do. It's not a drug, not really. And believe it or not, I didn't really have any plans to do it again. No Son of Saila conversations with my cat, I'm afraid . . ."*

She looked at Paris with one hazel eye and one eye, unnervingly, the color of chlorinated water. Cyndy had lost a lens. "Pretty guh-good . . ." she said, her throat now grown dry, the loss of blood sapping her last caches of energy. She closed her eyes.

Paris heard the EMS unit shriek to a halt at the other end of the alley and knew it was time to get down to business. He got very close.

"Where's the razor?" he asked.

Cyndy's head lolled on her shoulders. Her skin had taken on the color and texture of well-worn putty. *"Drazer . . ."* she said.

"The *razor,* Cyndy."

She opened her eyes briefly, then closed them again, the whites giving way to the green mucus gathering at her lower lids. She was beginning her death throes. He poked her with the barrel of his Colt.

"Where's the fucking razor?"

Paris could hear the rattle of the aluminum gurney starting down the alley, a hundred feet away. The blue lights swirling on the dirty brick walls around him also told him that at least one black-and-white cruiser had already arrived at the scene. The call had gone out "shots fired." They would be coming down the alley with their weapons drawn.

"The tape for the razor, Cyndy. Where is it?" He extracted the cassette from the recorder, its thin brown tape spewing out of the housing in a spiraled mass. "Come *on,* Cyndy . . ."

Paris shook Cyndy Taggart once, violently, drawing thick bubbles of blood from her mouth and nose.

"Okay," she said, soporose now, near the extreme edge of consciousness. "Okay . . ."

"Where is it?"

"Isssss . . ." was all Cyndy Taggart would manage before slumping heavily onto her side, giving her body over to the ground, to the jagged circle of moon-blackened blood on the asphalt.

"Police!"

The shout came from the other side of the green Buick to his left. Twenty feet away.

Paris began to rummage through Cyndy's purse—Kleenex, Life Savers, Nivea, Tampax, Rolaids—but the razor was nowhere to be found. He was just about to search Cyndy's pockets when his hand closed around a plastic sandwich bag with a weighty, flat metal object inside. The feel of the scrolled tip and the small, smooth rivet told Paris it was the straight razor. He could also feel that the inside of the bag was still moist.

"Police!"

Much closer now. Near the back end of the Buick. Paris could hear the adrenaline streaking through that voice. The cop was young and pumped: inner-city call, shots fired, clear night, dark alley. Jack Paris remembered it well.

Paris worked open the zipped top of the plastic bag with one hand. He upended it, dumped the straight razor into the blackness of Cyndy's purse and began to move it furiously around with the back of his hand, the side of his hand, up against a leather glove, up against something that felt like an eelskin wallet, up against—

"Drop it!" came the voice from directly behind him.

Had he been seen with his hand in the purse?

"Now, motherfucker!"

Had he obscured his fingerprints?

Paris didn't know.

He dropped his weapon and held his badge high.

48

THE CANDY STRIPER COULDN'T HAVE BEEN MORE THAN twenty-two, but Paris managed to charm her into it. She had most likely grown up on syndicated television, so to her, at that hour, he must have looked like Barney Miller or somebody. Funny, slightly graying cop with a lame but lovable line.

"Okay, but you're not going to sneak him any food or liquor, are you?" she asked. "He's been driving us nuts with that stuff."

"Would a three-foot Genoa salami and a quart of fried peppers be considered food?" he asked with the arch of a solitary eyebrow.

The candy striper smiled and wagged a finger at him. "Don't be long. It's way after hours and I don't care if you *are* a cop."

"Thanks . . . uh . . ."

"Brenda," she said, and turned on her squeaky white shoes.

"Brenda," he echoed, and looked for 303.

o   o   o

HE ACTUALLY LOOKED BETTER THAN HE HAD BEFORE HE GOT SHOT. MORE robust, for some strange reason.

Because, although Paris learned a half-hour after the shooting that Nick had been knocked out cold in that alcove, and that it was not he, in fact, who fired the bullet that dropped Cyndy Taggart, he also found out that Nick Raposo had taken the bullet meant for Melissa. It had hit him in the upper left thigh and exited through his left buttock as he lay unconscious on the cement. Nick had missed everything that took place in the parking lot, but Paris had already filled him in.

The identity of the person who fired the bullet that hit Cyndy was still unknown.

Nick had been in Mt. Sinai for six days and he—like the staff, faculty, volunteers and support personnel around him—was more than ready for Nicholas Carmine Raposo to be discharged.

"What happened to the friggin' world when I wasn't looking?" Nick said in a front-row whisper, once the last of the nurse's aides had left the room. "A woman? A *woman*, Jack?" He raised his hands into the air, genetically incapable of making a point like this without the use of his appendages. "I mean . . . I remember when women were . . . what?"

"Ladies?"

"I guess that's what I mean. Pretty sexist, huh?"

"They've come a long way, baby."

"And this is progress?"

"I guess so," Paris said.

Nick leaned forward, getting down to business. "So . . . still no idea who bopped me? Or who shot Cyndy?"

"No," Paris said. "We have the slug but it's pretty commonplace. Standard nine-millimeter."

"Unbelievable," Nick said. "I mean, I'm standing there, I got a perfect view of the BMW, the next thing I know, I'm kissing the friggin' cement. *Man,* did that hurt. I haven't been hit that hard since I got jumped behind Leo's Casino when I was twenty-two years old."

"And you didn't see anything."

"Stars," Nick answered. "A whole shitload of stars."

"And you think that—"

"And cologne. I remember that whoever sapped me was wearing cologne."

Paris filed this morsel of information in its proper mental drawer. He'd add it to his final report.

"So tell me," Nick continued, "what's up with the case?"

"Well, the prosecutor's office says that there's a good chance that the tape I recorded in the alley won't be admissible in court," Paris said. "Seems that because Cyndy didn't know I was taping—"

"Yeah, but *you* did. I thought the law was that only one party has to know."

"That will probably be the argument. Who knows . . ."

"Do you need the tape to nail her?"

"I'm afraid it's all there is to link her to the Pharaoh killings. Otherwise, she skates on those charges. The arson team hasn't come up with a damn thing from the cottage on Tarleton Street. Not a fiber, not a hair, not an unburned piece of paper. The place was sixty years old and the wood was dry as hell. It went up like kindling. Just about the only thing they could identify was the serial number on my revolver. Fortunately that was explainable."

Nick shook his head.

"Fortunately also," Paris continued, his voice softening, "the coroner has ruled that Andrea Heller was already dead when her body was placed in the attic."

Nick met Paris's eyes, knowing what a relief it must have been for Jack to find out that he hadn't help set the house on fire while the woman was still alive. The two went silent for a few moments.

"Jesus . . ." Nick finally said. "And to think Cyndy's in *this* building, right at this minute."

"One floor up," Paris answered.

Nick lowered his voice and leaned slightly forward. "This *puta* shot me in the ass, you know," he said, pointing at the ceiling but fixing Paris in a hopeful stare. "I mean, before I check out of this place, do you think I could have some time with her alone?"

For a moment, Paris thought Nick Raposo was serious. "I don't think they'll let you do that, Nick," he replied, breaking a smile.

"Just a half-hour or so. Nothing fancy. Me and her, maybe a bottle of Chivas, a pipe wrench."

Paris laughed. "Uh, it seems to me that the last time the two of you hooked up, she shot you, my friend," he said. "I'd say leave well enough alone. Let the law take over here. Even this messed up, I think this woman is a little too dangerous for both of us."

"Maybe you're right," Nick said, thinking. "Okay then, let me at least play with the medicine cart outside her room. You know . . . move stuff around."

"Sure thing."

Nick poured himself some water and regarded Paris. "So tell me . . . how's Melissa? How's she taking all this?"

"My daughter," Paris began, "is taking this whole thing like Charles Bronson. I mean, *I'm* having the nightmares about Cyndy Taggart chasing me down the alley and she's fine with the whole thing. Her school newspaper is doing a cover story on how she foiled this psycho-killer. She's a star."

"It's the NTV, Jack. It's taken over their minds," Nick said, tapping his temple.

"I caught her using the word 'perpetrator' yesterday," Paris said. "*Perpetrator!* Can you imagine?"

"I'm telling you, it's the NTV."

"You got that right," Paris replied, finding no need at all to correct Nick Raposo on the proper initials for music video channels. "But I don't think her mother is ever going to speak to me again."

Nick nodded in understanding. He had been married thirty-three years. "And how's Rita doing?"

"She's good, Nick. She's tougher than all of us put together," Paris said. "The investigating team cleared her yesterday and she's going to visit her sister in Erie, Pennsylvania. I'm going to take her to the Greyhound station in a little while." Paris looked at his watch. "Actually, I'm due at her place in fifteen minutes."

"I'm telling you, Jack. If I was forty years younger . . ."

"Maybe that doesn't matter," Paris said. "I know for a fact that Rita likes older men."

"Nobody's this old, though."

Paris grabbed his coat from the rack near the door. "Yeah, you're so old that you saved my sorry ass in a dark alley."

"True," Nick said, summing up his advantages as a hero. "Okay . . . so go get me a pound of prosciutto and a couple of fresh breads from Alesci's. Some honeydew melon, too."

"You got it," Paris said from the hallway. "You get some rest."

"And what about that Diana? When am I gonna meet her?" Nick asked, doing his Italian-father get-the-fuck-married-already routine.

"Next time I see you. Hand to God."

"Tomorrow," Nick said, pointing a finger at him. "When you bring the food."

"Tomorrow," Paris replied. "I promise."

o   o   o

PARIS PULLED UP TO THE CURB IN FRONT OF THE GREYHOUND BUS TERMINAL on Chester. A light drizzle began to fall as he put the car in park.

"Well, I have to tell you, you're a hell of a date, Jack Paris," Rita said, opening the passenger door. "I mean . . . what else could a girl ask for? Dress-up, barhopping, assault and battery, handcuffs . . ."

Paris smiled. "I can't tell you how much I appreciate what you did, Rita."

"I'll let you make it up to me someday," she said, pointing over Paris's left shoulder in the general direction of Chung Wah's. "Just get your VISA card paid up before you do it. You're not getting off cheap." She leaned over and kissed Paris on the cheek, her face looking impossibly young and unlined in the blue-gray light of the overcast afternoon. "Thanks for the ride."

"Need help with the suitcase?" Paris asked.

Rita just glared at him. She stepped out of the car, grabbed her bag and shut the door.

"Sorry . . ." Paris said in surrender, hoping he hadn't trodden on any feminist doctrine.

Rita smiled and looked back in the half-open window. "See you on the dance floor, detective."

"Sure thing," Paris replied.

He watched her walk toward the tattered art deco building, a bright, capable young woman in faded jeans and white Reeboks, and wondered if Melissa would one day be as resourceful and independent as Rita Constance Weisinger.

He had a feeling she would.

4 9   SHE WAS STILL DRESSED FOR WORK. AND SHE HAD CUT her hair. But although Paris preferred long flowing tresses on a woman, she actually looked better. Sexier, if that was possible, although he didn't see how.

"I can't say it's the way I wanted to get ahead in this town," Diana said, pouring the last of the Chardonnay into their glasses, evidencing the effects of the first two thirds of the bottle. They were in front of the fire at Diana's condominium in South Euclid. It was small and furnished for one in shades of peach and white and gray. A baby grand graced the wall opposite the fireplace. "I mean, the BMW-accessory jokes are already up and down the Justice Center."

Paris had to suppress a chuckle. He had heard a few. "It's the price of fame, I guess," he said, composing himself, stroking the back of her newly cropped hair. He was fascinated. Her neck was long and slender and smooth in the firelight. "Price of fame . . ."

He had decided not to pursue the photograph of Diana and Tommy he had found. It really was none of his business what she did before he stumbled into her life. God knows, he was no altar boy either, so what gave him the right to judge?

"Well, I would have preferred fame for some other reasons," Diana said. "Busting corruption, maybe. Putting *away* people like Cyndy Taggart. I mean, I'm a lawyer, Jack, and a damn good one. I want to be known for something other than my ability to be victim of the week."

"You will. Doesn't matter *how* people get to know about you, see, it's how you dazzle them once you've gotten their attention." He leaned forward and kissed her, gently, at the corners of her mouth. "And I *know* you'll dazzle them."

They clinked glasses one more time, sipped, then fell into each other's arms for a few eager, impassioned moments.

Diana pulled back, smiling.

"What?" Paris asked.

"Got two questions for you," she said, demurely now. "Personal ones."

"Okay," Paris said.

"Did you think I was unbelievably forward our first night together? I mean, me showing up with condoms and controlled substances?"

Paris *had* considered the fact that she was rather predatory that night. But compared to the other things he had suspected her of, being forward was well within the confines of acceptable adult behavior. "Nah. I'm used to it. Women are always showing up in the middle of the night with rubbers and reefer. It's why I had to get such a killer dog. Keep them at bay." Paris sipped from his glass. "And what was question number two?"

"Have you ever . . . uh . . . done it in the trunk of a car?" Diana burst out laughing, snorting once, bringing her hand to her mouth.

Paris smiled and rolled his eyes. "Criminally unhumorous, counselor."

"Oh yeah?" She poked him with a stiff index finger. "Then why'd you smile?"

"Because it was funny, I guess . . ."

"You know, that's one of the things I like about you," Diana said, unbuttoning his shirt.

"What's that?"

"Actually, now that I think about it, I'm not sure how to describe it. It's a certain way you have about you. Sexy way. Ambiguous way."

"It's true," he said. "Huge part of my mystique."

She straddled his lap and kissed him deeply.

Five minutes later, as he removed Diana's blouse—the two them adrift in the thrall of their new and strange and genuine passion—Paris looked over her shoulder and thought of the door to room 419 at Mt. Sinai Hospital, the veiled visage of Cyndy Taggart lying so still in her hospital bed, her once perfect body plugged into machines, connected to IV bags, guarded by one of Cleveland's finest.

An hour after that, as they lay near the chasm of dreams, Jack Paris considered, as he sometimes would for years to come, the one photograph he had not taken with him to the Motel Riverview that night. The one that sat, at that moment, in a safe deposit box, in an envelope, in a twice-folded piece of bright white typing paper, all sealed up in an even bigger envelope.

A nine-by-twelve-inch brown kraft envelope with a signature along the flap.

Epilogue

IT HAD BEEN EIGHT MONTHS SINCE THE LAST OF THE Pharaoh killings. The Swing Set had moved three times and the people of Cleveland had since voted to retain Mayor Michael R. Brown.

It was the Friday before the Wednesday that would be Christmas Day.

Seven forty-five P.M.

The phone rang and I answered. "Hello?"

"Danny . . . it's Jack Paris."

Jack Paris was the cop who had killed Saila. Actually, he had lured her to a deserted parking lot to do the job himself, but I had put the bullet in her. She did her actual dying in the hospital a week or so later—during my watch guarding her door, ironically, some sort of blockage in her respirator, I believe—but for all intents and purposes, Jack Paris had killed her.

I knew he'd call me, socially speaking. A lot of men hated me for my looks, my sense of style, my wardrobe, but, for the very same reasons, a lot of men wanted to be my friend, too.

The spillover and all.

"Jack," I said, full of piss and vinegar and cop camaraderie. "How are you?"

"Same old shit, Danny. Just a little older."

"Merry Christmas."

"Merry Christmas to you . . ."

"So . . . what's doin'?" I asked, as if I didn't know the answer. Once it gets under your skin, see, you never really shake it. So I *knew*.

"I was wondering," Paris said, "if you weren't doing anything tonight, if you wanted to hit the Caprice. Or maybe go somewhere where the crowd has . . . you know . . . *active* DNA. Beachwood, maybe. You up for it?"

"Jack," I said. "You have to ask?"

"What do you mean?"

I laughed. "It's *Friday*."